WILDFIRE

Her brows knitted with worry as she watched him wordlessly. She must find a way to keep him warm. She had to. If only . . .

Coming to a decision, she unbuttoned her damp shirt and slipped out of her britches quickly. Pulling back the blanket, she crawled into the bedroll.

He was burning up with fever and shivering at the same time. Her heart beat fast inside her chest, and little shivers ran down her body. She could not lose him now that she'd finally found him.

She was half asleep when she felt his lips brush softly against hers.

"Angel," he muttered.

His mouth closed over hers with tantalizing gentleness. When she made no protest, the pressure of his lips increased. Wildfire coursed through her veins.

She melted against him, her body arching against the lean hardness of his, and her fingers entangling in the thick darkness of his hair. This was her man. Of that she was certain. . . .

MORE TANTALIZING ROMANCES

SATIN SURRENDER (1861, $3.95)
by Carol Finch
Dante Fowler found innocent Erica Bennett in his bed in the most fashionable whorehouse in New Orleans. Expecting a woman of experience, Dante instead stole the innocence of the most magnificent creature he'd ever seen. He would forever make her succumb to . . . *Satin Surrender.*

CAPTIVE BRIDE (1984, $3.95)
by Carol Finch
Feisty Rozalyn DuBois had to pretend affection for roguish Dominic Baudelair; her only wish was to trick him into falling in love and then drop him cold. But Dominic had his own plans: To become the richest trapper in the territory by making Rozalyn his *Captive Bride.*

MOONLIT SPLENDOR (2008, $3.95)
by Wanda Owen
When the handsome stranger emerged from the shadows and pulled Charmaine Lamoureux into his strong embrace, she knew she should scream, but instead she sighed with pleasure at his seductive caresses. She would be wed against her will on the morrow—but tonight she would succumb to this passionate MOONLIT SPLENDOR.

UNTAMED CAPTIVE (2159, $3.95)
by Elaine Barbieri
Cheyenne warrior Black Wolf fully intended to make Faith Durham, the lily-skinned white woman he'd captured, pay for her people's crimes against the Indians. Then he looked into her sky-blue eyes and it was impossible to stem his desire . . . he was compelled to make her surrender as his UNTAMED CAPTIVE.

WILD FOR LOVE (2161, $3.95)
by Linda Benjamin
All Callandra wanted was to go to Yellowstone and hunt for buried treasure. Then her wagon broke down and she had no choice but to get mixed up with that arrogant golden-haired cowboy, Trace McCord. But before she knew it, the only treasure she wanted was to make him hers forever.

Available wherever paperbacks are sold, or order direct from the Publisher. Send cover price plus 50¢ per copy for mailing and handling to Zebra Books, Dept. 2198, 475 Park Avenue South, New York, N.Y. 10016. Residents of New York, New Jersey and Pennsylvania must include sales tax. DO NOT SEND CASH.

ZEBRA BOOKS
KENSINGTON PUBLISHING CORP.

Also by Betty Brooks:

Savage Flame

ZEBRA BOOKS

are published by

Kensington Publishing Corp.
475 Park Avenue South
New York, NY 10016

First printing: October 1987

Printed in the United States of America

This book is dedicated to:

Becky, my beautiful firstborn daughter whose love and encouragement has never faltered, and,

Kathy, my lovely youngest daughter who faithfully read countless manuscripts, listened to a thousand plots and never once told me to trash it. *And,*

Jamie, my son, the spittin' image of his father (don't dare call him handsome, his Dad might get a big head) who offered encouragement—as well as his Time Life reference books of The Old West.

Chapter One

New Mexico, Territory
September, 1882

The vision woke her.

Trembling, Angellee sat up on her bedroll, sweat beading her forehead. The freckles stood out starkly on her pale face as snatches of the dream filled the air before her. A man, his shirt tattered and bloody, his flesh lacerated from hundreds of cuts, was spread-eagled between two trees, his lifeblood seeping slowly away.

Angellee blinked rapidly, and the vision disappeared, leaving only the shadowy outlines of bushes and junipers seen by the pale light of the full moon.

Breathing in deeply, she lay back down, trying to relax her tense muscles. She closed her eyes but quickly opened them again, for a remnant of the nightmare had appeared: a dark-haired man, his face bruised and misshapen, held in the throes of agony.

She shuddered, chilled to the bone.

Who was he? Where was he? And more to the point, what was she supposed to do?

You cain't just ignore him, Angel. You got the gift. It was give to you a-purpose. Now you got to use it. Her father's words were so strong in her memory, he could almost have been standing before her now.

"I can't, Pa," she whispered, clenching her hands tightly. She held her green eyes wide open, afraid to close them again. "I don't rightly know who's got him or where he's at."

Find him.

Angellee turned restlessly on her side. She desperately wanted her mother. She had a sudden need to be loved and sheltered. Drawing a shuddery sigh, she blinked back the weak tears gathering on her thick lashes.

She wasn't going to cry.

Crying was a weakness, a woman's way, and she had no time for such nonsense. Crying wouldn't bring back her mother. Nothing would.

Find him.

"Leave me alone," she muttered grimly to her intruding conscience. "I don't know where he's at. Pa wouldn't expect me to help him when I don't know where he's at."

Rolling over again, she closed her eyes, determined to get some sleep. Immediately, the bruised face appeared on the backs of her eyelids.

Uttering a startled cry, she jackknifed up. It was no use. Angellee knew she might as well get up because past experience had taught her there would be no rest for her this night.

Someone—some unknown man—was in terrible

danger and would soon be dead. Chances were, it was already too late to help him, but she had to find out.

Jake Logan regained consciousness slowly. His arms and shoulders ached. The muscles in his thighs throbbed with pain. In fact, Jake realized suddenly, his big body hurt all over. His head hung limply, his chin resting on the base of his throat, and he had the worst headache he'd ever before experienced. He opened his eyes, stifling a groan, wondering what had happened to him. His vision was hazy, and he blinked rapidly to clear it.

An Indian, dressed in nothing but a breechclout and moccasins, hunkered down beside a fire just a few yards away. Bright red thunderbolts were painted from his forehead to his chin. Jake's slitted glance took in the brave's three comrades sleeping near the fire, and his memory returned with a jolt.

Silently, he cursed himself for a fool. His desperate need to find Becky and Lone Wolf had caused him to forget everything he had learned about survival in the West, and fool that he was, he had walked right into a trap.

The next question was, how was he going to get out of it? The wind gusted, whipping through his dark brown hair and rustling the fallen leaves on the ground. The warrior shifted his position, and Jake, fearing it would be discovered he was conscious, dropped his head again, letting it hang limply as before. He waited with bated breath, but the Indian remained where he was.

* * *

Angellee worked her way quietly through the sycamore trees growing on the banks of the shallow creek. Her nostrils twitched at the smell of smoke, and she knew she wasn't far from someone's campfire.

Tension coiled inside of her, tightening her stomach into a knot as she inched her way closer, careful not to disturb the freshly fallen leaves.

Even without the smoke to guide her, Angellee would have known she was close, for there was no sound at all except the gurgling of the water as it flowed downstream and the wind rustling through the branches. There should have been other sounds along the creekbank—the croak of frogs, an owl—something.

Knowing the dangers that could befall a woman traveling alone, she had dressed in boy's attire. Her trousers were tucked into her boots, and her hip length red hair was braided and wound tightly around her head. A soft wide-brimmed hat, fastened tightly beneath her chin with thin, leather straps gave her the appearance of a young boy as her watchful gaze scanned the area, constantly searching for danger—and something else—something she sensed lay just ahead.

"More'n likely it's the Apaches that's got 'im. Too bad he ain't one of them varmints I been trailin' all week," Angellee muttered. "If it was, he'd get no help from me."

Her mouth tightened grimly as a picture of a gutted, burnt out wagon with two bodies lying beside it surfaced in her mind, and she swallowed back the nausea.

"Don't be a danged fool," she muttered. "Got no time to be a-thinkin' on that." A memory of the face from her vision, bruised and bloodied, pressed her forward.

Rounding a clump of junipers, Angellee climbed a boulder partially concealed by trees to obtain a better view.

Anchoring herself on her precarious perch with the toe of her boot in a small crevice, she leaned over the top and looked down on the space where the Indians had made their camp.

It came as no surprise to see the man spread-eagled between two thick sycamore trees about twenty feet from the campfire. He was a big man, and as she had already known, his body was covered with numerous wounds. Angellee was impressed by the size of his shoulders and chest. She couldn't see his face, for his head hung forward as though he were unconscious.

Her green eyes moved over the three Indians sleeping beside the fire, then returned to the one lone brave who stood watch over the prisoner. A strong breeze rustled the branches of the sycamore trees, and the warrior stiffened. Angellee flattened herself against the boulder as the brave stood and walked slowly around the camp. He stopped before the prisoner, grabbed a handful of dark brown hair and yanked the man's head upright.

Catching a sight of the prisoner's face in the moonlight, she caught her breath. Even from this distance she could see, despite the bruises and blood on his face, he was undoubtedly a handsome man.

A handsome, *unconscious* man.

Angellee had had occasion to see the Indians' handiwork before, and her senses rebelled against the mutilation the Apaches had planned for this man. She knew she couldn't leave without trying to free him.

The guard, evidently disgusted that his captive was still unconscious and, therefore, oblivious to pain, turned loose his captive's hair and returned to the warmth of the fire.

Angellee's green eyes narrowed intently as she studied the Indian, then widened in surprise. The warrior wasn't Apache. He was Comanche.

What were the Comanches doing this far west?

The bright red thunderbolts streaked down both of the warrior's cheeks told their own story. The Comanches were on the warpath. But why?

Her mouth tightened into a grim line. As soon as day broke, they would be sure to turn their hand to torture again. And this time, she felt certain, they wouldn't stop until the man was dead.

What could she do? Despite the fact that her father had taught her to shoot straight and trail and trap game with the best of men, she was still just one lone female against four Indians. No one but herself would point a blaming finger if she made her way back from where she had come and rode out of there as fast as she could.

Angellee's eyes found the prisoner again. Maybe he's dead anyways, she told herself. Maybe I'll just be riskin' my skin for nothin' if I go mixin' in other folks' business.

He ain't dead. His nose is bleedin' and dead men don't bleed.

Angellee crawled down from the boulder, stealthily working her way closer.

Mind the leaves, girl! Don't stir 'em none. Injuns and animals kin hear the least sound.

Her father had said the words over and over, imprinting them on her mind, and Angellee could move through the forest without startling even the creatures of the woods. She moved that way now, working her way through the underbrush. Finally, after what seemed eons, she knelt behind a clump of junipers.

With narrowed eyes, she waited patiently for the right moment to present itself—and it finally did. The painted warrior kneeling beside the fire bent to pick up a branch to replenish the flames.

Now.

Straightening up, Angellee pulled her Arkansas toothpick from its sheath on her right boot and let it fly. With a soft whoo-oo-sh, the knife sailed through the air, penetrating the Comanche's yielding flesh in the region of his heart. The warrior grunted, crumpling to the ground.

Her wary eyes moved over the sleeping Indians, afraid they might have heard the brave, but they slept on, totally unaware of their fallen comrade. As Angellee's eyes moved back to the captive, she drew in a sharp breath.

He was neither dead, nor even unconscious as she had suspected. He was completely alert and staring straight at her.

His dark gaze held hers, and she crossed her lips with a commanding finger. Going to the fallen brave, Angellee bent over him, averting her eyes from his face. She had never killed a man before, and her stomach lurched sickly as she jerked her knife from his chest. Then she wiped the blade on the grass before rising and returning to the captive.

Angellee worked quickly, slicing through the leather bonds that trapped a hand and foot to one of the trees. Then, she crossed to the other tree, freeing the hand with no trouble. But the strands that held his foot were tougher, harder to cut through; she gave no thought for the leather of his boot as her trembling fingers sawed at the knotted bonds, and only a sinew held the thong together when he growled his warning.

"Look out behind you!"

Angellee was no more than half turned before the enraged Comanche was upon her. With surprise as his ally, and her small, ninety pound frame defeating her, she was flung to the ground with a bone-wrenching jolt. While she lay stunned, he wrested the knife from her grasp. Breathless, she lay flat on the ground, her hands held tightly above her head, staring up into the murderous face of an Indian warrior.

She bucked and kicked, but it did no good. If she could just reach her gun . . . But she couldn't. Although she'd worked hard all her life, from sunup to sundown, and was stronger than anyone would suspect, her strength was still no match for the warrior.

Slowly, the Indian raised the knife. His confident leer sent a chill of apprehension through her. Was this to be the end of her, then? She could hear the crackling of the flames as they ate away at the sycamore branch the guard had dropped on the fire, and a curious sense of resignation washed over her.

Don't give up, girl. Don't never give up. When your strength ain't enough, use the sense God give you.

Renewing her struggles, she writhed beneath the Indian. His weight pressed the softness of her small breasts into her rib cage, and comprehension dawned in his eyes.

God in Heaven! He knew she was a woman.

Hoping to distract him, she spat in the face of the warrior.

The gesture was useless, serving only to anger him. His knees bit into her upper arms. His flat, black gaze held her in its grip, and she swallowed raggedly.

The warrior grinned wickedly at her and carefully laid the knife aside. His hand came out, and he twisted her breast cruelly. She squeezed her eyes shut, hating him with every breath in her body.

Suddenly, the Indian was pulled away, and she was free. Angellee sprang to her feet to see another Comanche brave sighting down the barrel of a rifle at the man who had saved her.

Shoot him. You got no more need to be silent.

Drawing her Colt, she took aim and fired. As the bullet struck, the brave turned to look at her, surprise etched on his face. The rifle lowered, then dropped with a clatter to the ground. Clutching at his bloody throat, the Comanche warrior gave a gurgling sound and crumpled like a rag in the dust.

Angellee had been vaguely aware of a scuffle taking place a few feet away from her, and she turned to watch the man who had saved her life wipe her knife across the leg of his trousers before returning, and offering it to her, handle first.

"Thanks," she said, accepting it. Her pulse leapt wildly as their fingers touched. She drew in a sharp breath, her eyes widening slightly. It was as though an electric current had flowed through her body.

Bemused, her gaze followed as, without a word, he returned to one of the fallen Indians. She watched him pull something—a watch with a gold chain—from a pouch at the Indian's waist and drop it in his pocket.

When he returned to her side, he said, "Thanks for the help. You're not alone, are you?" His eyes swept the area around them, then returned to her face.

Angellee nodded.

He swore softly. "That was a big risk you took, kid. But I'll have to admit I'm glad to see you." He looked around at the four dead Indians and gave her a slow smile. Clapping her on the shoulder, he said, "As they say out here in the West, you'll do to ride the river with."

Angellee was unable to answer. For some reason her gaze remained fastened on his face. His heavy-lidded eyes were brown, as was his hair. His brows were bushy, nearly meeting across the bridge of his nose. Even though he had numerous wounds and was covered with the dust of the trail, she still found him a handsome man, and she felt strangely ill at ease with him.

"Not very talkative, are you?" he asked, narrowing sleepy brown eyes on her.

"Ain't got nothin' to say," she muttered, her eyes sliding away from him. Her stomach felt peculiar, like a million grasshoppers were jumping around inside, and she had a funny feeling he was the cause of the odd way she felt.

He motioned with an abrupt movement of his head toward where four horses were picketed. "I'll need a horse. Thank God they left Daniel. I wouldn't relish riding a half-broke mount."

"Daniel?" She looked at him curiously.

"Yes. Daniel's that big gray."

She looked at the gray stallion placidly cropping grass. "He don't look like much," she commented.

"Looks don't always mean much," he said, his gaze wandering over her slim body, lingering thoughtfully on the double holster holding her guns. "Take you, for instance. You look to be about thirteen or fourteen years old. You can't weigh over a hundred pounds, and yet, you give the appearance of a walking arsenal. You just waded in and got me out of a rough situation." He shook his head. "No. Looks don't mean much."

"How come they's only four horses if one of 'em is yours?"

His eyes narrowed thoughtfully. "That's a good point," he said. "And it was very astute of you to notice. This bunch here isn't all of them."

"How many're they?"

"Six. For some reason, the other two left, taking my belongings with them, except Daniel and the saddle, that is."

"I don't think they had in mind leavin' 'im for you," she said grimly.

He nodded. "I'm sure you're right. My comfort wasn't high on their list of priorities." He strode to the Indian she had shot, stooped and picked up the rifle. He was moving slower when he returned to her. "Where's your mount," he asked. "You do have a horse, don't you? You're not on foot?"

"I got me a horse. Left him back up yonder." She nodded toward the draw.

"Good." It was a curt, bitten approval, but approval nonetheless. "You go get him while I saddle up Daniel and we'll get out of here just in case their friends"—he gestured toward the dead Indians—"come back."

Angellee nodded her agreement but stayed where she was. At his inquisitive look, she asked, "You hurt bad?"

"Haven't had much time to think about it," he said grimly. "Go on now."

She went. The trip back up the draw didn't take long. Star nickered softly, nudging her as she approached. Angellee rubbed the soft velvety nose affectionately.

By the time she rode into the camp, he had saddled the big gray. His eyes lit with approval as he saw the black Arabian stallion with a white star blazed on his forehead. "That looks like a damn good piece of horseflesh you've got there."

"He is," Angellee said shortly.

"You start down the trail while I see if I can wipe out our tracks. It'd be just my luck for their friends to come along and take after us," he said.

"I'll have to go get my gear first," she replied.

"Where did you leave it?" His glance was sharp, full of questions.

"I made camp about three miles back up the creek," Angellee replied.

"Three miles . . ." His brown eyes narrowed on her. "What were you doing prowling this far away from your camp in the middle of the night?"

Angellee didn't answer.

He studied her for a moment. "I guess it really doesn't matter. You'd better get back there and grab your belongings." He stared at her, obviously mystified. "Did you leave anyone back in your camp?"

"No."

He puzzled over that for a minute. "Well, then what are . . . never mind," he said, turning away. "We'll get to that later. Go on. Get your things together. I'll be along shortly."

"Wait," she said, drawing a pistol from her left holster and handing it to him butt first. "You might need this. A rifle ain't much use for quick shootin'."

"Thanks," he said, accepting the weapon. He looked upon the twin of the Colt Navy .36 in her right holster with approval before tucking it into the waistband of his Levi's. "Now, get out of here."

Angellee didn't have to be told twice. She turned Star back up the creek, and his powerful strides moved her away from the camp with a ground-eating pace. She looked back once to see the big man pick up a sycamore branch and begin sweeping away her tracks. She wondered where he was from. It was obvious he wasn't a Westerner. *As they say out here in the West, you'll do to ride the river with.*

No. He wasn't a native Westerner. His way of speaking was different than any she had ever had occasion to hear, and yet, he knew the importance of covering their trail from the Indians who would probably return looking for their comrades. He was a complete puzzle to her. One that she would like to solve. She smiled self-consciously. She'd have to be real careful or he'd think she was interested in him, and that would never do.

Suddenly, she gave a throaty laugh. Actually, she could ask him all the questions she liked, and he'd probably think nothing of it, for he believed her to be a boy. But, then again, to question him might not be so wise, for he was curious about her, too. Angellee had seen the puzzled way the man had studied her—the questions he would expect answers to, such as, how had she known of his danger? How could she answer him?

Oh, she could say, it ain't really no big thing. It's just that I'm a sight different from most folks. You see, I'm hexed.

Chapter Two

By the time Angellee reached her camp, storm clouds had rolled in, and there was the smell of rain on the cool night air. Thunder rumbled in the distance while she rolled her bedroll up and tied it securely behind her saddle.

"Good," she muttered. "Rain'll wipe out our tracks and make it harder for them Comanches to trail us." Worry knitted her brow as she looked anxiously down the trail. Surely, the stranger should have been here by now. What could have happened?

Gathering up Star's reins in one hand, Angellee stroked his smooth, velvety neck. "Wish that stranger'd hurry up, Star," she said. "I ain't likin' the idea of gettin' wet." She frowned. "Where's he at?" she asked the animal. The stallion snorted, tossing his head. "He's had more'n enough time already. Danged fool prob'ly done gone and got himself in trouble again. Reckon as how I'll have to go back."

Putting a foot into the stirrup, she swung into the saddle, reining the stallion around. Suddenly, Star's ears perked forward, alerting her. Then she heard it; the creak of saddle leather and the soft thud of hooves. Her green eyes narrowed, and her hand fell tensely, hovering just above her gun.

Angellee relaxed as the big gray stallion came into view. Horse and rider stopped just short of her. The stranger's horse bared his teeth and bit at the Arabian stallion. Star stepped back, and the other animal missed by mere inches.

"Behave, Daniel," the man said shortly.

"He ain't too friendly," Angellee said. The man ignored her remark. She noticed he was wearing a black hat, obviously having retrieved it from the Indians.

"All set?" he growled, his eyes fixed on her bulging saddlebags and bedroll. He seemed to be a shade paler than when she'd left him. He sat stiffly erect, one hand gripping the saddlehorn tightly.

Angellee nodded, eyeing him with concern. "You all right?" she asked.

"I've been better," he muttered grimly. "Let's get the hell out of here."

They rode along the trail at the edge of the forest for what seemed to be hours, through rugged country with juniper and pine trees clinging to the hillside. The going became rougher as more storm clouds blew in. Sometimes the moon was completely obscured, making it nearly impossible to see the trail. The wind had risen, coming in short bursts, and the temperature had dropped.

Angellee's eyes kept going to the stranger. He was clinging to the saddlehorn with both hands now, and he swayed constantly. She knew he was running out of strength.

"We gotta find a place to hole up," she said. "You ain't gonna last much longer."

"There's a cave a little way from here," he said wearily. "I found it a few days back. We'll stop there."

They worked their way upward for several miles until they reached a boulder strewn hill with an open space below.

Angellee reined Star to a halt beside a stream and dismounted. Her eyes found the man. "Horses need waterin'," she said. "You want to get down?"

"Better not," he gritted. "I might not be able to mount again. It's only a short distance now."

She nodded. Taking the reins of both horses in one hand, she led them to the stream. Daniel rolled his eyes at her and aimed a kick at her leg. She jumped back quickly. "What's the matter with him?" she asked angrily.

"He don't like people," he said. The two stallions lowered their heads to drink.

A jagged streak of lightning flared and thunder cracked. The sky above looked as if it was being ripped from one end to the other.

The horses jerked their heads up, whinneying nervously, and Angellee stared anxiously skyward. If they didn't hurry, they would surely be caught in the rain. The storm clouds were heavy, obliterating most of the stars, but they thinned out around the moon, causing a curious, ghostlike haze to encircle its silvery orb.

Angellee shuddered slightly. The mountainfolk back in the hills would say it was a night to be watchful of evil spirits.

The first drops of rain hit her skin. "That's enough, Star," she said, pulling his head up. She turned to the stranger. "Where's that cave of yours at? We got to get out of this real quick-like. And I got to find the horses some shelter."

"Don't worry about sheltering the animals," he said. "The cave's big enough to stable them." He pointed toward the hill. "It's up there."

She followed the line of his finger and led the Arabian stallion up the rocky slope, her gaze returning occasionally to the man who was clinging desperately to the saddlehorn of his mount.

As Angellee drew nearer to a rocky ledge, the sky opened up, and a torrent of rain poured down in blinding sheets. She cast a worried look behind her at the injured man who followed her, then lowered her head against the elements. Pulling harder on the reins, she forced the stallion to a faster pace.

She was nearly on the cave before she saw it. A flash of lightning revealed the dark opening partially hidden behind a clump of bushes. Higher up, another opening was barely visible, but it would be out of reach for the horses.

As she neared the lower opening, Star shied away, but she tugged on the reins, urging the stallion on toward the dark gap in the face of the slope. Daniel gave no sign of trouble, which was surprising, but he had been here before.

The cave had a narrow entrance, barely wide enough for the horses to go through. After five or six feet, the tunnel opened onto a large cavern about twenty feet in circumference. Farther on, Angellee could see another passageway running off the main one.

"We can leave the horses here," the man said, sliding wearily from the saddle. His mount neighed softly, nudging at him as his legs nearly crumpled beneath him. He grabbed the saddlehorn to steady himself.

"Let me help," she said, moving quickly to his side and putting a steadying arm around his waist.

"Sorry about this, kid," he said, wrapping an arm about her slender shoulder. "It's lucky for me you came along when you did." He shivered, leaning heavily on her. "There's a smaller cave behind this one where we can sleep."

Angellee cast an anxious look at him as they moved slowly through the passageway and into the smaller cave. Immediately it was obvious why he had chosen this over the larger one. Toward the back was a ledge about two feet off the ground. The ceiling had dropped at this point, and upon closer examination, she discovered a large hole in the roof, boring up into the darkness, forming a natural flue through which the smoke from their camp fire could travel.

"I'll build a fire," she said, lowering him as gently as she could to the ground. Despite all her efforts, he hit the cavern floor with a thud and uttered a hoarse cry of pain.

"Sorry," she said, her face paling.

"'Sall right," he gritted. "It wasn't your fault. I'm too big and heavy for a kid your size to haul around." He shuddered.

Angellee bit her lower lip. He could catch pneumonia in his weakened condition if he didn't get out of those wet clothes soon. "Uh—you—you'd better—" She flushed a dull red. "You'd better shuck those wet clothes," she finished rapidly.

"These're all I've got," he reminded her. "The Comanches that left took my belongings."

"Well, you can't stay in your wet clothes," she said huskily. "Soon as I get a fire goin', I'll fetch you a blanket to wrap around yourself."

Discovering some dead limbs in a corner of the cave, she used her knife and shaved some kindling. Soon, she had a fire going and warmed her hands for a moment, grateful for the illuminating warmth. Then, she turned her attention to the stranger.

"You're gonna need some doctorin'," she said, her eyes moving over him, taking in the wet, blood-stained shirt that was plastered to his large, well-muscled chest. Her gaze moved to the Levi's pants fitting close against his hips, outlining powerful thighs that tapered into tall, black boots.

As she looked back at his tattered shirt, a bloodstain much larger than the rest caught her attention, and she frowned. As she realized blood was still seeping from the wound, her gaze returned to his pale face and found his eyes on her.

"How bad is it?" Angellee asked.

"Bullet wound," he answered, his voice showing his complete disgust. His big body shivered again. "One of them used the rifle. Fool that I was, I thought they were Apaches and walked right into it."

"I don't see how bein' Apache woulda helped you none," she said. "Word is, them Apaches is even worse'n Comanche."

"So I've heard," he said. His hand went to the buttons of his shirt, and she stopped him.

"Wait'll I fetch a blanket."

She hurried out to the outer cave and untied the

bedroll from the back of her saddle. Star snorted impatiently, and she gave his neck a sympathetic rub. "I ain't got time for you yet," she said. "I'll be back directly."

Returning to the other cave, she found the stranger had removed his shirt and was working away unsuccessfully at his wet Levi's. As she had suspected, his chest and shoulders had numerous cuts and bruises, but the one that really concerned her was the bullet wound. It was hard to tell much about it because of the blood that flowed steadily from the hole. She folded his shirt and pressed it against the wound, trying to staunch the flow.

"You can get to that later," he said weakly. "Right now, I'm afraid I need help with these britches. Damn things are so wet they stick to my skin."

She blushed scarlet. She'd hoped to avoid this. But needs must when the devil drives, she decided. She laid the bloody shirt aside and tilted her hat over her eyes to shield her expression. Then, she looked at the wet britches.

"Uh—wh—what should I do?"

His brown eyes were grim, his mouth stretched into a thin line of pain. "I take my britches off the same way you do," he snapped. Suddenly, he gave a loud sigh, and the tension drained out of him. "Sorry about that," he muttered, summoning up a weak grin. "It's just that I don't like having to ask for help."

Nodding, Angellee reached hesitantly for the buttons of his fly. Her fingers trembled as they brushed the heavy, wet fabric, and she was sure he could hear the pounding of her heart. She worked at the button, trying to force it through a hole that seemed much too small. Her hand brushed against the swelling down lower, and she drew in a sharp breath, trying to control her trembling fingers.

He frowned at her. "You'll have to undo the belt first," he said.

"Oh, yes," she mumbled, her fingers moving to work at the belt buckle. Her heart was fluttering like a trapped bird as she unbuckled the belt. When it was done, she returned to the fly, keeping her head lowered, hoping he wouldn't notice the color riding high in her cheeks.

Finally, to her intense relief, the buttons were all freed. "Could . . . could you lift up a mite while I pull 'em down?" she asked timidly.

He lifted his hips while she peeled the wet garment down his body. She kept her eyes carefully averted, heaving a sigh of relief when she finally pulled the Levi's free of his legs. Moving to the bedroll, she quickly unrolled it. "Crawl into that," she said, rising to her feet. "You oughtta warm up real quick-like. I'll go unsaddle the horses now."

He grunted, and taking it to mean he didn't need her anymore, Angellee hurried from the cavern. Burying her flushed face in Star's neck, she held tightly to him until her breathing had steadied. Star nudged at her, reminding her the horses still needed to be unsaddled. She took care of it, moving carefully as she approached the stranger's mount, but he gave her no trouble. She returned to the inner cavern, breathing a sigh of relief to find the man lying on the bedroll wrapped in a blanket. Perspiration beaded his forehead, and he shifted his position, trying to ease the pain.

Angellee knelt beside him. "You'd better let me look

at that bullet hole now," she commanded. "The lead may still be in there."

"It is," he gritted. "And you're going to have to dig it out." He looked pointedly at the knife sheathed in her boot. "Seems to me that knife would have to be awful sharp to cut through leather so fast. Think it can dig out a bullet as well?"

"I reckon so," she said, suppressing a shudder. She'd never been called on to do anything like that before, but in this hard country, there were a lot of things she would have to learn to do that might not be to her liking. Thoughts of the men she'd been trailing for the past two weeks now filled her mind, and her eyes grew hard. Yes, a lot of things, she told herself, but some of them she would relish.

Pulling the knife from her boot, Angellee laid it down on a rock near the fire where it would be near to hand when she was ready for it. The blade was two-edged, razor sharp and had a point like a needle.

Her eyes returned to him. "I never did get your name," she said. "Reckon if I'm gonna cut on a body's shoulder, I oughtta at least know his name."

He grinned weakly. "My name's Jake Logan. I'm afraid I've been too busy trying to stay alive to bother with the social amenities." He looked at her searchingly. "I didn't catch your name."

"That's 'cause I didn't throw it nowheres," Angellee said, her green eyes suddenly glinting with humor. "You talk kinda funny, mister. What's that . . . social minutes . . . word mean?"

"Amenities," he corrected. "It means polite conversation."

"You mean they's a special word for it? Where'bouts

you from anyways."

"Pennsylvania," he said, grimacing as pain stabbed through him again. "Look, kid, at the rate we're going, I could bleed to death while I'm giving you a lesson in the English language. If you're worried about getting the bullet out, don't be. You've shown yourself to have plenty of courage, and I know you can do it."

"Sorry," she muttered, knowing he'd hit the nail right on the head. She pulled the blanket away from his chest and suppressed a shudder.

Steady. You can do what needs a-doin'.

Knowing she really had no choice, she swallowed thickly, forcing her green eyes to study the bullet hole thoroughly. The flesh surrounding the wound was black and swollen; Angellee's stomach rolled as she stared at it.

"You already lost a heapa blood," she said, hoarsely. Her fingers probed the wound, pulling the ragged edges apart, and he caught his breath at the sudden pain. Her stomach lurched, and her gaze flew to his pale face. "Ain't no sign of the lead," she mumbled. "It's prob'ly settin' against the shoulder blade."

As she examined the bullet hole, her brow furrowed with worry. Probing at the wound had caused the bleeding to start again. Now, thick red rivulets of blood oozed from the black hole.

"Well, what does it look like?" he asked harshly, breaking the silence.

"I reckon it could be better." Angellee's gaze met his.

"Then you'd better not waste any more time," he said, giving her a weak grin.

"All that jouncing from the ride didn't do you no good," she muttered grimly. "I'm mighty surprised you lasted out this long." She continued talking as she studied the wound, hoping it would help to distract him from his pain.

"What're you doin' out here in the West," she asked, passing the knife blade through the flames to sterilize it. What was coming was going to be painful for him. "And how'd you come to be took by the Comanches?"

"I came west searching for someone," he growled harshly. "Do you want my life story before you take this damn bullet out?"

"Wouldn't hurt none, I reckon," Angellee said. Her face was calm as she met his eyes. "I ain't got no whiskey. I figgered to keep your mind off what I'm doin'."

"Sorry," he muttered, his brown eyes intense as they held her in their grip. His gaze moved over her slender, five-foot frame, taking in the hat still lodged firmly on her head. "Don't you ever take that hat off?" he asked suddenly.

"Not much," she said, meeting his eyes squarely. "Bein' a redhead, I burn easy." She lowered her eyes to the wound. "I reckon I better start. Hold on."

He flinched, sucking in his breath sharply as she pushed the tip of the blade into the hole. "You never did tell me what you're doing out here alone. You could tell me now."

"You want my life story?" she asked. Her lips curled in a faint smile as she repeated his words.

"Why not?" His eyes glinted with sudden humor. "After all, you've got a captive audience."

Angellee's gaze flicked toward him, and she caught her breath. She'd never met anyone like him before. After all he'd been through, he could still keep his sense of humor. She marveled at the stamina that had kept him going all this time with such a wound.

"Hold still," she said, her eyes darkening as she returned her attention to the bullet hole. "This is gonna hurt."

"Just see you get the damn bullet out."

"No need frettin' 'bout that." Her lips tightened grimly as she probed deeper, forcing her mind to ignore what she was doing.

It ain't nothin' more'n diggin' a thorn outta somebody's foot, she told herself. The tip of her pink tongue came out, lodging in the corner of her mouth. Her green eyes were narrowed in concentration. I done that lotsa times. It's just a mite bigger an' a heap deeper than a thorn'd be.

"Relax," Angellee muttered, feeling his muscles tightening beneath her grip. Her hands had blood on them—his blood. She controlled a shudder, risking a look at his face. She immediately wished she hadn't, for it was devoid of color. Resolutely she tore her eyes away and kept them fixed on his shoulder.

"I'd like to see you relax with somebody digging away at you," he gritted out. "Keep on talking to me. You were going to tell me what you were doing out here alone."

She forced a smile to her lips. "I don't think I was goin' to do that," she said, pushing the tip of the blade deeper as she probed for the bullet. "But I guess it won't hurt none. I'm alone 'cause my folks're dead. They was killed by two polecats, and I been trailin' 'em for nigh on two weeks now."

He frowned at her. "What are you going to do when you find them?"

"What do you think?" Angellee snapped. "I sure ain't gonna walk up and say howdy." Her emerald eyes met his grimly before returning to the wound. She probed deeper and Jake groaned.

"Don't take it out on me, kid," he growled.

"Sorry," she muttered tightly. "Maybe talkin' ain't such a good idea after all."

"You're probably right," he agreed.

Angellee put her fingers to the wound, holding the edges apart as she probed with the tip of the knife, searching for the bullet. "Dang it," she said. "I can't find it. I gotta go deeper."

"Just do it, dammit!" he snapped. "Quit dragging it out! And talk to me! Where were you born?"

She flinched at the harshness in his voice, but rightly attributing it to the pain he was under, she said, "Well, I was borned in the Ozark Mountains. We lived there in a little cabin that Pa built when he and Ma got hitched." Her smile was pensive as her fingers continued working steadily. "My brother, Johnny . . . he was five years older'n me, and a wilder, handsomer lad you never did see. He was a great one for foolin', Johnny was."

Suddenly, her eyes darkened with sadness. "I thought Pa would go crazy when Johnny died. He went away for a while. Pa, that is. Ma and me, we wondered if he'd left home for good, but one day, nigh on to six months after he left, Pa just up and come home. He didn't never speak Johnny's name again as long as he lived. It were as if Ma had never even birthed him a son. That were when he pulled me outta school, and I never went back, though Ma was thinkin' as how I should. Tweren't proper, she said, for a young lady to—"

Angellee broke off, taking a quick glance at his face. But he hadn't noticed her slip. His face was white and clammy with beads of perspiration rolling down his forehead. She went back to her probing. He had been silent so long that she had gone on babbling, forgetting for a while who she was talking to.

Soon the knife was imbedded in his shoulder, and blood was flowing freely down his chest in thick scarlet waves. Angellee could taste blood in her own mouth and knew that she must have bitten her lip.

Suddenly, she felt the tip of her knife hit something with a metallic-sounding clink. At the same time, he gasped, sucking in a sharp breath.

"I found it," Angellee soothed. "Just hold on an' I'll have it out directly."

"Keep talking to me," he gritted, his brow covered in sweat, his eyes tightly closed. "You said your father took you out of school. Why?"

"My Pa wanted to learn me the ways of the forest," she explained huskily. She understood his need to have her talking. She wished she had some whiskey to dull his pain, but she didn't, so she talked. "He reckoned as how schoolin' would take too much time away from his teachin's. He learned me how to shoot straight, throw a knife true and all about the ways of the forest."

Angellee probed harder, managing to get the knife a little past the bullet. Just a bit more and the bullet would be out. "Ma and Pa, they disagreed some on the schoolin', but Pa said as how I could already read and cipher, and in the end, Ma held still." Angellee cautiously nudged aside skin and muscle, and felt the bullet loosen.

He groaned.

She spared him a quick glance, then continued. "My Pa, he were the best tracker in all Caleb County, barrin' none." She slipped the knife a little farther, then pulled.

"There," she said with relief, holding the bullet aloft. "I got it." She wiped her brow with her sleeve.

"So you have," he said drily. "Now, if you'll reheat that knife, you can cauterize the wound."

Instantly, she paled. Her heart began to pound, and her knees threatened to buckle.

Steady on, girl.

Her lips tightened grimly. She wiped the knife on her britches and placed the blade in the fire, keeping her face turned away. She didn't want him to see how she was affected. Soon, the blade was glowing red, and she picked it up with trembling hands and held it before her.

"Don't fade out on me now," he said, sensing her reaction. "You've done real good so far, kid. Now, go ahead and finish it."

Nodding, while at the same time bracing herself, she quickly placed the knife on the wound. The smell of burnt flesh was overwhelming. He went limp, uttering no word or sound. Quelling the sickness in the pit of her stomach, she went about the job of cleansing and binding the wound. It had just begun to dawn on Angellee that he might die, and somehow, she found the thought unbearable. She had been alone in this wilderness territory until she found him. It was as though he belonged to her now, and it was up to her to keep him alive. Somehow, she'd do it.

She [illegible] a [illegible] glance, then continued. [illegible] If he were [illegible] in all [illegible] [illegible] a little farther than [illegible].

"Thanks," she said with [illegible], holding the [illegible]. She wiped her brow with her sleeve.

"Do you [illegible]?" he [illegible] that smile, [illegible] the [illegible].

[illegible] the [illegible]-heart [illegible] her [illegible] to [illegible].

[illegible]

Her [illegible] [illegible] and placed the [illegible] in the [illegible] [illegible] [illegible] with [illegible] hands and [illegible] her.

[illegible]

[illegible]

[illegible]

Chapter Three

Angellee listened to the sounds of the night. The storm had passed while she worked on Jake, leaving the forest freshly laundered, crisp and clean. She picked up a deadwood branch and smacked it against her pants leg. It was too wet to burn, but it would dry. Hopefully by morning.

An owl screeched over her shoulder, a poignant cry as he went about his business of hunting among the trees. Leaves whispered in the wind, and there was a flutter of wings. A branch snapped, and she started, her heart beating wildly against her breastbone. A dark shadow near the ground caught her eye, and she had already drawn her knife before she realized that it was only a rabbit.

Good, we can use some fresh meat.

Silently, she crept nearer, drawing back her blade. Then, with a twist of the wrist, she threw it. The rabbit fell to the ground. She knelt, pulling the knife from the rabbit's head.

A few minutes later, she entered the outer cavern, carrying the rabbit by the hind legs. Star nickered in welcome, and Daniel shoved against him, snorting and shuffling toward her. She eyed him warily, but he stopped before her, flattening his ears and bowing his proud head.

"You ol' phony," she said softly, rubbing his velvet nose. "You ain't really mean, are you?"

He perked his ears forward, nuzzling at her. "Go on," she said firmly. "I've got work to do." She laid the rabbit on the floor and dressed it out quickly, burying the remains in a corner of the cavern. As she moved toward the other cavern, the gray stallion followed like a large dog. "You can't come," she said firmly. He stopped. Her lips curled into a smile. "I don't think you're as dumb as you look," she commented. "Go back and stay with Star." The animal turned around and, with one last look at her, went back to stand beside the black stallion.

Deciding a stew would be beneficial to her patient, Angellee returned to the smaller cavern, carrying the strips of meat and a cooking pot.

She cast a glance toward the unconscious man as she put a pot of water, the meat and some dried peas and spices on the fire to cook. They would have to eat well while they had the chance, never knowing what tomorrow might bring.

Having seen to the food, she returned to the outer cave to care for the horses. Star snorted as Angellee neared, eyeing her reproachfully as she ran a hand over the animal's flanks.

"I know," she said apologetically. "You're bound to be mighty hungry, but I had to tend to *him* first."

Star switched his tail disdainfully, and she laughed softly as she fed the horses. She didn't bother with covering them with blankets; the cave itself would provide enough warmth.

When she was finished, she gave Star one last pat and returned to the other cave to check on her patient. In the darkness, the man called Jake Logan was only another shadow among those that flickered in the orange light cast by the fire. The heat that poured from the blazing pile of wood was welcoming, drawing her forward. Summer was over and the nights had grown colder. Standing with her hands clasped behind her back, she looked up, watching as the natural flue drew the smoke up into the mountains, leaving only untainted air behind.

Angellee found her gaze returning to the man lying in her bedroll, and she shivered slightly. She wasn't sure exactly what it was, but he affected her strangely.

He hadn't moved since he had lost consciousness, and that worried her. Unable to stop herself, she knelt beside him and placed her hand on the side of his face. His flesh was warm beneath her palm, but the chills that had shaken his body seemed to have stopped.

Picking up his wet Levi's, she hung them from a protruding rock on the cavern wall. Something fell from one of the pockets, flashing brightly as it landed on the cavern floor. Curious, she bent to pick it up.

It was the gold watch.

She turned it over in her hand, examining it closely. Her thumb brushed the catch, and the lid sprang open, revealing a picture of a young woman.

An unfamiliar feeling that she correctly identified as jealousy stabbed through Angellee, and she drew in a sharp breath. Who was this woman? And what did she mean to Jake? She must be someone he cared about, or he wouldn't be carrying around her picture.

He groaned, and she moved quickly away to the other wall, sinking down to the rock floor, the gold watch clutched tightly in her hand. She kept her eyes on him wondering if he was waking, but he lay still.

Angellee stared with disgust at the watch and heaved a tired sigh. She wished she dared throw the timepiece away, but she couldn't. It wasn't hers, and it obviously meant a great deal to Jake.

Drawing her legs up, she wrapped her arms around them and rested her chin against her knees. The warmth that came from the fire felt good against her chilled flesh, and the aroma of the stewing meat made her mouth water.

Angellee looked at her small pile of dry firewood, wondering how long it would last. Although she had found the night air outside nippy, the cavern had retained some of the heat of the day. But she knew, after the fire died down, the cold could become intense in the cavern, and that could cause pneumonia for Jake Logan in his already weakened condition.

If only she'd had time to gather firewood before the rain, she could have kept a warm fire burning through the night.

She knew there was no need to worry about the smoke from the fire giving their location away. The mountain was tall, and the forest that grew on it would help conceal the smoke even if the flue had not gone all the way through, as it did.

Angellee hugged her knees tighter. The only sound in the cavern was the crackling of the fire and Jake's ragged breathing, punctuated by a snort from one of the horses stabled in the other cavern close by.

She wasn't the type to be nervous or uneasy in the dark, but this evening seemed to be an exception. She attributed part of it to the harrowing experience of the past few hours. Shivering slightly in the chill air, she huddled closer to the fire.

Despite herself, her mind traveled back over the past two weeks. She found herself repeating a tiresome refrain.

If only she had stayed with her parents.

If only her father hadn't sent her for fresh meat.

If only she had been there.

Her reasoning told her that she would only have been killed along with them, but still, maybe there would have been something she could have done. She forced the thoughts from her mind, shaking her head with regret. It did no good to dwell on what was past. It was done. Now she was alone in the world.

Or had been, until she met up with *him.*

Angellee's glance moved to the man lying still across the room. Now she wasn't alone, but she still had to track down her parents' murderers.

What'll you do then? After they're dead. What'll you do?

She pushed back the thought. At least, she told herself, she would have the satisfaction of knowing they'd paid for what they'd done. She cupped her chin in her hand, staring broodingly into the glowing embers of the fire.

A shower of sparks caused her to sit back slightly, and she looked again at the man who lay wounded on her bedroll. She wondered what would have happened to him if she hadn't come along.

He'd prob'ly be dead by now.

The thought was like a kick in the stomach. Angellee studied his features, feeling a compulsion to memorize every line. His face was like a bronze mask, drawn and a little paler than it had been before. In profile, it was sharply cut, as cold as stone. His lips, in repose, were sternly chiseled, almost bitter. Continuing to stare at him, oddly disturbed, she wondered at her feelings for him. He was just a stranger; why should it matter so much to her that he was hurt? But it did.

He had shoved the blanket away again, and she found herself unable to drag her eyes away from him; her gaze lingered on his upper body, which was still naked except for the bandage she had put on his wound, and on the dark curls that matted together on his chest and continued in a triangle down to the edge of the blanket.

Finally, she lifted her gaze up to his face and breathed in a quick, startled breath of air.

His eyes were open.

"Are you hurtin'?" she asked, blowing out that same huge breath.

"Do ducks fly?" he asked mirthlessly.

"Can I do somethin'?"

"No," he said. Then, at her worried look. "Don't worry, I'm tougher than I look. My hide's just about bullet proof."

Angellee snorted. "Then why are you layin' there with that hole in your shoulder?"

"I make a big target," he grinned weakly.

"Yes." Her eyes flitted over his large frame, one side of her mouth curling upward. "You do."

His upper body lifted, one arm stretching toward his shirt. Suddenly he dropped back down with an unwilling groan. He was silent for a moment, then he nodded toward the garment. "Roll me a cigarette, will you?"

Silently, she did so, locating the tobacco and paper and adeptly rolling the cigarette for him. When she finished, she lit it and placed it between his lips, and an unwanted tingle washed over her as her fingers brushed against his mouth. Biting back an astonished exclamation, she withdrew sharply, refusing to credit the unlikely emotions threatening to overwhelm her at the mere touch of a man.

Totally unaware of her personal struggle, he inhaled deeply, then sighed with satisfaction.

"Lucky for me you happened by, kid," Jake said. "Did you ever tell me your name?"

"I don't rightly remember. It's Lee . . . Lee Tucker," she said, omitting the first part of her name.

"Did I dream it, or did you really tell me you were trailing killers?"

Angellee studied the toes of her boots. He sure was nosy. "I told you I was trailin' 'em all right," she finally admitted. Then she grinned, peeping at him through thick lashes. "Looks like we both was followin' a trail. But . . . unlike you . . . I was lookin' out for ambushes."

He smiled sardonically. "Guess I deserved that one." He puffed deeply then blew out a stream of smoke, studying the cigarette thoughtfully. "So you were following the trail of the men who killed your parents." His eyes searched the lines of her face, and she longed to wiggle under his gaze. Instead, she held herself firm.

"Yes," she said, surprised he remembered what she'd

told him. She picked up a stick and idly moved it back and forth in the dirt.

"And . . . I wouldn't be a bit surprised to hear you're intent on killing them when you catch them. Do you plan on doing it by yourself?"

"Guess so," Angellee said, flicking a quick glance at him from beneath her thick lashes. "Unless you're figgerin' on comin' along with me."

He laughed. "I know I owe you one, kid, but I've got my own trail to follow. I really think you should turn it over to the law though."

Her green eyes lifted to meet his. "I'll do my own revengin'," she said grimly. "Don't have no faith in the law 'round these parts."

"Have you talked to them?"

"Ain't got no call to," she said. Her expression hardened. "We was just passin' through an' I don't know the law 'round here, mister. But that don't matter much nohow. Us hillfolks, we take care of our own."

He studied her thoughtfully. "You said those men killed your parents. How did it happen?"

"We was on our way to California," she said. "Our wagon wheel broke. Pa sent me off huntin' for fresh meat while he tinkered with it."

"California," he mused, looking at the glowing tip of his cigarette. "I suppose, like so many others, your folks were hoping to find gold?"

"That's right," she said, a trifle bitterly. "My pa heard gold was so thick you could scoop it outta the streams by the handfuls. We . . . we had to leave the Ozarks in . . . a kind of a hurry, so he bought the first rig he could. Like I said, the wheel broke, and he sent me off huntin'." Her eyes darkened with pain. "When I got back, the wagon was burned. . . . My ma . . . she was dead, and Pa . . . he weren't far behind her. He kept himself alive long enough to name the killers."

"So you found the trail and decided to go after them." His voice was matter of fact, as though he'd expected no less from her.

"Yes," she said grimly, her eyes hard. "And I most near caught up on the first day; but they come on rocky ground, and I lost their trail. It took me nigh on to three days of searching and doublin' back afore I found the trail again." Her eyes held his significantly. "That were this morning. It come too dark to read sign so I made camp."

He frowned. "You made camp several miles away from where the Indians had me. How did you know I needed help?"

"Just had me a notion," Angellee mumbled, lowering her eyes evasively.

"A notion?" His eyes narrowed on the small figure. Jake stared at the boy in silence. There was something here he didn't understand, but he couldn't worry about it right now. His shoulder hurt like hell, and if he wasn't mistaken, that savory aroma filling the cavern was stew. His stomach growled with hunger. "Do you think that food is about ready?"

"Yes," she said, nodding her head. "You want some?"

"I wouldn't mind a bit." He slanted an unreadable glance at her. "And neither would my stomach."

Dishing out a plate of the thick rabbit stew, Angellee brought it to him, setting it down on a smooth stone. Her heartbeat escalated as she put an arm behind him, gripping his naked body and levering him into an upright position. He leaned weakly against the wall of the cave, but there was no weakness in the gaze she so carefully avoided.

The darkness outside the circle of firelight closed around them, cloaking them in a dark blanket of intimacy. She moved away, and her body began shaking as though she were chilled.

Anxious to get out of his vicinity for a while, she mumbled something about checking the horses while he ate and stumbled into the outer cavern. She needed time to analyze the strange feelings that came over her when she touched him.

Star nickered as she approached, and Daniel rolled his eyes at her. Crooning softly to the animals, she rubbed Star down automatically. Daniel aimed a kick at the black stallion that narrowly missed its mark. "Stop that," she said sharply. "I'll get to you in a minute." She tried to close her thoughts to the man in the next cavern as she worked on the horses, but try as she would, her mind kept returning to him. Finally, Angellee gave Star one last caress on his velvety nose and, feeling unable to delay longer, wandered back into the smaller cave. She found Jake still sitting where she had left him although he had finished his stew. His plate lay on the ground beside him.

"Are the horses all right?" he asked quietly, watching her with his steady gaze.

"Yes," Angellee said, her voice slightly husky. "Daniel's actin' up a bit though."

"He just likes attention," Jake said. "What time is it?"

"Time?" She gave a guilty flush as she looked at the watch where she had left it on the ground. "I don't rightly know," she said. "It's still dark outside."

"Would you hand me my watch?"

Angellee picked it up and handed it over, watching as he released the catch.

"It's almost five," he said, uttering a weary sigh. "Not long before daylight." He slid back down in the bedroll, his thumb caressing the picture of the girl.

"Who is she?" Angellee asked, her voice grating harshly. "The girl in the picture."

"Her name is Becky," he said, his voice soft. He closed the watch, and held it in the palm of his hand. His eyes closed.

Angellee's lips tightened. Surely he wasn't going off to sleep without saying anything else. "This . . . Becky,"—the name filled her mouth with distaste—"Is she your . . . sister?"

The corners of his mouth lifted in a smile. "No. Becky's not my sister."

"Is . . . she . . . your wife?"

"No. Not my wife." His head turned suddenly, his eyes narrowed on her. "Why're you so interested?"

"Just curious."

"She's a little too old for you, lad," he said, his voice full of humor. "Besides which, if Becky were up for grabs, I'd already have her."

Angellee's green eyes held a spark. "I weren't askin' for that reason," she said. "Forget I mentioned it."

"All right." He grinned at her and slid down in the bedroll. Pulling the blanket up over his shoulders, he closed his eyes.

She stared at him in frustration. Was he just going to sleep, leaving her curiosity unsatisfied? She slumped down to the cavern floor staring furiously at the watch in his hand. She wished she had the courage to wrest it from him and fling it out into the night.

Dammit! Who is she?

"Jake?" Her voice was loud, echoing in the silence of the cavern. "Jake?" There was no response from the man lying on the bedroll. He was already asleep. Sighing, she tilted her hat over one eye and leaned back against the cavern wall.

Tomorrow was another day.

Chapter Four

Angellee sipped the hot coffee from the tin cup as she stared into the fire, occasionally turning to look at the man lying on her bedroll.

Jake had been unconscious for several hours now and showed signs of fever. He seemed restless and tossed repeatedly. Several times she had had to replace the blanket covering him. Although his breathing was shallow, his heartbeat was strong.

Questions filled her mind about the girl whose picture was in his watch. What did she mean to Jake, and where did she fit into his life? Suddenly, Jake groaned, and she turned to see him push the blanket away again. Angellee sighed, putting her coffee down on a flat rock.

And then it came.

There was nothing to indicate it was going to happen; it just did. She felt a chill creeping over her, a chill that had nothing to do with the recent rain or the time of year. It was a deep down chill of the soul, a sudden awareness that something was wrong. A vague outline had taken shape just behond Jake's inert form—a darkness, nothing more than a shadow, really, but it seemed to be charged with a terrible threat. It hovered there for only an instant, and then it was gone, making her wonder if it had only been an illusion after all. Perhaps her worry over Jake had been responsible. But, remembering the chill that came before it, she knew it couldn't be dismissed that easily. It was an omen, a warning of what was to come.

With a fast beating heart, she went to Jake. She hovered there for a moment as though to keep the dreaded thing at bay. Then, kneeling, she checked the bandage, noting the amount of blood that had seeped through. Unwilling to cauterize the wound again, she searched the cavern until she had a handful of spider webs. Placing them on the wound to clot the blood, she left the cavern, searching for some tree moss. Granny Bess had told her the green mold had some sort of healing agent in it.

It didn't take long to locate some of the moss on a tree growing near the creek. She washed it thoroughly, then returned to the cavern, making a poultice from the moss. Pulling the spider webs away from the wound, she applied the poultice. Then, she bandaged the wound again. During the process, Jake opened his eyes once and stared vacantly at her. She saw no recognition in his eyes before he closed them again.

When she finished, she moved back to the fire and sat down again, her eyes remaining on her patient in case he should wake and need her. She leaned her head wearily against the cavern wall, willing herself to stay awake. She intended to do everything in her power to see that he didn't die.

Despite her intentions, she dozed off. Jake woke her. He had turned over and was thrashing about wildly. She hurried to his side, kneeling beside him anxiously. Suddenly, his arm lashed out toward her. She jerked her head back quickly, but not quickly enough. His hand caught her hat, knocking it back to hang by the leather straps around her neck.

The hair prickled on the back of her neck, and Angellee lifted her eyes to find his open and staring at her.

"Where am I?" he whispered hoarsely. "Who are you?" His eyes dwelt on the long, red braids fastened about her head, then moved slowly over her face, taking in her wide, startled, green eyes.

"You're in a cave," she said, feeling suddenly alarmed. He didn't remember what happened. How sick was he? She knew he needed a doctor; even from here she could feel the heat from his body, and his breathing seemed to be more shallow than before.

Angellee placed a hand on his forehead, and her heart gave a lurch. He was burning up with fever! Her pulse leapt. With his wound, he could easily get blood poisoning and die.

"Do you think you could drink some broth off the stew?" she asked, trying to speak calmly. It wouldn't do to alarm him as well.

He shook his head, closing his eyes.

"You need to get some more nourishment inside your body," she encouraged.

"Why am I wounded?" His voice sounded weak, as though it was an effort to speak at all.

"You were shot by an Indian."

"Oh, yes," he mumbled, struggling to sit up.

Alarmed, she fought to restrain him. "Lemme go," he insisted, struggling weakly. "I've got to get up. Got to find Becky."

"You can't go nowhere," she said, holding him down with her body. "You have to build your strength up. You got a bad fever burnin' inside you."

She must have got through to him because he subsided, allowing her to hold the cup for him while he drank the soup. She felt his eyes on her hair, and suddenly his hand reached out and grasped a long, red braid, tugging it free.

"It's real," he said wonderingly. "Like fire and silk." He let the braid slide through his hand, seeming to savour the silky texture.

"Go back to sleep," she said, her heart beating rapidly. She wasn't sure why, but his fascination with her hair disturbed her.

"Can . . . can I have another blanket?" he asked.

"We don't have another blanket," Angellee said. She pulled the blanket up to his chin and tucked it firmly around him. "I'll put more wood on the fire," she said. "That oughtta help."

Angellee got up and threw the last log on the fire, watching the flames sizzle and spark. Then she searched the cave for something dry to burn. There was nothing to be found. Her eyes went back to her patient and found him asleep again, his breath coming harshly in the silence of the cavern.

She moved back to sit on the stone floor again, feeling the chill of the cavern. After the wood was gone, it was going to be cold. Sighing, wondering how she was going to keep Jake warm after the fire died down, she pulled her hat off and laid it aside. She decided she might as well unbraid her damp hair and let it dry while there was still some heat in the cave.

Casting another worried look at Jake, she let down her long hair and worked her comb through the snarls, smoothing it out to lay around her in a flaming cloud of glory. Jake was mumbling incoherently now, and she was afraid his fever had risen even more. She knew he was too sick to notice her hair if he woke up. Besides, it really didn't matter anymore. What did matter was getting him well.

Jake pushed the blanket off again, and Angellee got up, hurrying over to pull it up again. His face was beaded with sweat, and she picked up the canteen, lifting his head and holding it to his mouth. He swallowed thickly, then gave a shudder.

Picking up a cloth lying close to hand, she wet it down and wiped his face, smoothing his dark hair back from his forehead.

Suddenly, his eyes opened, and he stared directly at her. Her brows lifted, and her green eyes widened in shock as realization set in.

It was him.

Her breath caught, her pulse leapt wildly, and she was unable to tear her glance away.

It's him, Ma. The one you spoke of so long ago.

Did he know, too?

"An angel," he murmured, his brown eyes filled with wonder. His hand lifted to touch the hair that fell around her in soft waves. "A real live angel," he whispered, stroking her hair, then her face with his hot, fevered hands. "I'm not dreaming."

"You feel it too, Jake," she whispered, a smile lighting her face, her green eyes as brilliant as emeralds.

Placing the palms of her hands on the sides of his face, she said, "I didn't think you'd know, too. Ma didn't tell me it'd happen this way."

His hand covered hers, wonderingly. Then suddenly he shivered again, and she drew back.

"We're 'bout out of firewood," she said. "I got to find us some more."

"No. Don't go," he said. "Stay with me . . . for a while." His dark, feverish eyes glittered as they held hers. Suddenly, he began to shake violently. "I—I can't—can't seem to get warm enough," he said, through chattering teeth. He pulled the blanket up to his neck and squeezed his eyes tightly shut.

Her brows knit with worry as she watched him wordlessly. She must find a way to keep him warm. She had to. If only she could . . .

Coming to a decision, she unbuttoned her damp shirt and slipped out of her britches quickly. Pulling back the blanket, she crawled into the bedroll.

Although Jake's eyes had been closed, he felt the heat from her body and turned instinctively toward her. His eyes opened momentarily to gaze at her. "It's . . . it's my angel," he muttered. "You've come to keep me warm."

"Yes," she agreed.

Pleasure shot through her at the way he used her name. Her cheeks were flushed, and although she was worried about him, at the same time she felt wildly happy. His breath was soft against her face, and without hesitation she wrapped her arms around him, determined to keep him warm.

He was burning up with fever and shivering at the same time. Her heart best fast inside her chest, and little shivers ran down her body. She could not lose him now that she'd finally found him. She became intensely aware of their bodies pressed intimately together and smiled slightly. She had never slept next to a man before and found the act disturbed her senses.

Angellee lay in his arms, experiencing a strange sense of peace. She was hardly aware when their positions shifted and his good arm came around her. Although he was weak, there was a surprising strength in his arm.

She was half asleep when she felt his lips brush softly against hers.

"Angel," he muttered.

Her pulse accelerated as Jake lay still for a moment, then slowly, as if testing her response, his mouth closed over hers with tantalizing gentleness. When she made no protest, the pressure of his lips increased, and his mouth coaxed hers to open.

She felt the sudden intrusion of his tongue as it pierced her lips with sensual expertise. Wildfire coursed through her veins, and Angellee had no will to fight the desire that flowed through her.

Jake's body was hard against hers; his rough hands slid down her body to caress the hillocks of her breast, and she gasped at the pleasure that assailed her. His hands were eager, caressing, and her nipples grew taut beneath his fingertips. She felt his heart beating in a rhythm that exactly matched her own. His manhood was hard, throbbing with passion as it pressed against her thigh.

She melted against him, her body arching against the lean hardness of his and her fingers entangling in the thick darkness of his hair. This was her man. Of that she was certain. Their future lay together, and from this moment on, she would see to all his needs.

"Jake," she murmured in unconscious longing as his lips left hers to trail a path of fire down her neck all the way to the curve of her breast. She was ecstatic with unfamiliar longing, feeling light and boneless as her body fitted itself to his.

His mouth was moist as it teased first one nipple and then moved to give the other one satisfaction.

Moaning low in her throat, Angellee felt delicious shudders quiver through her as Jake continued the tactile stimulation. His hands stroked her body, inviting the rhythmic movement of her hips against him. His caress offered a vague satisfaction but not the complete kind that she craved.

Her fingers tightened in his hair, applying pressure to express the urgent needs of her flesh, and she felt his body weight shift. He raised his head as if to withdraw.

"Please," she whispered, wanting him desperately. "Don't stop now, Jake." She was nearly begging in her need for him to make love to her, but she didn't care. This man was the one she had always waited for. The one her mother had told her to wait for. He was the man who would be her husband.

"I'm not going to stop, Angel. I couldn't if I wanted to." Jake's voice was husky with passion. As his lips returned to hers in hard possession, her mouth opened to him like a flower to the sun.

His naked flesh was against hers, his hair-coarsened legs had a sensuality all their own as she felt the rough texture against her smoother flesh. His chest hairs rubbing on her breast drove her wild with desire, and Angellee was carried beyond the realms of reality.

She was mindless with a pleasure that overwhelmed

caution leaving only this aching need to be satisfied. Caught in a raging tide, she was too bemused to even consider fighting it. When Jake's hands slid down to her hips, lifting her slightly and coaxing her thighs apart with the burning heat of his own, she could feel the excitement racing through her body at the intimate contact with his.

His manhood probed for entrance, and when he took her, his possession was swift. She uttered a brief cry of pain, gasping at the sudden intrusion. Then incredible pleasure swept over her, pleasure that beat at her in ever increasing waves as Jake began to move.

Jake drove his shaft deeper and swifter until she was moaning involuntarily beneath the burning demand of his mouth. With her arms locked tightly around his neck, he carried her to heights she'd never dreamed possible. Then, when she thought she could stand no more, they reached their peak together. Her body arched with instinctive need to prolong the pleasure he was giving her, and then they were plunging together down the other side.

The exquisite fulfillment of their lovemaking stayed locked inside Angellee's mind, even when her body had relaxed into exhausted satisfaction.

She lay wrapped in his arms until his even breathing made her aware that he was asleep. Then, slowly, assured that he was all right, she allowed her eyes to drift shut. Soon, the warmth emanating from his body was more than her tired state could take, and despite her intentions to remain awake, she succumbed to sleep.

Chapter Five

Angellee rode Star through the valley, the hot, heavy air almost stifling in its intensity. Not even the length of Star's full running stride created enough of a disturbance in the atmosphere to cool the fire in Angellee's mind. Something was wrong. Terribly wrong. The fear, the certainty, ate at her as she pushed Star harder. She had to get back to the wagon. Please, Lord, let her be in time . . . this time.

Topping the last brush-covered hill, the wagon came into view. It was smoking, in ruins. She knew it was happening all over again. Clenching her fists on the reins, she beat them against Star's withers, but not even that hurried the horse's progress. No, nothing could stop this now. With no direction from her, Star slowed, pulling abreast of the wagon.

Her stomach knotted as the horse cantered on; she was terrified of what she would see. Still Star carried her closer. And Ma was there.

She lay in a huddle of petticoats and calico, between the still smoking campfire and the wagon. Angellee knew before she saw the blood that her mother was dead.

She bit into her lip, tasting blood as she felt anew the sharp pain of grief and despair, then slowly, inch by inch, she turned her head. She knew there was still more to come; there was always more to come.

Her father lay beside the wagon, his legs and arms angled awkwardly.

Swallowing bitterly, she dismounted and walked—each step an exercise in terror—to her father's side. Just as she reached him, his head moved, his eyes the same green as her own, turned toward her.

He lived.

"Pa." Her whisper was tortured as she knelt beside him, lifting his head to her breast.

"They did it, Angellee," he gasped, and a spurt of fresh blood trickled from the side of his mouth. "They was two . . ." His breath was raspy, his voice gurgling, but he talked on. "One . . . was—" he broke off, coughing up blood. ". . . called him . . . Bull." His hand moved in the dirt, his fingers clutching at the grass, and the rattle in his throat weakened his next words. But she understood them. They came from her gut as much as from her father's mouth. "Find 'em," he told her. "Make 'em pay . . . don't let . . . get away."

"I will, Pa," she grated. "I promise they'll pay for what they done."

But he couldn't hear her. He was gone. Angellee lowered him to the ground and clenched her teeth. She wouldn't cry. She wouldn't! She had a job to do.

Still, she buried her face in her hands and let her grief wash over her.

And then, there were arms engulfing her. Big, heavy,

sweaty arms. *No,* she screamed, struggling, fighting the evil that embraced her.

"You can't fight me," he sneered. His face was full and scarred; his eyes were mean as he leered down at her. His hands roamed, bruising her body.

"No," she spat, fighting to free herself from the grasping hands, gasping for breath and striving to lift her strangely heavy eyelids.

Suddenly her sleep-fogged eyes were open, and she blinked, taking in her unfamiliar surroundings.

The walls were rock, covered with a mossy growth, and the ceiling . . .

The ceiling. It was rock, too. She was in a cave. Angellee let out a relieved breath, her heartbeat slowing as awareness seeped through her.

She was lying in a bedroll in Jake's confining arms. It had been his arms that caused the strange ending to her nightmare.

A delicious warmth flowed through her as she felt his naked body pressed closely against her own. She arched her back sensuously in a movement of pure contentment, closing her eyes in extreme pleasure, and nestled against Jake feeling warm and cozy. A smile lifted the corner of her lips. This was her man, and she belonged to him heart and soul.

Wriggling around, she faced him. Though he held her firmly clamped to his body, his eyes were closed. Angellee's green eyes filled with love as she watched him tenderly. She had never dreamed there could be anything as wonderful as what she had experienced last night. She wanted to lay abed and continue to feast on his beloved features but knew she needed to get up and check on the animals.

It was hard work prying Jake's arms from around her. Though the right one was weak from his wound, his left one had the strength of steel. He moaned in protest when she finally managed to free herself and roll away. Then he shivered slightly, and she frowned, laying the palm of her hand upon his brow to check for fever. His forehead felt abnormally warm beneath her hand causing her instant concern. Surely his fever should have abated by now . . . unless . . . was it possible the wound had become infected?

Carefully, she pulled the blanket away from his shoulder. There was no sign of fresh blood showing through the bandages. She decided that a closer examination of the wound would have to wait until he was awake. The best thing for him at the moment was sleep.

Glancing toward the cave opening, Angellee saw the first streaks of gray light that heralded the coming dawn. She rose from the blanket.

After pulling on her boots, she ran her fingers through her thick mane of copper hair, pulling out most of the tangles. It wasn't enough though, so she went for her comb to finish the job. When she was done, she braided her hair, wound the braids tightly around her head again, and jammed her hat onto her head. It was no longer necessary to masquerade as a boy in front of Jake; but she had to go outside and scout around, and it would be unwise to go out there without her disguise.

"Water." The groaned request was scratchy, low.

Angellee whirled toward the sound, toward the man lying outstretched on the rumpled bedroll.

Jake ran his tongue over his parched, dry lips; his

brown eyes were overbright, but he appeared completely alert.

Picking up a canteen, she moved to his side, knelt, lifted his head tenderly and held the mouth of the bottle to his lips. He drank greedily until she pulled the canteen away.

"How long have I been out, boy?"

Her heart gave a wild leap. He called her boy. Didn't he remember last night? And her? Was he out of his head again? "It's been two days," she said, forcing herself to remain calm.

His eyes widened. "Two days! I've got to get up," he said, trying to rise. She shook her head, pushing him back down gently, mindful of his wound.

"You can't," she said, her voice husky. "You're too weak. Don't worry. When you're well enough, we'll ride on. It shouldn't take more'n a couple of days. . . ." He opened his mouth to object but she stopped him. "I promise you," she said soothingly. "Whoever you're trailin', we'll find. They's two of us now. When you're fit, we'll ride on."

He must have heard the determination in her voice because she saw the tension drain from his face. He sank back on the bedroll with a sigh and closed his eyes.

"All right," he said. "We'll do it your way and wait. But just until I can sit a horse. Then we'll go. Gotta find her. Gotta find Becky. Just as soon as I can ride, we'll have to go on. Can't go back without her, and time's running out."

"Quit frettin'," she said, a trifle bitterly. "I already said we'll go on soon as you're fit."

"What are you doing?" he asked faintly, his eyes opening to a mere slit as she pulled aside the blanket and began unbinding his shoulder.

"I gotta tend your wound," Angellee told him, her eyes intent on the bindings. *He still thinks I'm a boy.* Forcing herself to concentrate on his wound, she pulled the poultice away from the ragged hole and suppressed a shudder. It looked bad, but as far as she could determine, there was no sign of infection. Angellee glanced up and saw he was studying her features intently.

A smile flickered across Jake's face. "I don't suppose anyone's been here except you and me." It was more a statement than a question. Her heart lurched, but she shook her head. He sighed. "No. I didn't think so." He closed his eyes, missing the pain that appeared on her suddenly whitened features as he continued. "I had an odd dream last night. Real odd. Maybe if I go back to sleep, I'll have it again." His eyes began to close. "Yes," he added. "Maybe I will."

Angellee's face mirrored her anguish. He believed he had been dreaming last night. It had meant nothing to him.

Tears burned her eyes. She got up and turned abruptly away. She knew it must be the fever causing his disorientation, but the knowledge didn't lessen her pain. She had thought he loved her, but she should have known better. Heartsick, she left the inner cavern.

Star whinnied softly as she approached, obviously glad to see her. Angellee smiled sadly at the stallion, rubbing her hand over the soft velvety nose. "It wasn't the same for him, Star," she whispered into his neck. "He didn't love me."

The stallion nickered, rolling sympathetic eyes toward his mistress. Angellee clung tightly to the animal, the words echoing in her mind.

Didn't love me. Didn't love me.

How could she have been so wrong about him? You're just a dumb hillbilly, she told herself. A backwoods mountain girl. Why should he want you anyway? He's been educated right proper, and they was prob'ly plenty of fancy ladies in fancy city duds who wanted him.

She swallowed around the lump in her throat. Tears filled her eyes and she blinked rapidly, forcing them back. Her fists clenched, her nails digging into her palms. She'd be damned if she'd let some Eastern tenderfoot come in here and steal her heart. Who needed him anyway?

You do, Angel.

"It ain't fair, Star. It just ain't fair," she whispered, rubbing her face against the stallion's.

You cain't always 'spect life's gonna treat you fair, Angel. The onliest thin' you can do is to take what comes your way and make what use you can of it.

"What use could I make of a broken heart, Star," she asked.

Quit feelin' sorry for yourself. You're a Tucker, ain'tcha?

Yes. She was a Tucker. And the Tuckers were proud people. She straightened her shoulders and lifted her head at a defiant angle. Jake would never know he had twisted a knife in her heart.

Angellee moved to the entrance to gaze outside. A heavy fog lay over the valley, but the sun had just begun to peep over the mountains. A heavy shuffling noise brought her head around to see Daniel just behind her. His ears were flattened against his drooping head as he stared at her with a peculiar intelligence.

"Go away," she muttered, glaring at him. As the animal started backing away, she put out a hand and stopped him. Rubbing his long neck, she soothed. "None of it's your fault." Giving him a final pat, she moved again to the cavern entrance.

She kept a watchful eye as she clambered down the side of the hill until she came to the creek, then followed it upstream a short way to a deep, calm pool hidden in a thick stand of pines. Peering into the crystal clear water, she removed her hat and took a good close look at herself. Her green eyes were wide, her nose straight, but that's as far as the good points went. Her mouth was too wide, her lower lip too full, and the freckles—she stared at the hated freckles, wishing she could rid herself of them.

The rays of the sun fell on her coppery red hair, lighting it like a flame, and she grimaced. Why couldn't she have been born a blonde? Or even a brunette? That Becky person sure didn't have red hair. She frowned at her reflection. Dirty red hair at that. It needed a good wash. Her eyes lit up at the thought. If only she dared! She dipped her hand into the water. It was cold but she could dry herself as soon as she got out, and she needn't stay longer than it took to get herself clean.

Angellee returned to the cavern, her spirits considerably lighter at the thought of a bath. She searched through her saddlebags, found a cake of her mother's scented lye soap and returned to the pool of water. Laying her hat upon the gravel that edged the stream, she stripped off her clothes and stepped into the creek.

The water was cold, but she immersed her naked body quickly in its icy depths. Then, with chattering teeth, she washed herself, scrubbing away the dirt and grime of the past week. When she finished with her body, she dipped her head into the water and washed her hair, massaging her scalp thoroughly. She was rinsing the soap from her hair when the clatter of hoofbeats sounded, echoing loudly down the canyon.

Startled, aware of her nakedness, she hurried from the stream, grabbed up her clothes and boots and swiftly pulled them on.

Hurry.

The hoofbeats had grown louder, and realizing there wasn't time to reach the cover of the cave, she crouched low behind a bush, her hand poised above her knife. She watched the trail with narrowed eyes, forcing herself to remain calm, aware that the slightest noise would give away her position.

A moment passed, then another as she remained there waiting, scarcely daring to breathe. The hoofbeats grew closer, then a lanky brown horse came into view. He drew abreast, then passed her hiding place.

The horse was riderless.

Careful. Somethin' ain't right.

"Well, hell! If it ain't a scrap of a gal!"

Angellee scrambled to her feet, and her hand moved swiftly, closing on the knife in her right boot. She stood facing the intruder, feet apart, knees bent slightly, the wicked looking knife held protectively in front of her.

She cursed herself roundly for coming out without a gun. She hadn't heard him approach. One second there was empty space, the next, he was there. She realized she had made a bad mistake, one that could cost her dearly.

She stared at the man who confronted her. He was

slightly stooped and looked ancient. His wrinkled, lined face seemed to be made out of the same buckskin that clothed him, and a battered coonskin cap was pulled low over a beetled brow. Deep lines ran from the flare of his nose, disappearing into the snow white, walrus mustache. His chin was covered with a beard the same color and fullness of his mustache.

He was holding a Winchester rifle in the crook of his arm. He had to be up to no good, or else why would he send a riderless horse to fool her?

"Stay back," she warned, her voice deadly calm, her green eyes watchful.

"Put down thet pig-sticker afore you hurt yourself," he growled. Although his faded-blue eyes held a glint of humor, the serious tone of her voice held him still. His gaze was watchful as he took in the wet clothes clinging to the curves of her reed slender body. "You're a fool, gal, if you figger thet knife can hold off a bullet."

Angellee's cold steady eyes never wavered from him. "I can put this knife through your heart before you can level that rifle and pull the trigger, mister," she said.

She wondered who he was. He seemed able to take care of himself and not the least bit worried about her threat. He looked to be a mountain man, and there was no way she could tell if he presented a danger to either her or the man lying injured in the cavern.

"Looks like we got us a stand-off here," he said, spitting a stream of tobacco on the ground. "I reckon you prob'ly *could* put thet knife right where you said. So maybe we better stand back and take us another look at this here situation." He studied her with shrewd eyes. "I ain't meanin' you no harm. I just got a mind to set and rest for a spell." His eyes narrowed on the knife. "If'n you ain't got no objection, thet is."

She would have felt a whole lot better if he would just ride off; but then, what was to stop him from sneaking right back when she wasn't looking? Perhaps she'd better pretend to accept him.

Angellee straightened, her eyes on the rifle.

The old man got the message and lowered the rifle to the ground, his eyes never leaving hers.

She let out a breath and slipped the knife into its sheath.

"Where's your mount?" The old man asked.

"Where's yours?" she countered. "And why'd you send your horse through like that?"

"Heard you splashin' back yonder a-ways. Figgered it was a good way to draw you out. You gonna tell me where your horse is?"

Angellee wasn't ready to tell him. She still wasn't sure he could be trusted, and he would be certain to find Jake if he knew about the cavern. "I ain't got one," she said. "My horse broke a leg a few miles back, and I had to shoot him."

"Thet right?" The old man spat a wad of tobacco on the ground. He pulled a pouch off his belt and took out a plug of tobacco, then reached for his skinning knife. His hand stopped in mid-air as she tensed. "Where'd you lose thet horse?" he asked gruffly.

Her wary eyes held his steadily, and her hesitation was barely noticeable. The old man had come from the east. "Due west," she said.

"Sure about thet, are you?"

She sensed something in his voice but refused to back down. "Yes," she said, her gaze never wavering from his. "It was due west," she repeated.

"Now ain't thet funny," he said, his gaze dropping to the plug of tobacco he was still holding. Then his eyes lifted to meet hers. "Thet's the way I come in. West. Seems likely I'd have seen thet horse. If'n there was one to be seen." The humor in his eyes was more pronounced now.

"Now you got me a-wonderin' why you ain't tellin' me where your horse is. What're you hidin' gal?"

"You callin' me a liar?" she asked softly, her hand held out, ready to reach for her knife.

His eyes narrowed on her hand. "Reckon I am," he said gruffly. "If'n the truth is gonna make you reach for thet pig-sticker again, then reach away."

Her green eyes narrowed, searching his faded-blue ones, and she saw something there that made her believe she could trust him. They had reached an impasse, and she was so worried about Jake that she wouldn't mind having some help with him.

"I'm not alone," she admitted. "But my partner's wounded. He's out of his head with fever."

His gaze held hers. "What happened to him?"

"He got shot."

"Where's your horses?"

"I got 'em holed up in a cave up yonder." She eyed him steadily. He might as well have it all. "We're hidin' out from the Indians. They spread-eagled him to a couple of trees, waitin' for dawn to finish him. We killed that bunch, but they had friends."

"Okay," he said, shouldering the rifle. "Let's go take a look at him." He leveled his gaze on her. "Took him away from the Injuns, did you? How'd you manage thet? A little bit of a runt like you."

She grinned ruefully. "It weren't easy. I figured for a

while we was both done for. I guess I just had me a streak of luck. That's all that saved us."

"Musta been," he returned thoughtfully. "Yep!" His shrewd blue eyes never left her. "Musta been some kinda luck at thet!"

They found Jake just as she had left him. The old man crossed to his side, and his brows met in a frown. "It's Jake Logan," he exclaimed, kneeling down. "Why didn't you say so?"

"You know him?"

"You bet I do. Ran into him when he first came out west." His faded eyes met hers. "'Pears he's in a mighty bad way. How long's he been like this?"

"Since yesterday. I cut the bullet out but—"

Jake groaned, opened eyes still dazed with fever, and focused on her face. "Hi, kid," he said weakly. "Where you been?"

"Swimmin'!" the old man said. "And if I'd been an injun she'd a'been skelped by now."

Angellee's green eyes widened. The old man knew she wasn't a boy. Now Jake would be sure to find out, and her humiliation would be complete when Jake realized last night wasn't a dream.

Jake's eyes fell on the old man. "Buck, you old geezer. What're you doing here?"

Buck's face split into a wide grin, displaying tobacco-stained teeth. "I wandered on to your friend here takin' a bath down at the crick."

Jake grinned weakly at her. "You should be more careful, boy. You never can tell what kind of varmints will creep up on you around these parts."

Buck's eyes sharpened in perception. He stared first at Jake and then at Angellee. A guilty flush stole across her cheeks.

"How's Prairie Flower, Buck?"

"She died." The old man's voice was flat, hiding a world of pain.

"I'm sorry, Buck," Jake said, putting a weak hand on the mountain man's arm.

"Yeah. I knew you would be." He sighed. "Woman was too damn old to go havin' a baby, anyhow."

"The baby?" Jake inquired softly.

"Buried 'em together," Buck growled.

"Where are you headed now, Buck?"

"Don't make no never-mind to me." Buck sighed heavily. "Ain't nothin' worth trappin' no more. Ain't nobody left to see. All my old friends done up an' died on me." His eyes held a faraway look. "Jim Bridger was the last of 'em, an' he died last year down in Missouri." He snorted. "Hard for me to believe. Thet ol' scout was quite a frontiersman. We done a lotta trappin' an' huntin' together in the old days. He was a good friend to me. Yep. It's kinda hard to believe he died on a farm down in Missouri. Never figgered I'd see the day." He looked at Jake. "Now, me, I plan on doin' my dyin' right here in these mountains."

"Quit going on about dying, Buck," Jake said, pushing himself up on his elbows. "You're making me nervous. Me, with this hole in my chest. By the way, have you got any whiskey?"

"Would I go anywheres without my jug? Sure, I got whiskey. Just hold your horses while I fetch it."

He rose and left the cavern without a backward glance. Angellee waited for a moment, then followed him. She was waiting just outside the cave opening when he returned.

"Are you gonna tell 'im?"

He didn't even pretend not to understand. "Don't reckon so. If he's too blind to see for hisself, reckon as how he don't need to know." He scratched his grizzled head. "For the likes of me though, I cain't see how he mistook you for a boy to begin with." His eyes traveled over the masculine garb. "I reckon the clothes do hide what's under 'em well enough, but you look too soft to be a boy to me." He shook his head in disbelief. "Jake must not have all his wits about him," he mused. "Yeah, that's it. Seein' how he's shot up and all. Once the fever's gone, he won't be so easy to fool."

"By then I'll be gone and it won't matter," she said. "I'm only stayin' with him till he's well."

"Uh-huh." He seemed not at all surprised at her words.

"Buck," Jake called from within the cave. "What's taking you so long?"

"Guess I best get this jug to 'im. But you mark my word. Tell 'im afore he finds out for hisself. No man likes to feel he's been made a fool of." With these sage words of advice, he entered the caverns.

Chapter Six

Jake showed such an improvement by nightfall that Angellee decided it was cause for celebration. While Buck and Jake talked quietly on the other side of the cavern, Angellee prepared venison stew. Then, from her saddlebags she took a large corn pone that she had cooked several days ago and wrapped in a clear cloth. Setting a heavy, iron skillet on the hot coals, she added bacon fat from a jar, and while it was heating, she sliced the corn pone, putting it on to fry.

When the meal was done, she filled three plates with stew and fried corn pone.

"You two're gonna have to stop talkin' long enough to eat," she said, carrying the filled plates to the men. Her green eyes fell with approval on Jake. He looked much better since Buck's arrival, not quite so pale, and she was relieved that she no longer had the full responsibility of Jake's health to bear, for it had weighed heavy on her slender shoulders.

As the two men continued to ignore her, she frowned. "If you two ain't wantin' this food, I 'spect I'll have to throw it out," she warned severely.

"Don't reckon as how I'd 'low that," Buck growled, his gaze lifting to eye the steaming plates. "I'm hungry 'nough to eat a horse."

"That may be what he's cooking, Buck," Jake warned, reaching for the metal plate. His brown eyes glinted with humor as he searched the contents of the plate suspiciously. "I don't remember the kid going out hunting. Maybe you better go and check those horses. The last time I looked there were two. How many did you count when you rode in?"

"I'm feared I was too busy tryin' to keep this youngun' here from skinning me alive with thet pig sticker thet I didn't rightly think to count the horses."

"You two just mind your tongues if you figure on eatin'," she said, a warm feeling flowing through her. With so much joking and lighthearted conversation surrounding her, she could almost close her eyes and feel as though she were part of a family again. And although they had been, and still were, in grave danger, since Buck's arrival, the danger seemed to be minimized greatly. The improvement in Jake's condition was remarkable, and something very akin to happiness flowed within her, spreading its warmth throughout.

Buck's gaze lingered thoughtfully on her flushed cheeks, then he took the metal plate from her. "I reckon we better do like sh—" He stopped, coughed to cover his slip, and seemed to find something interesting in his plate of stew. Clearing his throat, he said. "Reckon the night air's gettin' to me these days. Settlin' into my bones."

Jake eyed him curiously as he lifted a spoonful of stew to his mouth, chewed a moment, and then swallowed. "It's getting colder every night," he said. "It won't be much longer before winter sets in." He frowned thoughtfully. "Then the snow will block the passes again. Before that happens, we've got to find a place for the boy."

Angellee ignored his words. Time enough to argue about that later. "Looks like I'm saddled with a broken-down old mountain man and a shot-up tenderfoot from the East."

"Hold on there, boy. Buck might take exception to being called broken-down. But I'm afraid I can't deny the shot-up tenderfoot part," Jake said. "Imagine having to be rescued by a boy."

Angellee's amusement touched her lips in a slight smile. Jake's disgust at being caught unawares would have been increased ten-fold if he ever realized he'd been rescued by a mere girl.

"I was only funnin'," she said quickly. "Buck ain't nowhere near broken-down,"—she threw Buck a curious half-smile—"but I can't deny the old part. And you—" She looked at Jake again. "You don't really look like a tenderfoot to me."

"You wouldn't have said that ten months ago." He grinned ruefully, and her stomach lurched. She put a hand on it. Her stomach had been acting might funny since she'd met up with him. "I was just about the greenest thing God ever put on this earth when I first came to New Mexico Territory and started my search for Becky. I had to learn a lot in a hurry or die trying." He threw a quick glance at Buck. "This old mountain man here taught me a lot, but I'm afraid I wasn't paying enough attention when I met those Comanches. They were the first Indians I'd seen in over a hundred miles, and I felt sure my search for Becky was at an end. I made a real bad mistake there."

"Yes," she said. "And it could've been your last."

"I know," he agreed, leaning back with a heavy sigh. "I'll have to be more careful in the future." He stared into the fire, and when he spoke next, it was in thoughtful rumination, as if he were unaware of his audience. "There's too much at risk for me to take chances. Not with Becky's future at stake."

Angellee's green eyes hardened. "This . . . Becky . . . you keep talkin' about. Why're you lookin' for her?"

His gaze was sharp-edged in the firelight. "You're a nosy kid, aren't you?"

She flushed, averting her eyes from Jake, feeling unaccountably hurt. Her gaze fell on Buck who seemed to be especially attentive to his plate.

"No business of mine, I guess," she mumbled, moving back to the fire and picking up her serving of food. She lifted a bite to her mouth but found it difficult to swallow around the lump that had formed in her throat.

"No," he agreed thoughtfully, his eyes on her shadowed face. "It's no business of yours, but I don't really mind telling you. After all, it's certainly not a secret. It's merely a long story." He stared into the flames, and his voice was suddenly harsh, his eyes chilled as he spoke. "Becky is . . . an old friend who came out here a few years ago. Now circumstances demand she return to Pittsburgh." He laughed, but there was no humor in the sound. "Initially, I thought it would be a simple matter to locate her. I was wrong."

Frustration rose up in Angellee. What kind of explanation was that? What kind of circumstances was he talking about? She didn't know any more now than she did before he started his explanation. But one thing was certain. Jake had some kind of personal stake in his search.

"I got some news, son," Buck said, chewing his meat thoughtfully. "Figgered you'd want to know 'bout it. Been waitin' for the right time to tell you; didn't want you goin' off half-cocked in your condition. I run across Muley Kincaid a few days back, and he told me them Apaches you been lookin' for was spotted. Recent like, too."

"Where?" Jake set his plate down slowly, his eyes intent on Buck.

"'Round Cimmaron Canyon."

"Cimmaron Canyon? How far is that?"

"Not more'n a couple of days."

"When were they seen?" Jake asked.

"Last month. Could be they's still hangin' 'round there. Might be gonna stay awhile. They's more places to hide from the cavalry in these mountains than in the desert. An' a lot more game for the huntin'."

"Dammit, Buck! Why didn't you tell me right away? You know how important this is."

"Didn't tell you right away 'cause it wouldn't a done no good. You ain't in no kinda shape to go runnin' off up there right now. You wouldn't get far down the trail afore you fell offa the horse."

Jake's jaw twitched. "Perhaps so," he conceded. "But I can't wait long. I've got to leave as soon as I can travel." His eyes dwelt for a moment on Angellee, then returned to the mountain man. "Where are you heading when you leave here?"

"Well, I reckoned as how I'd go down to Fort Union

for a spell." He stared into the dwindling fire, his faded eyes distant. "When Prairie Flower died, there weren't no reason to stay a-top that mountain no longer. Yep," he said. "I'm gonna miss thet little woman. Gonna miss her a lot." He laid his empty plate aside and reached for his pouch, pulling a plug of tobacco out and cutting it with his skinning knife. Then he stuck the chaw in his mouth. "Think I'll go outside for a spell," he said. He rose and looked at Jake thoughtfully. "I'll scout the area, boy. You'd best lay back and rest yourself."

Angellee watched the old-timer leave, then gathered the cooking pot and the plates together. "He's right, you know," she told Jake severely. "You'd best get some sleep."

As she approached the creek with the dishes, Buck stepped from the concealing shadows of the willows edging the shallow stream.

"What you doin' out here, gal?"

"What's it look like?" she asked, kneeling beside the stream.

"Ain't safe in the dark for a gal."

She laughed.

Suddenly he grinned. "'Course, I ain't allus sure if'n you're female or not. An' I reckon as how you got call to laugh. You 'pear mighty able to take care of yourself." He looked at her thoughtfully. "Thet lad in yonder ain't likely to take it kindly when he figgers out you ain't no boy. An' mark my words, little gal, he won't allus be so addlewitted. He'll find out."

"My pa always said live one day at a time," she said. "Reckon it's good advice."

"I see you ain't claimin' to be a-leavin' him no more."

"I would if I could, Buck," she said seriously. "'Cause

it's God's truth I can't rest till I find the men who killed Ma and Pa. I ain't givin' up the trail of them skunks that did them in. Even if I hadn't swore to Pa I'd get 'em, I couldn't stop. But I can't leave Jake just yet. He don't know it, but he's in mortal danger. Somethin' awful's gonna happen to him, lessen I can stop it."

"Somethin' awful?" His grizzled brow wrinkled with a scowl. "Now, thet's a mighty strange thing to say. Mighty strange." He studied her thoughtfully. "What makes you think somethin's gonna happen to 'im."

"You wouldn't believe me if I told you, Buck. Just take my word for it."

"What's gonna happen to him?"

"I don't know, and that's what's scarin' me the most. If I knew what it was, then maybe I could figure out a way to stop it."

"What kinda crazy talk is this?" Buck growled. "You say somethin's gonna happen, but you don't know what."

"All I can say is it's a certainty somethin' will. Somethin' mighty bad."

"How'dya know a thing like thet?"

"Buck . . ." She hesitated, searching the mountain man's eyes. Ma had said the secret must be kept. But something made her feel Buck could be trusted. Protecting Jake was her major concern, and if she told Buck the truth, perhaps he could help her keep Jake safe. "I don't know how you're gonna take this," she said grimly. "But I saw the evil around him." She held his gaze steadily, willing him to believe her.

"You seen somethin' *evil?*" Buck asked, studying her from beneath beetled brows. "What kinda talk is thet?" He snorted. "Hells bells, gal! You're talkin' in riddles."

Her eyes glittered darkly green. "It ain't no riddle, Buck. The evil was there. No mistake about that." Her voice dropped lower, became almost hushed. "It was all darky-like, and sure enough plumb-evil. An' I ain't gonna let it get him." She turned back to the creek, swishing a tin plate through the current. "But that's not what I want to talk to you about."

"Well, go on. Spit it out. Maybe it'll make more sense than what you been a'sayin'. Why *did* you foller me out here?"

Angellee's voice was muffled as she forced the words out. "Do you know why Jake's huntin' that woman? That . . . Becky person?"

"Reckon as how I do."

She looked up. "You gonna tell me?"

"Nope. If'n Jake wants you to know, then he'll likely tell you hisself."

Her eyes darkened. "Buck, it's damned important to me."

"Yep. I reckoned it was," he said gruffly. "But, like I done said, if'n he wants you to know, he'll tell you. The words ain't mine to tell."

She stood up. "Do . . . do you know her?"

"Yep."

"Is . . . is she as sightly as her picture shows?"

"Yep. Miss Rebecca's a sightly young lady, all right."

Her head dipped low, and she pushed a loose rock with the toe of her shoe. "She's got lottsa book learnin', too, I reckon."

"Yeah. I reckon she does," he said gruffly. "But book learnin' ain't so much out here in the wilderness, gal. You got what's needed out here. Why, you got spirit thet don't know where to quit."

"She don't?"

"Well, I reckon Miss Rebecca's got lottsa spirit rightly enough."

"Seems to me she's got just about ever'thing. Why'd Jake let her leave anyways?"

"Cain't rightly say." He shifted uncomfortably. "Best get your stuff and go to bed, missy."

But she wasn't done yet. "How'd you come to know her, Buck?"

He grinned. "I clumb down a tree and slap dab run into 'er. I reckon I was bein' a mite nosy. Thet was the closest I ever was to bein' skeered, too."

"Of her?"

"No. The spirits of the dead and buried."

Her eyes widened. "Spirits?"

"Yep. At least thet's what I was feared of when I first heard it. But it was only the wind a-whistlin' through the caves. Them Injuns, though, they believe it was the spirits of their dead kinfolks what was a-makin' them wailin' sounds."

"What's Becky got to do with the Indians?"

"She's married to one of 'em."

"Married?" Her eyes lit up. "She's married?"

"Wal, didn't I just say so?" Buck asked, testily.

Unable to control her exuberance, she threw her arms around his neck and hugged him tightly.

The old-timer stiffened, remaining still. Then he patted her on the back with a rough hand. "Reckon if'n I'd a-knowed it meant so much to ya, I'd a-told you afore," he said gruffly. "Now you'd best be a-gettin' back to the boy."

"I reckon," she said, smiling shyly at him. "And, Buck. You won't tell 'im I acted foolish-like, will you?"

"Don't be a damn fool," he growled. "Now go on with you. See after the boy. It's up to the two of us to get 'im back on his feet."

When she entered the cavern a few minutes later, she found Jake on the verge of sleep.

"Is everything all right outside?" he asked drowsily.

"Yes," she said. "And I've took care of the horses."

"Good. Then you'd better get some rest now." He scooted over a little on the bedroll. "Didn't mean to take up all the room."

Her eyes fell on the narrow space he'd allowed. He obviously expected her to sleep with him. "Uh . . . I'll be fine here beside the fire."

"Don't be stupid," he said. "Come on to bed. There's more than enough room here for both of us, and I recall you saying there wasn't any more blankets." His eyes narrowed. "You did sleep here last night, didn't you?"

She flushed. "Yes, but you're hurt. I might knock against your shoulder in my sleep."

"If you do, then you can be sure I'll yell. Now get on in here."

She knew she'd either have to give in or provoke his suspicions. "I ain't rightly sleepy yet," she said, sitting down by the fire.

"That's odd, considering the amount of sleep you had last night. But if that's what you want—" He shielded a yawn with the back of his hand. "Don't stay up too late."

"I won't." She wrapped her arms around her legs and rested her chin against her knees, allowing her muscles to relax as Jake settled down in the bedroll. Angellee gazed thoughtfully into the flames. After what had happened last night, she didn't dare crawl in bed with him. But what else could she do? She was still undecided when Buck entered the cavern.

"Better get some rest," he said gruffly. "You can have one of my blankets."

"There's no need in that, Buck," Jake's sleepy voice came out of the darkness. "The boy's going to sleep with me."

Buck's narrowed eyes studied her flushed face. "It'll be a mite crowded in there with you, Jake," he said.

"We'll manage," Jake said, stifling another yawn. "Come on to bed, kid."

Torn between her fear of arousing suspicion and her natural reluctance, Angellee stood, her gaze skittering away from Buck's. Then she squared her shoulders and strode to Jake's side. He was no longer delirious, and he thought her a boy. She couldn't be safer.

Pulling off her holsters and guns, she laid them on the ground within easy reach. Then, she lowered herself down, keeping to the edge of the blanket as she removed her boots and laid them aside.

"Scrunch up next to me, boy. Otherwise, you'll wake up freezing in the night."

She grunted, hoping he would take it for some kind of answer. Her heart pounded loudly as she carefully inched a little closer to Jake. The heat from his body burned into her through her clothing. When her leg brushed his, she stiffened but forced herself to remain calm. She was intensely aware of her thigh touching his, but his even breathing told her he was unaware—or uncaring—of the contact.

"Boy?" Jake's voice startled her, coming out of the

dusky darkness.

"Yeah?" she mumbled, her voice cracking with strain.

"Relax. Go to sleep. Buck'll be listening for trouble. He's got ears like a fox." His voice carried a hint of laughter. "Isn't that right, Buck?"

"Dammit! Cain't a body get no rest a-tall 'round here?" Buck complained. "Just shet up Jake, and let us sleep."

Despite the awkwardness of her situation, she grinned. Then, slowly, her body began to relax. She waited in the darkness until Jake's even breathing told her he was asleep, and then felt herself drifting off.

Something—some sound—woke her. She sighed deeply, snuggling closer to the warmth against her back. It moved, and so did she. Suddenly, she felt the cold air as the blanket was thrown back. There was a sharp tug on her hat, followed by a loud laugh, and she was instantly alert.

"Well, hell! Would you look at this, Buck? The kid actually sleeps in the damn thing!"

Another hard tug on her hat brought her scrambling to her feet, her knife in her hand. "Keep your hands offa my hat, you mangy polecat," she snarled, her voice shaking with fury.

Jake's sleepy brown eyes narrowed. He leaned back on one elbow, staring at her in surprise. "Hell, kid. Why're you making such a fuss?" His eyes moved to the knife held protectively in front of her. "And why in the devil are you waving that thing back and forth?" His voice held a hard note of anger. "Put it down before somebody gets hurt."

She stared at him.

"Get shet 'o the knife, young'un," Buck growled. "You know you ain't a-wantin' to hurt Jake none."

Her eyes widened slightly, and she drew a sharp breath. No. She didn't want to hurt Jake. She straightened, trying to still her fluttering heart as she sheathed her knife. Her green eyes were turbulent as she left the cavern.

"Now what got into him?" Jake asked, watching the small figure retreat stiffly.

"Reckon he don't like nobody foolin' with 'is hat." Buck said grimly. "You ain't ortta be a-funnin' the sprout, Jake. Reckon you're forgettin' might quick he went an' saved your mangy hide."

"I haven't forgotten anything, you old geezer." Jake eyed him with disfavor. "How was I to know he couldn't take a joke. And why in hell does he want to wear that hat all the time anyway? I've never seen him without it."

"Cain't see as how thet would make no nevermind. Why you want to see the young 'un without his hat anyway?"

Jake snorted with disgust. For God's sake! I don't give a damn about seeing him without his hat," he growled. "I just remarked on how odd it was that he was so peculiar about it." He sighed, running a hand through his dark, unruly hair. "Look, Buck. Do you think we could just forget about it? I'll apologize to the boy when he comes back."

"Least said, soonest mended," Buck commented sagely.

"Perhaps you're right, Buck. You usually are. I don't

know what's ailing the boy, but will you go and check on him? The mood he's in, I wouldn't put it past him to take it into his head to ride off without us."

"Don't reckon he'd do a thing like thet, but I'll check on him."

Jake watched the old-timer leave and sighed wearily. If only he could figure the boy out. He owed him a lot. If it hadn't been for the boy's help, he'd be laying dead right now. Hell, he hadn't meant to hurt the boy's feelings. There was something about the kid that made Jake feel protective toward him, a curious vulnerability. Nothwithstanding, the boy had saved his life. If it hadn't been for him, Jake's search for Becky and Lone Wolf would've ended right there.

Becky.

With the lead Buck had given him, perhaps it would only be a few days before he saw her again. Could his search really be nearly over?

How would he feel when he saw her again? And how would she react? He smiled. She was certain to be surprised. Her face rose in his memory as he'd last seen her. Then, curiously, a younger face intruded; the soft, almost feminine features of the boy who had saved his life. He scowled, wondering again why the boy was so touchy about his hat.

Chapter Seven

Although night had fallen, the cavern seemed unusually dark and still, giving the impression of emptiness as Angellee entered. She frowned slightly; then Star nickered quietly, one of the other horses blew through his nose, and Angellee's expression cleared. For a moment, she had thought the two men might have actually left her there alone.

Jake had improved immensely in the two days since Buck had arrived, and she was sure it wouldn't be long before he would be ready to continue his search for Becky. When he did, she intended to go with him.

Speaking softly to the Arabian stallion, she moved toward the passageway connecting the two caverns, where a slight flickering against the walls gave evidence of a fire burning inside.

As she stepped from the connecting passageway to the inner cavern, she saw Buck and Jake talking quietly. She smiled at them, then stopped abruptly. The warmth fled her body as coldness swept over her. Her cheeks were cold, her hands icy, almost numb. Her heart began to hammer with dread, and her breath caught in her throat as reality seemed to slip into a haze. She felt weak, and hollow, light, almost brittle in fact.

She felt unaccountably threatened, and her eyes swept the cavern, searching for the source of the impending danger, lingering for a moment on the two men. It wasn't Buck that caused this feeling and certainly wasn't Jake. The two men were totally engrossed in their conversation, neither of them paying her any attention whatsoever. Yet inexplicably, unreasonably, she was terrified.

Straining her eyes, she searched the shadows in the back regions of the cavern. Her gaze sharpened and she sensed, rather than saw, something—a force was the word she had named it in the past, for it had no form—hovering in the darkened shadows. As she watched, portions of the darkness seemed to move, to shift and form itself into something . . . not exactly a shape but a solid mass of coalescing doom, a pulsating darkness that was the embodiment of all evil. While she looked on, it moved forward, a great lump of throbbing blackness, and then stopped, hovering around Jake where he sat near the fire. Her eyes rounded with horror as she watched it dip threateningly, almost wrapping itself around him.

"What's the matter, boy?"

The words came from a great distance as though she were standing at the far end of a long, narrow hallway. Angellee's heart drummed loudly in her ears, almost deafening her with its beat. Her feet seemed to be weighted with lead as she stared at Jake and the menacing bulk that threatened to consume him.

"Boy?"

It hovered there . . . black, hidden . . . a swarm of pure maleficence . . . pulsating just beyond his shoulders.

Indefinable fear pressed down on her, but she couldn't take her eyes off the mass. It seemed to be reaching out—pushing her back—and she struggled against it. She wouldn't, couldn't let it have him.

Her heart beat loud: *thrum . . . thrum . . . thrum . . . Became faster: thrum, thrum, thrum, thrum.*

Push it away! Drive it away!

"Boy! Snap out of it!" She felt hands on her shoulders. Then she was shaken roughly. Raising her head, she blinked rapidly, her terror-blurred vision focusing on Jake as the mists slowly evaporated and cleared away.

"Jake?" She stared at him, shaking her head in confusion. Her face was so pale every freckle stood out starkly. Beads of sweat dotted her forehead, and she breathed in short gasps as though she had been running. But the vision had disappeared.

Angellee ran her tongue over her lips. Her mouth felt parched and dry, and her stomach was coiled into a knot. Above all this, she felt bewildered, for never before had a vision affected her so badly.

"What happened?" Jake asked quietly, his narrowed eyes studying her pale face intently.

"What?" She was having trouble thinking coherently, but at least her heartbeat was slowing down as the fear gradually subsided.

"I said, what happened?" he repeated slowly and distinctly as though speaking to a child.

"I . . . Jake . . . I saw—" She stopped. What was she

doing? Jake was the last person she could tell about her visions. If he found out, he would turn away from her.

He would leave her!

She lowered her eyes. "Nothin'," she whispered. "I didn't see nothin'."

His gaze was concerned as he studied her white face. "Something's bothering you, kid," he said softly, squeezing her shoulder gently. "I believe I could help you if you'd only let me. Remember, I owe you one."

"You don't owe me nothin'," she said, avoiding his eyes. "An' it wouldn't do no good to tell you nohow. Nobody can help me."

He sighed. "If that's the way you want it."

She started to move away, but he caught her arm, stopping her.

"Kid," he said hesitantly. "Buck and I were just discussing you and what would be the best thing to do about your problem."

"My problem?" She frowned, blinking at him in surprise. She wasn't sure what he meant.

"Yes." He cleared his throat as though uncomfortable. "What would be the best thing to do about your parents' murderers. Buck's going on to Taos tomorrow, and we talked it over and decided it would be best for all concerned if you went along with him."

Best for all concerned. Her green eyes darkened ominously, but he took no notice.

"I'm well enough now to continue my search for Becky," he continued, "and Buck'll see you safe to town where you can report your parents' murders to the marshal."

"No!" she said sharply, the fear returning ten-fold. "I ain't goin' anywhere with Buck, so you might as well forget about it."

"Now be reasonable, boy," Jake said. "You're only a kid, and no one knows what could be waiting ahead. It's foolish to consider going after those men alone."

She stared at him stonily.

"For chris—" he bit off a swear. "Don't you have any sense at all? You're only half-grown. You may strut around here like Billy the Kid with those two guns strapped to your hips and a knife hidden in your boot, but it's suicide to think you can take on a couple of killers single-handedly."

She stared at him, feeling curiously betrayed. Her green eyes began to sparkle with anger. "I had enough savvy to save your damn hide from them Indians!" she snapped.

"I'm not denying that," he said. "If it hadn't been for you, I'd be dead right now. But you had surprise on your side. What if those gunslingers are waiting for you along the trail? You wouldn't stand a chance against men like that."

"They ain't no use arguin' 'bout this." She turned away. "I already made up my mind I ain't goin' after them right away."

"Well, why in hell didn't you say so?" he said, a big grin splitting his face. "I knew you—"

"I'm a-goin' with you."

His big frame stilled ominously. "What did you say?" he asked softly.

"You heard what I said. I'm a-goin' with you. Way I see it, we can go find this Becky for you, then go look for them murderin' skunks that killed my folks."

"Now, wait just a minute," Jake said. "You can't go with me."

"Reckon I will."

"Why?" he gritted. He seemed to be having trouble holding his temper in the face of her obstinence.

"Well, I saved your life, didn't I? Way I figure it, you owe your life to me, and I should have some say over it. I sure as hell ain't gonna let you throw it away."

"If that's not the most ridiculous thing I've ever—" He stopped, drawing a long breath. "You're serious about this, aren't you? Well, forget it, boy. You can't go with me."

"I'm goin', Jake. There's somethin' bad waitin' out there. I gotta go with you an' see it don't get you. I may be 'just a kid' to you, but that didn't stop me from helpin' before. Whatever's waitin' out there, it's a certain fact you're gonna need my help."

"You're not making sense, boy. What do you think is waiting for me out there?"

"Don't know," she said shortly. "All I know's it could kill you."

"Hell! What nonsense is this you're talking?" he snarled. "I'm not taking you!"

"You ain't gonna have to take me," she said with stubborn determination. Her eyes were desperate as she stared at him. "I'm goin' anyway," she snapped fiercely. "No matter what you say, Jake Logan. I'm goin' with you! An' they ain't no way you can stop me. It's a free country, and I can ride anywheres I want to in it."

He sighed heavily. "Don't make this difficult for me, boy. It's not that I wouldn't like to take you with me. And I realize that I owe you a lot. It's just—"

She turned away. "Ain't no use talkin'," she said. "'Cause I ain't listenin'."

He grabbed her arm, but she yanked it away. He ran a hand through his dark hair, studying her mutinous face. "I'll tell you what," he said. "You go on with Buck, and when I do what I have to do, I'll come back and look you up."

"You ain't gonna have to do that," she said grimly, "'cause I ain't goin' nowhere." Her eyes remained steady on his. "You don't have to take care of me if that's what you're worryin' about. I can do for myself."

"I'm not doubting that for one minute, but you can't come with me." His voice was grim, determined. When she opened her mouth to protest, he held up a forestalling hand. "I mean it! Forget it."

"Jake . . . don't . . . don't do this. You can't leave without me. You just can't." She crumpled in the face of his determination. "Somethin' bad is gonna happen," she whispered, her voice husky. "I gotta be there when it does."

"What the hell are you talking about? You keep yammering on about this . . . something. Explain yourself!"

He wasn't going to listen. Maybe if she told him just a part of it. Maybe then he would listen. "Sometimes . . . sometimes I know . . . things," she said, reluctantly. "*Things* that other folks don't. My ma . . . well, she called it a gift."

"A gift?" His dark brows drew together in a frown. "You're still not making any sense."

She drew a shaky breath. "It never has made no sense to me neither. And it's downright scary knowin' things that other folks don't."

Amusement flared in his eyes.

"It ain't funny," she snapped. "I'm dead serious.

That's why I gotta stay with you. Maybe me knowin' about it will help to keep it away."

His eyes softened. "I can see you really believe what you're saying, boy. For some odd reason, you really think I need your protection. But I can assure you, even though you found me in a tough situation before, there's no need to worry about me. I can take care of myself. Now, I think it's about time we turned in. It's getting late."

"I ain't gonna be sent to bed like some damn, snot-nosed kid!" she snapped.

He frowned. "Someone needs to take you in hand. You swear entirely too much."

My God! The man don't have no sense! She was worried about his life, and all he could do was complain about her cussing.

"It ain't gonna be you!" she hissed.

"We'll see. Now get on in that bed. It's getting late. We'll finish this discussion tomorrow."

She considered standing her ground, but weariness had taken its toll. "I'm goin'," she said. "But it ain't 'cause you told me to."

"The point is taken," he said wryly. "And, kid. Don't worry so much. Things will look different after a good night's sleep."

She moved slowly to the bedroll. She didn't care what he said. Things would be no different tomorrow, and there was no way she was going to let him out of her sight. Somehow, some way, she'd find a way to protect him.

She had to!

Without Jake, she'd be alone again, and she couldn't bear the thought of that. She'd stick with him no matter how hard he tried to shake her loose. Yes. She'd stick as close as a burr no matter what he said.

Jake watched Angellee settle down in the bedroll, then he motioned for Buck to follow him. The two men went outside where they could speak without being overheard.

"For some reason that kid's determined to stay with me," Jake said. "The only way I'll be able to leave without him is to go while he's asleep."

"I 'spect you're right," Buck agreed. "But you better get yourself a few hours shut-eye afore you take off."

Jake nodded. "You're right." He lit a cigarette. "I'll rely on you to look after him, Buck. I feel responsible for him."

"I'll do what I can," Buck said. "Cain't promise nothin'. Thet youngun's got a mind of 'is own."

"I know," Jake said wryly. "Just do what you can for him. That's all I ask." Jake looked curiously at him. "You never have said much about yourself, Buck. How did you come to be a mountain man?"

"Didn't rightly choose it," the old-timer said gruffly. "Just kinda fell into it."

"How's that?"

"A long time ago, back in the year eighteen hundred and thirty-seven, when I was just a young man, I was scoutin' for the cavalry. When they discovered all thet gold in California, I figgered to go there and make my fortune. Hired on as a scout for a wagon train headin' thet way an' thet was my downfall."

"What happened?"

"Met up with a gal." He reached for his leather

pouch and pulled the plug of tobacco from it. Cutting a sizeable chaw, he popped it into his mouth, wedging it into his jaw.

"You were saying you met a girl," Jake prompted.

"Yep," Buck agreed. "Purtiest little thing I ever laid eyes on. Hair as dark as a raven's wing, and eyes thet a man could purt near drown in. She took this heart o' mine and twisted it aroun' her little bitty finger." A shadow crossed his grizzled face. "Trouble is, she never even knowed it."

"You didn't tell her?"

"No. I figgered she was too good for the likes o' me. She bein' a doctor's daughter and all. I figgered she belonged in some high-class fancy home wearin' the best clothes money could buy an'"—he stopped, swallowed hard, seeming to find it hard to continue—"jewels a-plenty. Pearls strung 'round her soft, white throat . . ." He paused, cleared his throat and continued. "But it didn't happen. None o' it. No pearls . . . no jewels, nor fancy dresses. No servants to wait on her in no fancy house." His voice had dropped low, a mere mumble. "I shoulda spoke up. I shoulda let 'er know how I felt."

Jake could actually feel the other man's pain. "Did she die?" he asked gently.

"No," Buck stated flatly. "She didn't die. Not until five years later. But I wished a thousand times she had."

At Jake's startled look, he explained. "Injuns took 'er. Killed 'er pa and took 'er away. I never saw 'er again." He spat out the wad of tobacco.

"Did you search for her?"

"Boy . . ." Buck looked at him steadily. "I searched fer 'er for five years. Thet's the way I got to know the

Injuns. I'd a-still been searchin' for 'er, if'n I hadn't found out she was dead." He averted his eyes. "Died whilst havin' a baby" he muttered. "Baby died, too, or I'd'a took 'im. I never did make it to them goldfields. Didn't have no urge to make it rich no more. Couldn't see no reason to. So . . . I stayed in the hills and took up trappin'."

Jake remained silent, unable to find words. What could he say? A moment later, they went to bed.

Angellee awoke slowly. She felt cold, and her limbs were stiff from being curled tightly into a ball. She moved cautiously, searching for Jake's warm body. She had grown so used to him being there it had become a habit. Feeling nothing but emptiness where Jake should have been, she reached out with her hand, encountering nothing but air. Her breath stilled, her eyes opened and she turned—and froze.

She was alone.

She caught her breath, opening her eyes. Frantically, she searched the cavern. For a moment, her mind refused to accept the evidence of her eyes. But eventually, she had to.

The cavern was empty.

Jake was gone.

"Jake!" she called, throwing back the blanket and scrambling quickly to her feet.

There was only silence.

"Jake! Dammit, answer me!"

"He's gone."

She turned to see the old-timer standing in the entrance to the cave, a currying brush in his hand.

"What do you mean?" she gritted harshly.

"What I said. He's gone."

"Why the hell didn't you wake me up?" she snarled, her eyes snapping furiously. "Why'd you let him take off without me?"

"Warn't none of my business if'n he wanted to take off. Warn't my place to stop him."

"Sure," she said sarcastically. "You're mighty good at just mindin' your own business, ain't you? Well, you just keep on mindin' it and don't be tryin' to stop me from what I gotta do."

"What do you reckon on doin'?" he asked, entering the cavern. His faded-blue gaze was shrewd as he watched her roll the bedroll together.

"I'm goin' after him! Not that it's any of your damn business!" She shot a fiery look at him. "Dang fool's in danger and don't even know it. Wouldn't pay me no mind when I tried to stop him. Well, I ain't about to let him up and die on me." She swiped a hand across her eyes, catching the tears that fell down her face. "I'll save his hide in spite of 'im."

"Ain't no call for all this fuss," he said. "The boy's got more sense than you give him credit for."

She ignored his words, concentrating instead on rolling up her bedroll and tying the straps tightly around it. "Which way'd he go?" she asked, throwing a quick glance at Buck as she gathered up the cooking utensils and threw them into a tow sack. Not waiting for an answer, she picked up the bedroll and hurried to the other cavern. Star nickered a welcome as she approached, and nudged her gently, reminding her he'd had no attention, but she didn't have time now.

With an economy of movement, she saddled the big

Arabian stallion and tied the supplies on the back of the saddle. Then she turned to look at Buck who had still not answered her question.

"You been sayin' all along you know the boy was in danger." Buck's eyes never left her face.

She nodded. "That's right."

"You was yammerin' on 'bout seein' it."

"I did!" she snapped.

"How could a thing like that be?"

"I don't rightly know." Her eyes held his gaze steadily. "It ain't the first time it's happened. An' it prob'ly ain't gonna be the last 'cause I ain't found a way to stop it. I don't like it none neither. It ain't no pleasure to see visions of what's to come."

He chewed that over in his mind for a moment, his gaze keen as he searched her face. "I reckon you ain't a-joshin' me. You're dead serious."

"Dead serious," she agreed.

He nodded thoughtfully. "The boy went north when he left here. But he ain't gonna take it kindly if'n you follow him," he warned. "I reckon he made it plain enough last night."

"I don't care!" she snapped. "Jake Logan's a damn fool that can't see no farther than the end of his nose. I'm aimin' to save his life even if he's hankerin' to throw it away."

"Boy was right," he muttered. "You cuss too much. But, I reckon it ain't up to me to object. I'm just a-thinkin' though, it'd made more sense if'n you took time to eat before you rode off."

"Ain't got time, Buck," she said. "How long's Jake been gone?"

"Couple of hours."

She swore beneath her breath. With that much head start, it would take her all day to catch up to him. Angel-lee swung herself into the saddle and sat looking down at the old-timer. She hated to leave Buck, but it was imperative that she catch Jake as soon as possible.

"Guess I'll see you around," she said, then picked up her reins and urged Star out of the cave. She had a long ride ahead of her, a long ride that was certain to be filled with danger somewhere along the trail. Whether the danger was for Jake alone, or for both of them, it didn't really matter. She intended to be in the middle of whatever fate had planned for him. Jake was her future, her destiny, and she would allow no force, evil though it was, to keep them apart. If Jake's destiny was death, then she would share it with him.

Chapter Eight

Angellee traveled north, climbing up out of the valley of pinyon and ponderosa pines, and into the higher hills. The air was remarkably cooler in the higher elevations, and she stopped momentarily to don a lightweight jacket. An hour later she had crossed over the ridge, and Jake's trail began to lead downward into another valley.

As she rode, she remembered confessing her ability to see the future. With each beat of the Arabian stallion's hooves, Jake's laughter rang in her head. Whatever she'd expected from him, it hadn't been that.

Uncle Silas Tucker hadn't laughed. He hadn't even looked at her when he came to warn her folks about the hillfolks' intentions. As she remembered, he had carefully avoided her eyes as though he was afraid if he looked at her she'd cast a spell on him. Her eyes clouded over with memory.

Uncle Silas, if you was afeared of me—me, that you doddled on your knee—why wasn't Jake afeared? Better laughter than fear, she mused.

The morning passed, turning into midday, and Angellee had made steady progress, gaining slowly on Jake. She had found several places where sign had indicated he had stopped to rest. She had a notion his shoulder was bothering him more than he'd expected.

For the most part, she let Star pick his own path through the forest. It was quicker that way, and she was intent on closing the gap between Jake and herself as soon as possible.

The vision was still clear in her mind, and fear for Jake squeezed her heart every time the wind rustled. In her mind's eye she could still see the darkness that had hovered over him. She felt angry with him for discarding her words so easily, and she felt an even greater anger with herself for falling in love with him. If she saved him from danger this time, would she spend the rest of her life worrying about him?

She refused to let her mind dwell on what she would do if Jake came to harm before she reached him. The mere thought caused her pain. No. It just didn't bear thinking about.

Turning her head constantly, Angellee sent her searching gaze skittering over the rough terrain. Aware of the dangers, her senses were acutely attuned to her surroundings. Her nostrils quivered at the pungent fragrance of the damp earth, still moist from yesterday's rain. The mournful wail of the wind through the pine branches seemed to issue a warning, and shivers of apprehension trailed down her spine. She dug her heels into Star's flanks, urging the stallion forward. She must catch up to Jake before it was too late.

These mountains seemed familiar, reminding her of her beloved Ozarks: the crisscrossing canyons of pines, the dry streambeds that would fill to overflowing in the spring, the upthrust ridges. Even the wildlife that lived here was much the same as those in her own mountains: the deer, the rodents, fox, and reptiles.

Seldom had she ever been lonely in her world, for the sounds of the forest were many. But right now, she was too worried about Jake to enjoy the singing of the birds or the sighing of the wind as it rustled the leaves on the ground. At the moment, the chuckling of the brook she crossed was just a noise that could cover the sound of approaching hoofbeats, as was the chattering of a squirrel that ran across the trail.

Today, Angellee had no time for the pleasures of the forest. She only felt her urgency to overtake Jake as quickly as possible. Star responded to her driving need and moved along swiftly.

Stopping at a shallow creek, she dismounted, allowing Star a moment to drink. While she waited, she hunkered down beside the animal, staring at her disheveled reflection in the water.

"You look like you've been in a hog wallow," she muttered to the face in the water. "What you need is a good wash."

Pushing back tendrils of red hair that had escaped from her hat to cling wetly about her face, she rose with a sigh. How far ahead was Jake now? How much longer before she caught up with him?

Her anxious gaze searched and found the rocks that had been overturned when a lone horse passed by—the small bunches of grass that were bent—and the corner of her lips lifted in a half smile. By the sign, he wasn't far ahead of her now. She looked longingly at the cool water, pushing her hat back on her head. A long tendril of hair, having escaped the braid that had become loose, fell against her neck.

"What the hell," she said. "Won't take long to splash my face with water. And it's sure I gotta braid this hair again."

Pulling the hat off, she laid it aside. Kneeling, Angellee splashed water on her face and unbraided her hair. She had just started to rebraid it when the sounds of creaking saddle leather and the muffled crunch of horses' hooves against the thick layers of pine needles alerted her to a rider on the trail behind her.

Apprehension filled her, and she grabbed her hat, putting it on and quickly pushing her hair up beneath it. Was this to be the danger following Jake? Could it be pursuing him instead of waiting up ahead as she had feared?

If so, it would have to pass through her first!

Mounting Star, Angellee reined the animal into the shelter of the dense forest, finding a spot where she could remain concealed, and waited.

A few moments later, a horse and rider came into view. It was Buck. He stopped at the creek, swung off his horse and leaned down to study the hoofprints in the sand as he allowed his mount to drink.

She left the concealing bushes, and he straightened to greet her.

"Reckon'd as how you'd be awaitin' for me," he said gruffly.

"You took a mighty big chance gettin' off that horse. I coulda been an Indian."

"Injuns don't ride shod ponies," he said, pointing to her tracks.

She blushed. Of course he had known that. Despite

her embarrassment, she was glad to see him. She felt a warm glow spread through her body and her lips twitched. "I thought you were headed for Taos."

He spat a long stream of tobacco juice on the ground and eyed her with a keen gaze. "Didn't have nuthin' to do in Taos. Thought you might need a little company while you was a-chasin' after the boy."

She grinned. "I'm glad you've come, Buck. I can use a second pair of eyes."

"How far ahead do you place him?"

"Maybe an hour. Signs showed he rested Daniel for a spell back at that last stream we crossed. He's travelin' slow. I think he must still be a mite shaky from the sickness that was in him. He ain't even tryin' to cover his tracks."

"Uh huh. I seen thet right away. But then, neither did you."

"Didn't figure I could take the time," she said. "Seemed more important to reach him soon as I could."

"You're prob'ly right at thet," Buck said. He spat out the wad of tobacco and pulled another plug from his pouch as his eyes studied the ground for sign. Cutting a sizeable chaw, he popped it into his mouth. "You know thet boy's gonna be mighty put out to see you an' me," he commented mildly.

"He'll get over it," she said grimly.

His faded-blue eyes lifted, cutting into her cleanly as if he were trying to see through to her soul. "You still believe he's a-gonna get hisself kilt?"

"I don't know what's gonna happen, Buck. I wish I did." She shivered. "I only saw that . . . that thing twice before. And both times meant death."

"These . . . pictures you been a-seein' . . ." His gaze was shrewd as he studied her pale face. "Was you a-tellin' it for true?"

"Yes. It's for true."

He sighed, turning his gaze searchingly to the dense forest around them. "I don't like it none, youngun'. I didn't say afore. Guess I warn't sure the boy wouldn't a-laughed at me. But, fact is, I heered o' this sort o' thin' afore. Long time ago, it was. Way down Missouri way when I warn't knee-high to a grasshopper."

Her eyes studied him curiously. "You come from Missouri?"

"Yep. Reckon I did. And back in them hills . . . wal, things sometimes happened thet a body couldn't rightly put a name to. Things thet was hard for commonfolk to believe. But hillfolks swore 'twas true. Now me, I never seed none o' them things happen, so I reckon I cain't say 'twas true, nor cain't say it warn't." He nodded his shaggy white head sagely.

Hope grew inside of her. If she could get Buck to believe, then at least she'd have his support. Maybe together, they could convince Jake. "Buck." She held his gaze steadily. "Why does moss grow on the north side of the tree?"

"Don't rightly know, youngun'," he growled. "Never thought about it much. Just know it does."

"Do you know why your bones ache when the cold is settin' in or how the geese know when to fly south?"

"Nope. Cain't say as I do. What're you gettin' at, sprout?"

Her eyes were unwavering as they held his. "You can't explain it away, but you know it's true. Just as true as what I been tellin' you. I can see the future,

Buck. It ain't somethin' that I want to do, and I got no say on when it happens; but it *does* happen. And always when I least expect. It happened last night in that cave. Jake's in danger from somethin' or some-*one.* He might die, and I can't let it happen."

"Wal, reckon I'll have to take your word for it." He scratched his beard thoughtfully. "'Spect these here horses've rested and watered enough. We better get on an' find the boy afore whatever's a-comin' at him gets there."

"Thank you, Buck," she whispered fervently, reaching out to squeeze his arm. She felt as if a great weight were suddenly lifted off her shoulders. She had told someone and he hadn't laughed. He hadn't called her a witch either.

"Thank you," she repeated.

It was late afternoon when they caught up with Jake. He had apparently heard them coming and had been waiting, partially hidden by the dense foliage that covered both sides of the trail.

He reined Daniel into the path, waiting for them to draw abreast. "What the hell are you doing here?" he snarled. His bushy brows were drawn together as he glowered at Angellee. "I thought you'd be safely in Taos by now."

The air bristled and popped with tension that streaked between Angellee and Jake.

"You had no call to go off like that and leave me while I was sleepin'," she gritted through clenched teeth. Sparks flew in her accusing green eyes, and her mouth was drawn into a tight line.

Jake ignored her words, turning instead to the old-timer. "Why didn't you take the kid on to Taos?"

he demanded.

"Warn't none 'o my bus'ness if'n the sprout wanted to follow you."

Jake's lips tightened. Until he'd met up with this kid, he hardly ever lost his temper. Now, his whole body was tense with it. He turned a grim look on Angellee. "Well, you can just turn around again because you're not going with me!"

"How are you gonna stop me?" she asked softly, her hand moving to rest against the butt of her pistol.

"None o' thet, young'un," Buck growled. "You know thet ain't the way."

"Well, I ain't goin' back," she snapped, darting him a furious glance. "He can't make me!"

Jake glared at her in exasperation. Then he heaved a long, frustrated sigh. "Look, kid," he reasoned, forcing himself to calm. "This is no good. I'm only thinking of your welfare. You'd be a whole lot better off going on and reporting your parents' deaths, than coming with me."

She scowled fiercely at him. "I'll make you a deal," she said. "I'll go to Taos on one condition."

Jake eyed her suspiciously. "Which is?"

"You come too."

His mouth twisted in frustration. "Dammit, boy! I can't. Can't you get it through your dumb head? I haven't spent ten months searching in this damn wilderness for Becky to let her slip through my fingers when I'm so close."

"Then shut up and let's ride," she snarled. Her hands clenched tightly on the saddlehorn. She refused to let Jake see how deeply he had wounded her. No one had ever called her dumb before. It was true she didn't have as much book learnin' as he did, but she had plenty of savvy about the ways of the forest. And that was what counted out here. No one could dispute that.

Jake looked at Buck. "I guess I've got no choice except to take him with me," he barked irritably. "He's such a stubborn little cuss. Probably the only way to prevent him following me would be to tie him to a tree."

"I'm glad you finally figgered thet out," Buck growled.

Jake's eyes flicked over Angellee, completely aware of her blazing eyes, her slight figure held stiffly erect. "Well, since I seem to have company, we'd better get a move on. I was hoping to find Becky before night set in."

The afternoon passed quickly. Too quickly, in fact. As the shadows lengthened, Jake knew his chances of finding the Apaches before dark were practically nonexistent.

He threw a frowning look at the boy who rode ahead of him, and his lips twitched wryly. The boy hadn't spoken at all since they'd set out. His shoulders were still hunched with resentment, and Jake felt a pang of regret.

The situation between the boy and himself had deteriorated, and that was unfortunate. He only hoped he could keep the boy from doing anything foolish. Although the boy was willful, he had plenty of courage. He had proven it well enough, but there's where the trouble lay. He seemed to feel he could handle anything and come out smelling like roses.

Someway, he had to persuade the boy to give up the trail of those gunmen. He'd hate like hell to see anything happen to the kid. Why couldn't he realize

Jake had left him with Buck for his own good? For some reason the boy had decided Jake needed protection and was intent on being the one to furnish it. He was a funny kid. Hard for Jake to figure out.

When this was all over, he'd have to see what he could do for the boy. Although he was obviously uneducated, it was apparent he'd had some schooling. Not much though. The boy, wise beyond his years, was getting beneath Jake's skin. Imagine him, Jake Logan, who'd never had anyone to worry about except himself, suddenly giving a damn what a snot-nosed kid thought about him. What was the world coming to?

Angellee pulled Star up. "Riders've been through here," she said, pointing to the ground. "Not long ago, either. I make it six of 'em."

"Youngun's right, Jake," Buck said, his eyes studying the ground. "Six horses all right. Unshod at thet. Reckon it's a bunch of Indians."

"It couldn't have been a bunch of wild horses?"

Angellee lifted her head and gave him an icy green stare. "Marks is too deep," she scorned. "Them horses is bein' rode, tenderfoot."

He stiffened in the saddle, but when he spoke, his voice was calm. "How far ahead?"

"Now how am I goin' to know that?" she asked sarcastically. "We ain't up ahead, are we? We're back here on the trail behind 'em."

"Ain't no call in talkin' thet away, sprout," Buck said. "An' I 'spect we better be keepin' our voices down. Less'n you want to announce us to the whole dang bunch."

Her cheeks flushed crimson. Buck was right. She was letting her resentment of Jake take over her good sense.

There were Indians up ahead. They could be waiting in ambush. Was this the danger the vision forecast? Did the unshod ponies belong to renegade Indians, or was it the Apaches Jake was looking for?

"What do we do now, Jake," Buck asked. "Do we turn back or take a chance of running into another renegade bunch?"

"I've come too far to turn back," Jake said. "We're nearly to the Cimmaron Canyon, aren't we? That bunch up ahead could be the Apaches I'm looking for." His voice betrayed his eagerness. "If it is, it'll mean I've found Becky." He touched his toes to Daniel's flanks, urging the animal forward. "Come on," he said. "Let's go and find out."

The [illegible] balloons up ahead. They could [illegible]
[illegible]
the [illegible] belong to [illegible]
the Apache [illegible] looking for.

[illegible]

[illegible] bright.

[illegible]

[illegible] and [illegible] out.

Chapter Nine

"Aaa-i-yee!"

A war-painted Indian dropped from an overhanging branch, knocking Angellee from her horse.

She fell to the ground with a heavy thud, the weight of the attacking brave carrying her to the ground. Jake and Buck had suffered the same fate.

Angellee recovered swiftly, and quick as a cat, she sprang to her feet, her fingers closing over the butt of her Colt Navy. She drew her gun, but it was struck from her hand before she could fire. Her fingers clawed at the other holster, and despair washed over her. The holster was empty. The gun had already been taken.

Surprise had been their attackers' ally, and their numbers had quickly overwhelmed the trio. Angellee spared a quick glance for her traveling companions, and her heart gave a sudden lurch. Buck was lying on the ground where he had fallen, his body ominously still, and Jake was struggling valiantly, but uselessly, against three Indian warriors.

Oh God! So this was it. This was the danger that had

hovered so ominously over Jake. She hadn't been able to divert it after all, had in fact, accomplished nothing by following him. Now, not only Jake would be killed, but so would she and Buck.

Don't give up, Angel. Don't never give up. Her father's words surfaced in her mind.

No. She wouldn't give up. She refused to make it easy for them to take her.

Although her arms were gripped tightly from behind, she lashed out desperately with her foot. Hearing a grunt as her boot connected with a shin, she felt the warrior's grip loosen. Swift to follow her advantage, she lashed out again, higher this time, connecting with soft tissue—and found herself free.

Eluding the clutching hands of the warrior, she retreated rapidly, her fingers reaching for the knife hidden in her boot. She felt the handle, smooth against her palm, and jerked it from the scabbard, brandishing it in front of her threateningly. Her small body was tensed with determination.

"I'll cut your heart out if you come any closer, you mangy, flea-bitten savage!" she snapped, waving the knife back and forth.

The brave looked startled, falling back a step as the wicked steel gleamed in her hand.

Suddenly, he lunged for her, and she lashed out, slashing his upper arm with the blade. He jumped back, watching her closely, unwaveringly with his dark, ebony eyes. She held her crouched position, stabbing out as the brave tried again to approach. He jumped away from the wicked steel, remaining just out of arm's reach.

They circled each other warily, his dark gaze never

wavering from hers. If she hadn't been so intent on defense, she would have seen the way his eyes suddenly flared with admiration for her courage. He had obviously not expected such a furious fight from one so small as she.

Sensing another presence behind her, Angellee moved quickly, but she wasn't fast enough. An arm looped around her neck, cutting off her air supply while the other arm grasped her wrist, applying pressure.

Beads of sweat stood out on her forehead as she was hauled back with such force that tears of pain gushed from her eyes. Angellee found herself lifted off the ground by the warrior, and the pain became so intense that she could no longer hold the knife. It dropped to the ground with a clatter. She clawed with both hands at the arm that was choking her. Just when she thought she would surely suffocate, the arm loosened, allowing her to draw great gulps of air into her tortured lungs.

The warrior in front of her walked deliberately to the knife, looking into her eyes all the while. Then, he bent, picked it up and stuck it into the band of his breechclout.

"Jake," she called frantically, casting a quick glance behind her where he was being held fast by two warriors. To her intense relief, he appeared unhurt.

"Leave the kid alone," he roared. His voice cracked. "Don't let them know you're scared, boy," he warned.

Angellee fought for control as the Indians stared at her. Jake was right. She couldn't show fear. She had been told the Indians admired bravery and skill above all else. Just as they despised any show of weakness.

She lifted her chin and stared at the brave who

confronted her. He was tall, probably six feet in height. His hair was long, black as a raven's wing and held back by a beaded headband around his forehead. His copper colored skin was smooth, and he was naked except for the breechclout and long moccasins which were pulled up to his knees. Lightning bolts were streaked down both cheeks of his classic features. A bright red streak of blood ran down his arm, flowing freely from the cut she had inflicted on him. Another brave stood behind her, holding her arms tightly behind her back, and in this awkward position, her shirt was pulled tightly against her heaving breasts. She saw sudden knowledge dawn in the ebony eyes of the brave in front of her. He moved closer, his dark gaze locked with hers, the knife extended toward her.

Shuttering her eyes against her anguish, she stifled an appeal for help before it could escape her lips. Jake couldn't help her. No one could. Fear gave way to a feeling of intense hatred for the savages who had captured them. Somehow, she'd live through this, she vowed. And then . . . then, she'd make them pay.

As though she had uttered her fear aloud, Jake's eyes began to blaze. He jerked violently, struggling with his captors. Swearing profusely, he tried to lunge forward but was hauled back roughly. Managing to free one arm, his fist lashed out savagely, colliding against the nose of the nearest warrior. The bone crunched beneath his clenched hand, and the Apache brave fell to the ground. The warrior was quickly replaced by two more, and Jake was roughly subdued.

Angellee, though vaguely aware of the scuffle taking place in the background, found herself completely mesmerized, watching the knife descend toward her.

But instead of feeling the penetration of the blade against her chest, she felt the shirt give as a button flew off the front. Then another button was cut free, and another.

She stared at the Apache warrior, her green eyes widened in amazement. What was he doing?

Feeling the cool air against her breasts, she squeezed her eyes tightly shut, unable, for a moment, to face the shame of her exposed flesh. Suddenly, she became aware of the silence. Everything had become completely still. Unable to bear the suspense, she opened her eyes again, searching for Jake.

He was standing to one side, slightly behind her. He had become aware that something unusual had occurred and had stopped fighting. At the continued silence, a puzzled look crossed his face. From where he stood, he was unable to see her bared breasts and obviously wondered what had captured the warrior's attention.

Swallowing thickly, Angellee threw a look of despair at Jake. If only he didn't have to discover her deception in this manner. Suddenly she knew Buck was right. Jake would never forgive her.

She watched, horrified, as the warrior reached out again with the knife. Amusement lurked in his dark eyes as, with an anticlimactic stroke, he sliced the strings on her hat, yanking it from her head and tossing it lightly somewhere out of her line of vision.

The hair that she'd loosened earlier in the day and never rebraided fell free. It tumbled in a fiery glory across her shoulders, swirling as if it had a life of its own, blazing in the sunlight as it cascaded down her back until it fell past her waist. Although she was totally unaware of it, she was radiantly beautiful in the orange light of the sunset.

A stunned stillness, almost of awe, settled over the Indians. Her gaze was beseeching as it clung to Jake's, pleading for understanding. He stood in stunned amazement, his eyes traveling over her hair, then moving on down to her petite, feminine form. Suddenly, knowledge dawned in his eyes. And with that knowledge, something else, something completely undefinable.

"It wasn't a dream." The words seemed to be dragged from somewhere deep within. Suddenly, he exploded with savage fury. "Dammit! It wasn't a dream," he shouted, resuming his futile struggles.

A guttural command from one of the savages caused the braves to bind the captives' wrists tightly behind them. Angellee fought desperately, accomplishing nothing but causing her shirt to open more. When she became aware that her heaving breasts kept drawing their attention, she stopped fighting them.

A comment from her captor caused the Indians to break out in ribald laughter, and she flushed with shame, hunching her shoulders forward. At least in that position, the edges of the shirt covered the biggest portion of her breasts although it left a wide gap in the middle.

The color flew high in her cheeks as her shame was exposed for all to see, but she stared straight ahead as if she wasn't tired, dirty and shamed at being stared at in such a lustful manner.

Somewhere in the dense pine forest, hidden by the thick foliage, a blue jay squawked. She could hear a wren scolding overhead, while nearby, a squirrel scolded, then scampered quickly away.

It was almost dark, and a command from the leader was apparently the signal for the Indians to make camp. While she waited, still standing in front of the Apache warrior, she was aware of a fire being built in the middle of the clearing. The warrior stared at her a moment longer, then shoved her roughly toward Jake. She stumbled and fell to the ground. Exhausted and discouraged, she lay unmoving where she fell.

Casting a quick, almost pleading, look at Jake, she encountered a stony visage. Angellee knew he was angry about her deception, but how could she explain why she had deceived him? Then, again, why should she have to explain? Surely, it was obvious why she hadn't been able to track her parents' murderers as a woman. Her mouth tightened in a grim line as she realized that if she didn't get out of this mess, she wouldn't be tracking anyone.

Her glance fell on Buck lying face down near them, and she felt ashamed that she had momentarily forgotten him.

"Is he dead?" she asked tearfully, breaking the silence that surrounded them.

"I don't think so," Jake said, almost grudgingly. "But I'm afraid he may be seriously injured."

"We've got to help him," she said, tugging at her bonds. But it was useless. The straps tying her wrists together were too tight. She looked at Buck again. He hadn't moved. Her eyes moved to the six warriors.

"Do you know what band of Indians these are?" she asked.

"I think they're Apaches." Jake was staring at the Indians, avoiding her eyes.

"Apaches. Then, why did they attack us? Weren't you looking for them?"

"Yes. But they don't speak English. I can't make them understand me." He grimaced, glancing at her then swiftly away. "I don't suppose you speak Apache?"

"No. I don't speak Apache, and apparently you don't either," she snapped, glaring at him, unaware she was pushing him to the limit of his endurance. "Well, that's real bright, mister. How the hell are you gonna keep 'em from burnin' us at the stake."

"Shut up," he snarled. His brown eyes regarded her hair, lying in a flaming cloud over her shoulders, and his mouth tightened grimly. "Goddammit, boy . . . hell . . . what in blazes were you trying to pull, kid?" He turned angry eyes on her. "What the hell happened anyway?"

"I don't know what you're talking about," she said stiffly. Her eyes darkened with pain.

"I'm talking about the night we slept together. What happened then? I thought you were just a dream, but you weren't, were you?"

A flush rose up her neck, staining her cheeks bright red.

"So I was right," he said, his eyes narrowing, taking in the rosy flush. "It wasn't a dream. It really did happen." He shook his head. "Why did you pretend to be a boy the next morning? You let me make love to you and—"

"I didn't let you. You—"

"Forced you?" he asked softly. "If I remember right, I was in a pretty weakened condition." His eyes were inscrutable. "Not strong enough to force anyone to do anything."

"Shut up, damn you!" she croaked. She swallowed around the lump in her throat. Tears welled up in her eyes, but she blinked rapidly, refusing to let them fall. She wouldn't let him see her cry. "Just shut up and let me forget what happened that night."

He was silent for a moment. "What's your real name?" he asked, his gaze carefully avoiding her body.

"It's Angellee. Angellee Tucker."

"Angel."

Her breath caught. "Angellee," she corrected huskily.

"Angel," he repeated as though she hadn't spoken. His eyes studied her over-bright face. "I called you that, didn't I?"

She nodded, lowering her eyes evasively. *His memory seems to be comin' back mighty fast.* "Do you have to keep goin' on about it," she asked.

"About what?"

"That—that night."

His gaze flicked toward the Indians a few feet away, and he lowered his voice. "Are you ashamed of what happened, Angel?"

"Yes, damn it! Of course I am. I've never—I'm not—" She broke off, finding herself unable to continue.

"Stop swearing," he said, mildly. "You're not a backwoods boy anymore."

Her green eyes widened in astonishment. "Are . . . are you crazy?" she stammered. "Here we are in danger of our lives, captured by a bunch of savage Indians. We don't know what's gonna happen—we might be tortured or burned at the stake—and you're settin' there goin' on about my language not bein' lady-like."

"Somebody should've taken you in hand long ago," he snapped. "I can't think what your parents were thinking of raising you like a boy."

"Don't you say nothin' about the way my folks raised me up, Jake Logan," she snapped.

A movement at the corner of her vision caught her eye, and she turned to see the warrior who had cut her shirt open staring at her. He sat on his heels, cleaning his rifle. His gaze held hers for a moment, then moved to Jake. He barked a command that was obviously meant for her, and she stared at him, puzzled. What was he saying? He glared at her, then rising to his feet, strode over to them. He stood over her, saying the same thing again.

She looked at Jake. "What does he want?"

"I don't have any idea," Jake muttered.

The brave barked a command at Jake, then spoke to her again. She shook her head in bewilderment, trying to let him know she didn't understand him. He spat out a word, then reached down and grasped her arm, pulling her roughly to her feet.

"Get your hands off her," Jake snarled furiously, struggling to his feet.

The warrior stared at him, casually lifted the rifle and struck Jake a sharp blow on the side of his head, knocking him to the ground.

"Jake!" Angellee cried, trying to wrench her arm free. She had to go to him. The warrior's grip tightened roughly. Angellee fought against him as he dragged her behind him. When they reached the other side of the encampment, he shoved her roughly to the ground, barking a harsh command at her.

Her eyes were anxious as she stared across at Jake.

He hadn't moved since he'd been knocked to the ground. Had he been killed? Her eyes sparked furiously as she turned on her captor.

"You stupid savage," she yelled. "You wouldn't be so brave if he wasn't tied up!"

Amusement flared in his eyes. He spoke softly to her. Reaching out, he ran his hand down her hair, seeming to savor the silky feel of it beneath his palm. She jerked her head away angrily, and he laughed.

Across the encampment, a warrior walked up to Jake and nudged him with a toe. Jake didn't move.

Oh God! They've killed him. Despair settled over her. Why hadn't she been able to help him?

Damn her visions anyway! What good were they when knowing a thing in advance didn't help her prevent it?

Ma was wrong. This ain't no gift. It's a curse.

She watched helplessly as the warrior standing above Jake bent over and began going through his pockets. When he straightened up, he held Jake's watch in his hand.

The watch with Becky's picture in it!

Her heart began to beat faster. They had forgotten the watch. If these were the Apaches, then they would know the girl in the picture. Perhaps that would be their salvation. She held her breath, waiting.

The warrior seemed fascinated by the watch, turning it over and over in his hand. He seemed puzzled by it. He called something across to his companions, holding the watch aloft for the others to see. One of the other braves joined him, and the first warrior passed the watch over to him. The second warrior studied it curiously before handing it back.

Open the watch, dammit!

The first warrior raised his hand as if he was going to throw the watch away.

"No!" Angellee called frantically. "Don't throw it away! Look inside! The picture of Becky is inside!"

Struck by something in her voice, her captor looked at her curiously.

"Look in the watch," she pleaded.

He rose slowly to his feet, his eyes never leaving hers. Then he moved to the warrior with the watch and took the timepiece from him, studying it intently. Puzzled, he lifted his eyes to look at Angellee. She sat stiffly erect, her body held tense . . . waiting.

"Open it!" she snapped furiously. "Open the damn watch."

Although he couldn't understand her, he obviously understood there was something about the watch that was vitally important to her. He studied the watch intently, then tried to insert a fingernail into the crack. His thumb accidentally brushed the catch. It tripped, and suddenly the watch snapped open. He started, dropping the timepiece in his surprise. Leaning over, he picked it up and stared intently at the picture revealed inside.

Angellee held her breath. Perhaps, they would know that they had come looking for the girl Jake called Becky. Even now they were throwing puzzled looks her way. The warrior who seemed to be in command spoke to Jake, nudging him with his toe, obviously wanting him to wake up.

"You hit him too damn hard!" she snapped, trying to control the panic welling from deep within. "Turn me loose. Let me help him."

Ignoring her, he nudged Jake again, barking a command at him. Jake groaned, rolling over. The warrior kicked him in the ribs, and Jake groaned loudly, putting a hand to his head. Angellee gave a heartfelt sigh of relief. At least Jake was still alive.

"Jake," she called urgently. "They found the watch. You've got to find a way to let 'em know we're friends of Becky."

"How the hell am I supposed to do that?" he gritted. He pulled himself upright, a thin trickle of blood dripping down the side of his head. "Sign language?"

"Might help," she muttered. "How bad are you hurt," she called, trying to still her rising panic.

"It probably looks worse than it is," he said.

If only Buck would wake up.

As if the thought had revived him, Buck gave a loud groan.

Chapter Ten

Buck groaned again and rolled over. Angellee drew a sharp breath when she saw his face, almost colorless where it wasn't covered with blood. It was hard to tell from this distance if the blood came from one wound or many.

"Buck," she called urgently. "Buck! Wake up!"

"Why'n hell should I?" he growled. "Damn head feels like a mountain fell on me. What'n hell's goin' on anyways?" He pushed himself up onto his elbows; but when he attempted to raise himself farther, a grimace of pain crossed his weathered face, and he fell back with another groan.

"Don't you dare pass out again," she said, her words coming in a rush. "We're in big trouble. Jake thinks these Indians are Apaches but can't make them understand we're friends. You gotta talk to 'em, Buck. You gotta make 'em understand."

When Buck didn't answer, she thought he must be lapsing into unconsciousness again, and her voice rose frantically. "Dammit, Buck. Do you hear me? You gotta wake up and make these damn savages understand."

"Quit yellin', youngun'," Buck growled. "I hear you good enough." He pushed himself groggily up on one elbow, his narrowed gaze falling on the Indians and moving to Jake who was nearest him. Then he looked at Angellee who was sitting alone with her hair streaming down her back, her shirt gaping open. He struggled to a sitting position, taking in the situation at a glance.

Running a shaky hand through his shaggy white hair, he glared fiercely at the Indian holding Jake's watch. His voice was harsh as he spoke, but although Angellee couldn't understand the Apache words, she recognized the weakness beneath them. Buck was obviously hurt badly.

Whatever he said seemed to surprise the Indians, for they all stared intently at him. When he spoke again, one brave, apparently the leader, walked over to the mountain man. First, the warrior spoke to him at length, then Buck replied.

The Indian turned his attention to the picture, studying it intently for a moment. He seemed to be looking for an answer there. Then he lifted his head and looked at Jake and Angellee, and his features darkened, his mouth tightening grimly. His voice was harsh as he spoke, but Buck's answer was equally harsh. They were arguing about something.

The brave glared furiously at the old man, then flashed a dark look at Jake nearby. His glance moved farther, to where Angellee was sitting, and she flinched. Apparently making up his mind, he gave a guttural command, and a warrior separated from the others, leaned over Jake and cut him free of his bonds.

Angellee sighed with relief and watched Jake rub his wrists. Her attention was diverted as her captor moved to stand over her. His dark eyes were penetrating as they moved over her flaming hair and decidedly feminine form. Then he pulled his knife, leaned over her and cut her bonds.

Angellee's eyes lowered, quickly shielding her gaze from the warriors. She wouldn't forget he was the cause of the indignity she had suffered. Grasping the ends of her shirttails, she tied them quickly together. Then, rubbing her sore, chafed wrists, she moved to kneel beside Jake and Buck.

"I gather they finally understood we were friends of Becky and Lone Wolf's," Jake said, wiping his hand across his forehead, smearing the blood across his face.

"Let's say they're willing to let it rest for now." Buck looked at Jake's blood-smeared forehead. "Looks like you didn't come out of the ruckus so good."

Jake touched the wound. "I don't think it's deep. It just bled a lot." He frowned. "You're the one who didn't fare so well. You were unconscious for a long time."

"I've lived through worse," Buck growled. "It was just our bad luck to stumble across a war party. Swift Arrow, the one that did all the talkin', is their leader." He motioned toward Angellee's captor. "He was kinda reluctant, but he finally agreed to takin' us to Chief Tall Feathers' village."

"It can't be too soon for me," Jake said. "When we get there, Becky will confirm we came as friends."

"Not for a while, she won't," Buck muttered. "So we gotta walk mighty careful-like."

"What do you mean?" Angellee asked.

"Seems Miss Becky and Lone Wolf ain't to home

right now, youngun'. And we may have to wait a spell 'til they get back to the village."

"They're not there?" Jake's expression was grim. "Where did they go? And how long will they be gone? Dammit! Time's running out. I've got to see them soon."

"Take it easy, son. Them Apaches over there excite mighty easy, and I don't know where Miss Becky and Lone Wolf went. Swift Arrow didn't say. Just kept sayin' they weren't there. I wish they was some way of gettin' out of goin' to thet village o' theirs."

"Why?" Jake asked.

"Don't know how safe it's a-gonna be."

"Surely having Becky's picture is enough to prove we're friends of hers. That should make us safe enough." Jake's expression was wry. "I really don't think Becky would be too happy if she returned to find they'd burned me at the stake."

"It ain't no laughin' matter," Buck said, grimly. His faded-blue gaze seemed more than a little worried as it moved to Angellee. "I ain't worryin' about losin' my hair none. Thet ain't all of the problem."

"Well, whatever it is, I'm sure it can be ironed out," Jake dismissed lightly. He seemed in high spirits, as if a great burden had been lifted from his shoulders.

The journey was nearly ended. Soon, he could return to Pittsburgh and— His sleepy brown eyes moved to Angellee, sitting quietly now that the immediate danger had been averted. His gaze took in her flaming hair, then moved over her petite form.

How could he have been so blind, he wondered. She had completely fooled him. His mouth tightened grimly. Made a complete fool of him was a better way to put it. His glance moved farther to where Swift

Arrow sat beside the fire. The warrior's eyes were still on Angellee. Jake felt a sudden, inexplicable tightening in his chest.

Jake watched the Indians build a rope corral for the horses in a grassy glade near the water. "The Indians appear to be settling in for the night," he said. "They're not planning on camping here, are they?"

"Swift Arrow said it's too late to go to the village. The Apaches don't travel at night. We'll break camp at dawn."

"I don't like camping with that group," Jake said, his narrowed gaze resting on the warriors.

The old-timer flicked a glance his way. "Reckon you ain't got much choice," he said.

"I guess you're right, Buck. Since we're outnumbered and without weapons, it wouldn't do any good to object." He rubbed the end of his nose, his voice rueful. "Too bad there's never a policeman around when you need him." He moved nearer to the old-timer. "Let me see about that wound. You're bleeding all over the place."

He probed the cut with his fingers. "Damn, this looks deep." He threw a look at Angellee. "Bring me some water and a clean cloth," he said. "I need to clean this up before it gets infected. It looks as if it could use a few stitches, too."

She nodded, moving to where the horses were stabled with the Indian ponies. As she reached for her saddlebag, a hand closed over her wrist, stopping her. She turned to find Swift Arrow.

"Damn you!" she snapped, trying to pull from his grasp. "Let go of my wrist!" Her eyes glittered furiously as she glared at the Apache warrior.

Amusement played in his eyes, and his free hand

came out to grasp a long, fiery curl. She jerked her head back, and tears stung her eyes at the sudden pain. Swift Arrow let the silky texture flow through his fingers.

"Buck," she snapped, holding herself stiffly erect, her gaze never wavering from Swift Arrow's. "Tell this damned savage to let me go!"

Buck spoke sharply, but the warrior spared him only a glance, snarling a few words at the old-timer; and then turned back to renew his study of Angellee's flushed face and flashing green eyes.

"Turn me loose," she demanded hotly. "Buck, did you tell him?" Despite her efforts at control, her voice held a hint of panic.

"I did, youngun', but it ain't doin' no good. Thet's the other problem I mentioned afore. Swift Arrow says you belong to him."

"Belong to him!" she squeaked. Her heart began to pound furiously in her chest. "He's crazy!" she exploded, turning panic-stricken eyes on the old-timer. "Tell him, Buck! Tell him he's crazy. Tell him I don't belong to him!"

"Won't do no good, sprout. I'm afeared he ain't in a mood to listen."

She glared at Swift Arrow, feeling a helpless sense of frustration, but more than that, a rising panic. Surely this couldn't be happening to her. It couldn't!

She was vaguely aware that Jake had risen to his feet, his attention caught by all the commotion. He stared at the both of them, and even from this distance, she could see his hardened features and the tense way he held his big body.

Angellee yanked at her wrist again. "I belong to no man," she snapped. "Get your hands off me!"

"Turn her loose!" Jake gritted, savagely. "Tell him,

Buck. Tell him to turn her loose or I'll take him apart with my bare hands."

"You're a dang idiot!" Buck growled. "You think I ain't already told him? He just ain't a-listenin' to me. He says he's keepin' her!" He struggled to his feet.

"Tell him he can't have her," Jake snarled, his eyes glittering fiercely as they held the warrior's gaze. "Tell him she's my woman."

Angellee gasped. Her green eyes rounded in surprise. Jake's woman? But until an hour ago he thought she was a boy. How could he claim she was his woman? Suddenly, the truth dawned on her. It was because Swift Arrow wanted her. Well, he didn't have to go that far! She could handle this without any help from him. Her green eyes glittered brightly.

"Don't tell him any such thing, Buck. I don't belong to nobody."

Buck didn't even spare her a glance. "I think you're bitin' off more'n you can chew, boy. You ain't up to fightin' yet. And I reckon if'n I tell him she's yours, you may have to fight for 'er." He looked at Angellee. "You afeared of him, lass?"

She shook her head, trying to hide her trembling.

"'Course I ain't," she managed. And even as she said it, she realized it was true. Although this warrior looked fierce, she sensed her life wasn't in danger from him.

Buck's narrowed gaze turned back to Jake. "Let it be," he growled. "The youngun' ain't afeared of Swift Arrow, an' he ain't hurtin' her none. Time enough to object if'n he does."

"Tell him," Jake insisted, refusing to back down. The hard lines of his face tightened even more. "Tell him she's mine."

Buck spoke to Swift Arrow at length. The warrior's face darkened with anger. He obviously didn't like what he was hearing. His hand tightened around Angellee's wrist. He glared at Jake and bit out a few short words.

"I told him," Buck said. "But he ain't a payin' no mind."

"Leave it lay, Jake," Angellee said, suddenly afraid for him. His wound had started bleeding again, and he would be no match for Swift Arrow in his weakened condition. He would only wind up getting himself killed. "Swift Arrow ain't hurtin' me."

"Shut up, Angel!" Jake snarled. "Tell him to turn her loose, Buck," he repeated.

Angellee flared instantly. "I ain't shuttin' up, Jake Logan! Don't you tell that Indian nothin', Buck!"

Buck ignored her. He spoke to Swift Arrow in that same guttural language as before, gesturing toward the watch the brave was still holding. The warrior hesitated. His eyes moved from the watch to Angellee. Then he spoke at length. Slowly, as though reluctant, he let go of Angellee's hand, and she sighed with relief.

"It ain't over by a long shot," Buck warned. "He's only leavin' it lay until we get to the village. He prob'ly won't make his move until you talk to Miss Becky." His eyes were penetrating as they met Jake's. "But, you just mark my words, boy. Swift Arrow ain't agonna let it rest. He's got a powerful hankerin' for this little gal. I reckon maybe it's her red hair. It ain't gonna be all that easy to get 'er away from thet village when it's time to leave."

"We'll worry about that when the time comes," Jake told him. Turning to Angellee, he said, "Get the canteen and those rags like I told you. Then get back over here and don't move a foot away from me and Buck."

Fury boiled up, surging through Angellee. Jake had no right to take his anger out on her. The idea of telling her not to move away from them! Where in hell did he think she would go?

Resentfully, she took the water canteen from the saddle and searched in the saddlebags for a clean rag. Then she brought the things to Jake.

He took them without a word and began to clean Buck's wound. When Angellee remained standing, he threw a hard look at her. "Quit hovering, Angel! Sit down on that log out of the way."

"Don't order me around, Jake Logan! I ain't gonna stand for it!"

"Don't say ain't."

"Damn you!" she exploded. "Don't you be tellin' me how to talk."

Jake stood up slowly, obviously intent on teaching her a lesson.

"Easy, boy!" Buck muttered low. "Swift Arrow ain't a likin' the way things're goin' over here."

Jake cast a quick look at the warrior, meeting Swift Arrow's angry stare. He took a deep breath, forcing himself to calm. "Would you please sit down, Miss Tucker?" he gritted through clenched teeth.

Put off by his attitude, Angellee wanted to refuse, but one look at Swift Arrow's tensely held body caused her to obey. She didn't want any more trouble with the Indians either.

Jake knelt beside Buck again and finished cleaning the blood from the old man's forehead, exposing a wound two inches long at the hairline. He studied the gaping edges. "I was afraid of that," he muttered. "It needs stitching. Do you have a needle and thread, Angel?"

"No," she said, eyeing Buck anxiously. Jake was right; the wound needed stitches. "What're we gonna do?"

"Nothin'. It'll heal if it's a-gonna. Just wrap it up with a clean rag and leave it alone."

"It seems we don't have any choice," Jake said, his gaze taking in Buck's pale face. "Get the bedroll, Angel, and I'll spread it out for—" He stopped abruptly. "On second thought, don't get it. I will."

He rose to his feet, moving to the horses. The warriors watched him as he removed the bedroll from the saddle on Buck's mount and returned to the old-timer. He untied the bedroll and rolled it out, telling Buck to lie down.

As he helped the mountain man onto the pallet, Jake swayed slightly, his face ashen. "Jake," Angellee said. "Your wound needs tendin'. Let me do it."

"I need to unsaddle the horses first," he said, getting unsteadily to his feet.

"I can do it."

His expression was grim. "I told you I don't want you moving from here, Angel. And I meant it."

She opened her mouth to argue but thought better of it. Swift Arrow's ears seemed to be tuned to hear any dissension from his white captives.

Jake unsaddled Daniel, then attended to the Arabian stallion. As he turned to Buck's mount, he swayed slightly. Panic rose inside Angellee, and she stood.

"Mind the boy."

Although the warning was spoken low, it startled her. She turned to the mountain man who had raised himself on his elbows. "He ain't gonna want no help."

Knowing Buck was right, she watched Jake remove the saddle and slide it from the horse. Turning from the horse, he seemed to falter, then with no warning, he collapsed to the ground.

"Jake." Her anguished cry brought the warrior's heads around, but she paid them no mind, rushing to Jake's side.

"I told you to stay there," he muttered weakly, opening his eyes to gaze at her.

Ignoring his words, she knelt beside him, putting her arm around his waist and helping him to his feet. She swayed beneath his weight.

"Don't pass out on me," she said, her voice husky with strain. "I don't like the way Swift Arrow's watchin' us."

As they staggered across the uneven ground toward Buck, Angellee could feel the eyes of the Apache leader on them. When they finally reached the mountain man, she lowered Jake nearby, then picked up the cloth, dampened it and began ministering to his wound. Her eyes met his and held, for something indefinable flickered deep within the brown depths of his.

A trembling excitement took hold of Angellee, starting with a warm glow burning deep inside her body, gradually building until it nearly overwhelmed her with its intensity. She couldn't break the contact with his gaze. In fact, she felt she was almost drowning in the dark, velvety depths of his eyes.

Her hand grew still on his forehead. Her pulse leaped with excitement, and her breath was raspy. She drew a shaky breath and swallowed hard. A rosy blush stained her cheeks.

Suddenly, her wrist was grasped, and she was pulled to her feet. Something was thrust in front of her face, and she blinked, staring at Swift Arrow in bewilderment.

Swift Arrow smiled—a smile that didn't quite reach his eyes. Holding her gaze, he waved something before her face, speaking softly in his language.

"He's offering you a piece of dried venison," Jake said drily.

"Oh. Uh, tha—thank you," she stammered, taking the piece of meat from him, and summoning up a smile. She tugged at her still captured wrist, breathing a sigh of relief when it was released. Kneeling down beside Buck and Jake, she broke the dried meat, offering each a piece.

"I'd be more careful if'n I was you," Buck growled, eyeing Jake severely.

"What are you talking about?" Jake asked.

"You know what I'm a-talkin' about. Swift Arrow's done made it known he wants the girl. Figgers to have her when we get to the village. So I'd be mighty careful in the meantime not to give him any excuse to stick a knife in me while I was asleep."

Angel felt a tingle of apprehension. She looked at Swift Arrow, then back at Buck. "Do you really think he'll try that?"

"Cain't rightly say, youngun', but I wouldn't put it past him a-tall. He don't seem to cotton to the way Jake's a-lookin' at you." Buck bit off a chunk of the meat and chewed thoughtfully.

Angellee shivered. "I won't be able to sleep tonight."

"You can sleep," Jake said, touching her cheek gently. "And don't worry about it. I'll keep watch."

His words grew within her, filling her with the most abiding sense of security she could ever recall feeling. Jake would watch over her.

Chapter Eleven

At daybreak they began the last lap—or what Angellee hoped was the last lap—of their journey. This morning, aside from issuing orders through Buck, Swift Arrow had largely ignored them. One of the braves wore her hat; the same one dangled her twin Colt and holster set around his neck.

Although the air felt cooler as they climbed steadily higher into the mountains, the sun beating down on her unprotected head was hot.

They proceeded two abreast, with an Apache brave in front and several others interspersed between the captives. Jake rode beside Angellee and Swift Arrow brought up the rear.

A tingling sensation on the back of her neck told her that Jake had turned slightly in the saddle, and his eyes were on her again as they had been so many times since she woke this morning. She found it disconcerting. Casting a furtive glance in his direction, her eyes dwelt on the long length of his legs, his lean hips and flat stomach and his wide chest. The sheer masculinity of him left her knees weak. She felt staggered by her reactions to him. They seemed to be magnified now that he was aware of her identity.

Her gaze traveled over his wide shoulders to set upon his firm chin, his well shaped lips, which had fit so well against her own, his nose and his eyes—She gasped as she encountered his darkened gaze. A slight frown creased his forehead, and his eyes seemed to burn into her. Averting her gaze quickly, she wondered at the intensity of feelings he aroused in her.

Needing to get away from his burning gaze, she turned in her saddle to check on Buck, who rode close behind her, just in time to see him sway in the saddle, then straighten himself slowly. He seemed to be growing weaker with each passing hour.

She fretted anxiously over him, but every time she expressed her concern, he kept assuring her he was all right; he would make it.

At midmorning though, when they had finally reached the narrow trail that led upward toward a high mesa, Buck lost consciousness, falling to the ground with hardly a sound. Since Buck brought up the rear, she was the only one to notice.

"Buck!" she cried out, pulling Star up and sliding from the saddle. In an instant she knelt beside him.

"What's wrong?" Jake asked, reining Daniel around.

"It's Buck," she said. "He's unconscious."

Before Jake could reach her, two braves had picked the old-timer up and slung him belly down across the saddle.

"Don't," she protested, pushing at the nearest warrior. "He's bleedin' again. He'll lose too much blood ridin' that way."

They ignored her, tying him securely to the saddle.

Jake dismounted and lifted Buck's head to check his wound.

"Stop them, Jake," she said, turning pleading eyes on him.

"It won't do any good to try to stop them, Angel," he replied. "They don't understand a word we're saying, and arguing with them would only serve to slow us down more. I think their village must be on top of the mesa." He nodded up the trail. "We're nearly there. A few more minutes won't make that much difference to him."

"It might!" she snapped, turning away from him and mounting Star. Her worried eyes fell on the bloodied bandage circling Buck's forehead. If only she could make the Apaches listen. Her lips tightened grimly. They wouldn't dismiss her so lightly if she had her weapons; even her knife would add more weight to her words, but Swift Arrow had kept it. Jake and Buck's weapons had been distributed between the other men.

She urged her mount forward, and the animal stumbled over the rough, rock strewn ground. She pulled hard on the reins until Star regained his footing.

As they neared the top of the mesa, a dog barked—the first indication she had that they had nearly reached their destination—and she sighed with relief. Now maybe they could get help for Buck. Soon they reached a clearing in which stood some sort of dome shaped dwellings. A campfire burned in front of each one of the frail hovels, which were made of sticks and brush and put together with dabs of mud.

Several Indians, alerted by the barking dog, emerged from these rounded brush huts, their attention focusing immediately on the small party approaching. Some of the men were dressed in white man's clothing, and others were dressed in buckskin and breechcloths. Most of the women wore their black hair twisted into coils at the napes of their necks and were clad in shapeless buckskin tops that hung past their hips. The buckskin skirts they wore came to mid-calf, and high moccasins that pulled above their knees covered the rest of their legs.

Although Angellee was relieved the long ride had finally come to an end, she still felt uneasy. Refusing to be intimidated by the villagers, Angellee met their hostile glares as she rode past. Swift Arrow led the captives on until they reached a dwelling at the far end of the village, then he stopped, sliding from his horse with an effortless, catlike grace. He gestured for them to dismount.

A tall man stepped from the hut, and Swift Arrow spoke to him in that strange, guttural language that Angellee could not understand, gesturing occasionally to the white captives.

The tall Apache's gaze moved to Angellee, taking in the fiery red hair streaming across her shoulders and down her back, then moved on, coming to rest on Jake. "I am Chief Tall Feathers," he said. "Swift Arrow has told me you have come to see Blue Eyes. Is this so?"

Jake introduced himself and extended a hand to Chief Tall Feathers. The chief stood, unmoving; his face was expressionless as he ignored Jake's proffered hand. Undaunted, Jake casually dropped his hand. His eyes held Chief Tall Feathers' steadily. "I think there's been a mistake," he said. "I don't know anyone called Blue Eyes. I came to see Rebecca and Lone Wolf."

"Blue Eyes is the Apache name for the girl the white eyes know as Rebecca."

"Oh," Jake said. "I didn't know."

"If you knew her as you claim, then why did she not tell you this?"

Angellee held her breath, her body rigid. After traveling all this way, was Jake going to be turned away? And what about Buck? He needed help. She watched Jake but could tell nothing of what he was feeling by his expressionless face.

"When Becky returned to Pittsburgh after her time with your people, she was in mourning. She never spoke of that period to anyone."

Chief Tall Feathers seemed to weigh Jake's words carefully. "What you say could be true. In the beginning, Blue Eyes' stay in our village was not a happy one."

Jake nodded. "Chief Tall Feathers, I have traveled a great distance to see Becky and Lone Wolf. Are they here?"

"No."

Although Swift Arrow had already told them Lone Wolf and Becky were gone, Jake's intense disappointment was evident. "Could you tell me where they are?" he asked. "I must see them immediately."

"If you wish to see them, you will have to wait for their return," the tall Apache said.

"When do you expect them?" Jake asked.

The chief shrugged. "Maybe tomorrow. Maybe next week." His dark eyes moved to the figure of Buck lying belly down across the saddle. "Your friend is injured," he commented, studying the bloody bandage.

"Yes," Jake said gravely. "Could you help him? He

was injured when your people mistakenly attacked us."

"Who is this man?" Moving over to Buck, the Apache lifted the old-timer's head and stared intently at him. Some fleeting expression crossed his face, then he turned and barked a guttural command. Swift Arrow and another brave moved to Buck, untying him and pulling him from the saddle. Buck's limp, unconscious body landed with a thump on the ground, and Angellee uttered a sharp protest at the rough treatment.

Jake made a move toward them, but Chief Tall Feathers stopped him. "I know this man. He will come to no harm from my people."

Jake's lips tightened grimly. "It's because of your people he's in that condition."

"Swift Arrow was hasty. Your friend will be taken to our medicine woman's wickiup. She will care for him." His eyes fastened curiously on Angellee. "Is this your woman?" he asked.

"Yes," Jake said.

"No," Angellee muttered at the same time, watching anxiously as the Apaches carried Buck to a wickiup nearby. Was the Apache chief telling the truth? Were they really going to help Buck? She made a move to follow, but Jake stopped her, his hand gripping her forearm firmly.

"Wait," he muttered, his fingers tightening into steel bands when she tried to pull away.

Chief Tall Feathers studied Angellee, his gaze lingering on the fiery red hair that tumbled in wild disorder around her face and down to her waist. Then his sharp gaze fastened on the arm that Jake gripped tightly. "She does not appear to think she is yours," he said thoughtfully.

"Nevertheless, it is so."

"That is too bad. Her beauty has caught Swift Arrow's eyes," the chief continued. "He wants her."

"Yet she is mine. You don't allow one man to take another's woman, do you?"

"Not if she really belongs to the first. There seems to be some doubt."

Angellee couldn't leave well enough alone. "Chief Tall Feathers . . ." she ventured.

"Angel, shut up. Don't you understand the situation? Or do you wish to be given to Swift Arrow?"

"Of course not!" she muttered, glancing quickly at Swift Arrow who stood nearby watching the confrontation.

"Then for God's sake, keep your mouth shut and let me do the talking."

Her lips tightened grimly, and her green eyes glittered as they met his and held. Jake had no right to speak to her that way, and it was all she could do to remain silent. But she did, for deep down she knew he was right.

Somewhere, she vaguely remembered hearing that Indian woman were given even less freedom than their white counterparts. It was said that any unattached women were sold to the highest bidder by the Indians. She didn't know whether or not the stories were true, but she was afraid to risk it. At least Jake was civilized. Swift Arrow was not. If complications developed because of her disagreement, she'd worry about them later. Right now, concern over Buck took precedence over anything else.

"Chief Tall Feathers, I'd like to stay with Buck for a

while if it's allowed."

"No one will stop you," he said. "He is considered a friend to our people, and until Lone Wolf returns, you will be treated the same."

"Thanks," she said, breathing a sigh of relief. That had been easier than she had thought possible. She saw Swift Arrow and the other brave emerge from the wickiup where they had left Buck. Swift Arrow still carried her knife. She turned back to the two men. "There is one other thing, Chief Tall Feathers."

He lifted a brow inquiringly.

"It's my weapons. Your warriors took them. May I have them back?"

"You have no need of weapons in this village," he said looking down his nose at her. "Not if you are friends."

"But—"

"Don't push your luck, Angel," Jake warned.

"But they—"

"Listen to me, dammit!"

"Jake. Let me finish. Them guns belonged to my brother. They're the only things I got left of him. I want 'em back!"

"Your weapons will be returned when you leave our village," Chief Tall Feathers said.

Angellee knew she had no choice but to accept the chief's will. "I guess that'll have to do," she said, turning away from them.

As she left, she felt the men's eyes on her but quickly put them from her mind as she entered the wickiup belonging to the medicine woman.

The light in the hut was dim, making Buck a barely discernible lump lying on a bed of hides. Kneeling, she placed her palm anxiously against his forehead. His skin was hot to the touch.

Removing the binding from his head, Angellee examined the angry, red skin around the wound. It had stopped bleeding, but it was puffy and swollen.

An elderly woman, not much taller than Angellee, entered. Like the other Apache women, her dark hair was coiled at her nape. After a quick glance at Angellee, she knelt beside Buck. She bent over him, examining the wound carefully. Then, with a frown, she spoke a few words to the young Indian girl who had entered behind her. The girl listened, nodded her head, then left.

"How did this happen?"

Angellee started. "You speak English?" she said, noticing at the same time the woman's eyes were brown with curious yellow lights. Cat eyes, she told herself. The woman has cat eyes.

"Yes. I speak your language," the woman said. Her face was as expressionless as her voice. "What happened to him?" she repeated.

"We—Jake and Buck and me—were on our way here when your warriors attacked us. They hurt Buck pretty bad."

"I was afraid there would be trouble when Swift Arrow and the warriors left," the woman murmured. "They are young and hot-headed and still fighting a war that was lost long ago."

Before Angellee could think of a response, the young girl arrived with the supplies she had obviously been sent for, and the medicine woman turned her attention to the wounded man. Angellee found herself staring curiously at the younger woman. She was slender, dark-haired and somewhere in her early twenties. As though aware of the white girl's scrutiny, she cast a swift look at Angellee from dark, luminous eyes and smiled shyly before leaving the wickiup.

The medicine woman dipped a cloth into an earthen bowl of water and washed Buck's wound.

"Is he gonna be all right?" Angellee asked.

The Apache woman threaded a needle with white cotton thread before she answered. "I do not know," she said, jabbing the threaded needle into the puffy edges of the wound. "He has lost a lot of blood, and he is no longer a young man." She began to stitch the gaping edges together.

Angellee forced herself to watch as the woman worked. Buck was still unconscious, and for that, she felt thankful. Her concentration was so great, the woman's voice startled her.

"I have heard the man's wife, Prairie Flower, has died," she said, tying the thread off. Then, taking some herbs from a leather pouch, she mixed them with a little water until she had made a paste. Smearing the mixture on the wound, she bound it tightly with a fresh, clean cloth.

"Did you know his wife?" Angellee asked.

"No," the small woman said. "Although Prairie Flower was an Apache, she was not from this tribe." She settled back on her heels. "Now all we can do is wait. If he has not lost too much blood, and we are able to keep the infection down, then he will recover. If not, then he will die. I think it does not make that much difference to him anymore."

"Of course it makes a difference to him," Angellee protested. "No one wants to die."

"He has had much pain in his lifetime," the woman said, quietly. "Much pain. Too much to expect one man to bear." Her eyes were saddened as they dwelt on Buck's gray face. "Finally, after all these years, he had found a woman to love him that he could love in return. I am sure he found great joy in the coming of his child." She shook her head sadly and picked up one of the gnarled hands. "Poor Buck," she said softly.

"You know him." Angellee was surprised.

"Yes," the woman replied. "Many years ago, I knew him well. Well enough to know he would not wish me to pity him. He learned long ago, as I did, that we must accept what we cannot change, for it is useless to fight against fate."

She looked at Angellee. "I know you do not understand. You probably think I am hard. Perhaps I have come to be, but so is the Apache way of life. I learned when I was very young that I must adapt to the changes in my life or I would not survive."

Angellee looked closer at the woman's tanned face. It was unlined, making it hard to determine her age. She could be anywhere from thirty to fifty years old.

As their gazes met and held, Angellee's green eyes rounded with surprise. "You're not an Indian."

"You are wrong." A smile softened the woman's velvety brown eyes. "I am Apache."

She opened her pouch and dropped some herbs into a bowl then added steaming water and stirred the brew. Then she laid it aside.

Angellee stared at the woman curiously. She had said she was an Apache. Why should she lie about such a thing. And yet—

"Rachel?"

Startled, both women turned to find Buck's eyes open, his gaze fixed wonderingly on the woman.

"Is it you, Rachel? Am I dead, then? Did I go to Heaven? Or am I only dreaming again?"

"You're not dreaming." The woman's lips curved into a smile. "And you aren't dead." She lifted his head gently and held the bowl she had prepared to his lips. "Drink this," she said.

He sipped the liquid. "I thought you were dead," he groaned as she laid his head back against the furs. His hand lifted weakly, clutching her arm. "They told me you were dead, Rachel."

"I know," she said gently. "It's what I told them to say."

"You told them. Why?"

"Because I finally came to realize you would never stop searching for me as long as I lived. And Panther would never have let me leave. One of you would have died."

"All these years," he whispered, weakly. His faded-blue eyes darkened with pain. "All these wasted years. You were here. Close enough for me to reach out and take. If I had just known." His eyes closed wearily, and he breathed heavily.

"Is he unconscious?" Angellee asked, her anxious gaze on the old-timer who had come to mean so much to her.

"He is just asleep," Rachel said. "I gave him a sleeping potion. It is the best thing for him." She smoothed back the grizzled white hair gently. "He will—"

She broke off as an Apache warrior, his dark hair streaked liberally with gray, stepped through the entrance. His face was inscrutable, his dark eyes piercing as they scanned the hut, coming to rest on Rachel.

"How is he," he asked, ignoring Angellee as he bent over the old mountain man.

"Very bad, I'm afraid. He's lost a lot of blood and is very weak. But I will make him well if it is humanly possible."

"I'm sure you will," he said, taking her arm and helping her to her feet. "I am sorry. It was not my wish that this should happen, White Dove. Please believe it is not my doing. I have honored my promise all these years, and I will continue to do so."

Her eyes held his. "You do not need to tell me that, my husband. I already knew what was in your heart."

He smiled gently at her. "Tall Feathers wishes to speak to his mother," he said.

"Then I must go to him," she said immediately.

"Wait, Rachel," Angellee called. "Suppose Buck needs you. Where will I find you?"

"You will not need to find me. I will be here if I am needed. And please, do not call me Rachel. My name is White Dove now."

Chapter Twelve

After White Dove and the warrior left, Angellee sat beside Buck. Her eyes looked over his grayed features, wondering at his association with the medicine woman. What had their relationship been? Could he have loved her? If so, how terrible for him to lose her in such a way, and perhaps even more terrible to find her again after all these years.

Her eyes had become used to the dim light in the hut, and her gaze left the wounded man to search her surroundings curiously. The wickiup was very primitive, and yet, it had been made comfortable. The walls were made of brush and sticks fused together with mud, sand and grass. Tanned hides covered the dirt floor, and sleeping mats had been woven from plant fibers and covered with furs. Ears of dried corn hung together in bunches from the ceiling, and buckskin bags obviously held food, herbs and other supplies.

On one side of the entrance a tomahawk was hung, along with a bow and a quiver of arrows. Closer at hand were several larger baskets holding blankets and other things that were necessary to a well run household.

With her curiosity satisfied, her attention turned back to Buck whose face seemed to have grayed even more. She was afraid his chances of recovery were slim. Reaching out, she picked up his wrist and felt for a pulse. White Dove had told her Buck might not care if he died? Could she be right? Anxiously, she searched for a spark of life, heaving a sigh of relief when she felt a faint, but steadily beating pulse beneath her thumb.

With her fears about Buck slightly allayed, Angellee's thoughts returned to the medicine woman. Was she really an Apache? Angellee didn't think so. Her name had been Rachel at one time. That, in itself, meant nothing, but there was some mystery involved. She had said Panther would never let her go. What had she meant?

Her brow wrinkled in thought. She had called the old man, husband. Was his name Panther? Was he the one who refused to let her go?

Tall Feathers wishes to speak to his mother.

That's what the old man said. Angellee's eyes flickered with surprise. Was White Dove Chief Tall Feathers' mother? It appeared to be so.

Angellee was still pondering the mystery of the medicine woman whose name had been Rachel when a movement in the doorway caught her attention. She looked up to see the young woman who had been there earlier.

"My name is Little Turtle," she said shyly, stepping into the dwelling. "Swift Arrow told me you are Rebecca's friend."

"Uh—no. Not exactly," said Angellee, caught off

guard by learning the young woman spoke English. But, unlike the older woman, there was no question that she was Indian.

"You do not like Rebecca?" the woman asked, her eyes clouding over.

"No. I mean . . . it ain't that I don't like her. I don't know her. It's Jake that's her friend."

"I see. And the man called Jake is your man?"

"No," Angellee denied. Then, remembering the Indian who wanted her, nodded her head. "Well, yes. I guess he is," she amended.

Little Turtle looked puzzled. "You do not know?"

"Yes," Angellee said, nodding her head emphatically. "It's . . . well, he ain't been my man very long."

"Oh." Something flickered in the depths of the Apache woman's luminous eyes. "Perhaps Rebecca's friend, Jake, has not grown attached to you yet. That would be good. Swift Arrow finds you pleasant to look upon. He desires you and means to possess you."

"Well, like I said, I belong to—to Jake." A blush stained her cheeks as she told the lie. But then, was it really a lie, for her heart did belong to him. He just didn't know it.

"It is of no great importance," Little Turtle said, a smile lifting the corners of her mouth. "Swift Arrow will make an offer for you. Perhaps Jake will sell you to him. I would like that."

"Why?" Angellee gasped, looking at the Apache woman in dismay. Although she knew Jake wouldn't consider selling her to the Apache warrior, her heartbeat quickened. "Why do you want Jake to sell me to Swift Arrow?"

"Because then you would live in the village, and it

would be nice to have you for a friend." Her luminous dark eyes moved admiringly over Angellee's red hair.

"I wouldn't make a good friend," Angellee said. "I'm not a nice person at all. And Jake—he—he would never sell me."

"Why?"

"Because—" Angellee looked at the woman in confusion. "Well, where I come from, we don't sell each other. It's not done in the white man's world."

Little Turtle laughed. "We are in the land of the Apache People, far from the white man's world. Here, it is done."

"Dammit! I don't care, Little Turtle. I ain't gonna be stayin' here. I'm goin' back to my world soon as Jake sees Rebecca."

"Not if your man sells you to Swift Arrow," Little Turtle said calmly.

Angellee stared, stupefied, at the little woman. What kind of place had she come to? For God's sake, what had she got herself into? Or rather, what had Jake got her into?

She frowned as a sudden thought struck her. "Where's Jake?" she asked.

"With Chief Tall Feathers and Swift Arrow. They sent me for you."

A feeling of impending doom swept through Angellee. "Why?" she whispered.

"Swift Arrow will offer for you. You must be present," Little Turtle said. Suddenly, she frowned. "Jake must agree. If he does not, Swift Arrow may challenge him. Then, Rebecca's friend could be hurt. He is already wounded, and Swift Arrow is a mighty warrior. He would be sure to kill Jake."

"Jake would have to fight for me?" Angellee's face drained of color at the possibility. Surely Chief Tall Feathers would never allow Swift Arrow to do that. He had said the warrior was too impetuous. That meant the chief didn't approve of his actions. Surely the chief had the final say over the tribe.

"Yes," Little Turtle said. "Jake must fight if he is challenged."

Angellee rose to her feet slowly. "Is there anything I can do to stop them?" she asked the small Apache woman. "Your friend, Rebecca, would be angry if Jake was hurt."

"Perhaps there is no need for worry," the woman said. "Perhaps Jake will sell you to Swift Arrow. Then there will be no trouble."

"He—he'd better not." Angellee said grimly. "But he can't fight him either."

"If he is challenged, he must fight," Little Turtle said. "He has no choice."

As they emerged from the hut, Angellee's eyes were drawn to the crowd that had formed. As they saw her, the crowd split, creating a path that allowed her to approach the three men standing in the center.

Angellee moved on leaden feet toward the three men, dreading the oncoming confrontation. What could they do without weapons? Her footsteps dragged as she forced herself forward. Then, too soon, she stood beside the three men.

"What's goin' on?" she asked, glancing covertly at Swift Arrow's expressionless face before lifting her eyes to Jake.

His expression was troubled, and he spared her only a swift glance. "I'm not sure. But whatever it is, keep quiet and let me handle it."

Chief Tall Feathers held up a hand for silence. "Swift Arrow wants the woman," he said, his eyes running over Angel's petite form before returning to Jake.

"That's already been settled," Jake said evenly. "The woman belongs to me."

"Swift Arrow has accepted that. He wishes to buy her. He will give three rifles and a horse." Chief Tall Feathers' lips split into a smile. "That is much wealth for only one woman."

"She's not for sale."

Swift Arrow's face darkened when Chief Tall Feathers translated. He stared grimly at Jake, then spoke at length to the chief. Not once had his glance strayed to Angellee.

"Swift Arrow says the woman is skinny and cannot provide much warmth in his bed for the cold winter that approaches. She has no knowledge of the Apache life and must be taught these things. She is not worth what he offered, but he will add another horse to his gifts."

"He's right," Jake said, ignoring Angellee's gasp of outrage. "The woman is worthless. She can't cook and she's lazy and always complaining. I could not take advantage of Swift Arrow's good nature by saddling him with such a useless woman."

Swift Arrow's face became red with rage as he listened to the translation. His voice was harsh as he drew Angellee's knife from his breechcloth and spoke again.

"Swift Arrow agrees the woman has no value, but he will buy her anyway." He spread his hands. "Just to relieve you of her worthless presence. He knows he is mad, but he will give you the three rifles, two horses and the knife."

"That's *my* knife!" Angellee snapped, grabbing Jake's arm and shaking it roughly. Her green eyes glittered angrily. "Dammit, Jake! That's my knife, and he can't use it to buy me."

"Shut up, Angel," Jake growled, shaking his arm loose from her grasp.

"The knife belongs to Swift Arrow," Chief Tall Feathers said, ignoring Angellee completely and speaking only to Jake. "It was taken in a fight."

"The answer is still no," Jake said. His mouth was tense, and there was a tight alertness about him. "The woman is mine, and she is not for sale."

Swift Arrow didn't wait for a translation. He spun angrily on his heels and pushed his way through the crowd, disappearing into the forest.

"Your woman is willful," Chief Tall Feathers said, eyeing Angellee with disfavor. "You must take her to the wickiup you have been given and punish her severely." He sighed deeply. "I will never understand the ways of the white eyes. You should have sold her. Swift Arrow will not give up so easily what he desires, and she can only bring you trouble."

While Angellee stood outraged, Jake took his leave of the chief, pulling the indignant girl toward one of the dwellings.

As they entered the wickiup, Jake reached for the canvas flap and let it drop in place, shutting out the rest of the world and leaving them in complete privacy. Then he turned to stare down at her with glittering eyes. A muscle twitched in his jaw, and the moment crackled with tension as she waited for him to speak. There was something menacing about him, almost primitive in his stance. He didn't even try to hide his anger from her.

Her heart fluttered, and she drew the tip of her tongue across lips which had suddenly become dry. As their eyes held, her heart began to pound wildly in her breast. She breathed deeply and became aware of the completely male scent of him—and of something else. Her nostrils twitched as she identified the clean fragrance of pine needles.

"You're determined to get both of us killed, aren't you?" he gritted, startling her into awareness. "I told you to keep your mouth shut out there and let me do the talking."

"I don't take orders from you, Jake Logan!" she snapped. Although she felt more like crying, she lifted her chin and stared defiantly at him, unwilling for him to see how he affected her.

His anger erupted. Grabbing her by both shoulders, he shook her savagely. Her head bobbed on her shoulders, and she was dizzy when he finally threw her away from him.

They stood facing each other without moving for several moments. She tried to control her trembling body, while he fought to control his rage.

"Why did you lie to me," he growled. "Why did you masquerade as a boy?"

"I never lied to you," she muttered, turning away from him so he wouldn't see how his anger affected her. "I never told you I was a boy."

"Don't hedge with me, Angel," he gritted. "Just don't do it."

Her body sagging in defeat, her head bowed submissively. Buck had said he would be angry, but deep down she had hoped he was wrong.

"It was Pa's idea for me to make folks think I was a boy," she whispered. "Pa said it was the safest way to travel. What're you so mad about?"

"How did you think I'd feel when I found out I'd been rescued by a mere child?"

"I ain't a child," she said, her eyes glittering brightly with unshed tears. "I'm seventeen, and where I come from, that's a woman growed."

"Seventeen is not a woman where I come from, Angel." He ran a hand through his disheveled hair. "I can't believe you're promiscuous, so I—"

"What's that?"

"Promiscuous?" She nodded her head and he blushed. "It's a woman who—who—never mind."

"I want to know what you called me," she insisted.

"I didn't call you that, Angel. I said I can't believe you are."

"Well, how in hell do I know if I am unless you tell me what it is?" she asked in exasperation.

"Dammit! Quit swearing. And the word means women who pursue men."

Her eyes grew round. "Like—like them ladies of the night? Them—them soiled doves?"

He nodded.

A blush crept up her neck staining her cheeks scarlet. "Jake Logan, I never—never—oh, what do you mean by a-callin' me somethin' like that?"

"I didn't call you that, Angel. You didn't let me finish. I was going to say I don't know why you let me make love to you."

She lowered her thick lashes quickly, hiding her gaze from him.

"You must have got quite a few laughs from deceiving me," he said harshly.

"I didn't laugh," she muttered.

"Didn't you?" he asked. "I believe you were laughing all the time."

"Do we have to talk about this? We're in an awful lot of trouble, and we should be trying to find a way out of it."

"What trouble is that?"

"You mulehead!" she snapped. "Didn't you hear what that chief said? Swift Arrow ain't done yet. You might have to fight him?"

"Why should I do that?"

"Well, if you want me—"

"Who said I did?"

"You didn't sell me."

"For God's sake, Angel!" he snapped. "I haven't been away from civilization so long that I'd sell a woman to the Indians."

"That was the only reason?" Despite all her efforts at control, her voice came out strangled.

"What other reason could I have?" he asked loftily.

"I d-don't know," she stammered. "I g-guess I thought—"

"What did you think?" he asked, prompting her. His hand cupped her chin, forcing her to meet his curious, heavy-lidded, brown gaze.

"Nothing!" she snapped, her eyes glittering brightly. "I didn't think nothin'."

"Good. Then that's settled."

"Yes. I guess it is."

They stared at each other in silence, and as she gazed, mesmerized, into the velvety brown depths of his eyes, her anger melted slowly away.

When his arms circled her, there was no thought of resistance. She trembled as she laid her head against his chest, feeling the steady beat of his heart beneath her ears.

He was silent for the duration of a few heartbeats. Then, incredibly, she felt his lips on her forehead, his breath warm against her flesh. Her eyes met his, and as if moving independently, her arms slid up around his neck twining in the hair at his nape. She lifted her mouth eagerly to meet his. His hand found the curve of her breast, moving upward to caress her nipple until it stood erect, and she shivered, her breathing suddenly restricted.

He raised his head, gazing deeply into her eyes. She was wary, unsure of him, but she wasn't frightened. She had never thought to meet a man such as he. He had plenty of courage but was also knowledgeable in the ways of the world. Her gaze moved to his lips, and she knew she had to taste them again.

Jake's magnetic gaze roamed over her flushed features. Her heart began to pound faster, and she was engulfed in waves of anticipation.

God! How she loved him. She felt a momentary embarrassment as his hand moved to the knot in her shirt. He worked at it until it fell free, then his callused fingers slipped inside to caress the bare flesh of her nipples.

The heat began to build up in her body as Jake stroked the tautened peaks. Hot, languorous passion, which she had never experienced before, began to build inside her body. His mouth left hers, leaving a trail of fire as his lips moved to caress her throat. Her skin tingled beneath his touch, and she arched her neck, inviting his lips. His mouth wandered down to her breasts, and tension mounted within her hungry body. Her senses were being clouded with each caress, each kiss, each stirring movement of his lips.

Angellee whimpered, pressing tighter against him, trying to ease the throbbing ache in her body, an ache that was rapidly turning into an all consuming fire. He moved her away long enough to strip the rest of her clothing away.

Picking her up, Jake carried her to the bed of furs lying on the other side of the wickiup. She moaned when he left her; but soon he was back, and his maleness was hard, throbbing against her thigh, ready to possess her. Eagerly, she thrust her hips against his.

"Wait," he whispered huskily. "Take it slow and easy. I want to make it good for you."

She stared at him in confusion. Her pulse raced frantically, and she whimpered, consumed by her overpowering need.

His lips found her breast, closing over her taut nipple, and he began to suck it gently. She quivered with delight, holding his head firmly to her breast. She hadn't known making love could be such a blend of anguish and pleasure.

Jake's lips left her breast, and she sighed with disappointment. Then, his lips moved down her body, halting briefly to tease her navel before they continued farther down. His tongue caressed her body gently, moving down—down—down . . .

Suddenly, she quivered. "Stop it, Jake," she gasped, twining her fingers in his dark hair and pushing frantically at him. "What're you doin'?"

Ignoring her efforts to push him away, he slipped his hands beneath her rounded bottom and lifted her as his lips fastened against the bud of her desire. Skillfully, his tongue invaded the area and lovingly labored to overcome her objections, bringing her to heights of eagerness that she had never believed possible.

Soft moans and pleas escaped her, and her breath came in short gasps. Her tongue snaked out, wetting her dry lips over and over again.

The blissful torture finally ended as he possessed her swiftly, and she was swept into a whirlpool of raging desire, drowning in the all consuming rapture. Her senses swirled as she was lifted higher and higher until finally the universe exploded and she was sliding—sliding down the other side.

She lay sated, tiny beads of perspiration dampening her skin. His rough hand smoothed a damp tendril of hair away from her face.

"I can't believe what just happened," he whispered huskily. "Why did you resist so long, Angel?"

She looked up at him, wanting again to drown in his eyes. "I—I guess it's because I'm stubborn," she said, huskily. "And—and maybe I'm used to havin' my own way?"

He laughed softly. "You can say that again. But I never thought you'd admit it."

"Pa always said faults wasn't so bad unless you pretended not to have any."

"Your father was a wise man, Angel." He picked up a strand of hair, wrapping it around his fingers. "You've had me worried. With Swift Arrow deciding you belonged to him . . ." His voice trailed off. "Why didn't you tell him you were my woman?"

"I didn't know you meant it," she said. Her eyes lifted, meeting his. "Did you mean it, Jake? Did you really mean it? I wanted it to be true."

He frowned. "You denied it because you wanted it to be true? That doesn't make much sense, Angel."

"I guess not," she sighed. "But you made me so damn mad." She noticed he had avoided answering her question.

"Angel," he said severely. "You have got to stop swearing so much."

"Why?"

He seemed taken aback by her question. "Hell, Angel. Where I come from, ladies don't swear."

The color drained from her face. "I'm sorry, Jake," she whispered. "I guess I ain't a lady." She turned her head away from him, feeling ashamed.

"Angel," he said gently, cupping her chin and forcing her to look at him. "I didn't mean to imply you weren't a lady. You're every inch a lady in every way that counts. I know that. But we'll have to teach you a few things so other people will know as well."

"What other people?"

"The people you will encounter when we leave here. The people who live back east."

"Will I be seein' them?"

"Of course you will. Did you think I would leave you here? After I've seen Lone Wolf and Becky, we must go to my home in Pittsburgh."

"You're gonna take me with you, Jake?" Her eyes were the color of emeralds, shining with happiness. "You mean it? You ain't just foolin' me?"

"Of course I mean it. Do you think I could bear to go

anywhere without my angel now that I've found her?"

"Jake," she said, cupping his face with her small hands and staring solemnly at him. "I'll try to stop cussin'. Really I will. And I promise I'll learn to control my temper." Her eyes darkened. "It sure ain't gonna be easy though," she sighed. "Seems like it just sorta explodes a-fore—"

"*Be*fore, Angel," Jake corrected firmly.

"—*be*fore I know it," she said obediently. "Jake. Will you teach me to talk like you do? I don't want you to feel shamed by bein' with me."

"I could never feel shame for anything you did, Angel. Please believe that. I just don't want you to feel badly, and people aren't always as nice as they could be. Especially when they meet someone that's different."

"I'm gonna learn, Jake," she said fervently, planting a butterfly kiss on his chin. "I swear I am. I ain't—ain't—" She broke off. "That's wrong. 'Ain't' ain't a good word, is it?"

"No. It isn't. You must say. I am not, instead of ain't."

"I *am not* gonna make you shamed with me," she said earnestly, gazing into his eyes. "I swear I ain't—" she stopped, clapping a hand over her mouth as she realized what she'd done. Then tears welled up in her eyes. "I ain't never gonna learn, Jake," she wailed. "I ain't never."

"Yes, you will, Angel," he said, cuddling her closely against him. "We'll take it one step at a time. You'll have to expect to slip every now and then. Don't worry about it so much. We're going to start right now, so you'll have it down pat by the time we go home."

"Right now?" she repeated, reaching up to place another kiss on his chin. "Do we have to start right this *very* minute?"

"No, you little minx. It doesn't have to be right this *very* minute." Then his lips found hers, covering them possessively with his own, and they sank into a world of passion.

Chapter Thirteen

The air was hot, almost stifling. Desperation filled Angellee as she rode Star through the valley, praying she wouldn't be too late this time. She topped the last brush-covered hill, and there was the smoking wagon. Like before, it lay in ruins. Was she destined to always be too late? Would she never arrive in time to save them? Maybe . . . maybe this time they would still be alive. She urged the big stallion forward, fear knotting in her stomach, her fists clenched tightly on the reins.

Ma lay broken, as before, in a huddle of petticoats and calico. There was no doubt in Angellee's mind she was dead, and an anguished scream escaped her.

No.

No. Don't let it happen. Knowing it wasn't over yet, her despairing eyes searched for her father. He lay beside the gutted wagon, his broken arms reaching for her as blood trickled from his mouth.

"Make 'em pay, Angel," he groaned. "Make 'em pay for what they done."

Suddenly, heavy arms engulfed her, and she struggled violently. "Pa," she cried. "Help me, Pa."

Her father stared at her with dead eyes, and she screamed and screamed and screamed, fighting against the arms that held her.

"Angel. Wake up. Wake up, Angel. You're having a nightmare."

The words finally penetrated her consciousness, pulling her from sleep. She opened her eyes and stared at Jake's concerned features.

"You were having a bad dream," he said softly. "Are you all right now?"

She nodded her head, staring at him with sleep-drugged eyes. "I . . . It's just a nightmare that I have sometimes," she said.

"About your parents?" he asked gently.

She nodded. "About when I found 'em. It . . . it wasn't very pretty. My ma was . . . they had . . . and my pa . . ." She shuddered, unable to continue.

"I'm so sorry, Angel," he whispered, pulling her close against him. His voice was ragged with emotion when he spoke. "If there was any way I could take the pain away, I wouldn't hesitate for an instant."

She snuggled against him, allowing him to comfort her. "I wish you could have known my ma and pa," she whispered. "They'd've liked you."

"Would they?" he asked. "I hope so." He kissed the tip of her nose, then pressed a butterfly kiss on her lips.

When he raised his head, the look in his sleepy brown eyes made her blush, and she turned her head, avoiding his gaze.

He laughed softly, aware of her confusion.

Turning her head cautiously, her gaze met Jake's, then quickly skittered away as memories of last night returned. Blushing, she reached for the blanket which had fallen to her waist, exposing her breasts to Jake's view.

"Don't be embarrassed," he said softly. "It happened. Just accept it."

Shyly, she lifted befuddled eyes to his. "I guess"—her voice sounded slightly strangled—"it'll take some gettin' used to."

He laughed. "You're a delight, Angel," he said, cupping one perfectly formed breast in his palm. "How long do you think it will take to get over that shyness with me?"

"I . . . don't think it'll take very long," she whispered, her breath catching swiftly as his mouth lowered to catch one pert nipple between his teeth. "If you keep that up, I don't think it'll take long at all."

She felt breathless, weak and not just a little giddy. He was working the same magic again as he had done last night, making her forget everything except his arms around her, his lips on her warm flesh.

"Jake," she said, arching against him breathlessly. "Is it right like this?"

"Like what?" he growled softly, biting gently on the tautened peak.

"Like this?" she gasped, squirming beneath him, reaching out to hold his dark head closer, pressing him tightly against her. "In the daylight? While the sun's shinin' down on everthin'."

A muffled sound reached her ears, making her aware that she was smothering him in her desire to get closer, to feel more of the intense pleasure that only he could bring. His body began to shake, and she let him go, startled. She stared at him, wide-eyed, as he raised his head. Suddenly she became aware he was laughing and drew back to stare at him in amazement.

"What're you laughin' at?" she demanded indignantly, her green eyes glinting.

"You," he sputtered. "Oh, God, Angel! You're priceless."

"You're makin' fun of me again," she said, feeling unaccountably hurt.

"No. No, Angel," he said gently, kissing her eyelids briefly. "I would never laugh at you. But you make me feel so damn good. I've never in my life met anyone like you." He clutched her to him tightly. "Thank God you came along."

"You really mean that, Jake?" she asked. "You're not just funnin'?"

"No, sweetheart. I'm not just funning, and I really do mean it." He gazed at her earnestly. "I would never laugh *at* you, Angel. Just *because* of you. There is a difference, you know."

"Truly?" she asked.

"Truly," he replied.

"You didn't answer my question," she said softly. "Is it all right to—to—well, you know."

"To make love?" he prompted.

"Yes," she blushed. "In—in the daylight like this. While the sun's shinin' down."

"Oh, yes. Anytime and anyplace. As long as we're alone and feel like it, we can make love whenever we want to."

"I like that idea, Jake," she said softly. "I like it a lot."

"So do I," he said, kissing the end of her nose. He looked regretfully at her mouth. "I'd like nothing better than to lay in this bed and make passionate love to you, but we'd better save it for later. I've got to go see how Buck's doing." He frowned. "I hope he's going to make it. He's been a good friend to me."

"And to me," she said softly. She sighed with disappointment as he reached for his clothes but knew he was right. The lovemaking would have to wait until later. Right now, they must make sure Buck was being taken care of.

Angellee dressed herself, then brushed her fiery hair and pulled it back at the nape, tying it with a piece of string. Then she prepared them a breakfast of cornmeal mush and dried fruit.

After they had eaten, Jake left to check on Buck. A few moments later Little Turtle appeared, offering to show Angellee the spring where she could fill her water *tus,* a small wicker jug woven out of sumac.

As they walked, Angellee learned that Little Turtle was married and had a son.

"His name is Little Crow," the Apache woman said proudly. "And he is five summers now."

"Where is he?" Angellee asked curiously.

"He is with the other boys. He learns to make spears from the old ones."

"Do they start so young?"

"The boys must start early, for there is much for them to learn if they are to grow up to be mighty warriors."

By now, the two women were approaching the narrow stream of water. Nearby, Angellee saw three warriors. One of them, she recognized as Swift Arrow. As she watched, one of the warriors drew back his tomahawk and let it fly. The blade buried itself with a muffled thud in the center of a red circle painted on the trunk of a large pine tree.

"What are they doin'?" Angellee asked, stepping on a stone and dipping the jug in the sparkling water. She allowed it to fill to the brim before lifting it out again.

"Playing a game of skill," Little Turtle replied. As Angellee stepped back, the Indian woman bent to fill her water container.

"Throwin' tomahawks is a game?" Angellee asked, keeping her voice low. She knew from the surreptitious glances they were receiving the warriors were perfectly aware of their presence.

"Yes. It is a favorite pastime of the young warriors when they are not hunting for meat. The men of our village must practice their skills constantly, for many lives depend on their skill."

Angellee watched another warrior bury his tomahawk in the tree. She was fascinated. Although only three warriors participated, she was reminded of the get-togethers they'd had in the Ozarks. Any excuse at all was used to get together for festivities in the hills. There'd been Corn Shuckin's, Quiltin's, House Raisin's, Pea Thrashin's, and Candy Pullin's. But the ones she'd liked best were the Turkey Shoots she had attended with her parents. There had always been knife throwing contests and games of horseshoes as well as shooting matches.

"Can we watch 'em?"

The Apache woman hesitated. "Perhaps it would be better if we returned to the wickiup," she said.

Angellee frowned. "Why?" she challenged, her green eyes glinting. "Do they have somethin' against women watchin' 'em?"

"No . . ." the little woman said slowly. "I do not think so, but—"

"Then we'll watch," Angel decided, setting her water container down.

In the face of Angellee's determination, the Apache woman gave in, setting her water jug down next to Angellee's. They moved closer to the men to obtain a better view. Angellee was quick to notice Swift Arrow wasn't using a tomahawk. He held a knife. As she watched, he let it fly. It landed on the edge of the target circle. Hoots and jeers from his fellow opponents accompanied his failure.

Angellee's eyes sparked, and her mouth thinned as she recognized the knife Swift Arrow was using to compete with. It was *her* knife.

Just then, Swift Arrow's dark gaze met hers, and something flared in his ebony eyes. As she watched, he lifted the knife and stroked his chin softly with the blade, seeming to taunt her with its possession.

Angellee's lips tightened grimly. Damn him! The knife was hers, given to her by her father. She'd get it back. She didn't know how just yet, but Pa had always said where there was a will, there was a way. And she meant to find it.

One of the other warriors spoke to Swift Arrow in that strange guttural language, obviously reminding him that it was his turn to throw, for the warrior drew the knife back and let it fly.

The knife buried itself just on the edge of the circle, quivering a moment before it became still.

Angellee's lips curled contemptuously. If only she could retrieve her knife, she'd show him up quick enough. Slowly, an idea formed in her mind. "Tell him

I'll play him for the knife," she said, turning to Little Turtle.

"Angel—"

"Tell him, Little Turtle."

Reluctantly, the young woman approached the warriors and spoke to Swift Arrow. His eyes flashed with humor as they played over Angel's face. Then he spoke and Little Turtle turned back to Angellee. "He says why should he? The knife is his."

Anger surged in Angellee's eyes, and she shuttered them quickly. "Tell him I'll buy it from him," she said, attempting a smile that didn't quite come off.

Eyeing Angellee's flushed face uneasily, Little Turtle spoke again to Swift Arrow, then gave Angellee the answer. "He wants to know what you'll give for it."

Angellee dug in her britches pocket, removing the few coins she found there. From these, she plucked a twenty dollar gold piece and offered it to him. He shook his head. Adding the few remaining coins, she held them out. Again, he shook his head.

"It's—it's all I've got," she said.

When Little Turtle translated, Swift Arrow grinned and spoke. Laughter broke out around them, and Little Turtle answered him sharply.

Angellee gritted her teeth and clenched her fists tightly, reminding herself of her promise to Jake. Holding Swift Arrow's gaze grimly, she asked. "What'd he say?"

"He—he says you can have the knife for a—a kiss."

Rage flowed through Angellee's body. The damned savage was making fun of her, throwing her offer in her face. Why she'd . . .

I swear I'll learn to control my temper, Jake.

Last night's words surged in her memory, and she took a deep, calming breath. No. She wouldn't fly at him, but he wasn't going to get off scott-free.

Angellee's green eyes flashed up at him with insolent appraisal. Putting a hand on each rounded hip, she spoke.

"I'd rather kiss a rattlesnake," she said, slowly and distinctly so there would be no mistaking her words.

She heard Little Turtle's gasp of dismay, but her gaze never wavered from Swift Arrow's. He studied her curiously, obviously puzzled, waiting for the Indian woman to translate her words.

When Little Turtle remained silent, her eyes lowered to the ground, Swift Arrow spoke to her.

"What's he sayin'?" Angellee asked.

"Swift Arrow wants your answer," the Apache woman said timidly, casting a desperate look at the fiery-haired girl with the matching temper.

"Tell him."

"I cannot tell him such a thing," Little Turtle said. "It is a bad thing to insult a warrior such as Swift Arrow. He—"

"Tell him," Angel insisted. "And make sure you get it right."

Little Turtle's voice quivered as she translated Angellee's words. The other braves broke out in laughter; but Swift Arrow's face darkened, and his eyes grew hard. Deliberately, he pulled a silky strand of long, red hair from the confining string. Holding it away from her head for a moment, he sliced through it with the blade.

Angellee was outraged. He had cut her hair. She stood motionless, her body rigid, trying to control her temper.

Holding the long strand aloft, Swift Arrow waved it in the air in front of her, tauntingly. When she stood unwavering, staring at him with glittering emerald eyes, he pulled another long strand from the string and cut through it.

Angellee exploded.

"Damn you, you mangy polecat. Gimme my knife!" She leapt toward him, but he danced away, laughing at her, waving the long strands tauntingly in front of her. Angellee balled her fist and took a swing at him. Quick as a cat, he sprang back and she missed.

Angel was vaguely aware the commotion had attracted a crowd. The three of them were surrounded by several of the villagers who seemed to laugh louder as she grew angrier.

"What the hell is going on?"

Both tormented and tormentor turned at the same moment to find Jake pushing his way through the crowd.

"I asked a question!" Jake growled. He looked big and dangerous as his gaze fell on Angellee's red, flushed face. Somehow, her fiery hair had escaped the confining string and tumbled in wild disorder about her face, streaming across her shoulders and down her back.

Jake's eyes narrowed on the long red locks in Swift Arrow's hand. "What's he doing with your hair?" he growled.

"What's it look like?" she spat. "He cut it off! All I was tryin' to do was get my knife back and—"

"You mule-headed little baggage!" Jake exploded. "Won't you ever learn?"

"Jake—" she protested, her eyes going round with surprise. His anger seemed to be directed at her, not Swift Arrow who was clearly to blame for the whole thing.

"Shut up, Angel!" Jake growled, grabbing her hand and dragging her along behind him. She dug in her heels, sending pebbles and dirt scattering, determined not to suffer the indignity of being dragged along behind him like a child. With a muffled oath, Jake threw her over his shoulder with hardly a break in his stride.

"Lemme go!" she shrieked, pounding Jake on the back. "Lemme go!"

Laughter, punctuated with her outraged shrieks, followed them all the way back to the wickiup.

As soon as they were inside, Jake threw her on the bed of furs. She landed with a thud, the breath knocked out of her, staring at the angry man who confronted her.

"Damn fool girl! Don't you have any sense at all? You told me last night you were going to keep that temper under control. But the minute my back is turned, what do you do?" He didn't wait for an answer. "You go and get in a fight with Swift Arrow over that damn knife!"

"Jake," she protested. "That knife is mine. It belonged to my pa. He gave it to me. It's all I have left. Swift Arrow had no right to—"

"Rights don't count here, Angel," Jake said grimly. "Strength does and he's got the whole damn village to back him. That makes him a hell of a lot stronger than us."

"I can't let him keep it," she said, her voice quivering.

"I have to—"

"Dammit! You don't have to do anything! If that knife is that important to you, then I'll think of some way to get the damn thing back."

"Will you?" she whispered. Her green eyes shone up at him, bright with unshed tears. "Would you really do that?"

"Yes. I guess I'd really do that." He came down on the bed of furs with her.

"And my guns?" she persisted, sliding an arm around his neck. "Will you get them, too?"

"Angel," he groaned, burying his face in her neck. "I don't see how—"

"I have to have 'em, Jake. I can't leave 'em here. My family's all gone. Them weapons are all I have left of 'em. Them Colts was Johnny's. When Pa gave 'em to me, I swore I'd always keep 'em by me."

"I'll see what I can do," he muttered, lifting his head to stare at her. "But I'm not making any promises, Angel. Those pistols are fancy and could be harder to recover than the knife."

"I don't care." She traced his jawline with a fingertip, watching him steadily. "I ain't one for cryin' uncle, Jake," she said. "I never was."

"What in the world does that mean?"

She frowned. "You may be smart on some things, but others you ain't. Back in the hills, when you're down, you gotta say uncle to be let up. I ain't never said uncle, an' I ain't gonna."

He grinned. "That doesn't surprise me in the least."

"Are you still mad?" she whispered softly.

He sighed. "No, Angel. I'm not *mad.* I just don't know what I'm going to do with you."

"You could try kissin' me," she suggested, huskily.

"That's the best offer I've had all day," he said. His softened brown eyes roamed hungrily over her flushed features.

A warm glow spread over her body as he lifted a finger and traced the outline of her lips ever so slowly. His hand captured her chin, tilting her face for a full view. His probing gaze caressed her with tenderness, and her heart began to race madly. His hands moved lightly down her throat grasping her shoulders tenderly. Then he leaned forward and fastened his lips eagerly against hers. His tongue darted into the moist cavern of her mouth searching out the inner softness there. Then he kissed her eyes, her earlobes, and teased the tender flesh of her throat.

When his questing fingertips found the hard button of her nipple, she shivered, overpowering desire racing through her body. She pressed herself tightly against him, feeling an immediate response in his body. Then he lifted his head and smiled gently down at her.

"I'd like nothing better than to stay here all day with you, Angel. But Brave Eagle, Little Turtle's husband, has asked me to go hunting with him. Since I don't know how long we'll be here, I figured I'd better lay in a fresh supply of meat."

She gazed at him in disappointment. But he was right. They needed more meat.

"Take me with you," she suggested.

"No." He grinned wryly. "You're expected to stay here and do women's work."

"I'd rather go huntin'," she said.

"I expect you would," he said. "But you'll have to stay here. It's Brave Eagle's hunt, and he wouldn't want a woman accompanying us."

She sighed with disappointment but accepted defeat gracefully. Her gaze roamed tenderly over his features. He was so vibrant, so alive. And she loved him. If anything happened to him . . .

Suddenly, a chill came over her, and a shadow crossed her face. Had the evil she'd seen passed him by? Or was it still to come?

"What's wrong?" Jake asked, huskily, tracing a gentle finger across her jawline.

"Jake." Her voice was hesitant. "You'll be careful, won't you?"

"Of course," he said. "You worry entirely too much." He leaned over, kissing her lightly, then rose to his feet. "I have to go." He smiled down at her. "I can hardly wait for tonight."

"Neither can I," she whispered softly. "Neither can I."

Chapter Fourteen

Angellee lay on the bed of furs where Jake had left her. Her green eyes glittered with remembered pleasure, her heart soared. Jake had given her a glimpse of heaven. His lovemaking had been skillful, tantalizing her until she had been mad with wanting him.

She could hardly believe he really cared for her.

She hugged herself, squeezing her eyes shut, laughing with pure pleasure. Jake loved her. He wanted her to go to Pittsburgh with him. She'd never dreamed there could be such happiness.

Suddenly, a thought intruded and she frowned. Jake hadn't really said he loved her, but he had to care. He had been so tender, so passionate.

Passion isn't love. She pushed the thought aside.

Angellee wanted his love, but if desire was all he could offer, then she would accept that. She wouldn't press him. She'd wait, and eventually he would come to love her. He hadn't mentioned marriage, but it had to be an oversight. Right now the important thing was this feeling he had awakened in her, this surging, overpowering urge to possess him. As soon as he completed his mission and talked to Becky and Lone Wolf they could . . .

A shadow crossed her face, and she closed her eyes in pain.

Jake had nearly completed his mission.

But she hadn't.

Oh, Pa. I'm sorry. For a moment I forgot.

She stared sorrowfully at the ceiling of the hut. She couldn't go with Jake. She had only delayed her search for her parents' killers, not completely abandoned it.

Initially, she had only meant to protect Jake. Instead, she had lost sight of who she was and her purpose in life. She had even forgotten she was gifted with "the sight." Though she had hinted of it to Jake, he had not believed her. Would his feelings change if he believed in the gift?

Would he look at her in hatred? Would he react as the hillfolks had done, avoiding her eyes in case she took a notion to put a spell on him? She hoped not. Perhaps he would take the news calmly, as Buck had.

Unable to stay with her thoughts any longer, Angellee rose and went to see how Buck was faring.

As she crossed to White Dove's hut, she met Little Turtle and arranged to meet her later. She found White Dove sitting beside Buck, her dark eyes on his weathered face. Hearing Angellee approach, she turned, smiling as she recognized her visitor.

"How's he doin'?" Angellee whispered, kneeling beside the wounded man.

"You don't have to whisper," Buck growled. "I ain't dead yet." He opened one eye to peer up at her. "What you been up to, youngun'? I heared all thet commotion goin' on out here awhile back, and Rachel said you was in the middle of it."

Angellee grimaced, hating to be reminded of the incident. "Weren't nothin' much," she muttered. "Swift Arrow's got my knife. I was tryin' to get it back."

Buck frowned. "Ain't he had it since they jumped on us?"

She nodded her head.

"Well, what's rilin' you all of a sudden about it?" he snapped.

She gazed at him with reproof. "It's mine, Buck," she said. "You know that. I told you it was give to me by my pa and—"

"I knowed where you got it, sprout," Buck growled. "But you mark my words and leave it be. It ain't worth gettin' them Injuns all riled up over a knife."

"It ain't just any old knife," she snapped. "You know that. And that ain't all. Swift Arrow cut off some of my hair with it and—"

"You got plenty of it left, don't'cha," he growled. "I don't see what you're squawkin' about."

Her green eyes mirrored hurt. "I thought you would understand," she muttered, looking away from him. "You're actin' just like Jake did."

"I understand, all right," he growled. "But, like I said, thet knife ain't what's important right now. So mind my words and leave it be." He licked his lips. "Damn, where's my tobacco chaw?"

"You don't need it, Buck." White Dove cut in. "You still have a fever. We must rid you of it before you have your tobacco again. Now, close your eyes and go back to sleep. You must rest to get your strength back."

Angellee was amazed to see Buck subside. He

heaved a long sigh and closed his eyes. "Don't you be a-gettin' in any trouble while I'm laid up youngun'," he muttered. "I'll sort things out later about that knife."

Angellee smiled at the old-timer. He hadn't turned against her after all. "I'll come back later," she whispered softly to White Dove. The woman nodded, not taking her eyes off Buck's face.

Angellee left the hut thinking of Buck's long hunt for the woman inside, which finally ended with him believing her dead. How sad life could be. He must have suffered terribly all these years.

"Is he not well?" Little Turtle asked, taking note of the frown on her friend's face.

"No. He's much better," Angellee said. "I was just thinking of your medicine woman, White Dove. Buck knew her before we came to your village."

"Yes," the woman said. "I heard the People discussing them."

"The People?"

"Yes. The old ones. The elders of our village."

"What did you hear?" Angellee asked, curiously.

"Just the elders speaking together. Even though White Dove is our medicine woman and is allowed many things other women aren't, they expressed surprise Panther would allow the mountain man into the wickiup."

"Panther's her husband, isn't he?"

"Yes. He is also the father of Chief Tall Feathers. Until a few years ago, Panther was the chief of our tribe. But he fell ill with the white man's disease called smallpox. Panther feared he would die like so many others of our tribe did. He knew it would leave the warriors without a leader. So he made Tall Feathers the chief."

"And he didn't die."

"No. Chief Tall Feathers offered to step down, but Panther told him the warriors needed a younger chief to lead them and refused."

Angellee wondered if White Dove cared for her husband. Was it possible to live with someone so many years and not care for him?

Little Turtle interrupted her reverie by asking if she was ready for her first lesson in basket weaving. She nodded, more than ready, needing something to keep her hands busy.

Angellee had often helped her mother back in the hills, and soon she had completed a small basket and began a larger one. They worked in companionable silence for a while, each busy with her own thoughts. Suddenly, a dark shadow passed over the basket Angellee was working on, and she looked up to see an ominously dark sky above. She turned to Little Turtle intending to comment on how quickly the sky had changed.

The Apache woman was not there.

Instead, Angellee saw a swiftly running stream. On the bank, a small boy stared across the water. She couldn't see his face, but something in the figure, possibly the slump of the shoulders and the angle of the head, gave him an air of tragedy.

"Angel?" The voice called from a great distance. "Is something wrong?"

Angellee blinked and Little Turtle's anxious face appeared in her line of vision.

"Where is your son?" Angellee heard a voice asking, a voice that she barely recognized as her own.

The Apache woman's face went still. "Little Crow is playing near the stream with his friend, Black Arrow."

"Show me where!" Angellee said urgently, jumping to her feet, sending the baskets scattering.

Reacting to Angellee's sense of urgency, the little woman didn't question her further. With Little Turtle leading the way, the women hurried to the stream but found no sign of the boys.

"This place ain't deep enough," Angellee muttered grimly. "It's a deep hole—some place deep enough for swimmin'."

"There is such a place," Little Turtle said in a shaky voice. "But the children have been warned to stay away from there. They cannot swim."

"Show me," Angel said. "And hurry."

Needing no further encouragement, Little Turtle took the lead again, and the two women started up the stream. As they rounded a curve, they saw a young boy standing on a gravelly shoal that fingered out into the water. He stared with horror-struck eyes into the depths of the stream.

While Little Turtle frantically questioned the boy, Angellee was pulling off her boots. She dove cleanly into the stream that had widened and deepened at this point. Her fear for the child was so great that she was hardly aware of the icy chill of the water. Her strokes were strong and sure, for she knew the exact spot. In a matter of moments she was there.

Taking a deep breath, she dove to the bottom. She opened her eyes, searching through the dimness for the child she knew was there. The bottom was covered by weeds that obstructed her view, but she pushed them aside. Her heart pounded with exertion, and her lungs began to burn, demanding air.

Angellee called upon inner reserves for strength. She must find the boy. A dull roar had begun in her ears, but she ignored it, threading her way through the reeds.

Suddenly she saw him.

The boy's body was limp, his foot wedged between two rocks. He looked lifeless.

Angellee reached for the child's foot, trying to tug it free of the obstruction. Bright flashes sparked beneath her eyelids, yet still she worked. Then—he was free.

Grabbing the boy's arm, she gave a desperate push with her feet, emerging seconds later on the surface, gasping for air in her tortured lungs.

Turning the boy on his back, she grasped him beneath the chin and began her swim back to shore, unaware of the silent crowd of women and children that had gathered to watch her struggle with the limp boy.

Her heart was pounding heavily in her ears as she pushed the boy onto the bank and heaved herself out of the water. She lay panting with the effort, vaguely aware of Little Turtle's anguished cries.

Struggling to a sitting position, Angellee stared at the child's inert body. His face was drained of color, his eyelids bruised. Turning the boy on to his stomach, she poised her body over his and began to rhythmically pump the water from his lungs. Water surged from his mouth, but his small body lay still, unaware of her ministrations.

She rolled the boy over on his back. Placing her mouth against his, she began to breathe into him, praying all the while. She had seen Granny Bess do this in the hills, and although she wasn't sure it would work, she knew she could do no less than try.

Someone grabbed her arm, trying to pull her off the boy, but she pulled it away and kept on breathing for him. Then she was grabbed again and yanked forcibly from him.

"Leave me alone, dammit," she shouted. "I'm tryin' to help him." Her arms were released, and she began to breathe for the boy again.

Suddenly, her efforts were rewarded. The boy's chest heaved, he took a big gulp of air and began to cry. Angellee's eyes filled with tears of relief, and she moved back, allowing Little Turtle to take her son into her arms and comfort him.

Over the little boy's dark head, the Indian woman's tear drenched eyes met hers, thanking her silently for saving her son. Little Turtle lifted the boy into her arms and, despite offers of help from several women, carried him back to their dwelling.

Although Angellee could feel the stares of the Indians as she trailed along behind them, no one spoke to her. She shivered as the chill wind penetrated her wet clothing. She began to feel slightly apprehensive as she returned to the hut she shared with Jake. How would the Apaches react to what she had done?

Changing into dry clothes, she willed her mind to forget what had happened. Then she dried her tumbled mass of red hair, worked the tangles free and brushed it smooth, leaving it hanging loose and shiny along her slender back.

At dusk the warriors returned to the village. She had prepared vegetables for a stew and made ash cakes. As Jake entered the wickiup, she ran to him, welcoming him home with a hug and a kiss on the mouth.

"I'll have to go away more often if that's what will be waiting when I return," he whispered in her ear. His lips tugged at an earlobe, and she felt a tingling sensation start in her toes.

She smiled at her reaction to him. It would take some getting used to. Her eyes met his and the smile faded.

"What's wrong," she asked, hesitantly.

He frowned. "Nothing's *wrong,* but I heard something peculiar when I got back to the village."

So he had heard. She pulled away from him.

"Don't do that," he said, giving her a shake. "Don't draw away from me. We have to talk about this, Angel."

"I don't know what you mean," she muttered. She wanted to look away, but he refused to allow it, taking her chin in a firm grip.

"Yes. You do. You weren't anywhere near that child and yet, somehow—someway—you knew he was in danger."

She remained silent.

"You knew he was in danger," he repeated, his gaze holding hers. "Just as you knew I had been captured by the Comanches. And you saved the boy after everyone thought he was dead."

"My Granny Bess did that back in the hills once when little Timmy Wilson fell in the river and folks thought he was drowned," she said. "It ain't no big thing. Sometimes it works and sometimes it don't."

"All right. I'll accept that. But what I want to talk about is how you knew we were in danger?"

"I tried to tell you that time in the caves," she whispered. "I tried to tell you about my visions, but you laughed at me."

"I did, didn't I?" he mused softly. "I'm sorry about that. So you have visions. How long have you had them?"

"Near all my life. At first, I didn't understand about it. Not until they came for Granny Bess. But then, I knew."

"Who came for your Granny Bess?" he asked gently.

"The hillfolks," she said, swallowing around a lump in her throat.

"Why did they come?"

"They said she was a witch and they burned her."

"Oh, my poor little girl," he said tenderly. "How you must have suffered."

She met his eyes. "What're you gonna do?" she muttered.

"Do? Nothing."

"Nothin'?"

"Of course not. What did you think I'd do?"

"Ain't you afeared of me now that you know?"

"Is that what you thought?"

She nodded slowly. "Folks usually are when they find out. That's the reason Ma said it had to be kept secret. Not even Pa was told."

"Your father didn't know?"

"No. Only Ma and Sara Fellowes, the birthin' lady, knew."

"How did the mid-wife know? Was there a sign?"

She nodded. "I was born with a caul, as was Granny Bess and her ol' Granny afore her." Her eyes studied her feet. "It's the sign of the witch, you know."

"What is?" he asked. "Being born with a caul?"

She nodded.

"Angel."

His voice was grim, and she flinched beneath it. *Here it comes. Now he'll hate me—or be afeared—or—"*

"Angel," he repeated. "Look at me."

Bravely, she lifted her chin and met his eyes. Then, confusion filled her mind. He didn't look angry, or scared, or anything else like that. What she saw was concern.

"Is that the reason your family left the hills?"

"Yes."

"And you actually thought it would make a difference in my feelings for you?"

She nodded.

"Come here," he said. "Let me show you how I feel."

He tilted her face up to his and covered her mouth possessively with his own. She responded with such fervor that he seemed momentarily taken by surprise. He recovered quickly.

When she was allowed to breathe again, she looked at him with relief. "I was afeared for you to find out."

"Never be afraid to tell me anything, Angel," he said.

His dark gaze fastened on her hair. Palming a long fiery curl, he let it slide through his fingers before he met her eyes. She felt as if she had been marked with his brand as his glittering gaze burned into her. And even though he had said it didn't matter to him, she sensed something was troubling him.

"What's wrong?" she asked.

"Nothing, really," he muttered. "But Swift Arrow tried to buy you again on that damn hunting trip. We nearly came to blows." He pulled her tighter against him.

"I thought all that was settled," she said. "I thought it was over."

"I'm not certain it is. He's determined to have you. I think it's that damned hair that he's so determined to possess."

"They's other ways of gettin' it, if that's all he wants," she said, laughing nervously at the memory of Swift Arrow's dark, ebony gaze on her. "Maybe he's thinkin' on tryin' to scalp me."

"Don't be silly," he said. "Of course it's not only the hair. He wants what's under it, too."

She smiled nervously. "He may change his mind when he hears what happened today."

"It could work the opposite way and make him more determined to have you," he muttered grimly.

"You ain't gonna sell me are you?"

He shook her gently. "Of course not."

"Then forget it."

"I've tried. But somehow, I can't. I guess it's just the thought of another man wanting what's mine."

"Why does it bother you?" she asked, hiding her delight at being referred to as his.

"I know men like Swift Arrow, my love. I've met his kind before. Lone Wolf is cut from the same cloth. Men like him have a habit of using any means at their disposal to acquire what they want. Especially, when they desire it as much as he does."

Mention of Lone Wolf made Angellee draw away from Jake, for she knew he must be remembering how Lone Wolf took Becky from him. When Jake tried to draw her back into his arms, she resisted. "I gotta get the stew on cookin'," she muttered.

He allowed her to go free, but she felt his eyes on her, and the minute she had everything in the pot, he pulled her down on the bed of furs beside him.

"Now tell me what's upsetting you," he murmured.

"I ain't upset," she denied, looking away from him. "I was just gettin' supper ready. I don't like you messin' with me when I'm fixin' the meal."

"You're not being truthful," he said, studying her flushed face. "What upset you?"

She wriggled, trying to escape him, but he refused to relent. Finally, she gave up and relaxed against him. "I guess . . . I guess I don't like to hear you talkin' about some other woman."

He stared at her in surprise. "Other woman? Do you mean Becky? What nonsense, Angel. Why should it bother you?"

"It shouldn't," she snapped. "But it does."

Comprehension dawned in his eyes and they softened. "Are you jealous of Becky, Angel?"

She nodded, refusing to look at him.

"Look at me," he commanded, cupping her chin in his palm and forcing her to meet his eyes. "There's no need for you to be jealous. Becky is an old friend. Nothing more."

"You mean it?"

"Come here," he said, his eyes gleaming with hunger. "I'll show you."

Needing no further encouragement, Angellee raised her face for his kiss. As his mouth closed over her own, she became aware of the thudding of his heart, of the feel of his strong arms that encircled her body.

Her breath was coming low and shallow; her senses were swamped by his subtle, entirely male fragrance. She felt as though she were on the edge of a precipice as Jake deepened the kiss, sending heat waves of lightning flashing through her nerves. His hard length seemed to be imprinted on her flesh, and her nipples tautened, pressing tightly against him.

His tongue probed her lips, demanding entrance to the moist cavern within, and her lips parted without hesitation, deepening the urgency of his. This was what she wanted, what she needed. She could feel his manhood pressing against her, throbbing with unrestrained passion, pulsing with a life of its own.

A golden tide of passion curled through her body as her tongue dueled with his, tasting the inner warmth of his mouth. She spread her hands over the rippling muscles of his back, delighting in his strength.

His heart beat unevenly against her own, and there was a labored edge to his breathing. He broke the kiss suddenly, lifting his head to meet her gaze with brightly gleaming eyes.

"I want you, Angel," he whispered huskily, his eyes darkened by passion. "I want you like hell."

"The—the meal, Jake. It—I n-need to—"

Jake's lips stopped her words as they settled on her mouth, tasting, nuzzling them, seeming to find satisfaction in their softness, before settling firmly on them again. His heady kiss dragged a response from deep inside her body, making her want to forget all else except the wonder of being held close against him. Her pulse was behaving erratically, speeding up, then skipping a beat. The sweetness of her pleasure bordered almost on pain.

His hand roamed caressingly, first cupping her breast, then moving down her hips, applying a gentle pressure that urged her closer—ever closer.

His muscular thighs created a burning heat through the thin barrier of their clothing. His mouth moved to her ear, and his warm breath acted as a sexual stimulus to the sensitive orifice, sending quivers of ecstasy across her skin. She tried to stifle the moan of pleasure, but the sound escaped her lips.

"Stop fighting it," he muttered, picking her up and carrying her to the bed of furs. He laid her gently down, removing her clothing piece by piece.

Her eyes were glazed with passion as she waited for him to finish. "Hurry, Jake," she whispered.

His breath rasped harshly as he finished undressing her and removed his own clothing.

Weakness assailed her as she felt his hands slide down to curve possessively over her buttocks. He pulled her tightly against his hardened thighs; then he plunged into her, deeper, fuller, so certain of his right to take her. He began to move. Slowly, at first, then faster and faster until she thought she would surely faint from the pure pleasure he was bringing her. When she thought she could stand no more, Jake gave a groan and they exploded, hanging from the cliff together—hanging—hanging—and then sliding down—down—until they lay entwined together on the bed of furs.

Chapter Fifteen

News of Angellee's rescue had traveled throughout the Apache village, reaching Chief Tall Feathers' ears. He decided their guest must be honored. A celebration was to take place that night. Brave Eagle, accompanied by his son, brought the word.

Prompted by his father, the dark-haired child thanked her in halting English for saving his life. Angellee received his thanks as formally as it was offered, feeling immensely relieved that the boy showed no outward sign of his brush with death. He gave her a cherubic smile; then, with the resilience of children the world over, he ran off to play with his friends.

"I apologize for my son," Brave Eagle said, solemnly. "He does not realize how close he was to death. He is not properly grateful."

"Don't scold 'im," Angellee said, looking anxiously at Brave Eagle. "I don't expect no—" She looked at Jake, then corrected herself. "—*any* thanks."

"Nevertheless, it is proper thanks is given." His gaze

dwelt on her flushed face, and he changed the subject abruptly. "We are going on a hunt, Jake, to supply meat for the celebration."

"That sounds like a good idea," Jake said. "I'll join you in a minute."

Brave Eagle nodded, then left the wickiup.

Jake smiled ruefully. "I think there's a conspiracy going around this place to keep us apart," he said. "I was hoping we'd have a chance to talk today." Tilting her chin, he planted a light kiss on her lips.

"I wish you didn't have to go," she muttered.

"Me too," he sighed, studying her flushed face. "Something's upsetting you. It's not the celebration, is it?"

"I don't like a fuss bein' made," she said, averting her eyes from him.

"Don't do that," he said. "Don't try to hide what you're feeling from me, Angel."

"I ain't—" She stopped, went on, "*am not* tryin' to hide my feelin's."

"No?" he asked, softly. His dark eyes were penetrating.

"Not really. I just never had nobody to share with afore—*be*fore," she corrected hurriedly, noting his raised eyebrows. "It'll take some gettin' used to I guess."

"Didn't you share your feelings with your parents?"

"I had a secret to keep, Jake. Ma said nobody could know. Not even Pa. It's mighty hard to talk when you're keepin' a secret."

"Yes. I suppose it would be." He looked deeply into her emerald eyes. "Angel, don't ever try to keep secrets from me. Don't hide your thoughts."

"I'll try, Jake," she said, her gaze lifting to his.

He kissed the tips of her fingers. "Try real hard," he said. Then he took his leave.

After Angellee did her household chores, she went with the other women to gather firewood and dig roots from the sun-baked earth with a sharpened stick. The women carried out their tasks with joyous camaraderie. Far from regarding these unceasing chores as drudgery, the Apache women found a sense of satisfaction as they foraged on their root-gathering expedition.

Angellee was surprised at the sense of belonging she felt as she worked with the women. Throughout the day she had received smiles from everyone she encountered. She had expected fear from some and was grateful there had been no sign of it. She had feared the Indians would react in the way the superstitious hillfolks had. By the end of the day, she felt embarrassed at all the good will she was receiving.

Angellee and Jake were not allowed a moment alone during the day, for they were caught up in the preparations as well. The men spent the day hunting and fishing. When they had plenty of food for the feast, they worked on their weapons, sharpening their hatchets and spearheads, restringing their bows. Although Jake had no weapons, he lent a hand wherever it was needed. The village was a bustle of activity as everyone prepared for the night to come.

The children, who had paid her no attention before, seemed to overcome their former timidity in favor of curiosity. While she gathered firewood with the other women, a boy about Little Crow's age approached her shyly.

"Hello," she said, watching him curiously.

Casting a quick glance at the other children who stood watching in awe, he reached out a cautious hand and touched her hair. She smiled at him, and he ran away with a laugh.

Twilight brought the sound of drums, and Little Turtle appeared in the entrance with a hide-wrapped package containing a buckskin dress which was fringed and encrusted with brilliantly colored beads and dyed porcupine quills.

Angellee held the dress up to admire, thanking the Apache woman profusely.

"It's a mighty pretty dress," she breathed. "But, Little Turtle, I can't rightly accept it."

"You must not refuse," the woman said. "You have saved my son's life. This is very little to offer in payment."

"I don't expect pay."

"I know. But you must take it."

Angellee's eyes misted over as she thanked Little Turtle. How could these people, referred to as savages by the white man, act in such a charitable way toward her? Happiness surged within her. For the first time in her life, she felt complete. She had Jake, and she had been accepted by others who knew what she was. She was no longer alone.

Decked out in the fringed and beaded dress, smelling of wild mint from the crushed leaves that had been rubbed into her skin, she was composed as she accompanied Jake to the celebration. It lasted late into the night, but she found a moment to leave the festivities to visit Buck.

"I heared what you done, youngun'," he said, studying her from beneath beetled brows.

"They ain't—*aren't* afeared, Buck," she said, her lips lifting in a delighted smile.

"Injuns is diff'rent than white folks," he said. "They don't worry 'bout the whys of a thing. They accept it as fact."

"I always thought of Indians as savages," she said, bowing her head. "I feel shamed."

"Injuns is people, youngun'. Same as anybody else. I figgered the same as you when I first started lookin' for Rachel."

"You loved her, didn't you?" she whispered, fearing she was intruding on his privacy, but her curiosity pushed her for answers.

"Yep." He sighed. "But it was a long time ago. Best forgot now."

"I'm sorry."

"Weren't your fault." A movement at the entrance caught his eye. "Looks like somebody's come for you," he commented.

She turned her head, and her eyes lit up as she recognized the tall figure watching her.

"How are you feeling, Buck?" Jake asked, transferring his attention to the old-timer. He sat down beside the sleeping mat.

"I'm 'bout ready to get up from here. Rachel is the one what's insistin' I stay abed." Buck reached for his ever present tobacco pouch, cut off a chaw and popped it into his mouth.

"Rachel?" Jake questioned, his brow furrowing.

"He means White Dove," Angellee offered hastily, casting a cautioning look at Jake. But his gaze was fixed on Buck.

"You called her Rachel?"

"Slip o' the tongue," Buck said. "Hand me thet bowl over there. She'll have a fit if I spit on her floor."

"Has she told you when you can get up from here?"

"Maybe tomorrow," Buck said. "She's been buildin' up my blood." He grinned. "Said I lost too much."

"You did. You're lucky to be alive."

"I reckon so." He eyed Angellee's ceremonial dress. "You better get back to thet celebration. Seein' as how it's in your honor."

"We're going," Jake said. "Although I can think of a lot of things I'd rather be doing." His eyes held a glint as they dwelt on Angellee, and she blushed.

Taking leave of the grizzled mountain man, they returned to the festivities. Swift Arrow's face was flushed as he watched them approach, making Jake wonder if there was going to be trouble yet.

When they were finally able to leave the celebration, they went to the wickiup, and Jake immediately pulled Angellee into his arms, burrowing his face against the tender skin of her neck.

Goosebumps appeared as his lips moved against her sensitive skin. She shivered delicately. Chuckling at her reaction, he nipped playfully at her earlobe.

Suddenly she felt an urgent need for his possession and wound her arms tightly around him. She breathed deeply of the purely male smell of him, pressing her body firmly against him.

He groaned low in his throat, his hand clasping the firmness of her breast.

"Love me, Jake," she murmured huskily.

He laid her gently on the mat, covering her body with his warmth, pressing his lips almost savagely against her own.

She opened her lips to him, feeling the same sense of urgency that seemed to possess him. She clung to him desperately, needing to fill the aching void that started somewhere in her loins.

He drew back long enough to rid them of their clothing, then his lips began a downward course, stirring her senses. Her breasts rose and fell with her quickened breathing. Then his lips were suckling at one breast while his fingers manipulated the taut peak on the other one. Threading her fingers through his thick hair, she held him tightly against her. Her back arched as she struggled to be closer to him. Then his lips left her breast, his tongue tracing a trail of fire as it worked down to her navel, pausing to dip inside before moving downward, ever downward. She writhed beneath him, her breath coming in short gasps as his teeth nipped gently at the flesh of her belly.

"Jake," she pleaded. "Don't wait. Don't wait."

His teeth closed gently on the tender flesh of her thighs, nipping, pulling at the smooth white flesh.

"God, Jake," she groaned. "I can't stand it."

Then his lips found the apex of her desire, closing on the soft mound. His tongue began to inflict torture as she moaned softly, thrashing wildly beneath him. When she thought she could stand no more, he covered her body with his own and entered her.

Angellee went wild, arching her hips, pushing against him, trying to take more of him in her. His body enflamed her senses. When he began to move with rhythm, she dug her nails into his shoulders, urging him nearer, closer. Her breathing was coming in parched gasps, her eyes glazed over. She began to climb the mountain, and he was with her.

Faster and faster he drove, igniting her senses, setting flame to her body. Wilder and wilder became his movements, until finally, with one last push, she was there—crying out—quivering beneath him with a wild rush of pleasure. With one last movement, he groaned out his release and collapsed on her still shaking form.

Angellee opened sleep-drugged eyes to find Jake leaning on his elbow, gazing down at her. Her head was pillowed against him. Leaning down, he kissed her on the tip of her nose.

"I wondered when you were going to wake up."

"Is it late?" she whispered, rubbing her cheek against his shoulder.

"The sun's up, but we're not going to worry about it. I was enjoying myself, watching you sleep."

"Can't have been all that much fun," she said, pushing away from him.

"No," he said, pulling her back. "I want to talk."

"What about?"

"You. Tell me about yourself. And your family. I want to know all about you."

So she did. She told him about growing up in the Ozark Mountains. Her eyes grew shuttered as she spoke of the gift, but he seemed so casual about it that soon she was telling him everything. She told about Father O'Brian, who'd been an educated man, and how he'd laughed when she'd told him old Abe would be kicked by his cow. When it happened, he wasn't laughing. He wouldn't even look at her. But at least he hadn't exposed her secret. She told how Rita Mae

Crockett had been her friend until the secret was exposed, then she'd run away in fear of being cursed. She spoke of her brother Johnny who'd only been sixteen when he'd fallen in with a bad lot and been caught rustling cattle. Her eyes were awash with pain, and her voice grew husky as she spoke of the posse who'd hunted him down and killed him. She didn't hold anything back.

When it was Jake's turn to talk, he told her about his life in Pittsburgh, how he'd been an orphan raised by his uncle. He had gone to law school and become a lawyer.

"So you see," he finished. "My life was very simple until I came west to find Becky. It consisted mostly of opera's, dinner parties, and—"

"What's an opera?" she interrupted.

He grinned. "It's a place where everyone dresses in their finest clothing and goes to sit in a big room to stare at each other, all accompanied by music."

"That's all?" She was disappointed.

"I'm afraid so," he said. "You can see I had a very dull life until I met you. Since then—" he sighed. "Well, I guess I'll manage to survive somehow."

"Are you funnin' me?" she demanded.

"Yes." His eyes glinted. "I'm having all kinds of fun. Let's have some more."

Chapter Sixteen

They had been at the village for a week when Becky and Lone Wolf returned. Buck, who had made a complete recovery, came for Jake, and the two left the wickiup together, leaving Angellee to clean the hut and begin the meal.

She was folding a blanket, unaware of anything unusual, when Little Turtle appeared in the doorway of the dwelling.

"Come, Angel," she said smiling. "My friend Rebecca has returned. I wish for you to meet her."

Angellee's movements stilled. Slowly, she rose to her feet, feeling a curious anxiety settle about her, an anxiety that she couldn't put a name to. Feeling as though her world was about to topple around her, she followed Little Turtle outside.

There was an air of contained excitement and bustling activity all around the rancheria. It seemed everyone there—men, women, and children—had turned out to welcome the travelers home. Chief Tall Feathers stood in front of his dwelling. Children raced back and forth between the wickiups, laughing and calling to each other. Angellee searched the faces in the crowd, recognizing the medicine woman standing with a group of women. Next to her was the almost fragile figure of the elderly Bird Woman. Angellee's gaze searched farther, traveling across the faces that had become familiar to her—searching—searching—until she found him. He stood next to Buck, his figure tall and straight as he waited among the Apache braves.

As Angellee watched, he turned to gaze at three riders who approached the village. Feeling as though she were an intruder somehow, Angellee stepped from the entranceway of the travelers' abode.

A babble of voices broke out as the three came abreast of the crowd. Angellee, intent on the slender figure dressed in a buckskin outfit with the skirt hiked up past her knees for ease in riding astride, was surprised to see one of the riders was a child. One of the village children must have gone to meet them. Her eyes never left the auburn-haired girl as she dismounted. Angellee's heart was stilled, waiting for the moment when the woman saw Jake. She didn't have long to wait. The girl saw him almost immediately. Angellee couldn't see her face, but she heard her voice ring out, clear as a bell.

"Jake!"

Angellee watched. The beautiful girl stopped short for a moment, then, with a squeal of delight, ran to Jake and threw herself at him.

Angellee's heart felt squeezed in a vise as Jake's arms closed about the slender woman. Picking her up, he swung her around and around, laughing loudly all the time. When he set her on her feet again, she hugged him to her fiercely, scattering kisses all over his face.

A thick, heavy pain nearly smothered Angellee. She stood frozen, tears slipping unheeded down her cheeks. Her eyes found the brave standing near Jake and the woman.

What was the matter with him? Didn't he have any gumption at all? Angellee had thought Becky belonged to him. If she did, would he allow this to happen right under his nose?

The auburn-haired woman finally stopped kissing Jake and was talking excitedly. She turned and called to the brave near her, and he stepped up and shook Jake's hand. He didn't really look like a coward; in fact, he looked strong and brave and fierce. But then, why hadn't he objected to the way Jake was kissing his wife.

Angellee brushed tears from her face, replacing them with a scowl. Maybe Lone Wolf had just been waiting for Jake to come so he could send Becky back to Pittsburgh with him. She wouldn't blame him at all. The woman looked too soft for the life the Apaches led. He would probably be glad to be rid of her when Jake took her away.

Burning with jealousy, rage and hurt, Angellee slipped quietly through the few villagers that had hung back to watch the greeting from afar. She'd had enough of the sickly performance. She knew that if anyone approached her, she was likely to snap the offender's head off. She wanted to get far away from them all.

No one noticed her as she left the Apache village, headed for the forests where she could come to terms with her feelings. Beneath the rage and pain, she knew she was being unreasonable, but seeing Jake with another girl in his arms was more than she could stand. If love could cause such intense feelings, she really didn't want any part of it. But of course, she realized, she really had no say in the matter. It was already too late for her.

Angellee walked quickly through the forest, intent on putting as much distance between her and the village as soon as possible.

"Jake," Rebecca said, her blue eyes still flashing with excitement. "I still can't believe it's true. What are you doing here? Never mind. Don't tell me now. You can tell me later." She turned to the small child clothed in buckskin who stood nearby, motioning him nearer. "Right now, I want you to see how much Forrest has grown."

"So this is my godson," Jake said, kneeling so he would not tower over the boy. "How are you, son? Do you know who I am?"

The boy nodded, his gray eyes serious as he studied Jake curiously. "You're my Uncle Jake," he said.

"That's right," Jake said. He took the boy's hand in his and shook it solemnly. "You're growing up to be quite a young man."

"I know," the boy said. "Someday I will be a great chief, and I will help my people."

Jake felt a curious pang at the boy's statement. "That's good," he said gently. "Your people need all the help they can get."

"I know," the boy said. "My mother and father told me this." He turned his serious little face toward his father. "I have greeted my godfather as you said. Is it not so?"

Lone Wolf nodded just as solemnly. "Yes, my son. You have done well."

The child's face split into a wide grin. "Then may I go to play warpath with my friends, Little Crow and Black Arrow?"

"Forrest," Rebecca gasped.

The child turned wide, inquiring eyes on her.

"Never mind, Forrest," Lone Wolf laughed. "Run along and play with your friends."

"You shouldn't let him get away wtih impudence, Lone Wolf," Rebecca said.

"Now, Rebecca," Lone Wolf admonished. "The boy wasn't being rude. He was very polite to Jake."

"Yes, he was," Jake agreed. "It wounds me to know I can't compete with his two friends . . ."

"See." She turned her head to Lone Wolf. "Jake was—"

"Don't be ridiculous, Becky. I was just teasing."

"Well . . ." she said hesitantly. "If you're really sure."

"Of course. I was a little boy once."

"How well I know," she said, smiling at him. "And you were an atrocious little boy."

"What are you doing out here anyway, Jake?" Lone Wolf asked. "Did you just decide you needed to breathe some fresh air for a while, or is there some purpose to your visit?"

Jake's eyes darkened. "There is a purpose all right. I'm afraid there's trouble back east."

"Oh? What kind of trouble?"

"Lone Wolf, I hate to interrupt," Becky said, "but

I'm tired and I'm dying to get unpacked. Why don't we go into the wickiup while Jake tells us what brought him."

"If it's all right with Jake."

"Sure. It'll keep for a few more minutes. And there's someone there I want you to meet."

"How long have you been here?" Becky asked as they entered the wickiup.

"We've been here for a week, now," Jake said, looking around at the empty dwelling. "That's funny," he said. "I thought she was here."

"Who?"

"The lady I wanted you to meet."

"Oh . . . I see . . ." she drawled, her eyes mischievous. "A lady, is it?" She turned to her husband. "Did you hear that, Lone Wolf? Jake has a lady friend. I believe I'm devastated."

"Well, I'm damn glad to hear it," Lone Wolf said. "It's about time. Now I won't have to worry about him trying to steal my wife."

"As if you ever had to worry about that," Jake said. "Although, there was a time when I gave it my best shot. I didn't have a snowball-in-hell's chance with her, even during that year when she thought you were dead."

Rebecca shuddered. "Don't remind me of that, Jake," she said seriously. "It was the worst year I ever spent in my entire life. Even to remember it now, I wonder how I survived."

"Don't worry, Little Blue Eyes," Lone Wolf said, putting his arm around her and pulling her close against him. "It's long past now."

"But it seems like it was only yesterday when Black

Bear wounded you so grievously." She shuddered. "It's a wonder you survived and a miracle that you found me after all that time had passed."

"I wonder that you fell in love with me after all the horrors you suffered at the hands of my people when you were captured and your escort killed."

"It could have been much worse if you hadn't fought Black Bear and won me from him."

"Let us forget the past, my love, and think only of the future." He turned to Jake. "You said there was trouble back east. What kind of trouble?"

"Do you know a man called Charles Craven, Grant?" Jake asked, reverting to Lone Wolf's white name.

"Yes," Grant frowned. "He's a distant cousin."

"Apparently not distant enough," Jake said grimly. "He turned up last year bent on trouble."

"How so?"

"You and Becky dropped completely out of sight over six years ago. You didn't even keep in touch with Robert."

"I know," Becky said. "We thought it best. After Grant was unable to get any satisfaction from Washington, we rejoined Chief Tall Feathers' band, and we figured there would be less worry for Robert if he didn't know where we were. That way, the cavalry would leave him alone."

"Well, Charles Craven used all that to his advantage. He's petitioned the court to declare you dead."

"Why should he do that?"

"You're a wealthy man, Grant."

"I'm afraid I have a tendency to forget about monetary matters, for what good is money here in the wilds of New Mexico Territory. That's the reason I left such things in your hands. You're a competent lawyer. All I want from the money is to insure that it's safeguarded until the time that Forrest may have need of it."

"That's the problem, Grant. If the court grants the petition, Craven will inherit everything you have. Forrest will be left penniless."

"The hell he will!" Grant snapped.

"Yes."

"But how can this be? If I'm declared dead, then Becky and Forrest should inherit. That's the way the will is set up, and that's the reason we went through a white man's wedding after we had already been married in my village."

"I guess I didn't explain it all," Jake said. "He wants you all declared dead."

"Surely the court will require proof."

"Well, there's the rub. He claimed to have proof of his allegations."

Grant raised an imperious brow. "What proof is this?"

Jake threw an uneasy look at Rebecca. "Perhaps we'd better discuss this in private," he said.

"Jake!" Rebecca protested.

"Whatever you've got to say," Grant said stiffly, "my wife can hear. We have no secrets from each other."

"Of course." Jake threw an apologetic glance at her. "It's just that it's a delicate matter. But if you don't mind, then I certainly don't."

"I don't," Grant said firmly. "Now what is this proof?"

"He's produced a witness that saw you shot down in

the street. I'm afraid the girl was able to convince the court, Grant. Since I didn't believe the story, I demanded the required time be allowed before declaring you dead. There's only two months of it left."

"Two months!" Grant exploded. "Damn it man! That's cutting it a little short, isn't it? Why didn't you come sooner?"

"I did," Jake said drily. "I've been searching for you for ten months. You weren't easy to find."

"Of course we weren't," Grant said. "I apologize for that outburst. We make it hard for anyone to find us on purpose. Especially the cavalry. Now tell me why the court is so willing to accept this unknown woman's story, and why my family wouldn't inherit even if I were declared dead."

Jake glanced at Rebecca, then away. "The blonde was a . . . soiled dove. She showed the judge the gold watch with your initials on it that Becky gave you the day you were married. She claimed the watch was for services rendered."

"That's ridiculous!" Rebecca snapped, outraged. "I sold the watch to a jeweler in Taos for enough money to buy medicines for our people two years ago. We were too far away from Silver City where my brother Robert lives to get our hands on the gold we had left there for emergencies."

"I'm afraid I'm still in the dark about why this was enough proof that I was dead," Grant said.

"Everyone who knew you agreed you would never part with that watch under ordinary circumstances."

"They should have known as well that I would never betray Rebecca with another woman."

"That's the clincher. The woman said you told her

that Forrest and Becky had died in a smallpox epidemic. She said you were wild with grief and even that you were . . ." he hesitated, then cleared his throat, "uh . . . unable to—"

"Never mind," Grant said drily. "I get the picture." He looked at the color fluctuating wildly in his wife's cheeks. "He did warn us, love. You did insist on hearing."

"Well," she said indignantly. "Of course I should hear. And the woman was stupid. I can't imagine you not being able to—" Suddenly, her eyes widened, her hands flying to her flushed cheeks. Flustered, she quickly began preparations for a meal, keeping one ear tuned to the men's voices.

"You said the court believed the woman?" Grant asked.

"Yes. Completely. It didn't help matters that all three of you had dropped completely out of sight six years ago."

"Like I said, we've just managed to keep one step ahead of the cavalry. We have no intention of being confined on a reservation."

"Wouldn't you be better off going into politics, Grant? I believe you would have a much better chance of helping them that way."

"If it comes to the worst, and the tribe is sent to the reservation, then that's what I'll do," Grant said. "Meanwhile, all the time I can buy for my son with his people, I'll take."

"I don't blame you, but I'm afraid you'll have to make a trip to Pittsburgh and get this thing cleared up as soon as possible."

"I know. We'll rest from this journey then make

preparations to leave tomorrow."

Buck walked in. "Have you seen the sprout, Jake?"

Jake frowned. "No. Maybe she's with Little Turtle."

Grant frowned. The words sounded vaguely familiar. Suddenly, he recalled the time Black Bear had caught Rebecca alone in the forest and kidnapped her.

"I saw her outside when Miss Becky and her family got here," Buck announced. "She didn't look too happy, either."

"She didn't?"

"No."

"I wonder what was wrong? She was all right when I left here a few minutes before."

"There's something I haven't told you, Jake," Grant said. "Rebecca and I were ambushed by two men on our way back from Silver City. I had a feeling the men were after the gold we carried. I intended to tell the council to warn everyone, for it's possible we were followed. If the girl has gone into the forest, she could be in danger."

"I don't think she would have gone off alone," Jake said with a frown. But even as he spoke the denial, he remembered how willful Angel was. Willful, headstrong, and exasperating. But certainly not foolish.

She's at home in the forest. Why shouldn't she go there?

Even as the thought intruded, Buck spoke. "I think you're wrong, boy. I think that's exactly what she'd a-done."

"But why, Buck?" Jake asked. "She wasn't even armed."

"She seen you a-kissin' Miss Becky. Don't think she was too happy about it."

"Oh, Jake," Rebecca exclaimed. "I'm sorry. Of course she would have minded." She turned to Lone Wolf. "You've got to help him find her."

"Yes, Little Blue Eyes," Grant said gravely. "Come, Jake. I will call the villagers to help in the search."

As they left the wickiup, Jake felt a great anxiety. What he had felt for Rebecca had been small compared to the overwhelming attraction he felt for Angellee. Even when he had thought of her as nothing but a boy, she had touched his heart. Now, knowing what she was, having loved her in all the ways a man could love a woman, he wavered between the desire to make love to her passionately when he found her and an urge to spank her on her nicely rounded bottom for worrying him so.

Why had she left the security of the village? Buck had said she was jealous.

Foolish, spunky, brave, little Angel.

She had fought like a she-cat to rescue him from the Comanches. If anything happened to her . . .

Chapter Seventeen

Angellee walked quietly along the forest path, her thoughts still on the scene that remained printed vividly in her mind. The air was crisp and cool, the earth moist and pungent after last night's rain. But she was hardly aware of these things from which she usually took such delight. How could she enjoy such things when her world was falling apart? She had thought Jake was beginning to love her, but she had been wrong. He couldn't love her and greet the auburn-haired girl the way he had done.

How could you, Jake? her heart cried. I thought you loved me.

Leaning against the trunk of a pine tree, Angellee closed her eyes and recalled the blissful moments of the past two weeks.

From the moment she had met him, she had been mesmerized by his handsome physique and drawn to his gentle manner. He had appeared as the epitome of masculinity to her absorbing senses, a provocative blending of strength and sensitivity. No power in existence could have prevented her attraction to him. She had experienced a burning love that no woman could hope for more than once in a lifetime.

A tear welled in Angellee's eyes, and she choked back a sob. Sighing, she pushed herself away from the tree and started to retrace her steps along the path that led to the village.

Suddenly, she stilled, her eyes narrowing alertly. Something was wrong. She looked around but saw nothing out of the ordinary. Nothing moved at all. And there was no sound.

She cocked an ear, listening, but only silence prevailed. Then it struck her. That's what was wrong. It was the silence. There should be sound: jays chattering, squirrels scampering—something.

She waited, her body tense, her breath caught, all her senses screaming out a warning. Fear caused the back of her neck to tingle, and her hands were wet from tension. For an instant she thought she heard something on the path ahead. She strained to catch the sound, but it was no use. Now she could hear nothing.

She began to move down the path again, hoping to gain the safety of the village before whatever danger threatened broke loose. She breathed easier as she rounded a curve. Thank God! The village was in sight.

Suddenly, a dark shape moved from behind a large pine tree and blocked her path. She stopped, rigid with shock, the color draining from her face. Confronting her was one of the men who had killed her parents.

The big one with the scarred face—Bull.

And she was weaponless.

Angellee stood frozen, dry-mouthed. Her wits scattered about her like leaves in the wind, her emerald eyes slitted, hiding her hatred behind a thick fringe of dark lashes.

He moved swiftly for such a big man, wrapping one burly arm around her waist and lifting her off the ground while the other arm snaked around her neck, choking her.

"Well, just lookee what we got here," he growled.

Angellee grabbed the arm cutting off her air supply, but her efforts were puny beside his great strength. As she grew dizzy with the effort to breathe, he carried her farther into the forest. Her vision was becoming blurry, and she knew she was on the verge of passing out.

"Let her go, Bull!" snapped an angry male voice. "Can't you see she's choking? I don't want her dead!"

Instantly she was released. Her legs refused to hold her, and she crumpled to the ground, coughing as she took in huge gulps of air to her tortured lungs.

"You okay, girl?"

A small man dressed in black swam into her line of vision. He looked to be only a couple of inches above her own five feet. Hatred flared in her eyes, quickly disguised. He was the other man who had a hand in killing her parents.

"What do you want with me?" she asked.

He grinned. "We got sort of lonesome out here all alone. We thought you might keep us company for a while."

"You got a funny way of askin'!" she snapped.

"I'll admit Bull forgets himself at times." He studied her through narrowed eyes. "What's your name?"

"Angellee Tucker," she said. She wanted to tell him to go to hell; but her only chance was to escape them, and to do that, she must make them feel they had no worry from her.

"Tucker," he repeated thoughtfully. "I've heard that name recently somewheres."

When you killed my ma and pa!

She quickly averted her gaze, hiding the hatred that flared in the green depths. She couldn't allow them to see it yet. She had to make them believe she offered no resistance.

"We gonna stand around and talk all day?" Bull asked, eyeing the man in black resentfully.

"No," the smaller man said. "I believe we're ready now. You can bring the horses."

Angellee tensed. Now was her chance. While the big man went for the horses, the smaller man was the only one she would have to worry about. And although he was armed, and she was weaponless, he wouldn't dare fire his weapons this close to the village.

As he extended a hand to help her up, she smiled sweetly and took it in a light grip. Before he could brace himself, she tightened her grip and yanked, pulling him off balance and sending him tumbling to the ground. Quick as a cat she was on her feet and running, running as fast as her legs could carry her. She heard a thrashing as he followed closely behind but knew safety would soon be in her grasp. Just a little more and surely she would be seen by the villagers.

Suddenly, she became aware that she was running the wrong way. Her panic stricken flight had carried her farther away instead of closer to the village, and her pursuers were gaining on her. Her breath was coming in gasps, and her heart was drumming loudly in her ears.

It was almost anti-climactic when Bull grabbed her

and threw her down against the soft, moist earth. She clawed and kicked, fighting in every way she knew how even though she knew it was a battle that she couldn't possibly win. She heard the tearing sound of cloth as her shirt ripped, then, before Angellee could react, she was yanked to her feet. She stumbled, her legs threatening to buckle beneath her, but found herself caught close to Bull's big, brutish body. His thick fingers pawed clumsily at her breasts, and his teeth fastened on her neck.

Angellee went wild, snapping out of her daze. In desperation, she lashed out with a foot connecting with his shin. The only sign he gave was to tighten his mauling grip on her breasts. Her breath came in short gasps as she curled her fingers into claws and slashed out at his face. Raking a path down one cheek, her sharp nails sliced into the flesh of his face.

Bull snapped his head back. His eyes glinted with fury as he wiped his hand across his face and came away with the blood. He stared incredulously at the blood on his palms. Then, bellowing with rage, he balled up one brutish fist and struck her a numbing blow to the side of the head.

Blinding lights exploded in Angellee's head. She reeled, a soft whimper escaping. As she crumpled, she heard an evil chuckle from somewhere above her head.

Stunned and weak, Angellee was vaguely aware of being lifted and carried. Only half-conscious, she was thrown across a horse, belly down—then darkness descended.

She came around once when they were splashing through a stream. She could hardly breathe as she was jolted and tossed about. Her body was aching all over, and she knew she should try to rouse herself enough to scream or fight, but it required too much effort. The pounding of hooves as they struck hard-packed ground drummed in her head over and over until she finally welcomed the darkness enveloping her.

When she regained consciousness again, the movement had ceased. She opened pain-filled eyes to see the moon wavering fuzzily above her. She squinted, bringing the pale orb riding high in the star sprinkled sky, into focus. It seemed almost ghostly, casting its silvery glow over the dry ground and scrub.

Angellee lay in a motionless huddle where she had been dropped. Painfully, she tried to straighten her legs and discovered they had been tightly bound. As were her wrists.

She was numb with pain and fatigue, half frozen by the chill night air. Her ribs and jaw felt bruised. She moved and a groan escaped her lips.

"So, sleeping beauty finally awakens" came a soft male voice from close by.

She turned her head, recognizing Slade immediately. He brushed a tangled streamer of red hair from her face, and she flinched away from his touch, watching him from beneath lowered lashes.

"Why are you doin' this?" she asked. "What do you want from me? I ain't got nothin' of value."

He smiled thinly, his eyes traveling over her soft, feminine form. "I beg to differ with you, young lady. I'd say you've got plenty of value."

She felt chilled by his words but refused to let him see. For some reason, she felt there was no immediate danger to her person.

Angellee shivered, looking longingly at the fire

where Bull sat on a rock stirring something in an iron skillet. She wanted to move closer, but pride and stubbornness demanded she show no weakness to them. She was unable to control the shiver that shook her body.

"Get closer to the fire," Slade said. "We can't have you getting sick on us. Then you'd be useless, and I'd have to give you to Bull."

"What do you mean useless?"

"Why'n't you tell 'er, Slade?" Bull asked, rising to his feet and coming toward her with an evil grin splitting his face. His thick, brutish body stood above her, blotting out the light from the moon. "Did'ja think I'd fergot you?" he asked, laughing down at her.

She didn't answer him.

"Me an' Slade," he continued. "We been a-talkin' and a-plannin' on what we're gonna do with the money you're gonna bring us."

Angellee didn't answer him, and he kicked her in the ribs with the toe of his boot. A sharp pain cut through her like a knife, but she tightened her lips, refusing to utter a sound, determined not to allow him the satisfaction of knowing just how much he had hurt her.

"You hear me, bitch?" Bull growled, prodding her with the toe of his boot again.

"Take it easy, Bull!" Slade snapped. "She's bruised up enough already."

"Well, hell, Slade," Bull whined. "It's her own fault. She needs bein' taught a good lesson. Needs learnin' her place. She's too uppity by far. Just let me have her for an hour, and she'll be nice and cowed fer them mexes."

"Shut up, you fool! Them *mexes* don't want cowed

women. The more fire they've got, the better they like it. She won't be worth as much if you break her spirit."

Them mexes.

God! What're they gonna do?

"You'll never get away with this," she said, hatred spitting from her green eyes.

"Aw . . . lookee thet, Slade," mocked Bull. "She *can* still talk. As fer gettin' away with takin' you, I'd say we already done it."

Bull laughed harshly, his slitted eyes mean in the dim light. "Did'ja hear thet, Slade. She says we ain't a-gonna get away with it. Now ain't thet a laugh?"

Angellee's hatred overcame her caution. Her green eyes were hard as she stared coldly up at the two men. Slade smiled down at her.

"You rotten bastard," she said, enunciating each word slowly. "You're lower than a snake's belly in a wagon rut, an' I'll see you dead and burning in hell for what you done to my ma and pa."

The smile slowly faded from Slade's face. His eyes were puzzled as he returned her gaze. "What're you talking about?" he asked softly. "I've never seen you before in my life. If I had, I'd remember because I haven't run across many women with beauty to equal yours."

She glared at him. "No, you ain't never seen me, but I know you. I trailed you for two weeks, an' if I hadn't been sidetracked, you'd be dead right now instead of standin' here in front of me."

"You trailed me? Why?"

"Because you killed my folks," she hissed. "You an' that damn animal you travel with."

Slade drew back from the blazing look of fury on her

face. "I don't know what you're talking about," he said.

"We were headin' for the gold fields when our wagon wheel broke," she said. "That was about a month ago. I went huntin' for fresh meat while Pa fixed the wheel. While I was gone, you and your friend there bushwhacked my folks and left 'em for dead. My pa lived long enough to say who done it and ask for vengeance."

"Yeah," Slade said, his eyes turning cold. He studied her thoughtfully with his cold, killer's eyes. "Too bad your pa won't get his vengeance; you don't look in any kind of shape to do anybody much harm."

She stared at him, refusing to show fear. "He'll get it," she said. "I won't rest until I see you both in hell." For a fleeting moment, she thought she saw a begrudging admiration cross his face, then it was just as suddenly gone, replaced by savage amusement.

"That's probably where I'll be going eventually, all right," he laughed. "But I have my doubts that you'll ever see it. Meanwhile, I plan on having a good time before I leave this world, and good times cost money, my sweet. If I'd been able to get more from your folks, then we wouldn't be here now."

"You're gonna bring us a purty little penny where we're gonna take you," Bull smirked.

Angellee would rather have remained silent and not spoken to these men, but she knew forewarned is forearmed. "What do you mean?" she asked. "Where you taking me?"

Bull's mouth split into a wide grin, showing rotten, tobacco-stained teeth. "Reckon we oughtta tell her, Slade?" he asked the smaller man.

"Why not?" Slade asked. He stared at her with

amusement. "After all, we must give her time to savor the excitement that's in store for her. It would hardly be fair to spring it on her with no warning at all."

"Yep," said Bull. "I bet she'll be mighty excited all right, and mighty anxious to get there after she finds out where we're takin' her."

She gritted her teeth. Her green eyes glittered with anger and hatred, but she forced herself to remain calm. "So where's this place you two polecats have in mind for me?"

"Polecats?" Slade raised an eyebrow. "Just for that, I've a good mind not to tell you. But then again . . . why not? Well, little lady, we're taking you to Mexico." Slade said, watching her with those cold, snake eyes.

"Yeah," Bull said. "Mexico." He snickered. "I 'spose you're wonderin' what we're takin' you for?"

She stared coldly at him.

"I don't think the lady's interested, Bull," Slade drawled.

"She's just pretendin', Slade. She's interested all right. But I've a good mind not to tell her."

"Now, Bull," Slade admonished, gently. "That wouldn't be very nice of you. After all, you've got the lady's interest whetted. Just think of how disappointed she would be if we don't satisfy it."

"Yeah," agreed Bull. "An' on top of thet, if she knows where she's goin' she'll be good and hot by the time we get to thet hoar-house. And I 'spect the hotter she is, the more she'll be worth."

Angellee's face paled as the meaning of their words sunk in. It was as she'd suspected. They planned to take her to Mexico and sell her to a bordello!

"Get her some food and water, Bull," Slade ordered.

"We don't want her dying on us. She'd be worthless dead."

"I'll feed and water 'er," Bull growled, taking his canteen from the back of the saddle. "Then I've got somethin' else I'm a'dyin' to give 'er." He rubbed his bulging crotch.

"No," Slade said, sharply, his eyes on Bull. "You leave her alone."

"Leave 'er alone?" Bull's mouth dropped open. "What do you mean by that, Slade?" he asked angrily. "You ain't a-goin' to keep 'er fer yourself. I'm the one thet seed 'er. If'n it hadn't a-been fer me, we'd a-still been waitin' outside thet Injun village hopin' fer a chance to get at thet gold."

"Kidnapping the girl is a damn sight safer way to get money. We don't have to fight a whole village of Indians for it either. But we'll get a lot more money out of her if she's untouched when we get there."

"What do you mean—untouched?"

"My God!" Slade sneered. "Are you blind? The girl is a virgin, you fool!"

"A virgin?" Bull stared at her in consternation. "Is thet right, gal?"

Knowing she was safer in the circumstances if they believed the lie, she nodded her head vigorously.

"Hell! Now what'd you have to go and be a virgin for?" His eyes narrowed. "How do I know you're tellin' the truth."

"Hell, Bull! It's as plain as the nose on your face. Now quit griping. There'll be more women than even you can handle when we get where we're going."

"Thet's nearly a week from now." Bull's eyes never left Angellee's face. "How much more do you think she'll bring if'n we leave her cherry."

"Forget it, Bull!" Slade snapped. "She'll bring at least three times as much."

"Well, I don't know if'n it's worth it," Bull muttered. "I ain't had all thet many cherries myself."

"Well, you're not getting this one!" Slade said coldly. "We didn't get much from her folks. I figure she can make up the difference."

"Like she kinda owes us, huh?" Bull asked.

"Yeah," Slade drawled. "I guess you could say that. She owes us for what her folks didn't have."

"Her ma sure weren't cherry," Bull remarked. "But she was a mighty fine piece a' ass anyways."

Angellee gave a strangled cry of rage and tried to get to her feet. Bull grinned and kicked her with the toe of his boot.

"Bull!" Slade snapped. "Leave her alone. You're bruising the merchandise."

"Hell, Slade," Bull whined. "Didn't you see 'er? If'n she'd a-had a gun, I reckon she'd a-tried to kill me."

"If I had a gun, you'd both be dead men," Angellee snarled, her eyes blazing with hatred for the two men.

Slade laughed in amusement. Then, seeming to grow tired of tormenting her, he turned away from her. "Is that food ready?" he asked Bull.

"Yeah," Bull growled, moving to dish up the beans and bacon.

Her mind whirled, trying to devise a plan of escape. She refused to accept defeat. A sharp crack from a nearby juniper brought both men to their feet, their guns already drawn. Slade laughed nervously as a rabbit hopped into view. A shot rang out, and the rabbit lay twitching on the ground.

"What did you do that for?" Slade asked Bull who stood watching the animal in its final throes of agony with a grin on his face.

"Why not?" Bull asked.

"You know, Bull. She's right. You are an animal," Slade said thoughtfully.

"Hell, Slade," Bull growled. "It was just a rabbit. Nobody cares nothin' fer a rabbit."

"His death served no purpose."

Angellee stared at him in amazement. What purpose had her mother's and father's deaths served? Couldn't he have taken their money and left them alive? Rage boiled within her anew. She forced herself to calm down before they brought her food. Knowing she couldn't do any good without her weapons, she wondered if it would help to play on their obvious nervousness.

Before she could devise a plan, Bull brought her a plate of food. He untied her wrists to allow her to eat. She rubbed them briskly, trying to start the blood circulating again, watching him beneath lowered lashes.

"You ain't gonna make it to Mexico," she said, trying to instill confidence in her voice.

Slade turned from the fire and stared at her with cold, mean eyes. "Why do you say a thing like that?" he asked. "Of course we'll make it. There's no one to stop us."

"My friends'll stop you. They'll be lookin' for me."

"Your friends are a long way behind us," Bull sneered. "It was prob'ly dark before you was missed."

"Why do you say that?" she asked casually.

"'Cause I watched you leave. You snuck out, didn't

you? Thet bunch was all excited about them other three comin' home, and they prob'ly won't even miss you before dark. And last time I looked, Injuns couldn't see in the dark to track."

"Are you sure they didn't see her leave?" Slade asked, his voice betraying a slight uneasiness. "I don't want to tangle with a whole village of braves."

"You ain't a-gonna have to. We got us a good start, an' I don't think they'll go very far a-lookin' fer her. They's too big a chance they'd run into the cavalry."

"My friends ain't Indians," she said, deciding she was definitely on the right track. She'd play it for all it was worth. "They'll go as far as they have to, to find me. And they won't rest until they do."

"Is that so?" Slade asked. "Thanks for warning us. When they come, we'll be ready for them. But even so, they still can't track us at night. And we'll get an early start tomorrow and be on our way. We'll go along faster than them because we won't be having to watch for tracks."

"She's God-awful sure they's gonna foller us, Slade," Bull said nervously. "What if they figger out where we're takin' her. If they don't have to track us, they might catch up to us."

"Don't worry, my friend. If we keep a close watch on our back trail, we can spot them before they see us and take them by surprise."

Chapter Eighteen

Angellee took deep gulps of fresh night air. She felt sick. Her nerves were drawn as tight as a bowstring, and her body shook uncontrollably.

The nightmarish mental image was still before her: Jake and Buck, guns drawn and blazing, the deafening roar of gunfire echoing through the valley and Jake falling, blood flowing freely from his wounds.

She closed her eyes tightly, an icy chill sweeping over her. Fear emanated from her. She was afraid to open her eyes, for the vision had been so clear that she was afraid she would see her beloved lying in a pool of blood nearby. She feared if she did, she would surely go mad.

Cold sweat beaded her forehead; her palms were damp. Her ears rang with the pounding of her blood as her heart threatened to burst from her chest. She had no doubt that she hadn't just suffered a nightmare. She had seen the future—a future in which Jake was killed—unless she was able to prevent it.

You gotta get away, Angel. You gotta save 'im.

Forcing herself to a calm she didn't feel, she flexed her hands which had grown numb from the lack of circulation. But they were bound tightly, and she found very little slack. Then she tried her legs which were cramped from being tied at the ankles. No use there either.

Opening her eyes to mere slits, she looked at the two men sitting beside the fire. Somehow, someway, they were to be the instruments in the death of her love. They talked quietly, unaware that she had wakened. She was afraid the slightest movement—the slightest sound—would attract their attention. She fought against the hot tears that threatened to choke her as the muted tones of their voices came to her ears.

"I think we ort to wait and ambush 'em," Bull was saying.

"Could be you're right," said Slade. "She seemed certain they'd come."

"It'll take 'em a while to catch up, won't it?" Bull questioned. "If we cut out at first light, thet ort to give us plenty head start."

"Not if they discovered her missing soon after we took her," Slade said. "If they started after us right away, they may find us by midmorning."

"Wouldn't it make more sense for us to back track in the mornin' and pick our spot to wait for 'em? Thet'd give us an edge, an' we can use the girl as bait."

Angellee lay motionless, almost afraid to breathe for fear they would know they had been overheard.

"I think you're probably right," agreed Slade. He rose to his feet. "We'd better turn in now. We'll want our wits about us when we take on her friends."

She heard the flames sizzle and spark as the dregs of

a coffeecup were thrown into the fire. Then came the jingle of spurs and the muted sounds of swishing blankets as the two lay down on their bedrolls.

Angellee waited for what seemed like hours, listening to the sounds of the night, before she finally opened her eyes. She moved her head enough for her to make out the bulky figures of the two men lying near the glowing embers of the fire. Bull was snoring loudly, but his big body was as motionless as Slade's.

Moving quietly, she wriggled around, pushing herself to a sitting position, sending her sweeping gaze searching—searching, for something—for some way to free herself. When she saw the blade gleaming in the firelight, her eyes widened. Bull had been careless. He had left a small hunting knife beside the fire. But then, he had known she was securely tied.

His carelessness could be the means of saving Jake's life. If she could just work her way over to the knife without waking them up . . .

Using her bound hands as leverage, Angellee inched her way toward the fire. It was slow going because each rock she encountered had to be avoided or carefully moved. But she was determined, and before long, she had grasped the knife between her bound hands.

Carefully wedging the knife between two rocks, she began to saw away at the leather thongs. When the bindings finally parted, elation flowed through her. Grasping the handle firmly, she cut through the bindings around her ankles, and with a cat-like movement, sprang to her feet.

Angellee's emerald eyes glittered vengefully as she stared at the two sleeping men. Her fingers tightened around the knife, and her mouth thinned grimly.

Although the knife was small, it was big enough to make them pay for what they had done. She moved toward the two men, and Bull snorted. Angellee stopped mid-stride. The big man mumbled something and turned restlessly in the bedroll.

She stood motionless, poised on the balls of her feet, hesitating. She was torn between an overpowering urge to kill her enemies, and a sense of urgency to find Jake in case something should go wrong. Memories of Jake lying in a pool of blood surfaced, and she knew she had no choice; she couldn't take chances with Jake's life. He had to be warned.

The guns. Take their weapons.

Sheathing the small knife in her boot, her narrowed gaze searched the area around the sleeping men, but the guns were nowhere in sight. Her lips tightened grimly. They must have taken their weapons to bed.

She left the camp silently, damping down the urge to slit their throats where they lay. She cut a wide berth around the horses, fearing they would be disturbed and wake the sleeping men. Her every action—every thought—was concentrated on putting as much distance as possible between the two men and herself before they woke up.

Jake stared broodingly into the flames, his face set into hard lines. His eyes were alight with a burning need for vengeance. What would he do if they harmed Angel? How could he face life without her now that he'd found her?

Angel.

The hard lines of Jake's face softened when he

thought of her. She had brought meaning to his life—had made it worth living.

Angel.

Lying upon a bed of furs, warm and willing, arms eagerly outstretched, her lips parted in a shy smile, her eyes shining like emeralds as she waited for him.

"Better turn in now, boy," Buck growled from his bedroll. "You ain't gonna help the sprout none by starin' into thet fire."

"I shouldn't be sitting here like this!" Jake muttered. "Dammit, Buck! We should have gone on!"

"They wasn't no trail to foller in the dark," Buck growled. "You done all you could fer tonight. Now try to rest."

"There's no telling what she's going through," Jake groaned, his head sinking into his hands. "God, Buck! What're they doing to her?"

"Don't think about it," Buck advised. "Thoughts like thet can drive a man crazy. It durn near happened to me nigh on to fifty years ago. Put 'em outta your head, boy. Don't think about it none."

Jake knew Buck was right, but there was no way he could turn off his thoughts. He leaned over and filled his cup from the coffeepot left near the coals.

"Pour me some o' thet," Buck said, gruffly. He pushed his blanket aside and came to sit near the fire. "I reckon I cain't sleep yet, neither. We might as well talk fer a spell."

Jake poured the old-timer a cup of the strong brew and handed the steaming cup to him. "I never did thank you for coming with me, Buck. I guess I ought to do that now."

"Don't require no thanks," Buck muttered, taking a

sip from the cup. "I done it fer the sprout, too."

Jake nodded. "She has a way of growing on you, doesn't she?"

"I reckon," agreed Buck. He eyed Jake steadily. "Think a lot of 'er don't you?"

Jake nodded. "I plan on marrying her, Buck."

"She know it?"

"Yes." He hesitated. "At least, I think she does."

"You ain't sure?"

"No." Jake shook his head. "I guess I'm not."

"Don't make the mistake I did, boy," Buck said. "When we get 'er back, make sure she knows it."

"I intend to," Jake said grimly.

"I wished a thousand times I'd'a told Rachel how I felt. It might'a made a difference to 'er. But she didn't know there was somebody thet cared fer 'er."

"Rachel is the girl you told me about? The one who was taken by the Indians?"

"Yeah." Buck sighed heavily. He gazed into the cup, swirling the liquid around, remembering the past. "She shore was a purty little thing. Still is. If things'd been different, we could'a had a mighty good life."

Putting his cup down, he reached for his leather pouch and pulled the plug of tobacco from it. Cutting a sizeable chaw, he popped it into his mouth and continued his study of the flames.

"You said she still is," Jake said, slowly, his puzzled gaze on the old-timer.

"Yep. I did," Buck agreed. "Didn't tell you, boy, but I seed 'er again."

"You saw her?" Jake stared at him, wondering if Buck's mind was wandering. "You said she was dead."

"Thought she was," Buck said.

"She wasn't?"

"No. She warn't."

Jake studied the grizzled face thoughtfully. "You're not making sense, Buck. You told me in the caverns that she was dead. Now you say she's not. Have you been—"

"I ain't seein' things." Buck interrupted. "An' I ain't losin' my mind neither. Rachel's alive all right. She's livin' in thet Apache village we just left."

"In the . . ." Jake stared at him. "You found her alive—after all these years?"

"Yep."

"But you searched for her—"

"Boy . . ." Buck looked at him steadily. "I searched a'plenty, an' I'd still be searchin' if'n them Injuns hadn't told me she was dead."

"You didn't ask for proof of her death?"

"Never figgered it fer a lie. 'Paches despise lyin' more'n anythin' else. Their whole way of life depends on 'em tellin' the truth. They don't have no written language to put on paper. They depend on runners. The lives of several tribes could hang on a runner carryin' the chief's exact words." He shifted restlessly, staring thoughtfully at the flames. "They treat liars as outcasts, yet thet whole damn village lied to me. They told me she was dead, and I believed 'em."

"If you found her, you should have stayed with her, Buck. You shouldn't have come along with me." He looked at the old-timer. "You *are* going back for her?"

"Wouldn't do no good," Buck said. "She wouldn't come away with me now." He looked at Jake sadly. "It's been forty-five years, boy. She's got a husband and son in thet village. It's too late fer us. I reckon it allus was too late." He sighed heavily.

"My, God!" Jake exclaimed softly. "I'm sorry as hell, Buck."

"Weren't none o' your doin'," Buck said.

"She wouldn't consider leaving them?" Jake asked thoughtfully.

"It's too late fer me, boy," the old-timer said. "I know thet. But it ain't too late fer you. When we find thet little gal, you make damn sure she knows you want 'er."

"She'll have no doubts at all, Buck," Jake said. "I'll see to that."

Buck sipped from the cup, then tossed the remains on the ground. "Ain't worth drinkin' noway," he grumbled. "Past time to get some rest, anyway. I'm gonna turn in, and you better be doin' the same. We'll need to break camp at first light."

"In a minute, Buck," Jake said. "I'll bank the fire first."

Angellee stood at the edge of the forest watching the sun peep over the horizon, topping the pine trees with a glorious burst of color. She was tired, having traveled most of the night, stopping to rest for only short periods of time.

Although she had kept a careful watch on her back trail, she had seen no sign of pursuit as yet. A grim smile crossed her face as she imagined her captors' consternation when they woke to find her gone. She knelt beside a stream that was a mere trickle and heaved a weary sigh. She had been jogging steadily for the past hour and was perspiring freely despite the cold night air. As she gathered up a handful of water, she heard a metallic clink and turned quickly. The small knife had fallen from the sheath of her boot. She'd have to replace it as soon as she'd refreshed herself. She splashed the cooling water on her face, then lay on her stomach to drink. The liquid was cool, refreshing. She drank deeply.

Sitting up, she took a moment to rest. Her narrowed gaze searched her back trail again, but there was still no sign of pursuit. She found solid ground and, lying down, placed her ear against the earth. A soft drumming of hoofbeats told her someone was coming—two shod horses—and they weren't far away.

Angel felt a thrill of hope rising within her breast. It was Jake. It had to be. He had followed quicker than she had dreamed possible. She smiled with happiness. Soon, she would see him again—be held in his arms.

Last night's vision surfaced, and suddenly a niggling worry worked into her mind. Suppose the outlaws had discovered her absence after she left. Suppose they had followed her.

No!

Her mind rejected the thought. God couldn't be so cruel as to allow her so close to her love, then snatch him away from her.

But, had she come close to him? Perhaps it wasn't Jake who followed the trail. Perhaps she would do better to keep herself hidden until she knew for certain who was coming.

With these thoughts in mind, she hid herself behind a clump of bushes on one side of a small clearing and settled down to wait. If the riders were following their trail from the village, they would emerge from the forest shortly.

It seemed forever before the riders came into view. As they did, her heart surged with gladness. It was Buck and Jake.

She started to rise, then frowned, a slight sense of uneasiness filling her. Something about the scene was vaguely familiar. She wrinkled her forehead in concentration. What was wrong? She remained frozen as the riders dismounted to water their animals at the stream. Her mind worried the problem, turning it over and over, for she sensed the answer was important, even urgent.

Suddenly she remembered. At the moment of memory she was aware of a dazzling sparkle of light—the sun glinting off metal—perhaps a rifle barrel.

The vision.

Oh my God! The vision—it was happening—it was happening *now*.

Chapter Nineteen

For a moment, Angellee's fear held her motionless. Her breath stopped completely as her gaze moved from Jake to the glinting rifle barrel.

No, God. No. The words pounded heavily in her brain. *Please, God. Don't take Jake, too.*

Each second measured an eternity as time ceased to exist for her. *He was hers.* God couldn't be so cruel as to allow him to die.

Then she was up, running toward Jake, moving against what seemed to be insurmountable resistance. Briars clung to her legs, trying to hold her back, and fear lay heavy in her chest.

She had to reach him.

He rose from the stream, still unaware of the threatening danger. As he saw her, his face reflected surprise, then happiness.

He still didn't know.

"Jake," she screamed, her voice expressing the anguish on her face. "It's a trap."

As her words penetrated, his expression grew fierce.

His gaze searched for the danger, but still, he didn't move. "Get under cover, Angel," he yelled, but she didn't falter. Her swiftly moving feet carried her straight toward him.

Then she was there, her body held protectively in front of him, shielding him against the bullets, her arms wrapped tightly around his neck, her face pressing hard against his chest.

"Dammit, Angel," he snapped. "Get out of the way." His hands were like bands of steel as he ripped her arms loose from him, pushing her roughly away. At the same time, he twisted, falling to one side.

Jake's Colt was out and blazing as she hit the ground with a heavy thud. Rolling over, she sprang to her feet, reaching for the knife. Her fingers encountered emptiness. *She had forgotten to replace the knife.* But Jake was safe. She watched Bull fall beneath his gun.

Suddenly, without any warning, Slade darted from the cover of the nearby trees, wrapping an arm around her neck. He held her tightly, using her as a shield. Jake let out a string of curses as Slade backed away, dragging her along.

"Shoot, Jake," she screamed, terror for her love washing over her as she struggled wildly against Slade. "Never mind me. Kill him!"

Even as the words left her mouth, she saw Jake flinch as the bullets from Slade's gun hit him. Her horrified mind was only vaguely aware of Buck crawling into the concealing brush. But her eyes remained glued to Jake, lying mortally wounded on the ground, his lifeblood flowing away.

Just as she had foreseen in the vision.

Despite her efforts, it had come true.

Jake was dead.

She hadn't been able to prevent it any more than she had been able to prevent the deaths of her parents. She had, in fact, been the one to bring his death about, for Jake and Buck had fallen into a trap her captors had carefully laid for them—using her as the bait.

There was a moment of silence. And then she screamed. Slade continued pulling her backward, and she continued screaming.

Then, something inside Angellee snapped. Just as abruptly, a violent explosion of anger and hatred washed over her. It was far more intense than any emotion she had ever known. She struggled wildly, lashing out with fists and feet, releasing the hatred that had been festering like a thorn inside.

Angellee despised this man who had caused her so much pain. He wasn't fit to live. All she wanted was a chance to hurt him as badly as he had hurt her.

She wanted him down. She wanted to cut him, slice every inch of skin from his body, beat him and torture him until he screamed out with pain, begging for mercy.

Letting out a string of curses, Slade evaded her blows, fear in his eyes at her unrestrained wrath. Bringing the gun barrel up he struck her a hard blow on the back of the head. She reeled from the blow, her senses swimming and sank to her knees, vaguely aware of Slade dragging her back to the horses. Then darkness closed around her, shutting out the sight of Jake lying in his own blood. Angellee was not aware of being loaded belly down on Bull's horse. In fact, Angellee wasn't aware of anything at all.

Buck watched from his hiding place as Slade rode off

with Angellee. Although his heart was heavy, he knew he was lucky to be alive. If he had thought he could have helped her, he would have followed them. But Buck had lived a long time. He knew his limitations. He had been shot in the leg, and Jake lay wounded, perhaps already dead, a few yards away.

Buck felt Angellee was in no immediate danger. Jake was. He could help both of them more by obtaining some help. If Jake was still alive, he required immediate attention. Buck had learned long ago that staying alive meant there would be another day to fight.

Buck waited only a matter of moments to make certain Slade wasn't laying an ambush; then he hobbled toward Jake. His heart filled with dread as he saw Jake's blood-soaked shirt. He was afraid Jake was beyond help already. Then he saw a faint movement of his chest.

Kneeling and putting his ear against Jake's chest, he listened until he heard the faint beat of the other man's heart. His craggy face split into a smile.

"You ain't dead yet, boy. An' if'n it's up to me, you ain't gonna be. I owe thet little gal, an' if I can't help her, at least I can help her man."

He went to the saddlebag and took a shirt from it, ripping it in strips for bandages. Working as swiftly as he could, he opened Jake's shirt and bared his chest. His faded-blue gaze found the two wounds. One was high on the shoulder, and the other was down around the rib area.

"Thet bullet come mighty close to the heart, son," Buck muttered, wadding up strips of cloth and pressing the pieces against the wounded areas to try to stop the bleeding. Then he bound them securely to hold them in place.

"Way it looks to me, Jake," he muttered grimly, "you got a chance. It might be mighty slim, but it's shore a chance. Now if'n I kin get you back to thet village where Rachel is a-fore you die, then thet'll make the odds even better."

The old mountain man was breathing hard by the time he finished bandaging Jake's wounds. Knowing he was losing blood himself and everything depended on him getting back to the Apaches, he took the time to bind his wounded leg.

When it came to getting Jake on his horse, he found he had a problem. Jake was heavy, Daniel had been made skittish by the blood and noise and Buck's wounded leg threatened to buckle beneath him. The problem took Buck the better part of an hour to solve, and he was panting with exertion by the time he had completed the task.

Angellee regained consciousness slowly and blinked, trying to clear her blurred vision. Closing her eyes against the pain that stabbed through her head, she tried to focus her mind, clear it of disorientation. It was several moments before she remembered what had caused her mental stress and physical discomfort. Then, as the image of Jake falling beneath Slade's blazing guns intruded, she wished she hadn't remembered.

She was lying face-down on the ground where Slade had thrown her. Rocks and gravel dug into her cheeks. Her body felt bruised all over, and when she tried to move, she discovered her wrists and ankles were bound tightly. Rolling over, she saw Slade. He was sitting on a log, watching her with his snake eyes.

His expression was cruel as he stared down at her. "We can have it two ways," he growled. "You can make the journey belly down on that horse or riding him astride. The choice is yours."

Although she remained silent, her emerald eyes sparkled with hatred before she shuttered them beneath thick lashes.

"I'm gonna cut your feet loose so you can sit the saddle, but you give me any trouble and you'll be out cold."

Again she was silent, her eyes never leaving him. Slade was a dead man; he just didn't know it yet. But he must be put off guard—must be made to think she had lost her spirit. Then, when he least suspected, she would strike.

She lowered her eyes. "You can cut me loose," she muttered. "I ain't gonna give you no trouble."

"You'd better not," he growled.

A few minutes later they headed southwest toward the desert. Beyond that, Angellee knew, lay the border of Mexico.

Angellee was hot; her shirt was damp with perspiration. Her fiery hair tumbled wildly around her head and shoulders, streaming in wild disorder down her back. Wisps of hair lay wetly about her face, and she lifted her bound hands, using her sleeve to blot the moisture that beaded her upper lip.

Turning in the saddle, she stared dry-eyed back at the mountains. She swallowed around the lump in her throat and straightened wearily in the saddle.

Her pain was too great to be assuaged by the release of tears.

Casting another look back toward the mountains, she watched a lone vulture circle in the sky. Its wings seemed to scarcely move as it drifted lazily downward then rose again. The great black bird's eyes seemed to scan the desert below, then he dipped lower, lower, until he dropped completely out of sight.

Angellee shivered, then cast a look of intense hatred at the back of the man who had caused her so much heartache and pain. Somehow—someway—she vowed, she would get her revenge. She wouldn't rest until Slade had paid with his life for what he had done.

Darkness had fallen by the time Buck reached the Apache village. The Indians watched with impassive faces as the two men arrived: one, lying belly down across the saddle, the other, barely able to sit a horse.

Buck pulled the horses up and sat swaying in the saddle. His fever-glazed eyes scanned the crowd of Apaches, looking for the familiar faces of Becky and Lone Wolf. They were not there. A figure detached itself from the group, and Brave Eagle stepped forward, followed closely by Little Turtle.

"What has happened?" she asked anxiously, forestalling her husband. "Where is my friend, Angel?" Her dark eyes fell on Jake, widened, then returned to the old-timer.

"Is that Jake?" she whispered. "Is he—he—" She broke off, unable to continue.

Beads of sweat dotted his forehead as Buck forced himself to sit erect.

"He weren't dead the last time I checked," he muttered. "But the hard fact of the matter is, thet's been some while back. Been afeared for the last few hours to git off'n this here horse to check 'im over—afeared I wouldn't make it back on again."

"Do not worry," Brave Eagle said. "We will care for your friend now."

Buck watched two braves pull Jake from the horse. "Is Lone Wolf and Miss Becky still here?"

"No. They left this morning," Brave Eagle replied. "But you will be well taken care of. You are a friend of the people, Buck. We have not forgotten. The medicine woman has been sent for. White Dove can help you. Her medicine is powerful. She will care for you both. Come now, let me help you to Lone Wolf's wickiup."

"Never mind me," Buck muttered his knuckles whitening as he clenched his hands on the saddlehorn. "See to the boy first. He needs help more'n me."

"Others are already caring for him," Little Turtle said. "Let Brave Eagle help you dismount." Her eyes were anxious. "Is—is my friend, Angel—dead?"

"Last time I seed her, she weren't," Buck said grimly. "Jake got one of them varmints what took 'er, but t'other one got away with the youngun'. Reckon she's gonna need some help."

A shadow crossed Brave Eagle's face. "The horse-soldiers have been seen in the desert near the mountains, Buck," he said. "We cannot go into the desert. And we must make ready to move our people to a safer place if they come into the mountains. I am afraid we cannot help her."

"I understand," Buck growled. "The youngun' wouldn't expect help if the helpin' caused your people hurt."

"Yes," Little Turtle said gently. "Angel would understand. That is her way. Come. Let Brave Eagle help you. You must follow them and rescue her."

Angellee's shoulders were slumped as she rode behind Slade. Reaction had set in, and try as she would, she could not suppress the memory of Jake's death. She had lived it over and over again in her mind. If only he hadn't shoved her away. She would gladly have taken the bullet for him. But wishing did no good. He had refused to allow her to shield him with her body.

Her eyes fell on Slade, riding just ahead, and she shivered, dreading the coming of the night. For the last three nights, Slade had made her sleep with him so he would know if she tried again to escape.

He needn't have bothered had he but known it. She had given up fighting for the moment; it served no purpose. Fighting only brought painful retributions. She already had bruises from the painful slaps and punches Slade had inflicted on her. And her nose had bled several times. Angry about his partner's death, Slade had ceased to worry about bruising his merchandise.

For a time, Angellee had almost given up hope. Jake was dead, so what use was there in resisting? With Jake gone, her life had no meaning—no purpose. There had even been times when vengeance had lost its appeal. Angellee knew the blame for Jake's death lay at her door. Granted, Slade had done the killing, but if she had not let her jealousy over Becky send her unprotected into the forest, Slade and Bull could not have kidnapped her.

And Jake would be alive.

Angellee blinked back tears, pushing memories of Jake away. She forced herself to concentrate on her own circumstances. At least she didn't have to worry about being ravaged. Not as long as Slade believed in her virginity. That fact alone allowed her a little time before the inevitable, for Slade still hoped to sell her as a virgin in Mexico. If he ever suspected that she and Jake had been lovers, he would lose no time in raping her. She shuddered, her mind refusing to dwell on what it would be like to be forcefully violated by a man.

Angellee had been forced to do the cooking and the other work when they made camp. Through it all, she was made to suffer Slade's crude remarks about what he would like to do to her and his pawing hands that never tired of tormenting her. His rage at Bull's death was made apparent over and over again. Angellee both hated and feared him. But she hid her fear well, allowing him to see only her hatred.

She was aware that her intense hatred for him stemmed more from what he had done to Jake and her parents, than what he was doing to her. She hadn't fully realized, until he was dead, just how much she had come to love Jake.

Her eyes misted over. How could she go through life without Jake? Rage glittered brightly in her eyes as they returned to the man in black. She would live through what Slade planned for her. No matter what, she would survive. For now her only purpose in life was to make him pay.

Chapter Twenty

The town was an ugly place although Angellee's circumstances may have been responsible for making it appear even more so.

It lay crouched against the desert floor like some huge monstrous spider, perpetually waiting, ready to seduce the unwary traveler. Somehow, Angellee knew that only the dregs of humanity would be found in such a town. She would certainly find no help here.

Some of the buildings were constructed of wood while others were made of adobe, and they lay along both sides of the wide dusty road. All of the buildings had one thing in common: they were crude and ugly, erected in a haphazard fashion by uncaring hands with only the thought of shelter from the weather.

Most of the structures were cribs and cantinas with a few ramshackle houses thrown in here and there. The only sign of life was a lone horse, reins tied to the rail of the nearest saloon.

Slade pulled his horse to a stop in front of a large, two-story building located in the center of town. The weatherbeaten sign hanging over the unpainted door was faded, giving her no clue as to what kind of business went on inside.

Slade dismounted and pulled Angel from the horse. Taking her arm with a rough hand, he hustled her up the sagging steps to the front door.

Angellee shuddered. What kind of life lay behind those closed doors and drawn shades? At that moment her courage waned, and her eyes held a look of hopelessness. Slade opened the door and dragged her inside the darkened room.

Angellee blinked rapidly as her eyes tried to adjust to the difference in the light. Expecting to find a dirty, dingy brothel that smelled of stale whiskey and unwashed bodies, her eyes rounded with surprise, for she found herself in a richly furnished entranceway.

"Get on in there," Slade snapped, pushing her into a large, spacious room.

Heavy, purple velvet draperies covered the windows, blocking out the light from the scorching sun. Thick carpeting covered the floor, muffling their footsteps. From every wall hung gilt-edged mirrors interspersed with paintings of amply-endowed women in various stages of undress.

Angellee averted her eyes from the paintings in disgust, wondering at the sort of woman it took to pose for such a thing. Her gaze avoided the walls, traveling instead over the heavy mahogany sofas and high-backed chairs that made up the room's furnishings. They were covered in the same purple fabric that adorned the windows.

"So you're back, Slade." The husky, feminine voice broke the hushed stillness.

Slade and Angellee turned at the same time to stare at the young girl who had come quietly into the room. As Slade's eyes roamed over the girl's red silk clad body, her mouth thinned.

"Where's Bart, Heather?" Slade asked.

"Mr. Cantrell to you, Slade," her voice taunted.

"Don't get smart with me," he snarled, his mean eyes narrowing cruelly. "One of these days Bart's going to be tired of you."

"It won't make any difference to you if he does, Slade," she drawled. "What've you got there?" Her eyes studied Angellee's drawn, disheveled features, dwelling for a moment on her bound hands. "Are you bringing your own entertainment these days?"

Slade flushed and Angellee wondered at the audacity of the girl in challenging him. Obviously, she wasn't the least bit afraid of him.

Angellee studied the pale oval of the girl's face: the springing blond curls that framed it, the large, shadowed hollows of her eyes and the too-wide mouth and small nose. She guessed the girl's age somewhere between fifteen and sixteen years.

"Bart's not going to like you keeping me waiting when he finds out why I'm here," Slade growled. "Where is he?"

"In his office," the girl replied, seeming not in the least put out by his threat.

Slade strode to a nearby door, pulling Angellee with him. He knocked, then waited.

"Enter."

Slade opened the door, and Angel searched for the owner of the deep voice in the eerie flickering light. Finally, she found him sitting near a window. He was a man of medium build, his hair thick and dark, his eyes mere shadows in the darkness of the room. It was difficult to see clearly, but she could make out a square jaw with a cleft chin. As he approached, he appeared almost diabolical in the dim light, and she shivered as fear sent electric fingers traveling through her body.

"Hello, Slade."

"Mr. Cantrell." Slade licked his lips and smiled nervously. "I brought someone I thought you might be interested in." His hands gripped like claws as he pushed Angellee toward the other man.

Bart Cantrell's dark eyes were intense as they traveled appraisingly over Angellee, studying her inch by inch, lingering on the feminine form dressed in boy's clothing. He took special note of the bruises and dirt on her face and the wildly disordered hair falling about her shoulders and waist in silky fiery flames.

"Nice," he agreed. "Yes. Very nice indeed." He picked up a silky red strand and let it slide through his fingers. "Where'd you get her?"

"Now, Bart," Slade laughed uneasily. "What difference does that make."

"None, I suppose," Cantrell said, turning away from her as though suddenly disinterested. "What do you want for her?"

"I thought—maybe two thousand," Slade said, clearing his throat as he watched the other man uneasily. "And worth every penny," he added quickly.

"Five hundred," Bart countered, his voice smooth as silk.

"She's worth more than that!" her captor burst out. His expression grew sullen as he stared at the other man.

"Not from where I'm standing," Bart said. "If we weren't such good friends, I wouldn't offer a penny more than two hundred. She's already pretty well used up."

Angellee's face flushed at the insult.

"Dammit, Bart!" Slade snarled. "She hasn't been used at all. The girl's a virgin. She hasn't been touched."

"Hasn't been touched?" Bart drawled softly, turning his intense gaze on her again. He touched a bruise on her cheek, then met the other man's gaze. "Don't play me for a fool, Slade."

"Well, what the hell," Slade blustered. "I'll admit I roughed her up a little. But, dammit, Bull's dead because of her. I couldn't let her get away with it."

"The world's probably better off without him anyway," Bart said, dismissing the other man's death easily. He cupped Angellee's chin in his hand, tilting her face to his interested gaze. She suffered his touch, but hatred burned in her eyes.

"Is he telling the truth girl?" he asked softly. "Are you still a virgin?"

Angel didn't want to help Slade make a bigger profit off of her, but she knew instinctively that her position would be much better if they believed her to be a virgin, so she nodded her head.

Bart Cantrell turned to Slade. "I'll give you a thousand," he said. "But not a penny more."

"Dammit, Bart. That's not enough. A thousand dollars won't last me any time at all."

"Then steal another girl for me," Bart said amiably. "Or steal two and make twice as much."

"That won't be so easy to do without Bull to help me.

And anyway, I was thinking seriously of retiring from this business with the money I get from this girl."

"Getting scared, Slade?" Bart asked, eyeing the gunman with amusement.

"Not exactly. But there's a lot healthier businesses to be in than kidnapping. Robbing stagecoaches, for instance. When you steal a man's gold, he gets mad. But when you steal his woman, he doesn't forget it."

"Nevertheless, a thousand is all I'll pay," Bart said. He moved to the desk, picking up a cigar and examining it thoughtfully. His eyes were narrowed as he raised his gaze to Slade again. "Make up your mind, Slade. You can take my offer or leave it."

"Then I'll damn well leave it and take her elsewhere. You aren't the only one who deals in white slaves. I know this girl is worth a fortune. Dammit, she's the most beautiful girl I've ever brought you, Bart. You get rich men in this place. You could earn her price back in a week's time. You paid me fifteen hundred for Heather and—"

"Leave Heather out of this," Bart snapped. "Besides, Heather was young and pliable."

"And so is this girl. Look at her. She can't be more'n fifteen or sixteen."

"If she's so pliable, then why's she still tied up?"

"Hell, Bart. I'm not crazy. She'd run off if she got half a chance. She's got more spirit than any girl I've ever brought you. Them mexes'll pay plenty for her."

"Spirit?" Bart flicked a glance at him beneath scowling brows. "I don't see much sign of it. Looks like you've done away with it with your rough treatment."

"Don't you believe it. She'd have killed me if I'd've turned my back on her. That's why she's tied."

"I can't say as I'd have blamed her," Bart said, glancing at Angel again.

She glared her hatred at Slade. "It ain't over yet," she snarled. "I'll kill you. I don't care where you go. I'll find you." Her voice lowered menacingly. "And when I do, I'm gonna cut your mangy heart out and feed it to the buzzards."

Bart smiled at her. "I believe you might do just that." He looked at Slade. "All right," he agreed, not batting an eyelash. "Two thousand it is." His mouth thinned. "Just a word of advice, Slade. Take your money and leave without delay."

"I intend to," Slade said, his good humor restored at the prospect of getting his way about the money. "Just as soon as I've had a chance to rest and enjoy the women."

"I meant now," Bart said. His voice was cold and deadly. "Not tonight, or tomorrow, or the next day. But right now. Just as soon as I give you the money."

Confusion crossed Slade's face. "Why should I do that?"

"Because if she doesn't kill you," Cantrell said coldly, "I will."

While Slade stared at him, completely stupefied, Bart Cantrell strode to the door and jerked it open. "Heather," he barked harshly.

"Yes, Bart?" The blonde dressed in the red silk wrapper appeared in the doorway.

"Take this girl . . ." He paused, looking at Angellee. "What's your name girl?" he asked.

"Angel," she muttered.

"Angel," he repeated. "How appropriate. Heather, take Angel with you. Cut those damn rope bindings off her wrists and put some ointment on them. They look raw. Then clean her up, get some food in her and leave her to rest awhile. When you're finished, come back here to my office."

"All right." The Irish girl took Angel's arm in a firm grip. "Come with me," she said, leading her from the room.

Heather was silent as they moved up the stairway, but as they entered what appeared to be a bedroom, she turned to Angel. "How'd you get mixed up with the likes of Slade?" she asked.

"I reckon the same as you," Angel muttered. "I heard Slade say he got fifteen hundred dollars for you."

"He did," Heather said cheerfully. "And I'm worth every cent."

Angel stared at her in surprise. From the conversation between the two men, she had thought Heather had been kidnapped as she had.

Heather laughed at the expression on Angel's face. "I can see you're confused," she said. "Don't be. They kidnapped me too." Searching through a drawer, she found a jackknife and sawed through Angel's bonds.

Angellee flexed her hands then rubbed her wrists trying to ease the pain. She threw a quick look at the door, which the other girl intercepted.

"It won't do any good to run." She kept her voice low, watching Angellee with sympathy. "Erin ran and they killed her."

"Erin?"

Heather nodded. "She was my sister. Slade and Bull killed my folks when they took both of us."

"I'm sorry," Angel muttered. "I know how you feel. They killed my folks too." Her eyes darkened. "Bull's already paid. And Slade'll pay too. I'm gonna see to it."

"How? You can't escape from here. Bart Cantrell has the stables guarded day and night. Without horses, there's no chance of survival. Even if you escaped from town, they'd find you and bring you back." She shivered slightly. "Then he'd send you to that room in the cellar."

"The cellar?"

"Yes," Heather said grimly. "You wouldn't like it there."

"You don't look like a prisoner," Angel said. "You seem happy here."

Heather smiled wryly. "There are varying degrees of happiness. As long as I do what I'm told they treat me decent enough. And after three years—" She shrugged. "Well, I learned to accept what I can't change. I had to, or lose my sanity."

"Three years?" Angellee's eyes narrowed on the young girl's face. "You've been here that long?"

The blond girl nodded.

"Do you—uh—work here?"

Heather's eyes sparkled with laughter. "I do work, but not like you mean." She moved to the dresser, picked up a brush and pulled it through her blond curls. Her eyes met Angel's in the mirror. "I fetch and carry for Bart and entertain him."

"Entertain him?" Angellee's voice sounded strangled.

"I sing to him," Heather explained. "So far, I've managed to remain a virgin." She smiled, a dimple appearing in each cheek. "Bart thinks I'm resigned to my fate, and it suits me to foster that idea." Her blue eyes clouded over. "Time is running out, though. I'll be sixteen next month." Her eyes were speculative as they rested on Angellee. "Maybe together we could . . ."

Angellee remained silent, studying the younger girl who had spent three years in this hellish place. How had she been able to endure it?

I've learned to accept what I can't change.

As she recalled the girl's words, Angellee knew that she, herself, was doing the same thing. Her indomitable will to survive would never allow her to do otherwise.

"You said your time was running out. What did you mean by that?"

Heather moved to the window. "I came here when I was twelve. My sister Erin was thirteen. He—Bart—took Erin and it nearly killed her." She shuddered. "She—she bled a lot. When she got well enough, she ran away. I never saw her again."

"She might've made it."

"No. She didn't. Bart Cantrell wanted me. I could see it in his eyes. But I'm not very big, and that's what saved me. After what he did to Erin, he was afraid he'd kill me if he took me. He told me he'd wait until my sixteenth birthday." She stared pensively out the window. "It's next month. November twelfth. I've got to find a way to leave before then."

Hope sprang alive in Angellee's breast. "We'll *both* get away, Heather," she said. "Ma always said two heads was better'n one any day. We'll find a way to bust out of here."

"I'm afraid it may be too late for you by then, Angel," Heather muttered.

"What do you mean?"

"You're past sixteen, aren't you?"

"I'm seventeen. Does it make a difference?"

"I think it does," Heather said softly, her eyes filling

with tears. "I'm afraid tomorrow will be too late for you." She pushed Angel toward the water stand in the corner. "You'd better clean up now. Bart doesn't like to be disobeyed. He expects to see you clean and well rested later on in the evening."

"Tonight?" Angel asked in a strangled voice.

"I'm afraid so. As far as I know, I'm the only one he's given a reprieve to. There's a bunch of men coming in tonight, and I expect you'll be entertaining them."

"I can't," Angellee whispered. Despite her efforts to be brave, she swayed on her feet, feeling suddenly dizzy.

Suddenly Heather's blue eyes began to sparkle brilliantly. "That's it," she muttered. "I think I know how we can buy you some time. Just think real hard about what they're going to do to you. Those men are going to come in here and rape you. They're going to rip your clothes off and ravish you. They'll listen to you scream and they'll laugh."

"I ain't gonna scream," Angellee muttered, tightening her lips grimly. "No matter what they do, I ain't gonna scream."

"Don't be stupid," the Irish girl snapped, pinching her arm. "You're only a weak female. *Be* terrified. Slade has put you through a terrible ordeal. Think about it. Think about anything, but for God's sake, scream until you pass out with fright."

Understanding slowly dawned on Angellee. Drawing a deep breath, she let out a series of piercing shrieks, interrupted only long enough to draw fresh air into her lungs. She was still screaming when she heard heavy footsteps thudding up the stairway. As the door burst open, she clasped her hand to her head, collapsing on the floor in a dead faint.

"What in hell's going on?" Bart roared. "What did you do to her, Heather?"

"Wasn't me," Heather answered calmly. "She started crying as soon as the door closed behind her. She pleaded with me to tell her what was going to happen. I couldn't stand all the noise she was making, so I tried to explain about Señor Ramirez and the others."

"Dammit, Heather. Why didn't you keep your mouth shut?" He moved to the fallen woman, stooped, picked her up and laid her down on the bed.

"I told her the same thing you told me, Bart," Heather said.

"And what was that?" he asked suspiciously.

"You know. About it not hurting so much after the first time and all." Heather looked at him pitifully. "Are you mad at me, Bart?" she asked, her voice trembling suddenly as though she were not far from tears. "I was just trying to help. I guess after all she's been through, she couldn't face what was going to happen."

His expression cleared. He squeezed her shoulder comfortingly. "I guess you couldn't help it. It's really Slade's fault. He roughed her up some before he brought her in. Dammit. The customers don't like cowed women." His dark brows drew together in a scowl. "I'm not sure what I'll do about her yet." Leaning over, he pulled her shirt open, examining one small, perfectly formed breast. He stroked it gently with a fingertip, unaware of Angellee's surging fury. "Who knows," he continued. "I might find it amusing to keep her for myself."

"You—you'd use her?" Heather's voice trembled.

"Bart, remember Erin . . . this girl's not very big. Not even as big as I am. And she appears fragile. If you're as big—as big as I've heard—" She broke off as he turned his gaze on her. Flushing a deep red, she said quietly, "Would it harm her?"

"I don't know," he said thoughtfully. "I'm not sure." He stood up, his narrowed gaze still on Angellee's limp form. "The interesting thing about lovemaking, Heather," he said, "is that a woman can take more if she's willing. If she's not, then, yes, she could be permanently damaged—even killed—by someone like me." A curious expression crossed his face as he ran his eyes over the Irish girl. "Smaller than you are, is she? That's something to think about. When did you say you'd be sixteen?"

"Next month," she whispered huskily, licking suddenly dry lips.

"Yes," he mused, his gaze traveling over the slender form dressed in red satin, dwelling a moment on the generous swells of her breasts. "November twelfth, isn't it? I've got it marked on my calendar with a big, red pencil." He smiled slightly, turning to go. "Anyway, it looks like I'm going to have to rearrange tonight's entertainment. But no matter. Whether I sell Angel's services or use her for myself, she'll be worth every cent she cost me."

Angellee waited until the door closed behind him before she sat up. "That bastard," she muttered to the white-faced girl. "He's just playin' with you."

Heather stood motionless by the window, staring down into the street. Her shoulders were slumped with defeat, and there was an indescribable expression on her face.

"I'm scared, Angel," the blond girl said, her voice shaking slightly. "He's not going to wait until next month. I just know he's not."

Angel's sympathy went out to the other girl. Laying an arm across her shoulder, she said. "We'll think of something. I owe you for getting me through tonight. I ain't gonna forget it. I won't let him hurt you." She moved to the washstand and picked up the jackknife Heather had used earlier. "It ain't like we're helpless," she said, a slight smile curling her lips. "Not as long as I've got a knife. Don't worry none. We'll get out of this mess, and we'll do it together."

Chapter Twenty-One

Angel stood at the window staring into the darkness below. Covering her ears, she tried to drown out the sounds of bedsprings squeaking in the next room as one of the *girls* of the establishment went to work. But try as she would, she was unable to shut out the muffled cries and squeals as the whore pleasured her customer.

"Dammit, not so rough," roared a drunken, male voice. The sound of a blow was followed by a loud cry of protest.

Angel, dressed in a yellow satin wrapper, paced the floor furiously. While she was bathing, her britches and shirt had disappeared, forcing her to plunder the wardrobe or go naked. Her eyes sparked with anger, and her fingers gripped the handle of the small jack-knife hidden in her pocket.

Her brain worked furiously examining and discarding plans as she tried to devise a way out of this hell-hole for Heather and herself. She had almost given up after Jake's death, feeling there was nothing left to live for. Meeting Heather had been good for her because now she had something to fight for. And she would fight. For she refused to meekly accept the fate Bart had planned for the Irish girl and herself. Heather had no one to help her before. Now, she had Angel.

As the door opened, she stiffened tensely and turned to see the Irish girl sweeping into the room. Heather wore an emerald satin gown with black lace trim. Her blond hair was piled high on top of her head and decorated with a green ostrich plume that curled down around one cheek.

"Bart wants you downstairs," Heather said hurriedly, moving swiftly to the wardrobe and extracting a gold satin gown. "Put that on and hurry up, or he'll be angry with both of us."

"I ain't goin'," Angel said flatly. Her expression was grim as she met the other girl's alarmed gaze. "I ain't gonna be no part of that." She nodded her head toward the adjoining room.

"Don't worry," Heather said briskly. "Our ruse worked and you've been given a reprieve. Bart's not expecting you to work tonight. He said nothing would be required of you except to look beautiful. Personally, I think he wants to show you off and make all those rich dons who come here jealous."

When Angel didn't budge, Heather crossed to her and tossed the gown on the bed. "Hurry up," she snapped. "We haven't got all day. Bart Cantrell's not a patient man. When he says jump, you better jump. Because when he gets angry, everyone in his vicinity suffers for it."

Angel arched an eyebrow, wondering if the other girl wasn't exaggerating. The saloon owner had expressed a great deal of concern over Slade's treatment of her.

"Funny," she remarked. "He didn't appear that way to me." She unfastened her wrapper and pulled if off, tossing it on the bed.

"Appearances can be deceiving," Heather said, pulling the gown over Angel's red hair and settling it about her shoulders. As the Irish girl buttoned the gown, Angellee glanced down at herself and gasped with dismay at the amount of skin left exposed.

"I ain't wearin' this," she muttered.

"You've got no choice," the blonde said. "Bart knows every gown in this place, and he said you were to wear this one. And Angel . . ." she paused, her troubled gaze on the other girl. "I don't want you taking this wrong. But . . . please try not to say ain't. And don't drop your g's all the time. Bart puts great store in the way people speak. We don't want him thinking you're not a lady."

"I don't give a damn what he thinks," Angel snapped. Her mouth thinned. "And I ain't wearin' this dress, Heather. It ain't decent." She lowered her eyes to the generous swells of her breasts exposed by the extremely low-cut gown and flushed a bright crimson.

"Don't make such a fuss," Heather warned. "The gown covers more than most of those we have in this place. And as for not caring what Bart thinks—well—all I can say is you'd damn well better care." Angel's green eyes glinted with anger and the other girl continued hurriedly. "Don't you see? If Bart thinks you're not a lady, he might decide to give you to the men. You'll get used to the low-cut gowns after a while. I did." She tossed a pair of black net stockings and a pair of gold high-heeled shoes on the bed.

Angellee stared at the objects in dismay. She would

look like a tart wearing all those vulgar trappings.

Growing impatient, Heather grabbed her by the shoulders and shook her. Despite her small stature, she was surprisingly strong. "Hurry up, dammit. I mean it. Bart may look like butter wouldn't melt in his mouth, but don't you believe it. I've had enough of that room in the cellar to last me a lifetime." She shuddered. "I don't think I could stand another session in there."

Having decided that Heather's fears might be justified, Angellee picked up the stockings with trembling fingers and pulled them on her legs. "You keep talkin' about a room in the cellar," she muttered. "What's so awful about it?"

"If we don't hurry, you'll find out," Heather said sharply. Grabbing the hairbrush, she pulled it impatiently through the fiery hair.

A few minutes later they descended the stairs and entered the large room. Heather moved across the room and opened a door. Instantly barroom noises filled the air. This, then, was the cantina. Angellee's hesitation was slight, barely discernible. Lifting her chin at a defiant angle, she followed the other girl across the room, trying to ignore the lewd comments from the drunken men that lined the bar.

Across the room, Bart, dressed in a dark suit with an embroidered vest, was deep in conversation with several well-dressed men.

Angellee fought down the urge to squirm beneath the appraisal of the men and met Bart Cantrell's gaze steadily. She refused to feel shame for circumstances beyond her control.

"Here she is, gentlemen," Bart said, his lips forming a smile that managed to soften his features. "Just as

I promised."

Reaching out a well-manicured hand, he traced Angellee's delicate features with a long finger, then drew it slowly down her neck watching her color fluctuate madly as he reached the fullness of her bosom. Despite all her efforts to appear uncaring, she flinched away from his caress.

"You see, gentlemen," he said softly as though he had proved a point. He seemed not in the least upset by her movement. "This is my latest acquisition. As you can see, she has that peculiar blend of shyness and fire that makes her such an exquisite prize." Picking up a glass of amber colored liquid off the table, he took a long sip, eyeing her over the rim of the glass. "Her name is Angel," he said, placing the glass carefully back on the table. "Now tell me, what do you think of my flaming Angel?"

"Exquisite, as you said," murmured an elderly man wearing a pearl gray suit. He carried a thin black cane, and Angellee guessed his age to be seventy, at least.

The same age as preacher Jacob.

The thought shocked her, and she stared at the man with chagrin. The others murmured an agreement with the older man's statement but had nothing to add.

"How much will you take for her, Cantrell?" boomed a loud male voice from across the room.

Bart turned to stare down his nose at the man with unkempt blond hair sporting a day's growth of beard on his face. He wore an embroidered vest over a wrinkled red shirt, and his close set watery eyes were fixed on Angellee as he approached the group.

"Were you speaking to me, Jasper?" Bart asked, his eyes narrowed on the other man.

"None other," the man said. "You *did* say she belonged to you, didn't you?"

"I did."

"Well, I'm askin' the price for her."

"Now did I say she was for sale?" Bart asked mildly, flicking a piece of lint from his suit.

"Hell, Cantrell," the man growled. "Everyone knows all your whores are for sale. Why should this one be any different."

"I don't have to explain myself to you," Bart said sharply. "But just for the record, Angel is different from the girls Slade usually brings."

"Cain't tell it from where I'm standin'," Jasper said, running an experienced eye down Angellee's slender body. "She's got all the right parts."

Bart's face flushed with anger. "She isn't a whore," he said coldly. "Angel's a lady and I'm thinking of keeping her for myself."

As loud protests issued from all the men present, Angellee held her breath. Her eyes met Heather's for a moment. The Irish girl had been right. Bart apparently did put a lot of stock in being a lady. And, if she and Heather were to remain together, she'd just have to keep him thinking that way. She would have to consider each word carefully before it left her mouth.

"Aw . . . come on, Cantrell," Jasper said. "I don't mind waiting until you go first, but I sure as hell want a piece of that." He reached out a hand to caress Angel and found it knocked roughly aside. Bart's eyes were darkened with contempt as they stared into the other man's.

"Keep your hands off, Jasper," he said in a menacing voice. "You know the rules around here. If it belongs to me, you can look but don't touch. Not unless you have my permission, and in this case, you don't."

"Hell, Cantrell," Jasper growled. "That ain't fair. You bring 'er in here all gussied up, and then say we cain't touch. What in hell . . ." His voice trailed away as something caught his attention. Suddenly, he licked his lips nervously. Angellee followed his gaze, catching sight of the two burly men who were moving toward the group, menace in every line of their bodies.

Jasper held up a hand. "Now, wait a minute, Cantrell," he said, giving a nervous laugh. "I didn't mean nothin'. Nothin' at all."

The blond man began to edge quickly away from the group but found himself grabbed by the neck by one of the men.

"He givin' you trouble, boss," asked the beefy man. Angellee was amazed at the size of the man. Standing around six feet four inches, he must have weighed at least three hundred pounds.

"Nothing I can't handle, Bruno," Bart said. "But I'm afraid Jasper's making the ladies nervous. Remove him from the cantina."

"Right, boss," Bruno said, his wide mouth splitting into a grin.

Picking up Jasper, Bruno carried the protesting man toward the door. The other man walked in front, and by the time Bruno arrived with his prisoner, the door was thrust open. Before Jasper could gather his scattered wits about him, he was thrown head first out the door, hitting the dusty street with a muffled thud and a loud cry of pain.

"Sorry about that," Bart apologized, studying Angellee's pale face thoughtfully. He snapped his fingers, and a bosomy blonde with brighly painted red lips, wearing a garish pink costume decorated with black fringe, appeared holding a glass in front of him. He took it from her extended hand, holding it out to Angel.

"Drink this," he commanded. "You look like you could use it."

"I'd rather not if you don't mind," Angel said. Her lips thinned slightly, but she succeeded in evading his eyes.

Bart's eyes darkened and a muscle twitched in his jaw. "I do," he said coldly.

"What?" Her green eyes snapped up to his.

"You heard me," he snapped. "I said I do mind. Drink it." His voice still held an edge as he turned to Heather who had been waiting silently by his side. "As soon as Angel's drained that glass, take her to the bar and have her sit on the end so the customers can get a good look at her. I want her to stay there the rest of the night."

Angel's green eyes sparkled with fury. Her lips tightened grimly, but before she could open her mouth, she noticed Heather's warning look. Taking a calming breath, she drank from the glass and choked. Her eyes watered, but she forced herself to swallow the rest. As she set the empty glass down, the Irish girl grabbed her arm and hustled her across the smoke-filled room.

"Stop it, Heather," she snapped. "He can't—"

"Shut, up, Angel!" the blond girl muttered. "Bart can do anything he damn well pleases. Don't you understand yet that he owns you?"

"It ain't right for one human being to own another,"

Angellee said. "That's what the Civil War was all about."

"I told you not to say ain't," Heather hissed. "And it may not be right, but here it's a fact. Bart Cantrell can make you wish you'd never been born. Remember the room in the cellar and do as you're told."

Angel quit resisting and allowed Heather to drag her toward the long, oak bar situated along one wall. It was ornately carved, bedecked with mirrors. The bottles and glasses lining it were polished to a high sheen. On these, she focused her gaze. She tried to ignore the painted women in their scanty costumes being pawed by the drunken men.

"Here we are," Heather said cheerfully, climbing up on the bar and motioning for Angel to do the same.

Reluctantly, Angel joined her. "I don't know why I'm doin' this," she muttered. "I haven't even seen that damn room in the cellar. I don't even know what's so bad about it."

"I'll tell you later," Heather hissed. "Now shut up and smile. Bart's getting angry, and if you goad him anymore, I won't have to explain that room. You'll be learning from first hand experience."

"Would you like a drink before you sing, Mees Heather?"

The Irish girl smiled at the bartender. "No, thanks, Pedro."

When the bartender looked inquiringly at Angellee, the blond girl introduced them. Pedro's dark eyes were filled with sympathy as he offered Angellee a drink. When she refused, he turned his attention back to Heather, asking her to sing the song about Irish eyes.

She agreed with a smile, and as if just waiting for his signal, the piano player struck up the song. Heather's voice rang clear and true as she sang the Irish ballad to a suddenly hushed crowd. Angellee felt a deep sadness that someone with such a beautiful voice had no one to listen to her except the patrons of a cantina.

When Heather finished the song, she curtsied to the clapping crowd, then resumed her seat beside Angellee.

"You have a beautiful voice," Angel said.

"Thank you," she replied. "My mother was a singer before she married my father. She left the stage to marry him."

Angellee's eyes were sad as they roamed the cantina, watching the scantily clad women serve drinks to the customers, sometimes winding up on their laps with thick, meaty hands pulling at what few garments they wore. It wasn't fair that Heather was exposed daily to these surroundings. How had she managed to live in a place like this and still retain her innocence.

Shuddering, Angellee averted her gaze from a pretty Mexican girl dressed in a short, red satin dress. She was being pawed by a burly man with curly black hair. Angellee tried to concentrate on the men sitting around a table playing a hand of blackjack, but her eyes kept returning to the girl and the man who was mauling her so roughly.

"No, Señor Curley," the girl protested in a loud voice. Her dark eyes took on a look of desperation as she tried to free herself. "I cannot go with you, señor. I only serve the dreenks."

"We'll see about that," the beefy man said, standing up abruptly and dumping her on the floor. He laughed loudly as she cried out in pain. Reaching down, he grabbed a slender arm and dragged her, protesting, across the room. "Hey, Cantrell," he hollered. "How much for the little mex?"

"Twenty dollars," the cantina owner said, not even turning from his conversation with the men.

"Done," the man called Curley yelled, extracting a twenty dollar gold piece from his pocket and tossing it to the bartender.

"No, no," protested the girl, her flushed face taking on a terrified expression. "Please, señor. I only serve the dreenks."

Curley laughed, eyeing her suggestively. "That's okay, honey. I'll serve you up a drink that'll knock your eyes out."

Angellee's body stiffened, and her green eyes narrowed on the man. The girl was obviously frightened out of her wits. She felt for the jackknife she had hidden in the folds of her skirt.

"Don't be a little fool," Heather hissed in her ear. "You can't help her. If you try to interfere, you'll probably wind up taking her place. Curley Joe won't be the first customer Rosa has serviced."

Angellee's startled gaze flew to Heather's. "Are you sure? She seems so scared."

"I imagine she is. But it's not because she hasn't had a man. She's had plenty. But Curley Joe can be pretty rough sometimes. Especially when he's drunk. The last time he was here, he broke two of Juanita's ribs and cut her up some. Bart didn't seem to mind about the ribs, but he was mad as hell about the slashes the knife made." Her voice was wry. "Bart doesn't like his girls marked."

Angellee felt a shiver slide down her spine. That

explained a lot. It hadn't been concern for her personally that had made him angry with Slade. He just didn't want his merchandise damaged. "If he's so concerned about the girls' appearances, why does Cantrell let Curley Joe get away with it?"

"Curley pays well for the privilege," the Irish girl replied. "He paid twenty dollars for Rosa, and she usually only brings in two dollars a trick."

Angellee's gaze was dark with sympathy as she met Heather's eyes. "How have you survived all this time and still kept your sanity, Heather," she asked softly.

Heather's lips trembled. "It hasn't always been easy," she murmured. "And I think the hardest part has been not having anyone to confide in. The other girls have all accepted the situation." She touched Angel's hand. "I'm so glad you're here."

Suddenly, she turned, smiling brightly as one of the men who had been with Bart approached. "Señor Lopez, how nice to see you," she trilled. "It's been absolute ages since you were here last." She shaped her full lips in a pout. "How could you desert us for so long? I've been utterly devastated."

"I had to go to California on a business trip, Señorita Heather," the man said. "I only arrived back at the rancho tonight, and I came here straight away. I have missed talking with you and listening to you sing in that beautiful voice."

Heather laughed, leaning over to allow the man to gaze at her bosom. "How sweet of you to say so," she cooed, extending a dainty white hand to him. "No one else ever pays me such extravagant compliments."

He took her hand and raised it to his lips. Then he sighed. "Now I can go home and sleep the night away since I have seen my little dove."

"Don't be so long coming back next time," Heather called gaily as he moved away. "Old goat," she muttered under her breath.

Angellee's lips twitched. She stole a sideways glance at her companion, deciding that she was going to like this Irish girl who was able to poke fun at her circumstances.

Heather's eyes were sparkling like sapphires, and to the casual observer, she seemed to be having a marvelous time. But Angellee was aware that Heather liked the cantina and its patrons no better than she did. Heather continued watching Señor Lopez until he reached the door. She seemed to know exactly what the man was going to do next, and Angellee decided it must be a nightly ritual between them.

Señor Lopez turned and waved at her, remaining just inside the door until the Irish girl kissed the palm of her hand, raising it slowly to her pouting lips, and blew the kiss to the waiting man

"Don't look so surprised," Heather said, throwing a glance at her companion on the bar. "I learned a long time ago to do exactly what Barts wants me to. He planned every detail of that little act." She sighed deeply. "Look, I know that doesn't make me look so good, but when you wind up in a place like this, you do whatever you can to survive."

"I'm not blaming you, Heather. But Señor Lopez thinks you like him. Won't that lead to complications?"

"So far it hasn't. He's never tried to get me alone. One thing I've learned is to live one day at a time. Everyone around these parts knows that Bart has been saving me for himself. Hell. They've probably even got my birthday marked with a red pencil on *their* calendars." She examined a fingernail thoroughly. "So far, Bart has kept the others away from me. But when he's had his way with me . . ." She sighed despairingly. "I just don't know. Who can predict what will happen. Bart could even be planning on selling me to Señor Lopez when he's finished with me. That may be what that little game is all about. No one knows except Bart." Her eyes had lost their sparkle when she looked at Angellee. "All I know is that I'd do almost anything to keep Bart Cantrell from being angry with me. It's a lesson that took me a long time to learn but one I'll never forget. In time, you'll learn it as well."

"No. I won't," Angel said grimly. "I won't be here that long, Heather. I'll find a way to bust out of this place, and I'll take you with me."

"Shut up," Heather whispered, her fingers gripping Angellee's arm tightly. "Don't you know that even the walls have ears in this place." Her nails dug into Angellee's arm. "Smile, Angel. Bart's coming this way."

Although everything in her protested, Angel managed some semblance of a smile for the man who seemed to have total control over everyone he came in contact with. Although his face remained impassive, his dark eyes warmed at her obvious efforts to conform to his rules.

Patting her arm softly, he smiled his satisfaction. "You're learning, Angel," he said before leaving them to circulate around the room.

For the rest of the night, Angel sat on the end of the bar with Heather. Throughout the long hours that followed, she was forced to listen to men of the most vile sort telling her in lurid detail what they would like to do to her. She learned much that night, things that she would rather not have known about. For these men were without conscience; they existed without morals and were devoid of the least bit of compassion. But, although they viewed her with lustful eyes, they kept their hands off, and for that, at least, she was grateful.

It was past two in the morning when Angellee fell into bed, utterly exhausted. She was asleep the moment her head touched the pillow.

Chapter Twenty-Two

Angellee lay on the bed, staring into the darkness. Sweet memories filled with Jake's tender love touched her mind. She allowed the warmth of them to reach out and enfold her. Although Jake was lost to her forever, she knew with complete certainty no one would ever be able to reach inside her to the depth that Jake had.

It had taken only one touch from Jake, the merest kiss, to send her passions soaring, rendering her mindless to everything except the fiery love she had for him. If only she possessed the power to change what had happened.

Angellee had wanted a future with him, a child. But it was not to be. And now, she was alone again, as she had been before.

Although Jake's wounds were far greater than Buck's, he was the first to recover. Even though the medicine woman's power was great, Buck's leg wound had gone untreated so long that it had become infected. For more than a week fever had raged through his body, and he had wavered in and out of delirium. Finally, the fever that had laid siege to his body had abated, and he was now on the road to recovery. But the sickness had left him in a weakened condition. He would need time to recover his strength, and Jake refused to delay a moment longer, for each moment that passed, each hour that swept by, could mean an eternity to his love.

As soon as Jake was able to ride, he told Brave Eagle he could delay no longer, and resigned to his going, the Apaches provided him with several parfleches filled with provisions for the trip.

The morning Jake left, Brave Eagle found him saddling Daniel at the rope corral. With Brave Eagle was a warrior rigged out in white men's britches, boots and shirt, topped off with a brown felt hat.

Brave Eagle stood politely waiting until Jake finished tightening the cinch on the saddle. Then he spoke. "Swift Arrow wishes to ride with you."

Jake's dark eyes flew to the warrior in britches, resting for a moment on the white man's garb then moving to meet his eyes. "I'm afraid I didn't recognize him," he said.

Brave Eagle nodded gravely. "That is the reason he is dressed in such a way. We hope, dressed as he is, he will be taken for your guide. For it is the practice of many white men to hire Apache guides to take them across the desert. It is the only way Swift Arrow will be safe in the land where the horse-soldiers ride in such great numbers."

"If he goes with me, I'll see he has safe passage," Jake said, his eyes dwelling thoughtfully on the warrior.

"But I can't help but wonder why he's willing to help me this way."

"He feels responsible for the white girl's capture. It is said she is a mighty warrior with great power. If she had not been deprived of her weapons, she could not have been overpowered so easily. Swift Arrow was responsible for the weapons being taken, so he is responsible for her capture."

"He doesn't need to blame himself," Jake said grimly. "It wasn't his fault. But I would be grateful for his help. It's been over two weeks now, and the trail will be cold."

"That does not matter. Swift Arrow does not need to follow a trail. He knows where the white girl has been taken."

Jake's heart gave a sudden leap as hope sprang strong within his body. "He knows where she is?" Jake's voice was sharp. "Why wasn't I told?"

Brave Eagle spoke to the warrior, listened gravely, then translated his words for Jake. "He says you were ill and unable to follow her. Knowing where she was would not have helped you. Now it will, so he has spoken."

"Dammit." Jake swore softly at the rigid, Apache logic. "I wish I could talk to him. It's going to be difficult for us to understand each other without someone along to translate."

"I am sure it is a difficulty that you will soon overcome," Brave Eagle said. "You must travel swiftly, for more than the white girl's life is at stake."

Jake felt an icy chill run down his spine. "What do you mean by that?"

"Your woman has been taken to Paso Diablo."

"Paso Diablo?" Jake frowned. The name seemed to strike a chord in Jake's memory, but try as he would, he couldn't bring it to the surface. "The name has a familiar ring, but I can't place it."

"Paso Diablo means the devil's pass. You will find it across the border in the land of the dark-skinned ones. It is a place of unspeakable evil where women are sold for a few pieces of silver to provide pleasure for the men."

Jake paled. "White slavery," he muttered. "God! Angel won't be able to survive in a place like that. Can he be certain she was taken there?"

"Yes. There is no mistake. When you were brought back wounded, Swift Arrow took up the trail, knowing it would be gone when you recovered. They left the security of the mountains and headed across the desert. He followed them to the house of one of the dark-skinned ones, an old Mexican who provided her captor with supplies for the trip. Believing you to be dead, her captor did not try to hide his destination."

"And Angel?" Jake asked gruffly. "Did Swift Arrow inquire about her?"

"Yes. But he has very little information. The only thing he learned is she still lives."

Jake found a little comfort from Brave Eagle's words. At least Angel was alive, and where there was life there was always hope.

"Will you go after her?" Brave Eagle asked, his ebony eyes never wavering from Jake's.

"Of course," Jake growled. "Why should I change my mind?"

"Because now you know she has probably been used by other men. She has been gone for many days."

Agonizing pain flickered in Jake's dark eyes. "I know," he grated harshly. His hands clenched and unclenched. Until Angel was kidnapped, he'd never felt the need to see a man die. He did now. He wouldn't rest until he found her . . . and the man who'd dared steal her away from him.

"You still want her even though she may have been defiled?"

"Yes. Of course." His dark eyes narrowed on Brave Eagle's expressionless face. "What are you getting at? Don't beat around the bush. If you've got something to say, then spit it out."

Brave Eagle frowned, his lips thinning tightly. "I would like to know what you intend for her."

"I'll find her and bring her back of course."

"It is the Apache way to cut off the nose of an unfaithful wife," Brave Eagle continued, his eyes never wavering from Jake's. "I would not like to see such beauty marred."

Jake's face drained of color. "Dammit, man," he swore softly. "What's happening to Angel isn't her fault. She can't be blamed if she's forced to—forced to—" He choked, but made himself say the words. "—submit to animals." Turning blindly away, he pushed Daniel aside and picked up Angellee's saddle. Then, he put it on the Arabian stallion, leaning down to catch the cinch, keeping his face averted from the other two men.

Brave Eagle and Swift Arrow spoke at length. Then, Swift Arrow mounted the paint pony standing nearby and looked down at Jake, his gaze slightly challenging.

"Swift Arrow told me to say that he would not have helped you find her if you had intended her harm. He believes Angel gets her warrior's skills from her flaming hair and her great beauty, and he would not see it taken from her."

"Tell him I'm glad he feels that way," Jake said tensely, tightening the cinch on the saddle. "I'm grateful for his help."

Gathering up the black stallion's reins, Jake moved to the big gray horse and swung easily into the saddle. Then, with one last glance for Brave Eagle, the two men rode away.

There were no tracks to follow, for they had long been erased by the elements and time. But with their destination in mind, the two men rode tirelessly, Jake, driven by his love for Angellee, and Swift Arrow urged on by his admiration for her and his feeling of responsibility for her capture.

They left the mountains behind and began their trek across the dry, desert land.

They traveled well into the night, pushing themselves hard, stopping for short periods only when their mounts needed rest.

At midday of their third day out, Swift Arrow held up his hand, calling for a halt. Sliding from his mount, the warrior went swiftly to the ground. He listened for a moment, then turned his eyes to the southwest, squinting against the sunlight. The two men watched as a cloud of dust became a band of Indians.

"Geronimo," Swift Arrow said, pointing to the approaching horsemen.

Soon, it was all Jake could do to hold Daniel as he alternately kicked out, then shied away from the Indian ponies. Jake and Swift Arrow were surrounded in a cloud of dust, steaming horseflesh and sweating bodies.

Jake felt the hostile stares of the Apaches on him as Swift Arrow held up a hand and greeted an Indian who looked to be about middle-aged. Despite his squat stature, he was a forbidding figure, and Jake knew he was facing the legendary Geronimo.

Geronimo turned in his saddle to stare at Jake with a fierce expression.

"My brother Swift Arrow says you go to Paso Diablo," he said, speaking in perfect English. His dark eyes seemed to see into Jake's soul.

"That's right," Jake answered. "My woman was stolen from me two weeks ago. We have reason to believe she was taken there, and we're going after her."

"If your woman was taken to Paso Diablo, she will be sold to Cantrell to be used as a whore in his cantina."

Despite himself, Jake flinched, although Geronimo was only confirming what he had already been told. "Do you know of the place?"

"Yes. I know of it. It is a bad place you seek. Only evil men travel there. Anyone else would not be allowed to live."

Jake took his words to mean that only robbers and murderers were allowed in Paso Diablo—only those running from the law. "If that's what it takes, then I'll pretend to be running from the law."

"That is good," Geronimo said. "To enter an evil place and leave it, you must become evil. His gaze swept admiringly over the black stallion, then passed disdainfully over Daniel. He looked at Jake's two saddlebags and the bedroll tied on behind Daniel.

"You will need much gold in Paso Diablo," he remarked.

Jake wondered if the crafty chief was thinking about stealing what he had. He took a chance and answered. "Yes. I think I have enough to buy her back."

"I have heard much of this man, Cantrell. If the woman is good to look upon, he will not sell her until he grows tired of her. Swift Arrow will ride with you to the mountains near Paso Diablo, but he must not enter the place of evil, for to do so would mean his death."

"I understand," Jake said, hiding his disappointment well. The warrior could have made a lot of difference in his plan to rescue Angel, but he knew Angellee well enough to know she would not expect the other man to risk his life for her.

"Would you explain to Swift Arrow that it will be enough for him to show me the way. Then he must leave me there and return to his people."

Geronimo translated his words, and Swift Arrow listened impassively, replying in the same guttural language. Then the Apaches turned as one and went on their way.

It seemed an eternity before they reached the mountains outside Paso Diablo. Swift Arrow dismounted, motioning for Jake to join him. Jake swung stiffly from the saddle and looked enquiringly at the warrior.

Swift Arrow knelt, and with a stick, he drew seven blocks in the sand. Alongside these, he drew a straight line. Across the line, he made five more blocks.

Jake squatted beside him, studying the drawing closely.

The warrior swept an open palm over the drawing.

"Paso Diablo," he said, his flat, black gaze on Jake.

Jake nodded. "I understand. It's the town of Paso Diablo."

Swift Arrow nodded. "Town. Paso Diablo." He pointed to one building several times. "Cantrell," he said harshly. "Bad." His eyes glittered with hatred.

"Cantrell's Cantina," Jake said grimly. "That's where they took Angel."

The warrior nodded. "Angel," he repeated, pointing to the building. He stood, his gaze holding Jake's. Drawing Angellee's knife from his belt, he held it out to Jake. "You find," he said gruffly. "Give, Angel."

Jake took the knife solemnly.

"Thank you," he said, sticking the knife in his belt. Putting a foot in the stirrup, he swung a long leg across the saddle. "God willing, I'll find her." With a farewell nod to the silent Indian, he rode away—into the devil's town.

[illegible] and put some ointment on them. They look

Chapter Twenty-Three

Angellee stood at the window, idly brushing her long hair. The hot, midday sun kept the street free of activity at this time of day. A brief knock preceded the door opening, and a dark-haired girl entered her bedroom, sinking down on the bed beside Heather.

"God. I'm tired," she said. "That Cyrus sure knows how to wear a girl out. But then, he sure can pleasure one, too." Her dark eyes flicked to the book Heather was reading. "Whatcha readin'?" she asked.

"Webster's dictionary," Heather said, sparing only a brief glance for the girl beside her.

"Webster's dictionary! My lands, can't you find anythin' else to read?"

"I like reading the dictionary," Heather said, tossing an impudent grin at the girl.

Bertha looked confused. "I didn't know you could read the dictionary. I thought it was just full of words."

"It is. But it also has their meanings. For instance, did you know my name comes from a plant that grows in Scotland?"

Bertha threw a disgusted look at Angellee. "Can you believe her?" she asked.

"Don't make fun of her, Bertha," Angellee said. "She's only trying to better herself."

"Well, gee. I didn't mean to do that," Bertha said in a hurt voice. "Heather an' me been friends for a long time. I wouldn't poke fun at her. I just never knew anyone who read the dictionary before."

"It has little flowers that are pinkish-purple," Heather murmured, seemingly unaware of the two girls' conversation.

"What did you say?" Bertha asked, her dark eyes uncomprehending.

"Heather. It's a small flower. Pinkish-purple in color."

"I thought you just said it was a plant," Bertha said aggressively.

Heather looked up with a frown. "Did you come in here for any particular reason, Bertha?"

"I just wanted a little company," Bertha muttered, in an aggrieved tone of voice. "You used to have time for me before Angel came. If you don't want me here—" She started to rise from the bed.

"Don't go, Bertha," Angellee said, feeling sorry for the other girl. She knew what lonesome was. She had experienced it personally. "We don't mind you joining us. Do we, Heather?"

"No. Of course not," Heather muttered.

"Does that book have my name in it?" Bertha asked, sinking back down on the bed, her ruffled feelings having been placated.

"Yes. I'm sure it does," Angellee said. "Find it for her Heather, and tell her what it means."

"All right," Heather agreed. "Let me go back to the B's." She began turning the pages, her eyes sweeping down the list of names. "Here they are. B-e, B-e-r, B-e-r-t-h-a, Bertha." She studied the words, then looked up with a smile. "It means bright."

"Bright?" Bertha's features registered disappointment. "Is that all it means?"

Heather nodded.

"Well, for Heaven's sake. What a thing for a name to mean." She looked at Heather. "What about Angel's name? Look it up and tell me what it means."

"I don't have to look it up," Heather said. "It means Angel."

"Like the ones you find in Heaven?"

"Yes."

"Oh." Bertha's brow furrowed as she thought about that for a moment. "I think I might change my name," she said.

"Why should you want to do that?" Angellee asked.

"Because I ain't too bright. If I was, I don't 'spect I'd be in a place like this."

"That's not your fault," Angellee consoled. "You couldn't help being kidnapped any more than we could."

"She wasn't kidnapped," Heather commented. "Bertha's folks own a farm. She ran away and came here looking for a job. She *likes* it here."

"And you don't, I suppose," Bertha sneered. "Just because Slade kidnapped you don't mean you don't like it now, same as I do." Her eyes darkened with suspicion. "Or at least you pretend to."

"I'm not saying it's all that bad," Heather said. "I guess you kind of get used to it."

"You may not like it so much after you turn sixteen," Bertha said.

"Oh. Why not?"

"You know what he's got planned for you."

"I know. He told me three years ago."

"Well. I'd worry a little if I were you. And so should Angel." She lowered her voice. "I heard the men talkin' last night. Bart's due back tomorrow."

"Oh?"

"Yeah. And I may not be too bright, but I think both of you got plenty to worry about. He ain't easy when he beds a woman. He likes it rough." Bertha's brow furrowed. "I kinda like you two. Even though you're a cut above the rest of us here, you ain't snippity."

"Thank you for warning us, Bertha," Angellee said, laying her hand on the other girl's arm. "We appreciate it."

The dark-haired girl's gaze dwelt on Angellee. "You've changed since you came here," she said. "I can't really figger out just what it is, but you've changed. Maybe it's the way you talk. Kind of refined and all."

"Heather has been teaching me to be a lady," Angellee said. "Being a lady was terribly important to someone I knew once."

"A man," Bertha stated.

Angel nodded.

"He love you?"

"I think so. But he's dead."

"That's too bad. What about your folks?"

"They're dead too."

"Then you ain't got nobody who cares about you? Nobody who'd help you?"

"No."

"That's too damn bad," Bertha sympathized. "I wish I could help, but I wouldn't dare. I've seen enough of that room in the cellar. It wouldn't do no good noway. You'd only get caught if you tried to get away."

"Who says we want to leave, anyways?" Heather asked, cheerfully. She laid the dictionary aside, her eyes hooded.

"Nobody, I guess," Bertha commented, studying her with shrewd eyes. She got up from the bed and smoothed down her dress. "Guess I'd better go," she said. Bidding the girls goodbye, she left the room.

"We've got to get away from here Angel," Heather said, keeping her voice low. "Something's going to happen, and whatever it is, it's not going to be very nice for either of us."

"I know," Angellee agreed. "I'll try to figure something out. We obviously can't wait any longer."

"I really am getting desperate about this. Bertha's right. Bart's not going to wait for my birthday. I think if he hadn't had to leave, he'd already have taken me to his bed."

"I think you're right, but I ain't gonna—uh—I'm *not going* to let it happen. We're going to leave tonight."

Heather's eyes widened. "But how?" she whispered. "If it had been all that easy, don't you think I'd have already gone?"

"I know. That's the reason I haven't got away from here yet. I can't figure out how. Bart Cantrell's got Cecil and Carlos both guarding the horses. And his watchdogs, Earl and Bruno guard the entrance to this place night and day, preventing us from even stepping outside in the sunlight."

"Earl and Bruno aren't here just to guard us. In case you haven't noticed lately, we're among a bunch of thieves and killers. Bart keeps a lot of money in this place. He wouldn't want to see anything happen to it," Heather stated.

Angellee strode to the window and pulled back the heavy drapes, gazing down at the street below. Her voice was muffled as she spoke.

"I didn't tell you before, Heather, but Bart came to my room the night before he left."

"He did?" The other girl looked up, startled. "What happened?"

"He—he touched me and told me he'd finally made up his mind about me."

"And?" Heather questioned, wide-eyed.

"And nothin'. He didn't say what it was, but the way he looked at me—like—like he was eatin' me with his eyes. He—he opened my gown and just stared at me all over." She shivered with revulsion as she remembered. "Dammit. I wanted to spit in his face!"

"God, Angel. You didn't!"

"No. I didn't. I remembered what you said about him getting mad and the room in the cellar with all the rats and such. Since it looked like he wasn't goin' to do nothin' else until he got back, I managed to keep what I was feeling inside hidden."

"Thank God for that," Heather breathed. "So that's what he's decided. What do you think he plans for me, then. Do you think I'll be sold to that rich don. If he does that, at least my chances of escape would be better from the don's rancho than here." She brightened a little. "If I were outside this place, maybe I could think of a way to get help to you."

"I have a bad feeling about that business with the don," Angellee said. "I think he has you act that way just to keep the rich men coming. They come here hoping they'll get you. He lets you get 'em all hot and bothered; then they don't feel like being so choosy, and they settle for someone like Juanita or Rosa or Flora or maybe even Bertha to spend the night with."

"You could be right," Heather said. "But what does he intend for me in the end?"

"I don't think he's changed his plans at all."

"But you said he wants you."

"And you."

"Well, dammit!" Heather exclaimed. "He told me I was going to be the only one."

Angellee couldn't help smiling at the other girl's righteous indignation. "He lied," she said.

"Well—well—," Heather sputtered. "Well, I'll be damned." Suddenly she burst out laughing.

"It ain't funny," Angellee snapped.

"Isn't," Heather corrected automatically. "I know. It's just that all these years, I guess I thought I was better than the others because I would at least be a sort of wife if I had to go through with it. And here I find I'll be nothing but another damned whore."

"No you won't," Angellee said calmly. "We're going to get away from here."

"How?" the other girl asked, her face betraying her abject misery. "Do you think you can help us with that little jackknife you've got hidden away?"

"I'll admit it's not much. But I feel a lot safer with it around." Her eyes narrowed thoughtfully. "I wonder if there's some way of getting our hands on a gun?"

"I wouldn't even know how to use one," Heather said.

"I can use it."

Heather's eyes widened. "Do you really think a gun would help us?"

"I know it would. With a gun and enough bullets, I could blow our way out of here."

"Could you really?" Heather was beginning to get excited. "You're not just saying that? Do you really think you could go up against men like Earl and Bruno?"

"What are you sayin'," Angellee asked, her narrowed gaze on the other girl. "Do you know how to get me a gun?"

"Answer me first," Heather whispered. "Could you outshoot Earl and Bruno."

"I can outshoot any man I ever met," Angel stated grimly. "Get me a gun and enough ammunition, and I could blow this place to Kingdom come. No. If you can get one gun, you can get me two. Two would be even better."

"I should have known it," Heather said, sinking back against the bed in defeat. "You're just bragging. You couldn't take on a man."

"You little fool!" Angellee snapped, grabbing the other girl by the shoulders and shaking her fiercely. "I *can* do it. That's the reason I don't have no more schoolin'. Pa took me out of school when I was only nine years old and put me in the forest. He taught me to shoot straight and true and put my blade in a squirrel's eye as far as it can be seen."

"God!" Heather breathed. "You're not kidding, are

you? You really mean it?"

"Yes. I mean it. Now answer me. Can you get me the guns?"

"Well. I might be able to. Bruno is in charge of the weapons room, and he has a tender for me. The only thing is, he know's he's a dead man if Bart ever catches him around me. He's afraid if he tries anything, I might tell Bart. If he thought I—"

"All right," Angellee interrupted. "Get busy. Go after him and get me those guns—and some ammunition, too. As much as you can get."

Heather scrambled off the bed and started for the door.

"And a hunting knife, Heather. If you can find one, bring it, too."

Heather turned back from the door. "How about a couple of horses?" she asked drily. "Don't you want me to get some horses?"

"Oh that would be great," Angellee exclaimed. "I thought you couldn't get any."

"I can't," Heather said. "We'll have to manage without them."

"Oh well. That's all right then. I'll get the horses. You just get me those weapons."

As soon as Heather left the room, Angellee went to the window, her gaze going straight to the stables where the horses were kept. Carl leaned against the corral, deep in conversation with Cecil. As she watched, Cecil glanced up—straight at her window. She moved quickly back into the shadows wondering if he had seen her. After a few moments, she peeked out again to see Carl leaving his companion and walking down the street toward the north end of town where

Heather had said his girlfriend Mabel lived.

Cecil stood where he was for a moment; then, with a furtive look around, he tossed his cigarette on the ground and headed for the cantina down the street.

Angel could hardly believe her luck. They had left the stables deserted. Now was her chance.

Opening the door, she stepped into the hall and collided with someone. Drawing a sharp breath, she turned to see Heather. The girl was dressed in a gown cut alarmingly low. Her lips were painted with bright red lip rouge, emphasizing the full lower lip.

"Where are you going?" Heather asked, obviously surprised, for Angellee rarely left her room unless forced to do so.

"The stable's deserted," she whispered, remembering what Heather said about the walls having ears. "I'm going to have a look at it while nobody's there."

"Deserted? Are you sure?"

"Yes. I think Carl must have gone to see his girlfriend Mabel."

"What about Cecil?"

"He went to the cantina across the street."

Heather nodded, her eyes wide. "There's a card game going on over there at this time every day." She smiled. "Bart'll have a fit when he finds out."

"Let's hope he doesn't."

"I don't give a damn if he does. I can't stand either one of them. I've a good mind to make sure he finds out about it."

"Don't be stupid, Heather," Angellee said sharply. "We'll use it to our advantage. If he doesn't know, then maybe they'll do it again. Remember, we're gonna bust out of here, and we're gonna need horses to do it."

"You're right, of course," Heather sighed. "But I sure would like to see those two in trouble with Bart."

"Forget it. Now get down there and charm those two gorillas and give me a chance to get out that front door."

Angellee waited a few minutes, allowing time for Heather to reach the big room, then she slipped silently down the stairs. She waited in the shadows of the curving staircase while the Irish girl approached the two watchdogs sitting at a table playing a game of cards. While Heather held their interest, Angellee moved on silent feet across the plush carpet into the entranceway. Opening the door slightly, she peered cautiously out into the empty street. Then, pausing only to make sure the large door of the barn was still open, she gathered up the hem of her gown and raced fleetly across the dusty road, taking the most direct path to the barns. The air was crisp, the sky a pale blue, but she hardly noticed these things as she slid into the building.

She could smell hay, its biting aroma filling her nostrils as she moved deeper into the building. Most of the stalls were full, and she could hear the noises of horses eating, blowing and bumping against the sides of the stalls.

She moved silently through the shadowed interior of the barn, with experienced eyes examining each horse for strength and endurance. There wasn't much she didn't know about horses, and it didn't take long before she had selected the two she would take for herself and Heather when the time came. Locating the tack room, she made sure she knew where the bridles and saddles were kept. Deciding she had been there long enough, she moved toward the entranceway.

The door swung back and she froze.

Cecil and Carl stood arguing with each other. They hadn't seen her so she darted quickly in the first stall, landing on a pile of hay, sending up a cloud of chaff and dust that threatened to choke her. She uttered prayers of thanks heavenward as she found the stall empty.

God. What'll I do now?

Nothing. Just lay low.

For what seemed forever, Angellee lay low, straw biting into her face and arms, wisps of hay and chaff clinging to her hair. She heard footsteps approaching and shrank farther in the corner.

"I don't give a damn what you saw," Carl said. "Mabel didn't have no greaser in there. She swore to it on a Bible."

Cecil laughed harshly. "I didn't figger Mabel even knew what a Bible was, much less that she'd have one. I wonder where she got it?"

"Said it was the family Bible. Not only that, she swore on both her ma's and pa's graves, too."

"Thet's a laugh. Mabel's ma ain't even dead. Cain't rightly say about her pa though. She don't know who he was."

"Damn you, Cecil. You're just makin' thet up. You want 'er fer yourself. Thet's what Mabel said."

"She should be so lucky. Why should I want her when I've got Carlotta to keep me company?"

There was silence for a moment. "How do you know Mabel's ma ain't dead?"

"Because Flossie's her ma."

"Flossie? You ain't meanin' thet old whore in Gonzales' Cantina who sells herself fer two bits?"

"Thet's the one."

Carl let out a string of curses. "I could wring thet wench's neck with my bare hands," he growled. "She ain't gonna get away with thet."

"Well, you're gonna have to wait 'til later. I'm supposed to meet Clancy down at the warehouse and go over some stuff with him." The sound of jingling spurs came to Angellee's ears.

"Wait a minute," Carl called. "I'll go with you. I can watch this place as easy from across the street. I want to talk to thet whore over at Gonzales' place." The door closed and the stables were left in silence.

Chapter Twenty-Four

When Angellee reached her room, she found Heather, white faced and trembling, sitting on the edge of her bed.

"What's wrong?" she asked, instantly alarmed. Closing the door behind her, she hurried to the other girl.

"I think Bruno is suspicious," Heather said, her voice trembling. She clenched her hands tightly in her lap, her terror-filled eyes meeting Angellee's. "I'm scared, Angel," she whispered. "If Bart finds out what I've done, he'll kill me."

"No, he won't," Angel said, sharply. Her green eyes glittered savagely. "I won't let him touch you, Heather." Her eyes narrowed suddenly. "You *did* get the weapons, didn't you?"

"Bruno wouldn't let me near the guns," the Irish girl said. She brushed a lock of blond hair from her eyes. "That's the reason I think he suspected."

"Oh, God!" Angellee whispered, sinking down beside Heather. How could she protect the girl without a weapon? "Tell me what happened," she said.

"I . . . I managed to convince Bruno that I wanted some time with him, and since Bart was gone he would never know. He tried to get me to the cellar." A tremor shook her slender body. "I didn't have to pretend to be afraid of that place. I allowed him to see how the place terrified me and suggested the weapons room instead." Her wide blues eyes held Angel's. "I . . . I think he suspected something because no matter how hard I tried, I couldn't get near the guns. I managed to steal this, though." She drew a hunting knife from the folds of her skirt. "But it's all I could get." Tears welled up in her eyes and flowed down her cheeks. "God, Angel! It was awful. His hands—mauling me—touching me that way. They were all over . . ." She stopped, obviously unable to continue.

"Don't think about it anymore," Angellee said gently. "I'm sorry I asked you to do it."

"You didn't ask me. The idea was mine. I just didn't know how bad it would be." She turned a tear-stained face to Angellee. "Angel, I'm scared to death. I couldn't get the guns! And what can you do with just a knife?"

"More than you'd think," Angel said, running her thumb along the edge of the twelve-inch blade. "This isn't just a knife, Heather. It's a Bowie knife, and I've worked with them before." She smiled grimly, her green eyes cold as ice. "And aren't we lucky that it's been kept good and sharp."

Suddenly, a loud commotion coming from the street below caught her attention, and she moved to the window, pulling the drapes aside and looking down on the crowd that had gathered around a man and woman. They were arguing in loud, angry voices.

"What's going on," Heather asked fearfully, seeming to shrink more into herself.

Angellee smiled grimly. "Nothing for us to worry about," she said. "But I think maybe Mabel has bought herself a little trouble."

"Mabel?"

"Yes," Angellee replied, turning to the other girl. "Come and see."

Heather rose from the bed and moved to stand beside Angellee. The two watched the man and woman arguing below to the jeers and taunts of the watching crowd.

"I wonder what that's all about?" Heather asked, and Angellee was relieved to note a little color had returned to her face.

"It seems Mabel's been dallyin' with the wrong man. Or should that be men?" At Heather's obvious puzzlement, she went on to explain what she had overheard in the stables.

Heather's laugh was spontaneous. Her blue eyes sparkled as her fears were momentarily put aside. "So Carl finally found out what Mabel was up to. Everyone in town knew. Everyone but Carl, that is."

"You don't feel the least bit sorry for her, do you?" Angellee inquired, studying Heather's animated face.

"Why should I?" Heather asked. "I had to put up with her taunts and insults for nearly three years. I was glad when Bart gave her to Carl as a bonus for one of his jobs."

"She used to work here?"

"Yes. And dealt me plenty of misery." She laughed, but there was no amusement in the sound. "The first time Bart sent me to that room in the cellar, it was because of her. I think she had eyes in the back of her head. None of the girls liked her. She tried to better her position here by running to Bart with the least little transgression. All of us were glad when Bart gave her to Carl."

"He sure is mad now." They watched as Carl grabbed Mabel and began to systematically cut the woman's garments off. She struggled wildly, cursing him roundly in a loud, vulgar voice, but he continued slashing until the woman stood naked in the street. Then he turned and walked up the dusty road carrying the torn rags in his hands.

The door to the bedroom opened and both girls turned to see Bertha standing there.

"Are you watchin'?" she asked gleefully, coming to the window. "Ain't it somethin'? She's finally gettin' what's comin' to her. The only thing is, she'll probably be coming back here now. Nobody else'll have her."

"Carl. Honey," Mabel's voice came to them, slightly muffled by the glass window. "You ain't gonna leave me like this are you?" The woman called after the retreating figure.

Carl didn't answer. He didn't even look back. He just walked on down the street to the house at the far end of town, opened the door and went in, slamming the door behind him.

Mabel stood where Carl had left her. Then, as if suddenly aware of her nakedness, she began to run. Her pendulous breasts bounced up and down as she hurried to the house Carl had entered. Casting a baleful look at the watching crowd, she climbed the steps and pulled on the door. When it didn't budge, she knocked timidly. When there was no answer, she began to bang on the door and scream abuses and threats at the man inside. Finally, defeated, she turned and came down the street, ignoring the hoots and jeers of the watching crowd.

"I knew it," Bertha said, her voice mirroring her disgust. "Here she comes, without a stitch on her back and no place to stay. Well, she ain't gonna get 'er old room back, 'cause it belongs to me now. An' I ain't gonna share with her neither."

"Damn!" Heather said. "Why'd Carl have to find out about her. She's trouble for sure." She looked hopefully at Bertha. "Maybe Bart won't let her come back."

"Don't be stupid," Bertha snorted. "She can work, can't she? Of course he'll let her come. All I can say is she better lay off my customers. I got me a nice bunch of guys to work with, an' I ain't about to share with her."

"You'll do whatever Bart says," Heather said quietly. "You don't have any choice."

"Yeah I know you're right. Dammit, why'd Carl have to find out? I wonder if someone told him?"

"Oh, God, no!"

Something in Heather's voice alerted Angellee. She turned to see the Irish girl's face draining of color. Wondering what could have caused her panic, she followed the girl's gaze up the street. Angellee's heart gave a sudden lurch.

"Hey look," Bertha said, barely containing her excitement. "There's Bart. He's back a day early." Her eyes darkened with greed. "I wonder if he brought me something."

"Does he usually?" Angellee asked, trying to keep

Bertha's attention distracted from Heather's whitened face.

"Yes." Bertha said, hurrying to the door. "I think I'll just fix myself up a little before I see him." She smiled at the girls, frowning slightly as her gaze fell on Heather. "You're lookin' a little pale, honey. You feelin' all right."

"Just an upset stomach, Bertha," the Irish girl said. "It'll go away."

"Maybe you better take something and lay down for a while. Since Bart's back, he'll want you downstairs tonight. Well, see you both later." She left the room, closing the door behind her.

"We waited too long," Heather said, her voice filled with despair. "Oh, God, Angel! What's going to happen?"

"Take it easy," Angellee consoled, leading the trembling girl to the bed. "Nothin's going to happen. Sit down and get hold of yourself."

"What if Bruno tells him?"

"Why should he do that?" Angellee asked, hiding her own fears from the shaken girl. "It would make him look bad, too."

Heather licked her dry lips. "I have a bad feeling about this, Angel," she whispered.

"Stop worryin'. Everything's going to be all right. My pa always said there's no need in borrowin' trouble." Angellee moved to the wash commode and poured a glass of water, returning to hand it to Heather. "Drink this," she said.

Heather took a big gulp, swallowing convulsively, then sputtered. "Water?" she asked. "I thought it was whiskey."

"I don't have no whiskey."

"Any whiskey, Angel," Heather corrected.

Angellee could have hugged the girl. Even as terrified as Heather was, she was still trying to help her become a lady.

"Any whiskey," she repeated obediently.

Angellee wasn't all that surprised when the door opened, and Bart came in followed closely by Earl.

Although he was smiling in a gentle manner, something about his eyes alerted Angellee. They looked about as inviting as a rattlesnake's.

"Hello, my dears," he said, coming into the room. Earl stepped in and shut the door behind him.

"H-hello, B-Bart," Heather stuttered, her face flushing with guilt.

"What have you been up to while I was away," he asked softly, his dark eyes narrowing on the Irish girl's flushed cheeks.

"N-nothing," she whispered, lowering her eyes evasively.

"And you, Angel?" the saloon owner asked, turning to look at her with narrowed eyes. "Have you been behaving while I was gone?"

"Of course," she said, coldly, her mouth tightening into a thin line. Bart hadn't waited for her answer before his eyes returned to Heather. "What else would I be doing since I can't leave this place."

"That's what I've been wondering," Bart said, sitting down in a straight-backed chair with his back to the window, leaving his face in the shadow. "I suppose it gets boring around here sometimes." His eyes were mere slits while he studied the two girls as if they were worms on a baited hook.

Earl hadn't moved from his stance near the door. He stood leaning against the doorframe watching the tableau unfold with an expressionless face. His eyes met hers then quickly slid away. Angellee subdued a shudder of fear. Heather was right to be afraid. Something was going on. Somehow, Bart had discovered what they were about.

Well, I don't give a damn. If he thinks he can scare me with that room in the cellar, then he can think again.

Reaching into his pocket, Bart removed a small jackknife. Heather seemed hypnotized by his hands. She blanched as he opened the blade. Anyone could see she was frightened out of her wits, and fury surged through Angellee as she realized that Bart knew and was deliberately tormenting her.

When Bart began to calmly clean his fingernails with the blade of the knife, Angellee found she couldn't keep still any longer.

"Did you want something in my room, *Mr.* Cantrell?" she asked in a cold, hard voice. Her eyes glittered savagely as they met his. "Or did you just come here to clean your fingernails?"

He smiled, seeming not in the least put out by her anger. "I like a girl with spunk," he said. "But there's a limit to what I'll allow. Now, you take Heather there . . ." He pointed the blade at the frightened girl. "She had too much spunk when she came here." His cold eyes returned to Angellee. "Just like you do," he added. "I had to take a little out of her, I'm afraid. I may have taken too much." He stared at the girl on the bed. Her head was bent, and she stared at her trembling hands which were clasped in her lap. "Yes. I guess I may have. Perhaps it was too many visits to the room in the cellar." He gave Angellee a cold smile. "Never mind though. I learn from my mistakes. I wouldn't want to subdue that fiery spirit of yours."

Angellee stared at him with hatred. Sitting down beside Heather, she rested a hand against her pillow, feeling the comforting hardness of the knife she had hidden there. While both men's eyes were on the trembling figure of the Irish girl, Angellee's hand slipped beneath the pillow and gripped the handle of the knife, hard.

"You know, Heather," Bart continued playing with her, obviously enjoying her terror. "Bruno was waiting for me when I got back. He had an interesting story to tell me."

Heather stiffened. Gathering her courage around her, she squared her shoulders and tilted her chin defiantly. "What's that got to do with me?" she asked, trying to bluff it out. Angellee could have cheered.

"The story concerned you," Bart said softly. "Bruno said you approached him and flirted openly with him, enticing him into the weapons room with the promise of a kiss. He said he knew right away what you were about but decided to go along with you and see how far you'd go." His cold eyes never wavered from hers. "Is that true?"

"Are you asking me?"

"Yes."

"Would you believe me if I told you Bruno was lying?" Heather asked, studying her hands intently.

"No."

"Then, why ask?" Her voice was calm.

"Where's this all leading, Cantrell," Angellee asked.

"Probably to the room in the cellar," he murmured.

Tension stiffened Angellee's body, and her fingers tightened around the knife handle.

Heather seemed to guess her intention, for she put a staying hand on Angellee's arm. She looked defiantly at Bart Cantrell. "Well, it won't be the first time, will it?" she asked calmly. "Those rats and me have become pals after all this time."

"Indeed?" Bart asked. He turned to Earl. "Perhaps solitary confinement isn't enough anymore," he said. "Perhaps Heather would benefit from the lash this time."

"The l-lash?" Heather gasped. Her body seemed to shrink into itself.

"The lash?" Earl asked at the same time. His gaze flickered uncertainly between Bart Cantrell and Heather. "Boss, remember what happened to Stella last year. When Bruno starts, he doesn't know when to stop."

"That's right," Bart said. "Stella didn't survive, did she?" He studied Heather, a smile playing over his face. "Then, perhaps you'd better apply it, Earl. We don't want Heather dead, do we. Dead bodies have no value."

"Me, boss?" Earl asked, his big body stiffening. "Why me? You know whipping's not my style."

"It will be," Bart Cantrell said. "I don't know how much longer Bruno will be serving me. It's time you learned to apply the whip, and you can start right now with Heather."

"Now?"

"Right now."

As Earl began to move toward Heather, Angellee

pulled the knife from under the pillow. Springing to her feet, she took a protective stance in front of the Irish girl. "Don't come any closer," she snapped. "Not if you want to live to see tomorrow."

"What the hell?" Earl said, staring at Angellee in amazement. His gaze flicked to the Bowie knife, then to Bart Cantrell.

"Well, well," Bart murmured, his eyes narrowing on Angellee. "Now I wonder where you got that big knife." Rather than being alarmed, he seemed to be amused. "Take it away from her before she hurts herself, Earl."

"Sure, boss." Earl grinned. "Put it down, Angel," he said, taking a step toward her.

"I'm warnin' you," she snapped. "Don't come any closer."

Earl ignored her, reaching for the knife, and she slashed out with the blade, cutting a long gash on his right arm. Cursing, he jumped back quickly, staring in confusion at the long, crimson streak that stained his sleeve. She slashed out again, and he yelled out in pain as bright crimson flowed from one hand. Then, cursing hoarsely, he reached for his gun.

Before he could raise the weapon and take aim, the knife left her hand and landed with a thud in his throat. Earl gave a gurgle and sank to the floor, clutching the knife handle with his hands, his dead eyes staring up at her in surprise.

While Bart was still trying to come to terms with what she had done, she had ripped the blade from Earl's throat and kicked the gun across the room out of Cantrell's reach. Then she turned to face Bart who had gained his feet and started toward them.

"Back off," she spat, her eyes glittering savagely. "What the hell?"

"Behind you!" Heather screamed the warning.

Whirling, Angellee saw Bruno come into the room. Then Bart had reached her, wrapping one big arm around her neck, cutting off her air supply. She slashed upward with the knife, cutting deeply into the arm that held her, and was immediately released.

"Unless you want Heather dead, you'd better drop the knife," Bart said.

Bruno had Heather by the neck with one hand, depriving her of air, and the Irish girl's face was already turning blue.

Fearing for Heather's life, Angellee dropped the knife. As soon as it left her hand, Bruno dropped Heather to the floor where she lay limp and gasping for air. Bart kicked the knife across the room to Bruno. Then he struck Angellee a blow to her face that knocked her backward, sending her sailing against the wall. She was dimly aware of pain as her head struck something solid with a loud thunk. Then she sank down into a welcoming blanket of darkness.

When Angellee came to, she was lying on the floor of her bedroom where she had fallen. There was no sign of Heather.

Struggling to a sitting position, she put a hand to her aching head. She felt nauseous, and her heart seemed to be pounding out a loud rhythm in her ears. She wondered what had happened to Heather.

Getting to her feet and moving to the washstand, she poured water into the bowl and splashed the cool liquid on her face, managing to clear her head of some of the cobwebs.

With her anxiety for Heather overcoming her pain, she moved to the door, intent on discovering what had happened to the Irish girl.

The door refused to budge. She had been locked in.

God! What do I do now?

Angellee paced the room frantically, her mind conjuring up a vivid picture of Heather, hanging from her bound hands, her body quivering beneath the weight of the lash, blood streaming from the cuts on her back.

Feeling helpless, she went to the wall that divided her room from Bertha's and tapped lightly on it, hoping the girl was on the other side.

"What do you want?" The voice was muffled as it came through the wall.

Angellee put her mouth closer to the wall. "Do you know where Heather is?" she asked.

"They took her downstairs to the cellar."

"Bertha—did they hurt her?"

"I don't know. Bart's got Bruno guarding the entrance."

"Bertha, will you help us? Will you get the key and unlock my door?"

"I can't. Bart would kill me. It wouldn't do no good to let you out anyway. You'd never get near her."

"Bertha," Angellee pleaded. "Please help me. I'm afraid they'll kill her."

There was no answer. Only silence.

"Bertha, do you hear me?"

"I hear. I can't help."

"Do you know what Bart plans to do with us?"

"He's givin' you both to the men. Heather later. You, tonight."

Tonight.

Time had run out.

She sank to the floor in despair, leaning her head on her knees.

"Did you hear me?" Bertha asked.

"I heard."

"I wish I could help, Angel. But I'm afraid. It would be worth my life if Bart found out. Anyway, maybe it won't be so bad," Bertha continued, her voice consoling. "There'll only be one man tonight."

Angellee remained silent.

"Did you hear what I said?" Bertha asked.

"Yes." Angellee's voice was filled with defeat.

"I'm sorry, Angel. I really am. But I'm too scared to help you." Bertha remained silent for a moment then asked. "Are you all right?"

"Yes. I'm all right." Angellee got up from the floor and went to the window, pulling the curtain aside to stare down at the empty street below. Across the dusty road, near the stables stood two men. Carl and Cecil. No, although there was something familiar about the gunman dressed in black, it wasn't Carl.

What the hell does it matter who he is? He isn't going to get Heather out of that cellar room. It's up to me to do that.

She allowed the curtain to drop and began to pace the floor, desperately trying to figure a way out for Heather and herself.

Chapter Twenty-Five

Jake sat at a table in the smoke-filled room, a bottle of whiskey and a glass in front of him while his narrowed gaze watched the entrance of the cantina. Had anyone looked close enough, they would have seen the bright, dangerous flash in his dark eyes, the hard set of his features. His lean, muscled body was coiled for action, even though he appeared casually relaxed.

He had been sitting there over two hours now, and the place was beginning to fill up. Still he waited, hoping to catch a glimpse of one particular face. Although several gaudily dressed women had entered, hips swaying suggestively, their rouged faces and brightly painted lips smiling invitingly at the customers, none of them had been Angel.

The girls had begun to circulate among the tables. Most of them were prettier, and younger, than were ordinarily found in a saloon.

Jake had been aware for some time now of the girl standing with her back to the bar giving him the once-over. Her dark hair was piled high on her head, and she looked to be barely out of her teens. The canary yellow dress trimmed with black fringe dipped excessively low in front, barely restraining her overlarge bosom. Catching his stare, she bestowed a practiced smile with her red, painted lips.

Although Jake had intended to remain alone at his table, hoping to gather information about Angel from the conversation around him should she fail to put in an appearance, something about the girl, perhaps the way she continued to stare boldly at him, changed his mind, and he smiled at her.

Taking his smile as an invitation, the girl made her way across the room toward him. Stopping beside his table, she brushed her hip against him.

"Want some company, big boy?" she asked in a pleasantly husky voice.

He nodded, and she smiled, drawing out a chair and sitting down at the table. She nodded at the bartender who reached beneath the counter, extracted a bottle, filled a glass, then brought it to the girl.

Jake waited until the bartender had left before he spoke. "There's quite a crowd here tonight."

"Yeah," she agreed, taking a sip of the amber colored liquid in her glass. Jake suspected it was tea.

"I'm surprised you're not busy."

Her fingers tightened on the glass. "The customers are all waitin'," she said grimly. Her smile seemed forced. "You got a name?"

"Jake."

She tilted her head provocatively, showing him her practiced smile. "Just Jake."

He nodded. "What's yours?" he inquired, although

he didn't really care.

"Bertha," the girl said, tossing a coquettish look at Jake from beneath her long lashes. "My name's Bertha. It means bright."

"Yes, I know," Jake replied.

"Well, don't that beat all—you knowin' a thing like that," Bertha exclaimed. "I didn't know it until Heather—" She broke off, a shadow crossing her face.

"You were saying?" Jake prompted. "Something about some heather?"

"Oh, it wasn't nothin'," Bertha replied. "Just one of the girls here. Her name's Heather. She's the one that told me." Her eyes lifted to meet Jake's, her smile weak. "Have you ever heard of a girl that reads dictionaries before?"

Jake poured himself another glass of whiskey. "No. I don't believe I have." He lifted the glass to his mouth and took a long swallow.

"Me neither. She's something else." Her eyes held a touch of sadness as she took a sip from her glass, watching him over the rim.

Bertha gave a long sigh, then seemed to remember she was supposed to be entertaining. "Been in town long?" she asked, her eyes flickering over his trail-weary body.

"Only a few hours."

"Stayin' long?"

"I'm not sure yet. It all depends."

"On what?" she asked, eyeing him boldly.

"On a lot of things," he replied. His eyes kept moving to the doorway, hoping to see Angel walk in. "Mostly, it depends on how soon I find what I'm looking for."

"Oh." She shifted uneasily.

He smiled grimly. The woman obviously knew better than to ask him questions about his business there. But he didn't want her to leave. The room was growing warm, and he was bone-weary from the long hours in the saddle. He had to stay alert.

He studied the woman, wondering how to go about questioning her without raising her suspicions. Something niggled at the back of his mind—a remark she'd made earlier.

"You said something peculiar earlier. Something about this crowd waiting. Waiting for what?"

"Bart's laid on some special entertainment tonight," she said, her lips tightening. "And everyone wants to get in on it. That's why none of the girls are busy. All them bums are waitin' to see if they get a chance at her." She sighed heavily. "After the auctioning, I guess we'll be kept busy enough with the losers."

"You said 'her'," Jake commented, his heart skipping a beat. "Was that a slip of the tongue, or is Cantrell selling some*one?*"

Bertha took a long swallow from the glass and set it back down on the table. "Guess you didn't hear about it," she muttered. "It's the new girl Bart bought."

Jake's dark gaze narrowed on the woman. "He's selling one of his girls?"

"Not exactly," Bertha grimaced. "He don't part with what he owns. He's only selling one night with her."

"I see," he mused, swirling the amber liquid in his glass and studying it intently. "Now that is interesting. Is there something special about this girl?"

"Yeah. I guess you could say that."

Jake gripped the glass until his knuckles whitened.

Damn. It was like pulling teeth to get the girl to say more than two words. "What's she look like?"

"You thinkin' about buyin' her?"

"I might be."

"I can tell you right now, she ain't gonna come cheap, mister. She's a little bitty thing with long red hair and green eyes and the face of an angel." She studied him thoughtfully. "That's her name, too." She added. "Angel."

A muscle twitched in Jake's jaw. It was his only show of emotion as he continued his perusal of the glass. "Any chance of seeing her?"

"No," Bertha said flatly. "There ain't a snowball's chance in hell, mister. Bart's got her locked in her room."

"I take it she doesn't like it here."

"You take it right," she muttered. "Poor little thing. Shouldn't have cut Bart that way. I've never seen him so mad before."

"She cut Cantrell?" His eyes whipped to her face.

Bertha whitened. "Could be I'm talkin' too much, mister," she muttered. "That ain't too healthy 'round here. Forget what I said."

"It's forgotten," he said, reaching out and covering her hand gently. He didn't want to frighten her away. "Don't worry about it. Anything you tell me will go no farther."

"Thanks," Bertha said, holding his gaze. "I think you mean it." She studied him with puzzled eyes. "You seem to be a man with a purpose," she murmured. "You mind my askin' what you're doin' in Paso Diablo?"

Knowing he would need all the help he could get,

Jake took a chance on trusting the woman. He lowered his voice. "I'm looking for my fiancée," he said. "She was kidnapped three weeks ago." His eyes were penetrating as he held her gaze. "She's a tiny little thing—not more than five feet tall—with long, red hair."

Her dark eyes flickered. "That so?" she asked casually. "Could be you found her."

"Thanks Bertha."

"Don't thank me," she said. "I can't help you. And you ain't gonna be able to just waltz outta here with 'er. You gotta have a plan."

"I realize that," Jake said, remembering the guards at the stables where he'd left the two horses. "But I'll think of something. I won't leave without her. How many guards does Cantrell have on this place anyway?"

"Two in here. Two at the stables. No, I forgot," she said. "She killed Earl."

"That makes three in all."

"Don't think they'll be easy to take. Especially for one man."

"If I can reach her, it won't be just one man," he said, thinking of the Arkansas toothpick stashed in his boot.

"You got any money?" she asked.

"Yes."

"It's gonna take a lot to outbid them other gents." Her eyes never wavered from his. "You are going to bid on Angel, aren't you?"

"Nothing could stop me," he said softly. "How much money do you think I'll need?"

"I don't know. But I've got a couple hundred stashed in my room if you need it."

He laid his hand over hers. "Thank you, Bertha," he said. "That's nice of you. Apparently she found a friend here."

"Two of 'em," Bertha said quickly. "The other'n is locked in a room in the cellar. That's the reason Angel's bein' auctioned off. She tried to defend Heather. Bart got mad when she cut him and killed Earl with that Bowie knife."

"When's the auction being held?"

"In a few minutes."

"Is the door to the cellar guarded?"

"Yes. Bruno's guardin' it, and he's a mighty big man. He never leaves the door to the cellar." She eyed him doubtfully. "The only way for a body to get around him would be to kill him."

Jake nodded. "I understand what you're saying, Bertha, and I'll give the matter some thought."

"Listen, Jake. I got to circulate. Bart's been looking over here the last few minutes. I hope you can do something for those girls. They ain't like the rest of us. They don't belong here."

He nodded, watching her leave and begin to circulate around the room. His heart was beating like a trip hammer. He had found Angel and she was alive. His gaze swept the room, stopping on three men standing near an open door. Beyond them, through the doorway, Jake could see a desk. The room was apparently Bart Cantrell's office. He studied the faces of the three men. Two he dismissed as gunslingers. The third had his arm in a sling.

Cantrell.

As Jake watched, Cantrell pushed his way through

the men, coming to a stop beside the bar. There was an expectant air about the room as he held up a silencing hand.

Immediately, the cantina became quiet.

Cantrell pulled a watch from his vest pocket and looked at it. Then he looked over the crowded cantina. "It's about that time, gentlemen. Shall we proceed?"

Shouts of agreement filled the room, swelling to ear-splitting proportions.

"All right," Bart said. "Does everyone know what's going on here tonight?"

"Sure, Cantrell," someone shouted. "We're finally gonna get a chance at Angel."

"That's right," Bart said, a cold smile playing across his features. "We're going to auction off our flaming Angel. Now, who'd like to start the bidding."

"I will if you'll give me credit," said a man nearby.

Laughter sounded in the cantina. "No credit," snapped Cantrell. "This transaction will be cash on the barrel head, gentlemen."

"I'll bid ten dollars."

Laughter accompanied the bid. "Hell, Curley Joe," taunted a man nearby. "You paid twenty dollars for Rosa, and she's nothin' but a whore."

"All right," Curley Joe growled. "I'll give you thirty."

"Fifty," shouted a voice from the back.

"Fifty-five," called another.

Bart looked around the cantina. "I don't believe I'm hearing this," he said. "Fifty-five dollars for a whole night with a fiery virgin like Angel?"

Jake had been watching Bart with brooding eyes. The saloon owner was passing her off as a virgin. Could it be he thought she was? Sudden hope surged through his body. Could it be possible Angel had remained untouched all the time she had been here? If only he dared believe that was true.

"I'll bid a hundred," called a voice from the corner. Jake's narrowed gaze found the well-dressed man seated at a poker table.

"That's better," Cantrell said. "Who'll raise it to two hundred?"

The men began to move restlessly but no one answered. Obviously the bidding was getting too steep for most of them.

"Do I hear two hundred?" Cantrell asked. "Come on, gentlemen. Surely you're not going to let Ezra get away with that little."

"Don't sound like a little to me," a man muttered from a nearby table. "A hundred dollars will last a feller a mighty long time. And they ain't easy to come by."

"Come on," the man called Ezra said. "Quit stalling, Cantrell. My bid was the highest."

"All right," Cantrell said, admitting defeat. "I have a bid of one hundred dollars for a whole night alone with the flaming Angel. Going once—going twice—"

"And fifty," Jake called, pushing his black hat back on his head.

Cantrell stopped, his gaze traveling over the crowd, coming to rest on Jake. "Did I hear a bid out there?" he asked.

Jake nodded.

Cantrell looked pleased. "Well, gentlemen," he said. "I have a bid of one hundred and fifty dollars."

"Two hundred," shouted Ezra, looking at Jake with contempt.

"I have a bid of—"

"And fifty," Jake said, cutting Cantrell off.

"Three hundred," Ezra roared, a red flush staining his neck and face.

"And fifty," countered Jake calmly.

Cantrell stood near the bar, his gaze moving between the two men who were now the only bidders for Angel.

"Four hundred," Ezra shouted, scraping his chair back and getting to his feet. Placing his hands on the table in front of him, he glared at Jake. As the silence continued, a triumphant smile spread over his face, and his tense body slowly relaxed.

"And fifty," Jake said.

"Dammit, Cantrell," Ezra shouted, striding to the front of the room. "I want that woman. Who is this drifter anyway?"

"It doesn't matter who he is, Ezra. His money is as good as yours."

Ezra pulled a wad of money from his pocket and began to count it. When he finished, he looked up. "I'll give you twelve hundred," he snapped. Turning, he threw a look of fury at Jake.

The crowd in the cantina had become hushed as everyone waited to see what would happen next. It was so quiet you could have heard a pin drop as everyone eyed the gunman dressed in black who had remained calmly seated at the table.

Jake's voice was quiet as it fell into the silent saloon. "And fifty."

Ezra let out an angry roar. "I don't believe you've got that much money, mister."

"How about it, mister?" Cantrell asked, pushing his way through the crowd to stand over Jake. "Let's see the color of your money."

"Is he finished bidding?" Jake asked, rising slowly to his feet

"Are you?" Bart asked, turning to the red-faced man who had followed him.

"You know I am, Bart," Ezra said. "Twelve hundred is every penny I got on me. If you'd trust me with the rest, I got more at the ranch."

"Won't do," Jake said, calmly. "Cantrell said cash on the barrel head."

"He's right, Ezra. I said cash." Cantrell eyed Jake coldly. "Do you have it on you?"

Jake dug in his pocket, extracted a roll of bills and counted out twelve hundred and fifty dollars. He handed it to the saloon owner. "Where's the girl?" Jake asked.

"Upstairs," Cantrell said. "Fourth door on the right." As Jake started to move away, Cantrell dug in his pocket and extracted a key. "You'll need this," he said. "And a lot of good luck." His harsh laughter followed Jake as he moved toward the door of the cantina.

Jake left the cantina, crossed the large room with the heavy purple furnishings and mounted the staircase. At the top of the stairs was a long, dim hallway with several doors on each side. He moved down the hallway, his ears tuned to the groans, muttered curses and steady rhythmic sounds coming from behind the closed doors.

His heart beat fast with anticipation as he passed the second door. How would Angel look? She had been in this place for at least two weeks now and had to have been affected by her surroundings. Although Cantrell was passing her off as a virgin, Jake dared not hope that she had remained untouched by other men during her confinement, but he refused to allow himself to dwell on it.

He stopped before the fourth door, knelt and inserted the key in the lock.

Chapter Twenty-Six

Angellee knelt beside the door, picking at the lock with a hairpin. She wasn't sure just how long she would have before someone came, and despite herself, her fingers trembled as she worked. She had to get Heather out of the cellar and then escape with her. She wasn't sure what had been done to her. She just hoped Heather would be able to travel. She felt the lock with the end of the hairpin and worked harder, wiggling it around. It bent and she swore softly.

Sighing with disappointment, she rose to her feet and began to search for something else to use on the door.

Dammit, Angel, she chided herself. You forgot the jackknife.

Hurrying to the wardrobe, she raised herself on tiptoe, searching in the farther regions of the shelf at the top. Her fingers closed over the jackknife, and she gave a sigh of relief, grasping it tightly with her fingers. Then, returning to the door, she began to work the blade in the lock.

Hearing heavy boots in the hallway, accompanied by the jingling of spurs, she froze, cool fingers of fear trailing down her spine as the sound stopped just outside her door.

Had she delayed too long?

For a moment there was silence as though whoever was out there was listening. Silently, she rose to her feet, the knife held protectively in front of her. Her eyes fell to the knife as a key grated in the lock.

Fool! That knife won't do more than prick his skin.

Her frantic gaze darted around the room, searching—searching—coming to rest on the stand that held the water pitcher and bowl. Silent as a cat, her feet carried her to the washstand. Picking up the water pitcher, she turned down the wick on the kerosene lamp until the flame sputtered and went out, leaving the darkness of the room alleviated only by the pale shaft of moonlight filtering through the window. Swallowing hard against the rapidly swelling panic that threatened to choke her, she crept back to the door and waited.

She was momentarily paralyzed as the knob turned slowly. For a breathless eternity she waited. The door squeaked as it swung slowly inward, concealing her from the silent male shadow filling the doorway.

Her heart beat raggedly, thundering loudly in her ears as she raised the pitcher full of water over her head. Her fingers trembled, and she remained motionless, hardly daring to breathe, waiting for the moment to present itself when she could strike.

The dark shadowy figure hesitated, then stepped fully into the darkened room, closing the door behind him.

No one will hear him fall.

She stepped forward as his head swiveled, bringing the pitcher down hard. With a muttered oath, he saw the blow coming and moved swiftly. The pitcher struck him a glancing blow on the shoulder, the water drenching his clothes thoroughly.

He whirled, reaching for her, and she shrank back, stifling a scream, knowing it would only bring others that would help her assailant.

"Hello, Angel," he said, his voice soft.

"Jake!"

She stared at him incredulously, her mind trying to assimilate what her eyes beheld. It *was* Jake. Although there was a faint air of weariness about his dark, heavy-lidded eyes, he seemed to be all right.

His strong arm snaked around her waist, drawing her closer against his familiar warmth. Then his hungry lips covered hers, and she was temporarily lost in his kiss under the assault of ragged, spontaneous emotions.

Visibly shaken, he tore his mouth from hers. His breathing was uneven, his voice hoarse and anxious. "Are you all right, Angel?"

She couldn't answer. She lifted her fingers to touch his face wonderingly.

He was alive.

Jake was alive, and he had come for her.

Hot tears welled up and flowed down her cheeks.

He lifted a tear off with a callused finger and stared wonderingly at it. "Crying?" he questioned, hoarsely. "My fierce Angel crying? What happened to all that fire?"

"I thought you were dead," she whispered, her voice breaking with emotion. Her heart pounded wildly in her breast, matching the beat of his own.

"As you can see, I'm very much alive."

"Thank God! How did you find me?"

"Swift Arrow helped me trail you."

"Then, he's with you?"

"Waiting in the hills outside the city. It would have been dangerous for him to come in. They don't like Apaches around here."

With great effort, Jake set her aside long enough to lock the door. "That's so we won't be disturbed," he said, his dark gaze glittering as it devoured her face. He wound one hand tightly in her hair and wrapped the other arm possessively around her, holding her tightly against him.

"How did you manage to get into town?"

"Pretended to be an outlaw on the run," he whispered hoarsely against her lips. "Dammit. I don't want to talk." His lips moved across her cheek, along the line of her jaw, caressing the slender column of her throat.

"You—you shouldn't have come," she said unsteadily. "You've put yourself in so much danger coming here like this. You don't know what Cantrell is like."

"Tell me you aren't glad to see me," he said, his voice ragged. "Tell me my lips don't sear you the way yours sear mine." His hands splayed wide, moving along her slender back, clasping her rounded buttocks and pressing her hard against the rise of his passion.

As her arms moved of their own accord to circle his neck, he added huskily. "Tell me your body doesn't ache for mine just as mine aches for yours."

With a low moan, she reached for his lips, and he laughed low in his throat as his mouth claimed hers, devouring her sweetness. She could hardly think when his lips left hers. But she knew she must.

"How did you get past Bart Cantrell?" she asked. "How did you get up here without him seeing you?"

"I didn't," he said, his lips nibbling at her ear. "Cantrell knows I'm here."

"He knows?" Her eyes were wide as she pulled away from him. "Jake, stop it," she said. "What do you mean, Cantrell knows?"

He sighed heavily. "God, Angel!" he exclaimed, pulling her back against him. "Do we have to go through this right now?"

"Yes," she said. "I want to know why Cantrell let you come up here."

"I paid for the privilege."

"How were you able to do that?" she asked, avoiding his arms as he reached for her again.

"All right," he said. "You win. We'll talk. Cantrell let me up here because I was the highest bidder."

"Highest bidder?"

"Yes. Didn't you know he was going to auction your services off for the night?"

"No," she said, shuddering. "I knew someone would be coming. That's why I used the pitcher to brain you. But I didn't know there was to be an auction." She buried her head in his shoulder. "Oh, Jake," she cried, her voice muffled. "I've never been so glad to see anyone in my life."

A knock sounded at the door, and Jake stiffened. He pushed her away, drawing the knife from his belt. The wicked blade glinted in the moonlight as Jake held the knife ready.

"Hey, mister." The male voice sounded muffled coming through the door. "Cantrell told me to see if you were still alive."

"Yeah, sure," Jake called gruffly. "Why shouldn't I be."

"Don't know. He didn't say."

"Tell Cantrell I don't expect to be disturbed again. I paid good money for the whole night."

"Yeah, sure. I'll tell him."

As they listened to heavy footsteps receding, Angellee's eyes were riveted to the knife. "That's mine," she whispered. "Did you take it away from Swift Arrow?"

"No. He sent it to you."

"He did?" Her eyes were misty. "I never thought I would see it again. I wish I could thank him."

"You can," Jake growled, pulling her hard against him. "Later."

Angellee gazed up at him with shining eyes. "How do I thank *you?*" she asked softly.

He showed her, lowering his mouth to hers. As his lips claimed hers again, she was aware of nothing but Jake's lips—Jake's arms—Jake's body, pressing against hers.

"Shouldn't we be tryin' to figure a way out of here?" she asked when he finally lifted his head.

"We'll wait until everyone settles down for the night," he whispered against her ear. "It shouldn't be more than a couple of hours now. They won't be expecting us to leave this room before morning."

"Oh, Jake," she said, twining her fingers in his dark hair and drawing him nearer. "I'm so glad to see you."

"Are you," he whispered huskily, his lips pressing butterfly kisses on her eyelids.

He lifted his dark head to stare down at her with possessive eyes. Picking her up, he carried her to the bed, standing her beside it. Then he unfastened the gown and began to peel it down her body, bending to kiss each newly exposed area as he went.

Her body began to tremble madly as an ache slowly built up in her body. His hands moved gently over her, and her flesh was wildly responsive to his touch.

Suddenly, a tremor shook Jake's big frame, and insistent now, he divested her smoothly of the rest of her clothing and laid her down on the bed. His eyes devoured her as he hurriedly removed his clothing and boots. Then he was beside her, and her slender hands reached for his face, drawing it down until his mouth met hers.

His hands found the softness of her body, and she trembled as he slowly teased it into a fierce, throbbing submission. Then, when he had her moaning, he shifted over her, coaxing her legs to move and admit the hard shaft of his manhood. His hands framed her flushed cheeks, and his mouth covered hers, his tongue probing deeply, searching out the moist sweetness within.

His body was so firm and powerful, his skin so warm against her own. His hips gently glided against her, moving down, penetrating. Then he began to move in a slow, building, age old rhythm, and she followed his motion with desperate abandon.

Suddenly, like a flash of lightning, she was there. Blinding colors came rushing down on her, reaching out and covering her, drowning her in a sweet hot flood.

As Angellee threw back her head and cried out, Jake covered her mouth with his hand, muffling the sound. Tension arched her body, and her nails raked his back, her teeth biting into the flesh of his shoulder as her body began to echo the feverish movements of his.

Angellee's body burst into flames, and they were crashing together as they reached their peak simultaneously and went soaring down the other side. She was vaguely aware of Jake shuddering and emitting a harsh groan; then her mind welcomed sweet oblivion, and she lay in the aftermath of their love.

As soon as the place grew quiet, Jake and Angellee donned their clothing. Jake frowned at the low cut bodice of the gaudy gown but didn't comment. He unlocked the door and peeked out into the hall. It was empty.

Angellee picked up a brass holder with a single candle in it, unsure if the cellar was lit or not. Jake nodded approvingly at her.

Silently, they crept down the stairway, making their way toward the cellar door where Angel knew Heather was incarcerated. They stayed well into the shadows, not wanting to be seen by anyone prowling around.

Bruno was sitting in front of the cellar door in a straight-backed chair, his head nodding against his chest. On a nail to the right of the door hung a big key. As they watched, Mabel came into the room from the cantina.

"You gonna sit here all night, Bruno?" she asked.

"Boss's orders," Bruno muttered.

"What's down there that need's guardin'?"

"Heather."

"The hell you say!" Mabel's eyes sparkled with malice. "What's the little bitch done?"

Bruno looked uncomfortable. "You'll have to ask the boss, Mabel. He's the one that put her there."

"You'd think after three years the little bitch would wise up enough to keep from making Bart mad."

"Yeah."

"Hey, you want a drink before I go back to bed?"

"Yeah," Bruno brightened.

"Come on, then."

"I can't," Bruno whined. "Boss said to stay here. I thought maybe you'd bring it to me."

"Oh, come on," she said. "I don't want to drink standing in this drafty hall. I ain't had a drink all night. I been too busy servin' the customers, seein' as it was a full house what with all the excitement goin' on. Anyway, who's to know? Cantrell's over visitin' Maisie. He won't be back tonight."

Bruno snorted. "His own whores ain't good enough fer him, I guess."

Mabel shrugged. "Who cares? Come on, let's get a drink."

"What about her?" Bruno nodded his head toward the cellar.

"You figger she's goin' someplace?"

Bruno laughed loudly. "Nope. Thet room down there's locked up good and tight."

"Why worry then?" Mabel asked. "You'll be back in that chair in half an hour. Who's to say you ever left it?"

Bruno still hesitated.

"Come on," she coaxed. "I hate to drink alone, and if you're real nice to me, you can even have a feel."

That obviously decided Bruno because he left with Mabel.

Jake glided silently across the hall, removed the key and unlocked the door. Then he and Angellee hurried through the door, closing it behind them. They found themselves on a landing. The cellar was dark and cold, and Angellee felt like she was closed in a coffin.

"Careful," Jake whispered. "We'd better wait until we reach the bottom before we light the candle. We'll have to feel our way down."

Angellee's foot groped for the first step, found it, then searched again. Slowly, they made their way down. At the bottom, Jake lit the candle and held it high, creating odd shadows on his face, making his features almost sinister in appearance.

The cellar was large, running the length of the house and the dim light of the candle did little to penetrate the darkness. It smelled dry and dusty. They made their way deeper into the darkness, searching for the room that Heather had spoken of. Angellee saw a bullwhip hanging along one wall and shuddered, hoping it hadn't been used on the Irish girl. They found a door at the far end of the passage. It had a big padlock on it.

Jake searched for the key while Angellee leaned closer to the door, rapping on the heavy wooden panel with her knuckles.

Silence.

Her heart lurched. Heather must be there! She rapped again. There was a scuttling movement inside. "Heather," she whispered. "Heather, are you there?"

"Angel?" Heather's terrified voice was muffled by the thick wooden door. "Is that you?"

"Yes. I've come to get you out."

"Bart will kill you if he finds out," Heather cried. "Oh, Angel, God! I'm scared."

"Just hold on now," Angellee said, her eyes searching for Jake, pleading with him to hurry. "We'll have you out in a minute, Heather."

Suddenly, Jake appeared beside her with a key in his hand. He inserted it in the lock and turned it. The door opened, and Heather was tumbling into Angel's arms, hugging her fiercely.

"Thank God!" Heather whispered, her voice shaking. "I was terrified." Her golden blond curls tumbled wildly around her face, her gown was stained and torn. She turned a tear-stained face up to Jake and froze, her face draining of color. She clutched Angellee's arm tightly with trembling fingers. "Who's he?"

"Jake."

"Your Jake?" Heather asked unsteadily.

Angel nodded.

"I thought he was dead."

"We'll explain later," Jake said. "Right now, we'd better get out of here before Bruno comes back." He closed the door, locked it again, and replaced the key where he had found it. Then, warning them to be silent, the trio crept up the stairs, stopping as they reached the landing while Jake opened the door a crack and peered cautiously out. He couldn't see anyone in the entranceway or in the large room beyond.

When Jake gave the word, they hurried through the door and across the room. Jake paused just long enough to relock the door and hang the key on the hook. He joined them in the shadows as they heard Bruno and Mabel returning.

"There," Mabel said. "I told you no one would find out you were gone."

Bruno grinned and sat back in the chair again.

Angellee looked at Jake with stricken eyes. Bruno would see them if they left the shadows. They couldn't make it to the front door.

Suddenly, footsteps sounded on the stairs and Heather uttered a cry of fright. Jake's hand covered her mouth, muffling the sound. They watched Bertha descend the stairs and look straight at them. The girl's dark eyes widened slightly, then flickered to Bruno, who was still guarding the cellar door. "What's going on, Bruno," she asked, huskily.

"Nothin'," he said, watching her as she descended the rest of the way. She smiled invitingly at him and moved to stand in front of him, tugging her gown off her shoulder and looking at him beneath her lashes.

Suddenly, it dawned on Angellee that Bertha was distracting him purposely. The others must have realized it at the same time, because Jake touched her arm, nodding toward the hallway, and one by one they crept down the hall and slipped out the front door.

Chapter Twenty-Seven

The streets were silent and dark, lit only by the pale light of the full moon. The stars glittered brightly overhead. The air was crisp, the temperature chill. The figure of a man stepped from the dimly lit stables. He stopped, leaned one shoulder against the corral and cupped his hands to light a cigarette. As the match flared, Angellee recognized Carl. He took a deep drag and the butt glowed red.

"Stay here while I check things out," Jake whispered. "The other guard may be inside the barn."

While the two girls waited in the shadows, Jake assumed a drunken pose and staggered across the dusty street to where Carl waited outside the stables.

"Well, lookee who's here," Carl said, his voice clearly discernible in the stillness. "I didn't figger you'd be outta that room before morning. Ain't you gonna stay all night with the Angel after you paid for her?"

"Bar's closed," Jake mumbled. "And my bottle's empty. Gotta 'nother one in my saddlebags."

"Looks to me like you had plenty already, mister,"

Carl said with a smirk. "You drink any more, and that little gal will be lookin' for another man." He grinned widely. "And wouldn't that be a pure-dee shame?"

"I can handle it," Jake growled, pushing past the other man. "Where's the other fellar?"

"Cecil's gone to visit a friend," he laughed. "He'll be back after a while, then I'll go *visiting.*"

"Care for a drink?" Jake asked. "I got plenty of booze in that bottle."

Carl seemed to consider for a moment. "Sure thing," he said. "Guess I could guard them horses inside as well as out. And I could use a snort."

Angellee's body was tense as the guard followed Jake into the barn. She held her breath, waiting. Would Jake be able to subdue Carl? She considered ignoring Jake's orders and following him. Her heartbeat quickened as she waited. Jake was taking a long time. Was he in trouble? She gripped Heather's arm, and the girl started with fear, turning wide, terror-filled blue eyes on her.

"I'm goin' in," Angellee whispered. "You wait here."

"No," Heather protested, clutching her arm convulsively. "Jake told us to wait here."

"I don't care," Angellee said grimly. "Something's gone wrong."

Leaving the Irish girl in the shadows, Angellee darted across the dusty road. As she reached the stables, Jake emerged from the barn.

His eyes glittered with anger as they fell on her. "I told you to stay put," he said harshly.

"I was afraid you might need some help," she said quickly.

"Dammit, Angel," he snapped. "One of these days

you're going to have to start trusting my judgment." He glared at her, then motioned for Heather to join them. The Irish girl hurried across the street, and Jake smiled his approval at her as he led the way into the gloomy recesses of the barn.

"Where's Carl?" Angellee asked.

"Over there," Jake said. A booted foot protruded from behind a stack of hay. "We're wasting time. We'd better saddle up and get out of here before the other guard comes back and discovers him missing."

"Is he dead?" Heather whispered, her throat moving convulsively.

"No," Jake replied, sparing the girl a sympathetic glance. "Only unconscious."

"You shoulda killed 'im," Angellee muttered. "If he wakes up, he'll lose no time lettin' the whole town know what's goin' on."

"I don't like killing, Angel."

Angellee noticed the censure in his voice but had no time to dwell on its cause. A sense of urgency possessed her. Cecil could return at any moment.

Moving to Carl's unconscious form, she unbuckled his gunbelt, fastening it securely around her slender waist. Carl was a thin man. If it hadn't been for that and her nicely rounded hips, the belt wouldn't have stayed up.

A horse moved restlessly in the nearest stall, his coat shimmering with blue-black hues. A familiar whinny swiveled her head around. Angellee's eyes rounded with pleasure at the sight of Star, her Arabian stallion.

"You beauty," she whispered, moving to stroke the stallion's long, velvety neck. "I thought I'd never see you again. You didn't tell me you brought him," she said, turning accusing green eyes on Jake.

"I had other things on my mind at the time." He cast an oblique smile at her. "Hurry up. You can admire that animal later."

Needing no further reminder of their situation, Angellee quickly saddled the horse while Jake saw to Daniel and the dun mare he had chosen for Heather's mount. They had finished and were on the point of leaving when a voice came from outside the barn.

"Carl? You in there, Carl?"

"Damn," Jake swore under his breath. "It's the other guard. He would have to come back. It's going to look suspicious when his partner doesn't answer. I'll try to talk my way around him. If I can't he'll bring the whole damn town down on us. Angel, you and Heather scrunch down in that stall and stay there until I tell you to come out."

The two girls ducked behind the stalls just as Cecil entered the barn. Angellee peered through a crack, watching Cecil stop abruptly. He frowned as his gaze fell on Jake and the three saddled horses. "Where's Carl," he asked. "And what are you doin' with them horses?"

"I'm getting ready to leave town," Jake said casually, moving toward the man.

"With three horses?" the guard asked suspiciously. His eyes narrowed on the dun mare. "Hey," he said, his body stiffening, his hand hovering just above his gun. "Be damn if that don't look like Earl's mare. What're you doin' with it?"

"I'm afraid I don't know anything about it," Jake said, moving closer. "The dun was already standing there when I came in."

"Something stinks here, mister," Cecil said. "And you can stop right there until I figger out what it is that smells so bad." His eyes darted around the dim interior of the building, then returned to Jake. "Supposin' you tell me what you're up to an' where Carl is."

"I'm afraid I don't know Carl," Jake said, in a remarkably cool voice. "And since I don't know who he is, it stands to reason I don't know where he is. Maybe he got thirsty and went for a drink."

The guard drew his gun and Angellee's body tensed. Her fingers found the handle of the knife in her boot, and she gripped it tightly. Jake couldn't afford to get in a gunfight with Cecil for fear of discovery, but they dared delay no longer.

"You don't need that gun," Jake said calmly, taking another step toward the man.

"I said hold it, mister." Cecil's finger tightened. "Move to the door real slow-like. I'm taking you to see the boss."

"Now wait a minute," Jake protested. "You're making a big mistake."

Cecil smiled grimly, his gunhand steady. "I'd be makin' a bigger mistake if I let you pass," he sneered. "Don't think the boss'd like that. Now, move if you figger on stayin' alive."

Heather shifted uneasily and Angellee shot her a warning glance—too late. The Irish girl's boot hit a board with a loud cra-ac-k. She drew in a sharp gasp, her eyes widening with apprehension.

"What was that?" the gunman asked, his eyes moving toward the stall hiding the two girls. He stiffened, his gaze falling on the toe of Carl's boot. "What the hell!" He edged sideways, until Carl's body lay in full view. As comprehension dawned suddenly, he brought the barrel of the gun to bear on Jake's chest, his finger tightening on the trigger.

Jake, realizing his intentions, made a dive for cover. He rolled when he hit the dirt and kept rolling. The crash of gunfire came, and hay flew as the impact of bullets struck the ground where he had been only a moment before. Jake pulled his gun, ready to snap off a shot.

Before he could act, Angellee, fearing for his life, had risen to her feet, pulling her knife in one smooth movement. She let it fly with a swoosh, and the blade buried deeply in the gunman's chest. Cecil stared at the knife protruding from his body, then, he looked at Jake, his mouth working soundlessly. He sank heavily to the ground falling on the scattered hay, sending up wisps of chaff.

As the guard fell, Angellee grabbed Heather by the arm and pulled her upright, hurrying her from the stall.

Jake's expression was grim as he stared at the dead gunman. His big body was tense. When he turned to look at her, his eyes were dark, filled with some emotion that she didn't understand.

"You shouldn't have done that," he grated harshly.

Angellee felt as if he'd struck her. Couldn't he see she'd feared for his life? "He would've killed you," she muttered. "Would you have liked that better?"

"Is—is he dead?" Heather whispered, her gaze filled with revulsion as it moved from the knife protruding from Cecil's body, to Jake's harsh expression then on to Angellee's wooden countenance.

A muscle twitched in Jake's jaw. His darkly hooded eyes bored into Angellee, studying her as though he were seeing her for the first time and didn't particularly like what he saw.

Her chin lifted defiantly as she held his gaze. "What's the matter?" she snapped, unwilling for him to see how much his attitude hurt. Didn't he know she had only killed Cecil because there was no other way? "You've seen me kill men before."

"With the others, there was no choice," he said, his voice cold.

"They're still just as dead," she said grimly. "And you ain't got no idea what Cantrell would do if he catches us. I do. We're not out of the woods yet."

"Then you'd better quit wasting time," Jake said. "We'll hash this out later."

We'll hash this out later. What did that mean? Angellee turned away, blinking back tears that threatened to overflow.

While Jake tied and gagged Carl, Angellee knelt beside Cecil, pulling the knife from his chest, trying to ignore the dead eyes staring accusingly up at her. Was Jake right? Was she too quick to kill? Wiping the knife blade on the straw littering the floor, Angellee slid it into the sheath in her boot. Then, with quick strides, she moved to where her mount stood waiting and swung smoothly into the saddle. She watched Jake help Heather mount the dun mare, and her throat worked convulsively.

Her eyes were dark with hidden pain as she watched Jake with the Irish girl. He was making it obvious that he preferred a woman like Heather—a woman he could protect—a lady. Not a backwoods girl with little schooling who had never even seen the outside of a mansion such as the one he lived in, much less been inside it.

Angellee knew of such places only from the pictures she had seen in the few magazines that had found their way into the Ozark Mountains where she had lived. Sometimes the pack peddler would bring to her family goods wrapped with newspapers. At such times her mother would smooth the creases out carefully and read the stories about the people who lived in the fancy houses and dressed in fancy store-bought clothes.

Deep inside, Angellee had always known that her relationship with Jake was destined to end one day. Coming from two such different worlds, there could never have been any kind of permanency in their affair.

But did it have to end so soon?

Her heart swelled with pain, which she was determined to keep hidden from him. For it seemed that her pride was all she had left.

Her Tucker pride.

We ain't got much left, Angel. But as long as we got our pride, we'll get by. Her father's words rose like bitter gall in her mind.

Oh Pa. If it'd get me Jake. I'd even give up my Tucker pride.

Wordlessly, she let Jake take the lead, motioning for Heather to go ahead so she could bring up the rear in case of pursuit. Then, quietly, they left the stables. Even though the street was deserted, Angellee wanted to dig her heels into Star's flanks and ride away from Paso Diablo as fast as she could, but she knew it would alert the town. Her narrowed gaze searched the shadows suspiciously as they walked the horses slowly out of town.

And then they rode like hell.

Chapter Twenty-Eight

Angellee was groggy with fatigue. They had finally reached the mountains, and Heather, who hadn't sat a saddle in three years, swayed constantly in the saddle. Jake, though, could not be dissuaded. He refused to allow them to rest. The Irish girl finally reached a point when she could no longer stay upright, and he stopped long enough to put her in front of him; then they rode on, not even stopping as they were joined by Swift Arrow.

Throughout the night they rode, finally stopping to rest as dawn broke over the horizon. They ate a sketchy meal of dried venison and fruit, which they washed down with water from the canteens, and Jake allowed them a couple of hours rest before they took to the trail again.

Jake pushed them hard for several days, allowing them only a few hours rest each night. Heather had become so exhausted that she hardly ever sat her horse alone. Jake and Swift Arrow took turns holding her in front of them, thus allowing their horses a reprieve from the double weight. At first, Heather had been terrified of Swift Arrow but in time had grown used to him and uttered no protest when he took her in front of him, allowing her to rest against his wide, solid chest.

As they traveled across the desert, Angellee's thoughts turned often to Slade and the promise she had made him. For a time, she had managed to put him out of her mind, but he was a constant intrusion now. Although Jake rarely spoke to her, Angellee felt his brooding gaze on her often, having become completely attuned to the touch of his glance.

What was going to happen to them now? Jake's mission was completed. He had found Becky, and presumably, she'd returned to Pittsburgh. She must have. Jake had said her future was at stake. Yes. Surely she had gone. And, just as surely, when Jake reached civilization, he would be returning to his home as well.

Agony pierced her. Her hands tightened on the reins, her nails digging into her palms. Where did that leave her? What was she to do?

Find Slade and kill him.

Yes. Of course. She had never had any choice. She had vowed vengeance to her father, and there would be no rest for her until she saw he had it.

There had been no more visions where Jake was concerned, so she assumed he would be safe now. And she could no longer afford to indulge in the emotions he raised within her, could not let the warm memories of his arms allow reality to slip from her mind. The bond that had been growing between them had somehow been broken, but even had it not, her first priority was—had always been—gaining vengeance for her dead parents. To that end she would dedicate her life and her thoughts.

Doubtlessly, Jake had had many intimate encounters such as theirs in his life, and just as surely there would be many others. The expertise in his lovemaking was undeniable. His caresses and the touch of his hands were gentle, knowing exactly how to arouse her to the fullest.

In Angellee's mind there wasn't the slightest doubt that Jake had only to snap his fingers and any number of beautiful and desirable women with a good education would immediately answer his call. When their ride was over, and he deemed it safe to leave them, he would return to his own world of luxury and wealth. She must not allow herself to forget that even had he wanted her, she would never fit into that world.

No. Her own destiny lay in the West.

Angellee had killed men, and for this, she apparently stood condemned in Jake's eyes. But she must not allow that to sway her. Before she had accomplished her task, at least one other would lie dead. There could be even more if Slade had taken on new partners because she was determined she would not be stopped.

Slade was evil. He couldn't be allowed to live, and she intended to be his executioner.

Her future could prove very limited, and she must face the fact that Jake did not fit into that future. She must face her destiny, and she must do it alone. A familiar pain assaulted her.

Alone.

Was she destined to always be alone? To never find the happiness she craved for? Perhaps that was why she had been chosen to bear the gift.

While camped in the shelter of a ravine, Angellee sat

in the shadows, watching the flames of their campfire dance in the slight breeze. Heather had barely eaten before she fell wearily into the bedroll; the long ride had taken its toll on the Irish girl who was unused to travel. Jake sat on the other side of the fire, as usual, avoiding conversation with her. Swift Arrow, like Angellee seemed to prefer the shadows, keeping well out of the lighted area.

Angellee despised herself for allowing Jake's silence to hurt. All during their flight he had seemed to go out of his way to avoid her. Sorrow lay heavy in her breast, but she could offer no apology for what she had done. Out here in this wilderness, it was kill or be killed.

The sound of a hoot owl reached her ears, and she took comfort from the familiar night sounds. She had often camped out with her father in the forest back home. The call was followed by the faint piping of a cactus wren, and she stirred uneasily. Something about it disturbed her. Swift Arrow rose smoothly to his feet, fading into the night as the sound was repeated, and something clicked in Angellee's mind.

She froze.

Her hand gripped the butt of Carl's pistol as she listened for the sound to be repeated, for the call was out of place. The cactus wren was a bird of the day, not of the night. She drew the gun and pulled back the hammer with her thumb.

She waited, ears strained for the slightest sound, hardly daring to breathe. Something—someone—was out there in the night. Friend or enemy? There was no way of knowing, but would a friend stay hidden? Wouldn't they announce their presence?

Jake had sensed her tension and the way Swift Arrow

had melted into the darkness. His Colt was drawn and ready, his gaze searching the shadowed moonlit night for danger.

There was a blur of movement as the shadows seemed to come together. Then Swift Arrow's guttural voice identified himself before his shape became discernible, and he emerged from the night, accompanied by another Indian.

"Geronimo," Jake said, holstering his gun. "We weren't expecting you."

Heather, alerted by the voices, sat up in the bedroll. As she saw Geronimo, her face drained of color, and she let out a piercing shriek.

"It's all right," Jake said quickly. "It's only Geronimo, and he means us no harm."

"Which one is your woman?" Geronimo asked, his gaze moving between Angellee and the Irish girl.

Jake nodded at Angel. "She's the one I went for."

Angellee couldn't help but notice that Jake avoided laying claim to her by the way he worded his reply.

Geronimo stared at Angellee, his face expressionless. "She is worth fighting for," he stated.

"You're welcome to sit at our fire," Jake said.

"We must continue our journey," Geronimo said. "We have been to the reservation for the rest of our people. We are tired of being treated like animals. We want to live free as our ancestors did. Now we go to a place where the horse-soldiers cannot follow. Swift Arrow wishes to go with us. It would not be safe for him to return to his people, for the horse-soldiers will search for us, and their numbers will be great."

"I understand," Jake said gravely. "I am sorry for what has happened to your people. If there was something I could do then I would. Be assured that no one will hear that we have spoken."

"I did not think otherwise," Geronimo said. "Swift Arrow has told me this." His gaze traveled between Angellee and Jake. "Swift Arrow has told me to say that he will still buy the woman with hair of fire if you do not wish to keep her."

"Tell him I thank him for his offer, but the answer is still no." Jake didn't look at Angellee as he answered Geronimo.

Swift Arrow listened to Geronimo's words, his face expressionless. Moving to his saddle, he knelt, picked up a large, leather bag and returned to stand before Angellee. He pulled her twin Colt navy pistols from the bag, presenting them to her.

Her face lit up as she took them from him, holding them almost reverently. "Thank you," she said softly.

He spoke to her in the guttural Apache language, and she looked at Geronimo. "What's he sayin'?"

"He said he was told the weapons belonged to your brother. And even though they are fine weapons, he is returning them to you."

"Tell him I don't know how to repay him," she said. Her green eyes were brilliant as she stroked Johnny's Colts. "They mean an awful lot to me." Her eyes held Swift Arrow's, and she wished she had a way of communicating with him. Unbuckling the holster and gun she was wearing, she held them out to him. "Please take these," she said.

He accepted them gravely, fastening them around his waist. Reaching out a hand, he smoothed it gently down her fiery hair. Angellee wondered at her reaction to his touch. He was a handsome man, and if she had not had the misfortune to fall in love with Jake, then perhaps she might have been inclined to accept his attentions.

Jake moved restlessly, and Angellee darted a swift glance at him. Although his face was expressionless, she knew he was angry. She could feel it.

Swift Arrow stepped away from her and spoke to Geronimo at length, making her wonder if he was going to try to change Jake's mind about selling her. He must want her badly.

"Swift Arrow says the white man's law does not allow one man to have two women. Since you do not want to part with the woman with hair of fire, then you may wish to sell the other one."

Jake's lips twitched, and Angellee's face flushed a dull red. "The other girl is a friend. She was sold to Cantrell by Slade and wishes to return to her world. We are only taking her home."

When the chief translated Jake's words, Swift Arrow nodded his head. Holding up his hand in the sign of friendship, he gathered up his supplies and saddled his horse. When he was finished, the travelers bid each other goodbye and safe journey, and the two Apaches went to join the band of Indians waiting in the darkness.

A few minutes later, they heard the subtle stirring of horses as the band moved out, continuing their flight from the white men who had stolen their lands and their freedom, imprisoning them on bare wastelands that could support no life, knowing all the while the only way they could escape this fate was to remain in hiding.

Jake slowed the big gray, looking up at the clear blue

sky. There wasn't a cloud in sight and not a whisper of a breeze. The heat was intense; a little rain would work wonders, but from the look of things, no relief was in sight.

His narrowed gaze moved to the horizon, to the hazy peaks thrusting skyward, and he tried to gauge their distance.

Heather shifted in the saddle of the dun horse, drawing his attention. The girl looked completely exhausted. She was a brave little thing, but the long ride had been rough on her. It had been easier on her when Swift Arrow had been with them. He was able to take her in front of him while Daniel rested from the double load. Now she had no choice except to ride the dun mare.

He pulled Daniel up beside the mare. "Would you like to come in front of me again?" he asked gently, completely unaware of Angellee's dark look.

"No," Heather said. "Your horse can't keep carrying double." She gave him a wan smile, and her dimples appeared momentarily. "I'll make it. I'm just not used to riding. I've got saddle sores on my saddle sores."

"You're a plucky little thing," Jake said. "You haven't uttered a word of complaint all through this trip."

"Believe me, if it would serve any purpose, I'd complain to High Heaven," she said, her blue eyes twinkling suddenly.

He grinned. "You'll do," he said. "We'll stop early today. We haven't seen any sign of Cantrell and his bunch, so it should be safe enough."

His gaze searched out, and found Angellee. He was startled to find her staring at him, her green eyes savage.

His dark brows drew together in a scowl. What had gotten into her these past few days?

Past few days.

Had it really started the past few days? Or was the beginning when she had been kidnapped? What had happened to her on the trail? Or at that cantina. His lips thinned, his gaze flicking down her body. Had any of that bunch defiled her? Nothing else made sense. He had to talk to her. He had to find out. But talking to her wasn't easy lately. She seemed angry at everything. And everyone. She had even been short with Heather a time or two. Mostly, she just didn't speak at all unless it was necessary.

When they made camp, he would make sure they talked. He had to get it out in the open. Whatever it was. He refused to let anything come between them. His gaze met and held her turbulent eyes, and he issued a silent warning. He was tired of waiting. He would have answers.

Tonight.

You'll do. What did Jake mean by those words. Angellee glared at him as he seemed to issue a silent warning. A warning about what?

He's concerned about Heather.

The thought closed her throat and her eyes stung. She pulled her gaze away from him and looked at the distant mountains. He hadn't bothered to inquire about her. He didn't care how uncomfortable she was. Not one whit.

Her chin tilted defiantly, and she blinked rapidly, clearing her eyes of the moisture threatening to spill over. The mountains were hazy, but they were visible in the distance. That must mean they weren't far from their destination. And then what? She refused to dwell on the future. She concentrated instead on the buzzards flying in the sky with lazy ease, riding high on the air currents, before dipping low, forever searching the desert with beady eyes.

Darkness had fallen by the time Jake pulled up beside a shallow stream of water.

"We'll camp here," he said. His dark gaze found hers. "This'll be our last night out."

She had been right. The trip was almost over.

They made camp, ate a silent meal, and Heather crawled wearily into her bedroll. Angellee, knowing she would be unable to sleep yet, sat beside the fire, staring into the flames. Jake sat on the other side of the fire, his big body filled with tension, his brooding gaze on her motionless form.

Suddenly, Jake uttered an expletive, jerked to his feet, and before she could react, he was around the campfire, his fingers like steel bands as they circled one slender wrist, yanking her to her feet.

"What do you think—" she began.

"Shut up and come with me," he growled, pulling her with him into the sheltering darkness.

"Now wait a min—"

"I said shut up!"

"You can't make me!" she snapped, struggling to free her wrist.

Jake pulled her toward him, stifling the cry of protest and outrage before it left her lips. His dark face swam before her, and she closed her eyes, blotting him out as his mouth began a ravaging assault of her lips. His hand held the back of her head as his lips ground bruisingly against hers.

Unable to move, hardly able to breathe, she could not escape as he imposed a deeper intimacy. Her hands were pinned helplessly to her sides by the long arm wrapped around her body. The warmth of his skin burned through her bodice.

When his assault on her mouth ended she was weakened, gasping for breath, unable to resist as he pulled her farther upstream. When he stopped, he dragged her into his arms again, covering her mouth with his punishing kiss. His arms were like steel bands surrounding her, imprisoning her against his hard, male body.

A lone tear escaped and found its way down her cheek. He stilled. Then unbelievably, his lips softened, became tender, persuasive. Angellee groaned softly, melting against him.

Jake's fingers found her bodice, slipping inside to manipulate her nipple. As his tongue dipped into the moistness of her mouth, searching out the inner sweetness, her nipples hardened into taut peaks of desire. She was hardly aware of his fingers unfastening her gown, pushing it down to her slender waist. When his hand slipped inside, tracing a downward course, the muscles of her belly quivered, and her body jerked with a blaze of heat.

Unable to wait longer, Jake divested her of the rest of her clothing, then laid her down on the hard ground. A moment later, he joined her, covering her naked body with his own.

Angellee, hungry for his possession, circled her arms around his neck, pulling him eagerly to her. Her hips rose to meet his, and she shuddered as he entered her, plunging wildly into her moist, willing body. His eyes never left hers as he began to move, almost violently, in the age old rhythm of passion. Her emotions were as violent as his thrusts and she raised her legs, taking more of him into her. Her breath came in sobbing gasps, and her nails raked his back. Her teeth bit into the flesh of his shoulder as he lifted her higher and higher until, finally, she exploded with a sudden burst of ecstasy, far greater than any she had ever experienced before.

Chapter Twenty-Nine

It was a bedraggled group that rode into the Shaw ranch late at night. Angellee was too weary to pay much attention to her surroundings, but the tall, slender man with piercing blue eyes who greeted them caught and held her attention.

Robert Shaw's brown hair was sprinkled generously with gray at the temples, his skin tanned by the sun. Although he seemed to find nothing unusual in Jake's appearance, his blue eyes flickered with surprise as they fell on Angellee and Heather. His gaze lingered overlong on their gaudy gowns, then narrowed thoughtfully on Jake, but he made no comment.

Once inside, Robert introduced them to Juanita, his housekeeper, asking her to show them to bedrooms upstairs. The housekeeper was a short, black-haired woman with dark features. Her brown eyes expressed sympathy for the weary travelers as she preceded the two girls up the stairs while Jake stayed behind to speak with Robert.

"Thees was Mees Becky's room," Juanita said,

opening the door to a large, airy room. The bedroom was scrupulously clean. The bed was covered by a patchwork quilt, and white lace curtains covered the windows. She smiled at Angellee. "You sleep here and Mees Heather, she will sleep in the next room. Meester Jake, he have own room down the hall."

"Oh, but . . ." Angellee's voice trailed off as she caught Heather's warning look. A red flush crept up her cheeks as she realized they had returned to civilization, and that meant she would be unable to share a room with Jake.

"Thank you," she muttered. "It's a very nice room."

Juanita showed them the bathroom that had just been installed, and after inquiring if there was anything else they needed, she left. The girls wasted no time in bathing, falling immediately into bed and to sleep.

The next morning, Angellee woke to the vibrant sound of robins singing in the old oak tree growing just outside the bedroom window. She opened her eyes, squinting against the bright sunlight streaming through sheer curtains, and stretched luxuriously. She loved the feel of the feather mattress after so many nights spent on the trail. Her nose curled in distaste as she remembered she had nothing but her soiled, sweaty and torn clothing to wear.

Sighing, she sat up and reached for the soiled gown that she had laid in a straight-backed chair the night before.

Her fingers touched fresh, crisply ironed fabric, and her emerald eyes sparked with delight as she discovered a beautiful, dove gray skirt and matching blouse where she had left the soiled clothing. With it was fresh undergarments. Juanita must have left it. The clothing was more than likely some that Rebecca had left behind.

Eager to see Jake, she hastily washed her face and brushed her fiery hair with the ivory backed brush she found on the dressing table, fastening it at the nape of her neck with a ribbon that matched the gown. Then, she slipped into the clothing which smelled faintly of violets, loving the feel of the fabric against her skin. The skirt proved to be a few inches too long, but she remedied that by tucking the waist beneath a cummerbund.

Finished with her toilet, Angellee moved to the balcony doors and flung them wide, stepping out into the crisp, fresh air which smelled of wisteria and dew-soaked grass. She gripped the wooden railing as memories of her beloved Ozarks surfaced. There had been wisteria outside her bedroom window. Her eyes moved to the distant snow-capped peaks, the tops hidden by low lying clouds. Farther on to the west, the sky was fresh and blue.

She stared for a moment longer, her eyes feasting on the wild, untamed beauty of New Mexico. Her thoughts dwelt for a moment on Swift Arrow who was unable to join his people in those same mountains. Instead, he followed the desert path with Geronimo. He had given up his family and his people to help her. Sighing, she went back into the room, closed the door and went in search of Heather.

The Irish girl answered her knock immediately. Juanita had brought her fresh clothing as well, and Heather stood at the window in a sapphire blue gown staring out toward the snow-peaked mountains.

"I still can't believe I'm free after all these years," she

said huskily. "I keep thinking I'm going to wake up in the cantina and Bart will be sitting there watching me with those eyes—waiting—like a big, hungry cat, just waiting for the time to spring on his victim."

"Don't think about it, Heather," Angellee said, moving to stand behind her friend. "It's behind us now, and you're free again."

"Yes," Heather said bleakly. Her blue eyes moved to the distant mountain peaks again. "I'm free again."

"What's wrong," Angellee asked, her gaze moving over the Irish girl's troubled face.

Heather turned to face her, managing to summon up a smile. "Nothing," she said, moving to the dressing table. She picked up a hairbrush and ran it through her blond curls. Her eyes were evasive. "Nothing at all. We're out of Bart Cantrell's clutches, and that's all that really matters."

"Maybe," Angellee said. "And maybe not. Something is bothering you. Tell me what it is."

The other girl frowned. "It's hard to put into words."

"You could try."

"It's just that I'm wondering what happens now. I've spent the last three years under Bart Cantrell's rule. I learned early on not to ask questions—just do what I was told—live one day at a time . . ." Her sapphire eyes held a curious expression. "Now I'm free. But free to do what?"

"What do you want to do?" Angellee asked, puzzled. She didn't understand the girl's problem. Heather should be happy. "Don't you see? You're free now. You can do anything you want. Or nothing at all."

"Can I?" Heather asked softly.

"Yes."

"Have you thought about how I'm going to support myself, Angel? There aren't many ways for a woman to earn a living."

A shadow crossed Angellee's face. "I guess I'm awful stupid," she said slowly. She tried to smile but her lips were stiff. "I guess that's somethin' both of us have to be thinkin' on."

"Both of us? But you'll be going with Jake."

"I don't reckon I will," Angellee said. "I guess I'll . . . rest for a few days, then I'll probably go find Slade and kill him."

"Angel!" Heather gasped, shocked. "You can't go near that man! Not after what he did to you."

Angellee's mouth tightened into a grim line. "He won't be doin' it again," she said. "I got my guns back now. I'm not gonna let Slade get away with what he done. He's gotta be stopped."

"Jake would never allow you to go after him."

"Jake won't know. He'll be goin' back home now," Angel said. "He finished what he came to do."

"You don't really believe Jake would go back east and leave you here, do you, Angel?"

"Yes." Angellee's eyes darkened with pain. "Jake never promised me a future. We both know I won't fit into his world, Heather. Jake's got a lot of money and a big fine house. I don't know nothin' about things like that. He needs a woman that's been taught to live in that kind of world. Someone who can fit in with all his friends—the rich people."

"Are you so certain you know what Jake wants?" Heather asked, softly.

"Yes," Angellee said huskily. "He told me he wants a lady. He even tried to teach me how to talk like one."

She looked at the floor. "I guess I embarrass him."

"I don't believe that," Heather said sharply. "That doesn't sound like Jake at all."

"It don't matter if you believe it or not," Angel said. She drew a deep, shaky breath. "I've known him a lot longer than you have. And I know it's the truth."

"Have you talked to him about this?"

"I don't have to talk to him about it," Angellee muttered, swiping at a tear that had found its way down her cheek. "Jake's made it plain enough how he feels."

"I still think you're wrong. Don't be a fool. Talk to him about it. Jake loves you. I know he does."

Before Angellee could reply, Juanita entered to announce breakfast and tell them the men were waiting.

"Thank you, Juanita," Heather said, smiling at the Mexican woman. Angellee envied the girl her poise. "We'll be right down."

Giving them a quick smile, the housekeeper left.

When the girls had descended the stairs, they found Robert and Jake deep in conversation in the living room. As they entered the room, Robert and Jake both looked up.

"Good morning," Jake said, coming to stand beside Angellee. He smiled down at her. "You're looking beautiful this morning." He picked up a long, fiery curl, letting it slide through his fingers. "You should always wear gowns. I want to see no more of those britches you used to wear." He turned to compliment Heather who waited with downcast eyes. She threw a grateful glance at him.

As Angellee slid into the chair Jake was holding,

something about Robert's expression caught her attention. His narrowed gaze rested on Heather momentarily, before moving away to study the table. As though sensing Angellee's curious stare, he looked up, his gaze meeting hers, then quickly sliding away. A red flush stained his neck as he picked up his knife and fork.

Wondering why Robert should feel embarrassed, Angellee's puzzled eyes found Jake's, searching for the answer. He raised his brows inquiringly, seeming to notice nothing amiss. Wondering if she had been mistaken, she picked up her silverware and began her meal, savoring each bite of crispy fried bacon, fluffy scrambled eggs, biscuits and gravy. She finished the meal off with a steaming cup of coffee.

"That's the best meal I've had in months," she said, setting her empty coffee cup down on the table. "I don't think I've eaten so much in years."

"I'll have to watch you, or you'll get fat," Jake commented lightly.

"That'll be the day," Heather murmured. A smile lit up her features as she studied Angellee's slender body. "It's me that's going to have to be careful. Angel could stand to put on a few pounds, but I can't." She turned to Robert. "It's so nice of you to put us up, Mr. Shaw," she said. "I realize it's an imposition for us to barge in this way."

"It's no imposition," Robert said, gruffly. "I'm glad to be of help."

"Nevertheless, we've put you out, and I do apologize," Heather said earnestly. "I assure you we'll leave just as soon as we can make other arrangements."

"That's what we were discussing earlier, Heather,"

Jake said. "We were wondering if you have any family."

"No. Not any more," she whispered huskily. Her face had paled. "Slade killed my parents when he kidnapped me and my sister."

"Your sister?" Jake frowned, casting a questioning look at Angellee who had tensed slightly. "I didn't know you had a sister."

"She doesn't," Angellee said quietly. "Erin was killed trying to escape from Paso Diablo."

"Damn," Jake muttered low. "I'm sorry as hell, Heather," His sympathetic gaze touched the Irish girl. He cleared his throat. "Well, that does present a problem."

Heather flushed and Angellee threw a hard look at Jake. "I don't see any problem," she commented.

"Of course there's a problem," Heather said. "But you needn't concern yourself with it, Jake. I'll figure something out. I have no intention of imposing on Mr. Shaw." Her blue eyes moved to Robert at the head of the table. "If you could just point me in the direction of the nearest town . . ." Her voice trailed off as a scowl crossed his features.

"What do you plan on doing in town, Miss O'Day?" Robert asked gruffly.

"I'll look for a job of course," she said, holding his gaze with her own. "There must be something I can do there."

"Supposing you find a job in Silver City? Where do you intend to stay?"

"I don't know," she said. "I've never been there so I don't know what the town is like. I'll have to wait and see, won't I?"

"Heather," Angellee inserted. "You can't go there alone. Just wait and I'll—" She had intended to tell her they would both go when Jake left, but he interrupted.

"No. Of course she can't. I'll figure out something for her."

"There's no need for anyone to feel responsible for me," Heather said stiffly. "I can manage my own life very well."

"Heather," Angellee's expression was anxious. Why was the other girl being so stubborn? "You're not even sixteen yet. You can't go off alone. If Mr. Shaw will let us stay here for a few days—"

"I don't want anyone's charity!" Heather snapped, her eyes filling with tears. "I can manage on my own."

"Heather—"

Robert cut Angellee off. "There's no need for you to manage on your own, Miss O'Day," he said firmly. "You can stay here. There's plenty of room in this big house."

"No!" Heather said, pushing her chair back and standing up. "For three years I've been totally dependent on someone's charity. I want no more of that. I intend to support myself. For the first time in my life, I'm going to be independent."

"What nonsense!" Robert snapped, scraping his chair back and rising to his feet. His expression was fierce. "You're just a child. You're too young to know what you want."

Angellee's gaze flickered between the two of them. Robert was scowling and Heather had raised her chin stubbornly, her blue eyes snapping with anger.

"I beg to differ with you, sir," she said. "I was a child three years ago when Slade killed my parents and took me to Paso Diablo to serve in Cantrell's Cantina." She took a deep breath then added with a shuddery sigh. "In a place like that a girl grows up fast. I'm a woman now."

"You've been working in Cantrell's Cantina?" Robert's voice was grim.

"Yes," she said, holding his gaze steadily. She seemed to be daring him to condemn her.

"Heather," Angellee said, putting a calming hand over the other girl's. "Sit down. Finish your breakfast. We'll get our heads together later and figure something out."

"I'm afraid I've lost my appetite," the Irish girl said. Although Angellee could feel her hand trembling beneath her own, the blonde remained outwardly calm. "Please excuse me," she said gravely. Then, with a graceful movement, she left the room.

Angellee's accusing gaze moved between the two men, then back to settle on Jake. She stood up. Her chair scraped against the wood floor, sounding loud in the silence that had descended with Heather's departure. She looked at Robert. "Thank you for the meal," she said politely. Then she hurried out of the room, intent on finding her friend.

Heather was seated on the bed, pleating her skirt between her fingers. She looked up as Angellee entered. "I don't think Mr. Shaw approves of me," she said in a dispirited voice as Angellee seated herself beside her.

"He ain't got no reason not to," Angellee said, deliberately lapsing into her old speech pattern.

"Has no reason," Heather corrected automatically.

Angellee's lips curled slightly at the corners. "Has no

reason," she murmured obediently.

"Some people would say otherwise," Heather whispered, refusing to be sidetracked.

Angellee had sensed something about Robert's attitude toward the girl, but she wasn't all that certain it was disapproval. "We can live without his approval," she said. "We won't have to stay here very long."

"I'm going to make certain I don't," Heather said, her lips tightening. "I refuse to stay where I'm not wanted." The look she turned on Angellee was envious. "You're lucky to have Jake."

Angellee flinched inwardly. Apparently Heather didn't know Jake would be leaving. If only . . . She shrugged the thought away, refusing to dwell on her own problems. Right now, Heather's took precedence. She looked at the girl's bowed head. "You don't have any kinfolks at all?"

"No," Heather's expression was forlorn, her shoulders hunched in misery. "I thought everything would be so simple if I could only escape from that place, Angel. But during all those years, I never once thought about what I'd do when I got away." She sighed. "How could I have been so naive? It takes money to live, and I don't have any."

"I've got a few dollars," Angellee mused, her brows drawing into a frown. "But it won't last long. We need more."

Heather studied her clasped hands. "Maybe I could wait tables. They must have eating establishments in the town. Or . . ." she paused, looking up, her voice suddenly excited. "If the town has a hotel, then perhaps I could hire on as a maid—to clean the rooms."

"I don't know," Angellee said. "I don't like the idea

of you working in a hotel. The men who stop there might give you trouble."

"What are you girls plotting?" Jake asked from the doorway.

Heather smiled at him. "We're just working out a plan."

Jake frowned, coming into the room and seating himself on the chair. "Are you still worrying? Don't. Something is sure to come up. You could even come to Pittsburgh."

Angellee blanched, but he didn't notice. His eyes were still on the Irish girl.

"I couldn't do that," Heather protested.

"Why not?" he asked lightly. "I think you'd like the East."

Angellee rose from the bed, moving unnoticed to the window. Jake wanted Heather to go with him. How could he even suggest such a thing with her in the room as well. She had hoped—but then, what did he need with someone like her? No. The Irish girl would fit in with his life. She swallowed around the lump in her throat.

"Thank you for the offer, Jake," Heather said, her voice slightly unsteady. "But I couldn't possibly accept." When he started to protest, she continued. "I don't want to return to the East. There's nothing for me there."

"What is there here for you, Heather?"

"The mountains," she whispered, her gaze moving to the window and the purple peaks thrusting in the distance. "And the plains. And plenty of breathing space where you can roam for miles and never see a soul. All of the things my father dreamed of when we left the East. He would have wanted me to stay here."

"What will you do here, Heather?" Jake asked.

"I'll go to town and find a job."

"What can you do?"

"I can wait tables, or clean rooms, or . . ." Her eyes took on a thoughtful look. "I can sing."

"Sing?" Jake raised a dark eyebrow. "I had no idea you could sing. But that won't help I'm afraid. No one employs singers except the saloons, and you wouldn't want to work in a place like that."

Heather lifted an eyebrow. "I've spent the last three years in a place worse than a saloon," she reminded him.

"If you're so bent on supporting yourself," came Robert's voice from the doorway, "I hear Mrs. Carter on the Bar C a few miles west of here needs an upstairs maid. The job pays wages as well as room and board. You could see her if you're interested. But keep in mind there's no hurry in leaving here. You can stay as long as you like."

"I have no mind to accept charity," Heather said, meeting his gaze squarely. "If you direct me to the Bar C, I'll apply for the job."

"As you wish," Robert said his voice stiff. "I'll send word over by one of the cowhands. He can see if the job is still open." He turned away abruptly, leaving them alone.

"Well, now that's settled," Heather said, briskly. As if against her will, her gaze returned to the empty doorway. "I think Mr. Shaw disapproves of me," she said in a wistful tone of voice.

"Nonsense," Jake said stoutly. "He's just not used to dealing with the fairer sex. That's what happens when you're raised in an all-male household."

"All male? What about his mother and his sister?"

"His mother died when Rebecca was a child. Killed in an Indian raid. Their father, the elder Mr. Shaw, sent Rebecca to live with her Aunt Bess in Pittsburgh. Robert came and visited her through the years. That's the way I met him." He turned to Angellee. "You two girls wander around and get acquainted with the place but don't leave the ranch today."

"Why not?" Angellee asked.

Jake's eyes were evasive. "I would just rather you didn't for a spell. I suppose I may be overly nervous since you were kidnapped. But I'd never forgive myself if it were to happen a second time."

"Are you worried about Slade and Cantrell coming after us?" Heather asked anxiously.

"Of course not," Jake said stoutly.

Somehow, Angellee felt he wasn't being quite truthful. Her green eyes hardened. If either of the men came for them—Slade *or* Cantrell—they would pay for what they'd done. She would see to it.

Chapter Thirty

It was late afternoon and Angellee leaned back in the chair, her emerald eyes watching the flames dance in the fireplace. Across the room Robert and Jake were deep in conversation, their voices lowered.

Heather, who had asked Juanita for something to occupy her hands, was completely absorbed in the pillowcase she was darning, pushing the threaded needle in and out of the material.

As she worked, the two men's eyes strayed constantly to the comfortable picture the Irish girl presented, sewing by the fireside. Angellee knew the blond girl was every man's dream of a wife, a home and a family.

A curious pain stabbed through Angellee's chest as Jake's gaze wandered to Heather again. She drew a sharp breath, averting her eyes from the Irish girl, trying to ignore the sudden, quick stab of jealousy.

You're not being fair to her, Ethan. Her mother's words of the past rose to her mind. *Someday, Angel won't care how far she can throw a knife, or how many turkeys she can bring home for the cooking pot. She ain't a man, an' no amount of wishin' can make it so. Someday, our girl will want a home of her own and a man to do for her and children beside the hearth.*

My Angel, Pa had laughed. *No-sir-ree-bob. Not this youngun' here. This'n won't need a man to do for her. She'll do it 'erself. She'll get her own food and build her own cabin and do her own protectin'. Thet's what I done for 'er. Same as I'd'a done fer our boy.*

She ain't Johnny, Ethan. Johnny's gone. You cain't find him in Angel.

Her father's face had darkened with a terrible anger and grief. Without a word, he had turned and left the cabin, not returning for two days. After that day, they never mentioned Johnny again. Her mother never interfered again, but sometimes, after bringing in fresh meat from the forest, Angellee would sense her mother's gaze on her. She would turn and find a look of sadness on her mother's face.

You knew, Ma. You knew someday I'd fall in love. And you knew what was gonna happen. You knew just how it would be.

"You're looking mighty sad, Angel," Robert commented suddenly, and she looked up to find him studying her intently.

Jake's attention had been on Heather; but at the other man's comment, he turned to study Angellee's face, and his brow knitted with worry.

"Something wrong, Angel?" he asked, frowning intently at her.

"No," she said, completely failing to hide the edge to her voice. She brushed back a stray lock of fiery red hair, feeling suddenly stifled. She had to get out of this room for a few minutes—had to be alone with her thoughts. "I think I'll go for a walk," Angellee said, rising abruptly to her feet.

"Wait a minute and I'll go with you," Jake said, making a move to rise.

"No!" she snapped. Silence spread away from her like ripples from a pebble dropped into a pond. "I'd rather be alone for a while," she said, forcing a calm into her voice that she didn't feel.

Noticing Heather's mildly puzzled gaze on her, she added. "If you don't mind."

Anger briefly shadowed Jake's face, then flitted away, leaving his features expressionless. "Do you feel all right?" he asked, studying her pale face.

"I've got a headache," she said. "I'll feel better after I get out in the fresh air."

She was aware of Jake's concerned gaze following her but kept going. Stepping on the porch she gazed out toward the distant mountains, a feeling of such intense loneliness about her. The sun was above the ridgeline, shading most of the yard. The sky overhead was azure blue. Angellee breathed deeply, filling her lungs with the sweetly scented air.

Shouts in the distance caught her attention, and she turned to see a flurry of activity down at the corrals. Stepping off the porch, she strode across the yard and opened the gate of the white picket fence which surrounded the big ranch house. She moved down to the corrals, arriving just in time to see a big gray stallion being led out of the barn.

She hoisted herself onto the top rail of the corral, her emerald eyes intent on the animal. Dust clouds swirled as he screamed, rearing high into the air. His neck and withers were white with foam as he eluded the lariats of the two cowboys, lashing out at them with his wicked hooves. A shrill whistle rang from him as he pawed the ground sending more dust clouds aloft.

Angellee thought he was magnificent as she studied the power and strength he displayed in his anger. Suddenly, seeming to become aware of Angellee sitting on the fence, the horse turned toward her shaking his mane, his eyes malevolent.

Spinning swiftly around, he raced toward her, his teeth bared and his ears laid low on his head. She was distantly aware of a voice shouting a warning, and everything seemed to be going in slow motion.

Suddenly she was pulled violently from the fence, her head pushed roughly against a solid male chest, and strong arms encircled her. Momentarily off balance, she clung to the muscular frame holding her tightly, gasping for breath. Slowly, she began disentangling herself from the arms that held her so closely.

With hands still resting on a chest, she looked up, way up, into a face devoid of color beneath the sun bronzed skin. Her startled eyes met Jake's darkened gaze.

"What the hell do you think you're doing? Don't you know you could have been killed?" He rapped the words out with punishing scorn, and she felt like a child caught in a mischievous prank. The feeling was uncomfortable and didn't sit well with her.

Angellee struggled to free herself, but his arms had the strength of steel. She knew she was sure to have bruises tomorrow. Angellee's emerald eyes glittered savagely as she glared at Jake, blaming his caustic censure for her discomfort.

"Would you let me go?" she demanded. Her frosty

voice crackled with distaste for his attitude as she looked pointedly at the hands gripping her with such strength.

"I'm still waiting for an explanation," Jake said, in a hard, determined voice.

Instantly her hackles rose and her green eyes narrowed. "Well, you'll wait until hell freezes over if you take that tone with me, Jake Logan! I don't have to answer to you for my actions."

"What the hell is the matter with you?" he asked, giving her a hard shake.

Angellee was flushed and suddenly very much aware of their audience. "Nothing's the matter with me," she muttered, struggling to recover her dignity.

"You're different than you were before." He stared at her oddly. "Something happened to change you." His eyes narrowed on her face. "Something . . ." he said slowly, his dark eyes intent, "happened to you in Paso Diablo, didn't it?"

"I don't know what you're talking about," she said stiffly.

"Yes. You do." His voice was certain. Suddenly he became aware of their audience and took her arm again, gripping it tightly when she tried to shrug it away. "It's time we had a talk," he said grimly. "I've put it off long enough."

"We don't have anything to talk about."

"We damn well do," he barked.

"Jake, could you come here for a minute?" called Robert who was standing with a group of cowboys near the barn.

Jake stared at her a moment longer, his expression wavering between confusion and anger. Anger won out. "Looks like we'll have to postpone our talk," he gritted savagely, "but don't think this lets you off the hook. We'll talk later on tonight."

Angellee watched Jake join the other men and slowly the tension unknotted between her shoulder blades. She had just turned to go back to the ranch house when she noticed Jake's body had gone tense. He threw a quick look at her, and something about his attitude made her suspicious. She continued on her way to the house, but as soon as she was out of sight, she doubled back and went around the barn, entering through a window at the back. Moving on silent feet she crossed the barn. The wall was only a few feet from the men, and she could hear every word they said.

"Are you sure it was Slade?" Jake was asking.

"Yes. It was him all right," the cowboy said. "I'd know him anywheres. You don't forget somebody like that."

"Do you know where he was going?"

"I made a point of askin' around. Seems like he bought hisself a piece of land with a cabin on it up along the Gila River a few miles north of Silver City."

"Keep quiet about it, Shandy. I don't want a word of this reaching Angel's ears," Jake said grimly.

Damn him!

Angellee burned with anger. Jake had planned on keeping Slade's whereabouts from her. Her expression was grim as she left the barn the same way she had entered and returned to the ranch house. As she passed the door to the livingroom, she paused for a moment to observe Heather.

The Irish girl knelt before the hearth, probing the coals with an iron poker, then she placed a billet of split oak on the glowing logs. Taking a branch of dried rosemary from beside the stack of wood, she tossed it onto the burning oak, and the shrub crackled and blazed, filling the room with the incense of coastal hills.

A burnt-out log split apart, sending sparks flying, and she raked them carefully back into the hearth. Then Heather moved to a spoke-backed rocker placed before the cozy fire, seated herself and moved smoothly back and forth like a giant pendulum, a rapt expression on her face.

Feeling suddenly like an intruder, Angellee moved away on silent feet to find Juanita, hoping the housekeeper could find something for her to do that would occupy her hands while her mind worked out the problem of Slade.

Angellee helped the housekeeper the rest of the afternoon, and she managed to stay out of Jake's way until they sat down for the evening meal. All through the meal she felt the curious glances cast her way by Heather and Robert, but Jake completely ignored her. She excused herself as soon as she had finished eating, claiming to be tired and went to her bedroom.

A short while later Heather knocked gently on the door. Her face was troubled when she came into the room.

"Is something wrong, Angel," she asked.

"No." Angel forced a smile. "Nothing."

"You and Jake had a fight didn't you?" she asked gently.

"Yes," Angellee admitted. She looked away from the other girl. "I don't even know why. It just—" She broke off. "I wish I were like you, Heather. Then maybe he'd fall in love with me."

"Is that what's wrong? You think Jake doesn't love you? You're wrong, you know. I'm sure that he does."

"No. He doesn't. Oh, there's no doubt he likes making love with me. But any woman would do, Heather." She rolled over and stared grimly at the ceiling. "I guess it's best that way though. I've still got a job to finish."

"Why don't you go find Jake and apologize? My father used to say you should never let the sun set on anger."

Angellee laughed. "That's pretty," she said. "But it don't work with me. I've got plenty of anger at Slade and Cantrell." She looked curiously at Heather. "Aren't you mad at them for what they done to you?"

"I guess I do harbor ill feelings toward them," Heather admitted. "I find it hard not to. But that's different. I think my father was speaking about someone you loved."

"Jake is better off without me anyway," Angellee said wistfully.

"Now that's a defeatist attitude. Why should you think that?"

"I'm not educated like you, Heather. And I haven't finished the job I set out to do. I been puttin' it off, wanting a little more time with Jake, knowing all the time I'd go find Slade when he left."

"What do you mean? Why do you have to go after Slade?"

"'Cause he ain't dead yet."

"Angel!" Heather gasped, her blue eyes going round with surprise. "You can't mean what you're saying."

"I mean it," Angellee said, her expression hardening, her voice deadly.

Heather drew back from her. "Jake won't allow it," she said, her expression troubled.

"Jake won't have no say in it."

"You're making a mistake, Angel. Put this idea out of your head. Don't go after Slade. You could get hurt bad. Maybe even killed."

"I'm not gonna let Slade live," Angellee said, her voice flat. "He's not fit to walk this earth."

Heather sighed. "You need some rest," she said. "I'll leave you alone, but for Heaven's sake, don't do anything foolish."

Angellee had nearly dozed off when the bedroom door opened and Jake entered the room. His gaze found her, never wavering as he moved aggressively across the room toward her. Her heart gave a violent leap, her pulse thundering in her ears. She stared up at him. Why had he come? Had Heather gone to Jake?

"We didn't have that talk yet," he said, a touch of steel in his voice. His heavy-lidded eyes were on her startled face.

She gave an inward sigh of relief, relaxing visibly. "Can't it wait until tomorrow?" she asked.

"No, Angel. We'll get this thing settled tonight. Scoot over."

Sighing, she moved over, allowing him room to sit on the edge of the bed. A pale moonbeam fell across her face, and he reached out and smoothed his hand down her cheek. Surprised by his action, her face nuzzled into his palm.

"You're very beautiful in the moonlight," he said gently. Then his head moved lower, his mouth hovering just above her lips. "I've missed you, my Angel," he whispered, his breath warm on her face.

Of their own volition, her arms moved up and circled his head, pulling it down to meet hers. Their lips met and clung, hungry for each other.

With a husky groan his arms slid around her, pulling her close against his hard body. She could feel his heart, pounding in rhythm with her own as their passions ignited. Her mouth opened beneath his, allowing him entrance to the sweet moistness within. One hand moved around until he found a breast, and his thumb caressed the hard nipple. His mouth was tender on her face, adoring it, cherishing it. Every movement was tender, calculated, and he was breathing as roughly as she was. She trembled beneath him, straining upward, trying to ease the ache that was building fast within her body.

Then he was moving back, stripping the nightgown from her body, and removing his garments as well. When he returned, his skin was roughly abrasive against hers. She tried to capture his mouth with hers, but he moved down to her neck, nipping at the tender skin with his teeth, then her shoulders, and on down until she felt the warmness envelop her nipple. He sucked on it gently, and she could feel the fire building up in her body. She moaned, clutching his head tighter against her breast, encouraging him. Then he moved to the other nipple and treated it to the same loving tenderness.

When his mouth left her breast and moved lower, she began to writhe and moan beneath him. His tongue dipped into her navel and she gasped. He was trailing the wet moistness lower, lower, until his lips closed over the center of her desire.

"No, Jake," she gasped, pushing at him. But he

ignored her, creating a tension in her body that had her arching beneath him, writhing violently, uttering moans in her throat. When Jake came back to her, she was sobbing. He possessed her swiftly, and she followed his movements with desperate abandon, helpless before the passion that swept through her. They both reached their peak at the same time, crashing together in a flash of blinding colors followed by a sweet warm flood.

Her body was damp all over, and she was trying to still her pounding heart as she clung to him, trembling with emotions. Tears stained her face, and she nuzzled her cheek against his damp chest, loving the feel of him, the clean male scent of him. He held her tightly against him until she fell asleep. When he was sure she was sleeping, he rose from the bed, dressed and left the room.

Chapter Thirty-One

Angellee moaned, thrashing about on the bed in the grip of a nightmare. It's not really happening, she thought, even as she urged Star into the raging, swollen river. She tried to tell herself there was no need to hurry, no need to feel such desperation. It was only a dream. A nightmare. Jake wasn't really in danger. None of it was real. If only she could open her eyes.

As the water crept higher, inching up the black stallion's flanks, she looked up, searching for the sun. At first, she couldn't see it. There were too many clouds in the sky. Then, miraculously, the clouds drifted away, and the sun burst through.

But what had happened to it?

It was blood red, and it hovered directly overhead. That meant it was midday. Yes. That's why she must hurry. She was late.

Despite the swift water, she urged her mount on. Jake was waiting, and she had to be there. She must help him, or he would die. She tried to remember why she knew this, but the answer eluded her. The water rose higher, and the Arabian stallion lost his footing. The water closed over her head. She could feel her mount's attempts to break the surface. Her lungs were bursting, she had to have air.

Jake! Where are you?

"Angel! Wake up, Angel! You're having a nightmare."

The voice barely penetrated her consciousness, but it succeeded in pulling her awake. Her green eyes were wild as they snapped open. Perspiration dotted her brow.

Heather was a pale figure in the shadowed room, leaning over her, a worried expression on her face.

"Are you all right now," she asked quietly.

"Jake!" Angellee said, her voice rising with hysteria. Her panic-stricken eyes searched the darkened room. "Where's Jake?"

"I imagine he's in bed asleep," Heather said quietly. "That's where I was until you began shouting. The walls are thin, and you sounded terrified. I knew you must be having a bad dream."

"It wasn't just a bad dream," Angel said. "Something's wrong with Jake." She sat up and pushed the quilt aside. As the chill air struck her flesh, she realized she was naked and quickly pulled the quilt up to her chin. "Hand me my nightgown," she said. "I have to find Jake."

"Jake's all right," Heather assured her, her embarrassed gaze moving from Angellee, falling to the clothing scattered on the floor, then skittering quickly away. "You were only having a nightmare, Angel."

"It wasn't just a nightmare," Angellee said, sliding a bare leg to the floor. Her voice had risen with her fear, and she was determined to see Jake herself. Suddenly, she paused, her eyes narrowing with suspicion on the girl's flushed features. "You're trying to keep me from seeing Jake, aren't you? He's not here."

"What's going on?"

Angellee and Heather turned startled eyes to the doorway. They saw Robert standing there, wearing nothing but a dressing gown.

"Angel had a nightmare," Heather explained. "Now she's convinced something is wrong with Jake."

"I know he's in danger." Angellee's emerald eyes locked with the man's. "He's not here. Tell me where he is."

"I imagine he's in bed," he said, coming into the darkened room. He halted abruptly as he eyes fell on the discarded clothing.

"In bed?" Her eyes held confusion. "Are you sure?"

"Well, I haven't looked, but—"

"Would you look?" she pleaded.

"It's not necessary, you know," he said quietly. "He would have no reason to be anywhere else."

"Would you look anyway? Or else I'll never be able to go back to sleep."

Robert and Heather exchanged glances, then Robert shrugged. "All right," he agreed. "I'll go look."

"What's all the commotion?"

Angellee turned to stare at Jake in the doorway, a silhouette against the lighted hallway. His hair was disheveled, he was barefooted and naked to the waist.

"Jake?" she whispered. Relief flowed through her, and she sank back on the bed, her eyes feasting on him. "You're here."

"Of course I'm here," he said, walking into the

shadowed room. He looked inquiringly at Robert and Heather, then moved to stand beside the bed, frowning down at her. "Where did you think I was?" he asked, taking her hand in his. She clutched it as though she were a drowning man who had been thrown a lifeline.

"She had a nightmare and thought something had happened to you," Heather explained. "We couldn't seem to convince her that you were in bed."

"A nightmare?" His darkened eyes were thoughtful as they studied her pale face. He spared a glance for Robert and Heather. "You two might as well go back to bed. I'll stay with her until she calms down."

"Perhaps it would be better for Heather to stay with her," Robert said, his eyes steady on Jake's.

The nightmare was still so vivid in her mind that Angellee's hand tightened convulsively on Jake's, her eyes silently begging him to stay.

Jake shook his head. "No. I'll stay. You can leave the door open if you want."

Robert signaled Heather to come with him. They slipped out, closing the door behind them.

When they left, Jake sat down on the bed beside her.

"Now what's this all about," he asked. "Was the nightmare the usual one?"

"No," she whispered huskily. Her hungry eyes devoured his features. "I thought something had happened to you. Slade's still loose and . . ." her voice trailed off. She had given him an opening to tell her about Slade. Maybe he would use it.

"Want to tell me about it?"

She shook her head.

"Why not? It might help get rid of your fears if we discuss it. Did Slade figure in your nightmare?"

"Only in the sense that I felt he might be the source of danger to you."

He remained silent.

"I feel silly," she muttered. "But it was all so vivid. I was supposed to meet you, and I was late. The river was flooding, and Star couldn't make it across. We went under and I couldn't breathe and the sun was drenched with blood, and there was the fear of danger . . ."

"Sounds like a real doozy," he said. "But try not to think about it anymore. It won't be long before the reason for your nightmares is gone. Was that all there was?"

She nodded her head.

He picked up a lock of hair and played with it. "You've been through a lot lately," he said softly. "It's no wonder you're having nightmares again. Just let your mind relax, close your eyes and go back to sleep."

Her troubled gaze held his. "Why did you leave me?" she asked.

He thought about that for a minute before answering. "It wasn't because I wanted to," he said. "But we're guests in Robert's home. It wouldn't be right for us to take advantage of his hospitality."

"Staying all night with me would have done that?"

"I think it would have," he said gently, brushing back a stray curl.

"How?"

He smiled wryly. "Robert is a pretty straight-laced individual, Angel. I'm afraid he doesn't see colors. To him, everything is either black or white. Because of it, he had a very hard time coming to terms with Becky's marriage to Lone Wolf."

She studied him with puzzled eyes. "I don't see what

that has to do with me sleeping alone."

"To put it a little more bluntly, Angel, to Robert's way of thinking, there are only two kinds of women: the kind you marry and the kind you don't. I don't want him to get the idea you're the kind of woman that men don't marry."

"He would think that if we slept together?"

"Yes," he sighed. "I'm afraid he would."

"Well, I don't care," she said defiantly.

"But I do," Jake reprimanded. "Robert's my friend. He comes to Pittsburgh quite often, and I don't want him to get the wrong idea about us."

Hurt stabbed through her. "I understand," she muttered, drawing her hand away from his. Yes. She understood. Robert was a part of Jake's future, and his opinion would matter a lot. Hers didn't. "You can go back to bed," she said, her voice slightly reserved. "I'm all right now."

"Are you sure?"

"Yes."

Leaning over, Jake kissed her on the forehead. His eyes were thoughtful as he studied her pale face. "We're going to have to rid you of those nightmares, you know," he said. "And we still haven't had that talk." His smile was wry. "I guess there's plenty of time for it yet." Then, with a soft goodnight, he left.

She lay dry-eyed, staring at the ceiling. Her thoughts were in a turmoil, her mind refusing to rest. Try as she would, she couldn't fall asleep. Sleep would have been an escape, a panacea. But she was not to get that relief. Instead, she lay there battling against an ominous feeling of danger. It made no sense. All was quiet and still. Yet, she felt unnerved. Was it her imagination, or was it too quiet? Was the absence of sound absolute? Deciding her imagination was playing tricks on her, she turned her head to the pillow. But still, there was no rest for her. She went over the conversation she and Jake had. Something about what he said bothered her.

We're going to have to do something about those nightmares, you know.

Did he mean he was going to do something about Slade?

It won't be long before the reason for your nightmares is gone.

Yes. That had to be what he meant. And the dream wasn't just a dream. It was another vision.

He was going after Slade!

No. She wouldn't let him. Slade was her job.

How will you stop him?

"Dammit, Jake," she muttered, flinging back the covers and jumping out of bed. "You ain't gonna beat me outta killin' him."

She found the divided skirt that Juanita had provided her with, knowing it was imperative that she move about unencumbered. She slipped into the skirt and blouse, then pulled on her boots. She buckled her gunbelt over the skirt, checked to make sure she had plenty of ammunition and quietly left the room.

The house was silent, and she had no problem leaving it.

When she reached the corral, she whistled softly, and Star whinnied, coming to her immediately. She saddled the stallion, then swung gracefully into the saddle. They left the ranch at a walk until they were well out of hearing range, and then she urged Star into a gallop and headed for Silver City.

It was late when Jake woke, having spent a restless night. He stretched and blinked a couple of times to bring the room into focus. Memories of last night surfaced, and he frowned. He wished he had been able to stay with Angel, but he didn't want her reputation ruined. News had a habit of traveling a long way. Especially if it was news involving someone's reputation. He knew Robert wouldn't talk, but things had a way of getting around. Especially if you didn't want them to.

Getting out of bed, he dressed and went downstairs, looking for Angel and a cup of coffee. He found Heather in the kitchen with Juanita. Angel was probably outside taking care of that stallion of hers.

"Hello, sleepy head," Heather said, cheerfully. "I was wondering if you were even going to wake up before I had to leave."

"Leave? Where are you going?"

"I have a job," Heather said eagerly, pouring him a cup of hot coffee and setting the steaming cup in front of him. "I'm so excited I could bust."

"That's great," Jake said, smiling at the Irish girl's enthusiasm. "Is it the job Robert told us about?"

"Yes. I'll be the upstairs maid for Mrs. Carter. And she wants me to start today."

"That soon?" His brow furrowed. "Heather, you don't have to do this you know. Angel and I would love to have you come live with us in Pittsburgh."

"I couldn't, Jake. But I appreciate the offer. You and

Angel don't need anyone living with you. And besides, like I said, I like it out here."

"Where is Angel?" Jake asked, taking a cautious sip of the steaming brew.

"She went for a ride."

"Did she say which way she was going?" Jake asked, thinking about joining her.

"I didn't have a chance to talk to her," Heather replied, pulling out a chair and sitting down at the table. "Shandy told Robert he saw her riding off just before dawn."

"Shandy?"

"Uh hunh. He's one of the cowboys. He said he was restless and couldn't sleep. He went out to the corral, but he didn't see her until she was riding away. I think she must have needed to do some thinking."

Jake put the coffee cup down on the table. "What did she have to think about?" he asked harshly.

"Oh. You know. She was worried about Slade and a lot of other things," Heather said, her brow knitted in thought.

"What about Slade?"

"She's got it into her head that she's got to kill him."

"When did she say that?"

"Last night. It seemed to be preying on her mind a lot."

"She doesn't know where he is, does she?"

"I don't know, Jake. I got the impression that she knew something she wasn't telling. That maybe she'd heard something to set her off."

"Damn!" Jake shot out of the chair, sending it crashing to the floor, alarm streaking through him. He didn't like the sound of this. Was it possible she had over heard them yesterday?

Jake left the house in a hurry and saddled Daniel, explaining his suspicions to Robert.

"You mean she would really go after a killer?" Robert asked, amazed.

"Yes, she would," Jake said grimly. "The little fool doesn't have any sense at all."

"Would you like me to go with you," Robert asked.

"No. I'll handle it," Jake said. After thanking Robert for his hospitality, he rode out.

Chapter Thirty-Two

A bullet struck the rock just above Angellee's head. She ducked and swore savagely. She had made a bad mistake, going up to the house and announcing her presence to Slade like that, a mistake that could prove to be her last.

The only excuse she had for what she'd done was the need to see Slade's face when she killed him. She wanted him to know who was doing it. And why. She hadn't planned on Slade not being alone. While he kept her talking in front, one of his cohorts—there were four of them—went out the back, circled around and surprised her.

Now the hardcase lay dead in front of the cabin.

She hadn't counted on there being a back door, as most of these one room cabins only had a front entrance. Alerted by the gunman she had downed, she had barely made it to the concealing rocks before the others opened fire on her.

She had been careless.

Peering out at the stand of pine trees a hundred yards

away, she saw a scurrying movement and sent a shot in that direction. A yelp of pain encouraged her. And she sent off another shot.

"Boyd," called a voice from her right. "You okay, Boyd?"

"Yeah" came the answer from the trees. "She just winged me."

Angellee's sharp gaze narrowed on the big rock that was concealing the other gunman on her right. He was apparently trying to work his way behind her.

"Slade said it was just a girl" came the voice from behind the rock again. "Said it should be easy for us to take her."

"Why's he still in that cabin, then?" The voice came from the wounded man in the trees. "Why ain't he out here helpin' us?"

"Claimed he was keepin' her pinned down from that direction."

"Bullshit! Truth is, he knew the girl was a she-cat. Why's she after him anyway? What'd he do? And who the hell is she? I ain't never seen no girl that could shoot that away before."

Angellee smiled grimly. They sure were noisy for a couple of gunmen, and they were getting nervous. The sun glinted off a gun barrel that poked over the edge of the rock. She took careful aim and fired, rewarded by the loud ping of steel against steel, followed by a string of curses.

"Hell! I've had 'bout enough," yelled the gunman concealed by the rock. "I didn't bargain for no gunfight with no girl. It ain't decent-like. If Slade wants her dead, let *him* do it. It's his fight. It don't have nothin' to do with us." The voice rose. "Slade, get out here."

Angellee glanced toward the cabin. Nothing stirred. She kept her gaze moving between the trees, the cabin and the rock. Another movement in the trees caused her to send several more shots winging that way.

The gunmen weren't the only ones getting nervous. The way they were situated, they could keep her pinned down until night. And there was every chance they would try an attack under cover of darkness.

Taking advantage of the silence, she emptied the spent shells from the cylinder of one of the Colts, keeping the other one close at hand. Then she loaded the gun with fresh bullets.

Uneasy, she eased along the rock until she could see around it. She detected no movement at first, then . . . a faint sound reached her ears: a boot crunching on a branch. A moment later, a shadow flitted, and she fired three times. She heard a loud grunt of pain, and something heavy crashed against the brush.

"Frank. You okay Frank?" The voice came from the right and slightly above her. "Dammit, Slade! I think she got Frank."

"Goddammit! Shut up, Boyd!" Angellee recognized Slade's voice. "Haven't you got any sense at all? You're giving your position away to the girl."

Somehow, he had gotten out of the cabin and was closing in on her. A bullet hit the rock, spraying her with fine particles of grit, and she ducked back behind the rock again.

Angellee's eyes searched for a way out. Between the two of them, they wouldn't have much trouble keeping her here. Unless she could figure a way out.

Despite her circumstances, her thoughts turned to

Jake. What had he thought when he discovered her missing? Would he search for her? She damped down the surge of hope. She could expect no help from him. No one had the slightest idea where she was.

She had to get herself out of this mess.

Or die trying.

"Cover me, Boyd," Slade shouted, pulling her attention back to the gunmen. "I'm going to get behind her."

"That's what you think," she muttered, sending a bullet in his direction.

"Goddammit! I said cover me, Boyd," Slade shouted, his voice shrill with both fear and anger.

Silence.

What was going on? Was Boyd keeping silent until he could get behind her? Her narrowed eyes searched the area, but she detected no movement nearby.

"Luke!" Slade shouted. "Where the hell is Boyd?"

"Don't know, Slade" came a voice from her left.

So there were more than she'd thought. Damn! And where the hell *was* Boyd? Were they just pretending not to know to throw her off guard?

She sank wearily down on the ground. God, she was tired. It seemed years since she had left the ranch. She'd give anything to forget she'd ever started this. But no. That wasn't fair to her parents. She had to see Slade dead. She had promised Pa.

"Slade." She identified the man as the one called Luke. "I think something's happened to Boyd. Suppose we just sit tight until . . . ugh . . ."

The groan was accompanied by the sound of crashing in the underbrush.

"Luke!" Slade yelled. "Was that you Luke? Answer

me, damn you!"

"He can't answer you, Slade" came a voice that sounded very much like Jake's. "And neither can Boyd. Frank's out of it, too. Now there's just me and you and the Angel."

Angellee felt a great weight roll off her shoulders. She didn't know how it happened, but Jake was here. She wasn't alone anymore.

There was a momentary silence, then it was broken by Slade's, slightly hysterical, voice. "What'd'ya want from me, dammit?"

"I don't want anything, Slade." Jake's voice held a touch of steel. "But the Angel does. She wants your life."

Three shots followed each other in quick succession, thudding into the trunk of the ponderosa pine concealing Jake. Then there was silence for the space of a heartbeat.

"I can keep you pinned down there as long as I like," Slade shouted. "But it doesn't make any sense. All three of us could get mighty tired before it's over. So I'll make you a deal. You throw down your guns, and I'll let you ride out of here safe."

A harsh laugh accompanied this announcement. "No deal, Slade."

"Wait a minute," Slade shouted. "Think about what I said. One of us could get killed this way. There's no need to keep on with this fight. I'm not holding any grudges."

"Ask the Angel."

"Angel," Slade shouted. "You heard him. It's up to you. What do you say? You won't gain anything by my death. Let's just let by-gones be by-gones."

"Go to hell!" she shouted. "You ain't fit to live. Jake, don't touch him. I want 'im. It's my right."

"I'm not gonna fight any more," Slade yelled. "You can kill me if you want to, but I'm throwing my gun down and coming out."

His words were matched by a gun landing on the ground between the rock where she was hidden and the trees where she had fixed Jake at.

"Don't you believe him, Jake!"

"You can't shoot an unarmed man," Slade called, stepping out of the concealing brush. "It's not legal." One hand was high up, and the other was angled awkwardly behind his head.

As Jake stepped out of his place of concealment, Slade's hand whipped down holding a pistol that he'd concealed behind his head. Before he could bring it up to bear, Jake had cleared leather and sent two slugs slamming into Slade.

Slade looked at him in amazement, then fell to the ground with a thud. Jake turned to see Angellee running at him. She threw herself into his arms, burying her face against his wide chest, hugging him tightly against her.

"I sure am glad to see you," she said. Her voice trembled despite her efforts at control.

"Are you?" he asked grimly. "I'm surprised. You couldn't wait to get away from me."

She sensed his displeasure and pulled back from him. "I wasn't tryin' to get away," she denied. "Not really."

"Weren't you?" His eyes were cold as they studied her flushed features. "Why did you sneak out while I was asleep?"

"I was afraid he would kill you."

His chest muscles tightened. A muscle twitched in his jaw. "I'm not a child that needs coddling, Angel. In case you haven't noticed, I'm a full-grown man, and I'd feel a lot better if I were allowed to do the protecting."

She realized he felt she had questioned his masculinity. "Jake—I—" She broke off, unable to find words to explain. Her gaze fell on the dead gunman. "What're you gonna do with Slade and his friends," she asked.

"Nothing," Jake replied, turning away from her. His voice was cool. "I have no use for dead men."

"It don't hardly seem decent to just leave them here," she muttered, her shoulders hunching in misery.

"We can notify the sheriff. He can do whatever needs doing."

A few moments later, they had mounted and headed back, leaving the gunmen where they lay. Jake remained silent as they rode, ignoring the fact that Angellee traveled with him. She knew he was angry with her, and she smarted as she realized he was purposely keeping her in the dark about his intentions. She gritted her teeth in frustration, feeling he had deliberately set out to irritate her.

Swallowing her resentment, she followed along behind him, her misery and confusion intensifying as he ignored the trail leading to Robert's, taking instead, the fork that led to the town of Silver City.

[illegible] as I would [illegible]

[illegible] expected [illegible] Amanda [illegible] on his face. [illegible] you [illegible] the [illegible] if I was allowed to do [illegible]

She [illegible] and [illegible] [illegible] of the [illegible] do with [illegible]

[illegible]

"It [illegible]

[illegible] He [illegible]

[illegible] they had [illegible] Amanda [illegible] her [illegible]

[illegible] to [illegible] of Silver Elk.

Chapter Thirty-Three

When they reached Silver City, Jake reined Daniel up in front of the hotel, dismounted and entered the building. Angellee stared after his disappearing figure. Unsure of what was expected of her, she dismounted, tied the black's reins to the hitching post, then followed him. Jake had already signed the register by the time she crossed the lobby and reached his side.

"Room 204," the clerk said, handing him a key.

Taking her arm in an iron grip, he ignored the gaping clerk, pulling her along behind him toward the curving staircase. She was out of breath when they reached the top of the stairs. Number 204 was the second door on the right. He unlocked the door, then held it open, waiting silently for her to precede him into the room.

Angellee's control was about ready to break. What lurked in the depths of Jake's eyes? Was it anger? Hatred? Or pity? Heaven forbid. Did he pity her? Her chin lifted another degree, but still, it took all of her courage just to turn around and face him. He was still standing in the doorway, his tall frame blocking the only exit, an air of tension about him.

"Well," she began, a trifle belligerently. "What's the matter? You've been lookin' at me like I suddenly sprouted two heads."

He stepped into the room and kicked the door shut behind him. "What are you trying to do to me, Angel?" he gritted, his nostrils flaring.

She flinched at the harshness. "I don't know what you mean," she said, her voice wobbling slightly despite her efforts at control. She veiled her eyes behind thick lashes, swallowing convulsively against the pain.

"That's just it," he grated. "You *don't* know. Seems like you're always trying to save my hide." Although his voice was low, his anger was barely controlled. "No man who's worth his salt is going to want his woman's protection. How do you suppose it felt to wake up and discover you'd gone after Slade alone. Dammit! Who the hell do you think you are anyway?"

Her defiance drained away, her green eyes mirrored regret. "Jake I never thought you'd—"

"You're right." His voice was thick with anger. "You don't think. You don't give a damn about anything except your revenge. Well, I apologize for killing Slade." He ran a frustrated hand through his dark hair. "How the hell do you think I'd feel introducing you to my friends at home? What would I say was your function? The woman who protects me? Who guns men down if they look cross-eyed at me? I don't think I'd care for that at all. There's something about it that emasculates a man."

"Jake. Don't," she protested in an anguished voice. The words sounded torn from her throat.

"Damn! I've had enough." He stared at her, his gaze dark with emotion. "Get cleaned up," he said harshly, his features as hard as his voice. "You look like you've been rolling in the mud."

Her cheeks flamed hotly as conflicting emotions churned inside her. What was wrong with him? Hurt was a thick knot in her throat. She lifted her chin, choking back tears, staring wordlessly at him.

His expression was frozen, harsh and unyielding. His silence was more than she could bear, and she turned away, moving to the window. She stared down into the street, watching a buggy stop before the feed store. The loud slam of the door startled her. She turned to find him gone.

Angellee was unable to contain herself any longer.

Jake was gone.

He had really left her—walked casually out of her life without a word. She would never have believed he could be so cold and unfeeling. Although he had never said he loved her, she had believed he cared.

Her back was rigid, her face ashen as she stared unblinkingly ahead. Her green eyes slowly filled, then overflowed. She threw herself on the bed, spasms shaking her slender body.

Jake was gone.

Muffling her sobs in the pillow, she gave release to her agony. When her sobs finally ceased, she lay on her back staring with glassy eyes at the ceiling.

A knock at the door startled her, bringing her to her feet. Her pulse gave a mighty leap; her heart took on the rhythm of pounding drums.

He had come back.

She wiped her face with the sleeve of her blouse,

trying to erase all signs of her weakness. Then she opened the door, staring in confusion at the young Mexican girl confronting her.

"The señor wishes to know if you need something." Her large brown eyes were curious as they studied Angellee's tear-drenched face.

Angellee shook her head. "No," she said, wearily. "I don't need nothin'." She closed the door, her shoulders slumping with defeat. She, who had never cried uncle, was down.

"Uncle," she whispered, her voice ragged with pain. "Uncle, Jake. I'm all the way down and I'm sayin' uncle."

She moved to the window, staring into the street below. It was empty. Just like her. Empty.

Sighing, she washed the dirt and grit off. She could refresh her body, but nothing could refresh her spirits. Nothing but Jake's return. Where had he gone? Probably back to the Shaw ranch. Had he only brought her here to leave her? Was he going to abandon her here in this hotel room?

What could she do? Her chin quivered, firmed, then lifted defiantly. She was no weak-willed ninny. She didn't need a man. She could manage on her own. All she had to do was make plans, decide what to do, which road to follow. But why did she feel such emptiness, such loneliness.

Jake was gone.

Her gaze moved around the empty hotel room, coming to rest on the doorway where she'd last seen him, and stopped. Her eyes darkened with pain, and she swallowed around the lump in her throat.

Jake was gone.

So what? She had accomplished what she'd set out to do. Slade and Bull were dead. Pa and Ma had been revenged . . . her duty was fulfilled. . . .

Her gaze returned to the window. Her lips quivered as she watched the white cotton curtains lift gently in the breeze.

Jake was gone.

There was nothing left for her. Nothing left, except—perhaps—to continue the trip she'd started with her parents. Her mind told her to go, but her heart told her to wait, give Jake a chance. He might only have gone for a walk.

She waited for what seemed hours, then indignation rose fierce in her breast. He couldn't do this to her. She'd find him. Face him down. Make him tell her he didn't want her. Then she'd tell him she didn't need him. She'd get on Star and—Star! She had left him in front of the hotel.

She left the hotel room and walked through the empty lobby. The Arabian stallion was no longer there. Jake must have taken him to the stables before he left. Angellee's gaze searched the town, locating the stable at the north end.

The big horse whinnied when she entered the building. She moved to his side, smoothing her hand down his silky neck.

"I don't know what to do, Star," she told the animal. "There's not many jobs for a woman. Leastways, not one like me. I can't be a schoolteacher; I haven't had enough schoolin'. I'm not hankerin' to be no maid, and I'm sure not gonna work in no saloon. Seems like all I got left is to go on to California and dig for gold. But I'd have to have money to outfit myself with. How'm I gonna get it?"

"That's a mighty fine animal you got there."

Angellee turned to see a middle-aged man with gray hair watching her.

"He yours?"

She nodded.

"Wouldn't want to sell him, would you?"

"No. I wouldn't," she said. "Me an' him, we go back a long ways."

He grinned. "Figgered as much. But it never hurts to ask." He ran a hand down the black stallion's side. "He's a mighty fine animal," he repeated. "Mighty fine."

"That he is," she agreed. Her eyes dwelt on him. "Wouldn't happen to know of any jobs around these parts, would you?"

"Grandy's hirin' over at the saloon," he said, eyeing her hesitantly.

"I don't want to work in a saloon."

"Well, the Bar C was lookin' fer a maid. Don't know if they found one."

"They did. Friend of mine hired on."

"I'm sorry, miss," he said. "That's all I know anything about."

She sighed. "I figgered as much. Reckon I'll have to move on. Where's the stage office?"

He pointed the way, and she left to inquire the price of a ticket to California. Her heart sank when the clerk told her the cost. "There's a stage out tonight and one early tomorrow mornin'," he said.

She left, making her way back to the stables. She leaned her head against the stallion, rubbing his long neck. "What'll I do, Star," she asked. "Where will I get the money?"

"My offer's still good" came the voice from behind her.

"How much would you pay?" she asked, huskily.

"Two hundred."

Enough to get her to California and grubstake her. But how could she sell the stallion? She had raised him from a colt. He was all she had left of family and home.

"Two fifty if you throw in the saddle."

She looked at the black horse, tears welling in her eyes. Blinking them back rapidly, she said. "I'll have to think on it some. I'll let you know later." Giving the horse one last pat, she left the stables and returned to the hotel. Entering her room, she sat in a chair by the window, staring down into the street. Dusk fell, darkness closed in, and still she waited. Throughout the long, lonely night she kept watch.

Just before dawn, she rose and made her way to the stables. "I got no choice," she told the man, who emerged yawning from the back room. "He's yours." She laid her head against the black stallion's neck. "I'm sorry," she whispered, swallowing around the lump in her throat. "But you see, I have to." She turned to the man. "You'll be good to him?"

"I respect good horseflesh," he said, his voice gruff with sympathy. "He'll come to no harm from me."

"Then it's a deal," she whispered.

"Come on back here," he said, nodding to the room in the back of the stables. "We'll fix it up."

An hour later she was on the stage bound for California.

* * *

Jake left the hotel and took the horses to the stables. Then he found the nearest saloon. Driven by anger, he downed several drinks in quick succession. He was frustrated. He was driven between the urge to shake her and the urge to kiss her until she couldn't protest. Angel had scared the living hell out of him going off the way she had to take on Slade alone. He felt a fleeting regret for losing his temper with her, but it was only a momentary thing. It was past time she learned who was boss.

His knuckles whitened as he gripped the glass full of whiskey in front of him. He drank it down quickly.

Angel was too aggressive by far. Too spunky to suit his taste. He'd pay hell taming her. His brow furrowed. She *was* spunky. A little thing like that. His lips twitched. She couldn't weigh over ninety pounds soaking wet, and she was determined to protect him. A smile tugged at his lips. Suddenly he grinned.

What the hell. What did he expect? That's what made him fall in love with her. The first time he met her, she was rescuing him. Why was he trying to change her all of a sudden? She couldn't help it. If there was anyone at fault, it was her father. He's the one that raised her. It didn't really matter anyway, did it?

Face facts, man. You love her. And you'd damn well better grab her before someone else does.

A reluctant smile spread across his features. "Where's the nearest preacher?" he asked the bartender.

Chapter Thirty-Four

Angellee stood on a gravel bar that extended into the middle of the stream in the high country, close to the headwaters of the Feather River. Her britches legs were rolled up, but that hadn't stopped them from getting soaked. She swished the water around in the flat pan until all the sand was washed out, looking for a few tiny, but heavy, yellow flakes of gold.

There was no sign of color.

She sighed, then emptied the water from the pan, dipping it into the gravel bed and straightening up slowly. Every muscle in her slim back ached. She had never worked so hard in her life, but she had gained a feeling of security, a feeling of confidence that whatever happened, she could support herself.

It was back-breaking work, and several days had passed since she'd had any sign of color to add to the pouch of gold dust and a few small nuggets that made up her poke.

Gold had been getting scarcer than hen's teeth lately. Her dreams of getting rich were fading fast, but at least she wasn't starving. She had been taking just enough gold from the streambed to keep her working at it.

When she'd first hit California, her every waking moment had been filled with memories of Jake. She'd dreamed of striking it rich and going back to school to finish her education. Then she'd buy herself some fancy duds, and perhaps she might find her way to Pittsburgh. And if, one day, she just happened by the Logan mansion—well—who could tell what might happen?

With the passing of time, she had come to face reality. Even if she struck it rich, Jake would probably have already married. After all, it had been three months since she'd left Silver City. If he hadn't married Heather, then he'd surely found himself some other lady of quality. When she'd finally accepted these facts, she'd worked hard at putting the past behind her, and she began to plan a future for herself. A future that didn't include Jake.

Unlike the other miners, Angellee had no use for spending her gold on whiskey or the loose women who frequented the boom towns. And her savings, although small, had slowly accumulated.

Surrounded by rough men, she'd been careful to keep her braids firmly tucked beneath her hat, to always wear loose boy's clothing that disguised her womanly curves.

All in all, she was making a good life for herself. She stopped for a moment, swiping a hand across her forehead, wondering if she ought to call it a day and get an early start tomorrow.

Something—some sound—caused her to look up, and her breath caught, her heart skittering madly, before taking off like a scalded cat. She stood frozen, immobile in the act of dipping the pan one last time. Then, slowly, she straightened.

He was leaner than when she'd last seen him. Leaner, rawboned and tough. She stared wordlessly, her gaze drinking in the sight of him.

"Angel," he said, the word almost a sigh but loud enough to carry across the stream to where she stood gazing at him with turbulent eyes.

"Jake." The word came out a croak.

As he started forward, realization flooded over her. This man was the cause of her pain. This man was the one who'd left her alone in a hotel room. This man . . .

She held up a hand, taking a backward step. "No, Jake."

He hesitated, frowning darkly. "What do you mean, no?" he grated.

"Stay where you are," she said, taking a backward step. "I mean it, Jake."

"Why'n hell should I?"

"I don't want you here." Even as she spoke the words, she knew them for a lie. Her gaze slid over his body hungrily, noticing the way his pants shaped his lean buttocks, his muscular thighs. She recalled how it felt to be pressed against his length, how . . .

"Why don't you want me here?" he asked in a deceptively soft voice. His big body was stiff with tension.

"I refuse to let you use me again."

"Use you?" His voice was ragged with emotion.

"Yes. You used me," she said. Her voice bristled with indignation. "I ain't gonna let you do it again. So just go away. Let me be." Her hands were balled into fists, her back rigid as she stared mutinously at him.

"I'm not going anywhere." He growled, stepping into the stream. "Do you realize how long I've been searching for you?" Holding her gaze steadily, he plowed through the water, coming to a stop just a few feet away.

"Why did you bother lookin'?" she asked, determined to hold her ground.

"Why?" He reached for her, and she drew in a sharp breath, stepping back quickly, avoiding his touch.

His lips thinned, his dark eyes glittered. "You know why, Angel. Don't play games with me. I'm not in any mood for it."

Angellee knew she was at a distinct disadvantage standing in the middle of the stream, and as he reached for her again, her courage failed. She broke, turning to run from him. But he was too fast. Reaching out, he snared her wrist with an iron grip.

"No," she protested, yanking at her arm, trying to pull it free. "Don't do this to me."

He ignored her, pulling her against him. She could feel the quivering tension in his muscles but held herself stiffly. His heart drummed loudly in her ears, his arms tightening roughly around her. Although her heart begged her to give in, she struggled ineffectually against his superior strength.

"God . . ." His voice was harsh, husky. "I've missed you so much." His breath was warm against her ear. "I've searched so long . . . I thought I'd never find you."

What was he saying? Why had he searched for her? Why did he have to come and fan the flames of love again? She was just beginning to find peace.

He pulled the hat from her head, tossing it into the stream. Then he ran a hand through her hair, releasing it, allowing it to flow in fiery waves down her back. He tilted her chin, forcing her to meet his eyes. She stared at him defiantly, her flushed cheeks only emphasizing the vulnerability of her mouth.

Suddenly, he gave a deep shudder, lowering his mouth to cover hers, tenderly at first, then the kiss deepened, displaying a passionate hunger. For the space of a heartbeat, she resisted. Then, despite her efforts at control, something stirred to life, something that had been asleep too long. She felt herself responding to his passionate need with a hunger of her own. It began to grow like a flame, licking at her, feeding on her desire until her whole body was on fire.

She moaned softly, her lips moving beneath his. Low, guttural sounds emanated from deep within his throat. He lifted his head, staring down into her flushed face with slumbrous passion. Then, lifting her into his arms, he carried her out of the stream. Standing her on the ground, he found her lips again. His mouth moved hungrily downward, tasting the tender flesh of her throat, her shoulders, pushing the shirt aside to caress the soft, golden curves of her breasts.

"Jake . . . no . . ." she murmured, weakly. "I'm beggin'. Please, don't do this to me."

He lifted his head, his hands stilled as he gazed deeply into her eyes, searching for something.

She sighed with disappointment. She wanted him. She wanted his hands on her, his mouth against her skin. She wanted him to feed this hunger he aroused within her, wanted him to fill her body.

"Why did you run away?" he whispered huskily, his

voice ragged with pain.

"I didn't run," she muttered, shuttering her eyes behind thick lashes.

"You left."

Her gaze flew to his and remained locked. "I wasn't the one to leave. You left me."

His brows drew together in a frown. "I only went for the preacher, Angel. When I returned to the hotel, you were gone."

Her heart gave a mighty leap, then she forced herself to calm down, face facts. "How long does it take to fetch a preacher?"

"All night if you have to go to the next town to get him."

"You went to the—" She stopped, wanting to believe him, but her mind insisted she proceed with caution. "If that's true, why didn't you tell me you were going?" Her eyes darkened with pain. "Don't do this to me, Jake. I was just getting myself straightened out. You have no right to come here like this and mess things up for me again."

"I don't know what you're talking about," he muttered. "But talking seems to get us nowhere. We do better with kissing." He lowered his head.

"No, Jake," she said, turning her head and shoving at his chest. "I don't want that."

"Don't lie to me, Angel," he said. "You want it as much as I do."

She flushed. "Maybe so. But I can't just—I don't want—"

"What don't you want," he asked, biting at her lower lip gently.

She shuddered. Her body was trying to betray her. "I

don't want you to do that. You said you went for the preacher but I—"

"You don't believe I did?" He frowned darkly. "Is that what this is all about? I love you, you little idiot. I'm going to marry you. I wouldn't dishonor you. Not for anything. You're going to be my wife. You're coming home with me to Pittsburgh."

She gazed up at him with heartfelt emotion in her eyes. He hadn't really asked her to marry him. He had arrogantly told her they would be married. It was presumptuous—even pompous—of him. And yet, strangely, she didn't care. She belonged to this man. She had belonged to him since he'd first possessed her. There had never been any doubt in her mind. And when they were married, he would belong to her.

Her gaze locked with his. Her hands moved of their own accord, circling his neck. She clutched handfuls of hair and pulled his mouth down to hers. She loved the feel of him. The warm, fresh, male smell. The taste . . .

"Love me, Jake," she murmured against his lips.

His lips locked on hers hungrily, grinding savagely. His tongue slid into her mouth, touching hers, delving into the sweetest depths of her wet moistness. A fierce ache began deep within her. She arched her body against his, wanting him, a fever surging through her blood.

His fingers worked at the buttons of her shirt, freeing them, then he tossed the garment aside. She could hardly wait and worked fiercely at his garments. Then they were free of the offending material, and he laid her on the ground, covering her body with his own.

His face pressed against the softness of her breasts, his tongue coaxing her nipples into taut little peaks.

Her body began to heat, flooding with waves of delicious warmth.

"Hurry, Jake," she whispered. "Please."

He needed no more prompting. He entered her, plunging deep inside, filling her moistness with his warm male strength. For a moment, he lay still. Then he began to move, building a fire inside Angellee that was soon burning out of control. Her nails dug into his shoulders, urging him onward and upward until finally they reached the peak together. With one last convulsive movement, he pushed inside of her, and then lay shuddering against her as she exploded into a million fragments and sank down into a peaceful silence where there was no one in the world except Jake and herself.

With her head resting in the crook of Jake's arm, she looked up at him. "How did you find me?" she asked.

"It wasn't easy," he said, pushing a stray curl aside and placing a butterfly kiss on one eyelid. "I didn't discover you'd left town until the morning after you'd left. You sold Star and that threw me off."

At the mention of the Arabian stallion, her eyes darkened with pain.

"Don't worry," he said, brushing a stray curl back from her face. "I bought him back."

"You bought Star?" she asked. "But where—"

"He threw a shoe. I was so close to where I thought I'd find you that I didn't want to wait. I left him with the blacksmith down at that little town . . ." He paused. "Chance, something or other."

"Chance Meeting," she said with a laugh.

"Don't bother telling me where the name came

from," he grimaced. "Anyway, after I talked to that old prospector, Zeke Myers, I knew that I'd finally found you. But I didn't want to delay getting here, so I left Star and came on ahead."

"I still don't see how you found where I was from old Zeke Myers. I never saw him 'ceptin' when I bought his claim. So how did he know—"

"Angel," he said with a grin. "That Ozark language of yours, combined with the description of a spunky, pint-sized boy—well, needless to say, you stood out like a sore thumb." He frowned. "I thought we'd cleaned that language of yours up."

"Didn't seem no—*any* reason no more to work on it. Nobody cared much out here."

"Well, this somebody cares. And I'd have found you a lot sooner, but I sat in that hotel room with the preacher waiting for you to come back. I thought it was anger keeping you away. I was a damn fool." His arms tightened. "By the time I found out you'd sold your horse and left on the stage, you'd been gone too long to catch. But still, I never dreamed it would take me this long to find you. I had no problem tracing you to California. It was after you left the stagecoach that the problems began."

His eyes were filled with pain. "If I hadn't found that old prospector who sold you his claim, I guess I'd still be looking." His lips tightened grimly. "That's the last time you're getting a chance to pull a stunt like that. We're getting married just as soon as I can arrange it."

Her lips lifted into a satisfied smile.

That suited her just fine.